D1056843

POKÉMON ADVENTURES:
DIAMOND AND PEARL/
PLATINUM
Volume 11
VIZ Kids Edition

Story by HIDENORI KUSAKA
Art by SATOSHI YAMAMOTO

© 2014 Pokémon.
© 1995-2014 Nintendo/Creatures Inc./GAME FREAK inc.
TM, ®, and character names are trademarks of Nintendo.
POCKET MONSTERS SPECIAL Vol. 11 (40)
by Hidenori KUSAKA, Satoshi YAMAMOTO
© 1997 Hidenori KUSAKA, Satoshi YAMAMOTO
All rights reserved.
Original Japanese edition published by SHOGAKUKAN.
English translation rights in the United States of America, Canada, United Kingdom,
Ireland, Australia and New Zealand arranged with SHOGAKUKAN.

Translation/Tetsuichiro Miyaki
English Adaptation/Bryant Turnage
Touch-up & Lettering/Annaliese Christman
Design/Yukiko Whitley
Editor/Annette Roman

Printed in the U.S.A.

Published by VIZ Media, LLC
P.O. Box 77010
San Francisco, CA 94107

10 9 8 7 6 5 4 3 2 1
First printing, June 2014

PARENTAL ADVISORY
POKÉMON ADVENTURES:
DIAMOND AND PEARL/
PLATINUM is rated A and is
suitable for readers of all ages.
ratings.viz.com

Pokémon Adventures
Diamond and Pearl Platinum

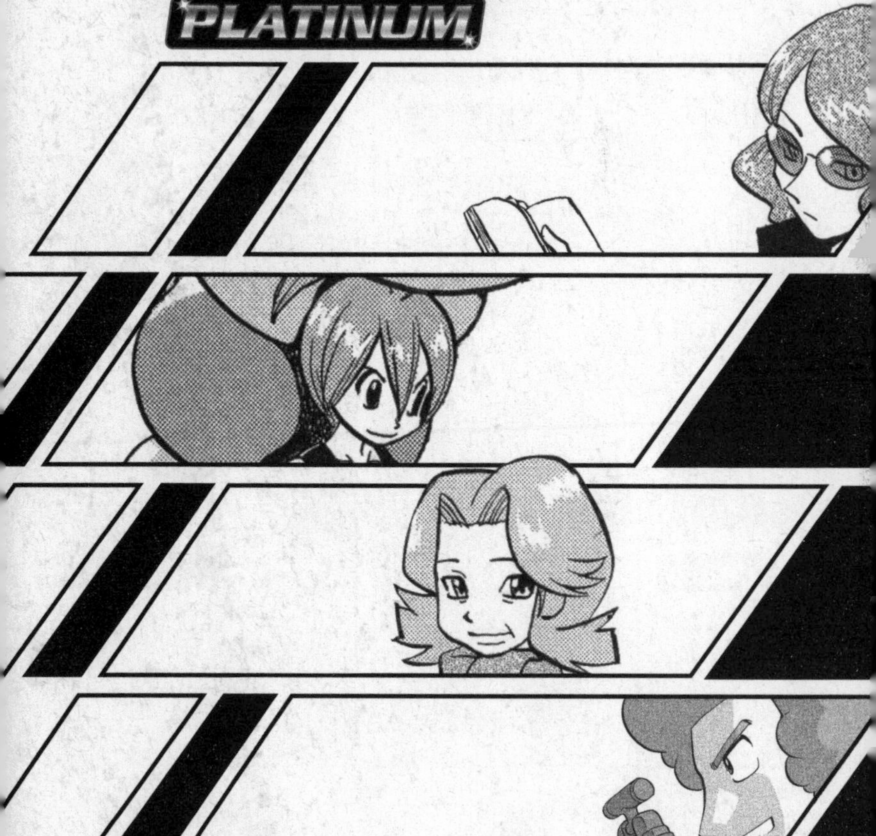

Art **Satoshi Yamamoto**

Story **Hidenori Kusaka**

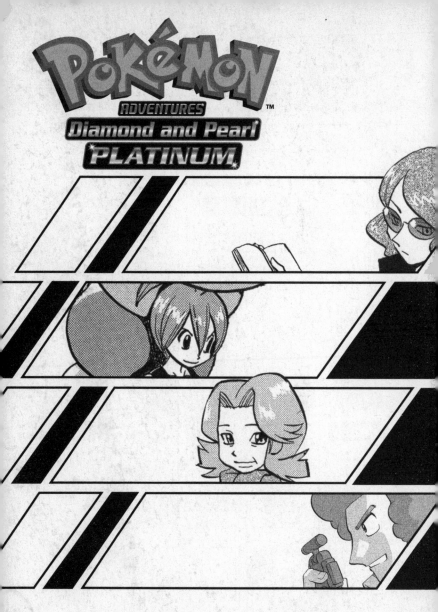

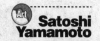

Our Story So Far…

A story about young people entrusted with Pokédexes by the world's leading Pokémon Researchers. Together with their Pokémon, they travel, battle and evolve!

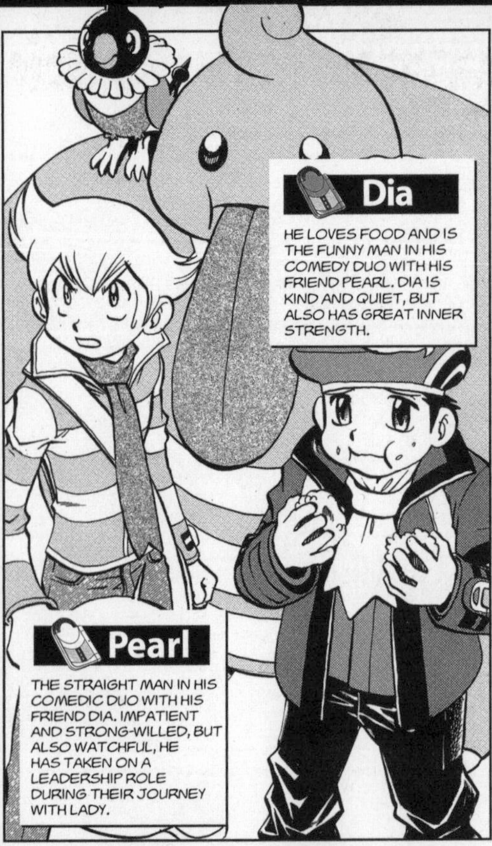

Dia

HE LOVES FOOD AND IS THE FUNNY MAN IN HIS COMEDY DUO WITH HIS FRIEND PEARL. DIA IS KIND AND QUIET, BUT ALSO HAS GREAT INNER STRENGTH.

Pearl

THE STRAIGHT MAN IN HIS COMEDIC DUO WITH HIS FRIEND DIA. IMPATIENT AND STRONG-WILLED, BUT ALSO WATCHFUL, HE HAS TAKEN ON A LEADERSHIP ROLE DURING THEIR JOURNEY WITH LADY.

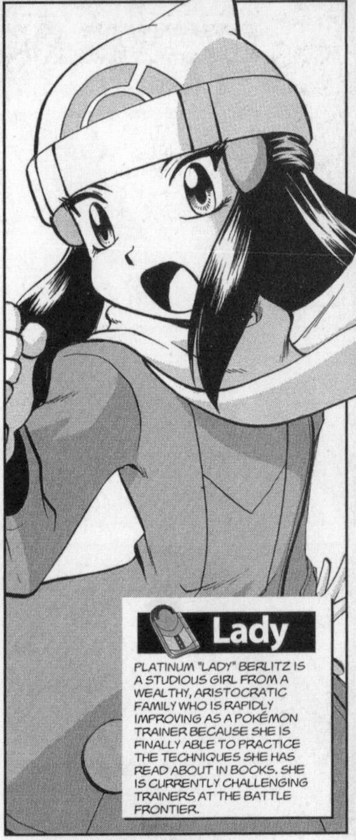

Lady

PLATINUM "LADY" BERLITZ IS A STUDIOUS GIRL FROM A WEALTHY, ARISTOCRATIC FAMILY WHO IS RAPIDLY IMPROVING AS A POKÉMON TRAINER BECAUSE SHE IS FINALLY ABLE TO PRACTICE THE TECHNIQUES SHE HAS READ ABOUT IN BOOKS. SHE IS CURRENTLY CHALLENGING TRAINERS AT THE BATTLE FRONTIER.

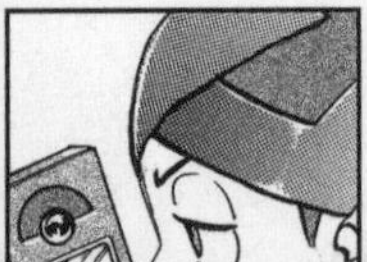

Thorton

THE FRONTIER BRAIN OF THE BATTLE FACTORY AND THE FACTORY HEAD.

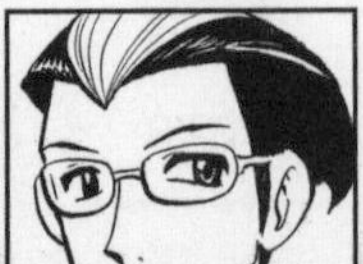

Darach

CAITLIN'S VALET, THE CASTLE BUTLER.

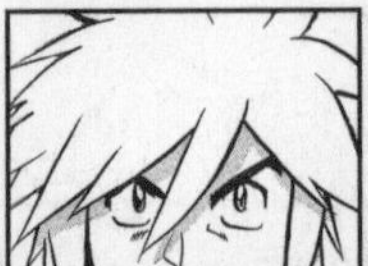

Palmer

THE TOWER TYCOON WHO PRESIDES OVER THE FIVE FRONTIER BRAINS AND BATTLE FRONTIER FACILITIES.

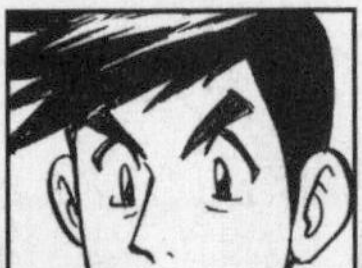

Looker

AN INTERNATIONAL POLICE OFFICER. HE IS STRIVING HARD TO INFILTRATE TEAM GALACTIC.

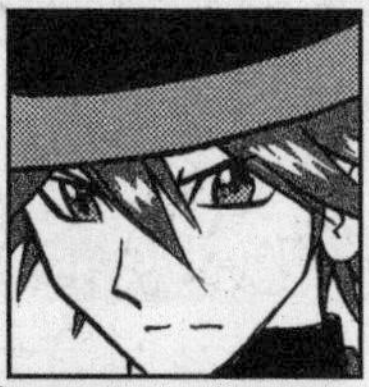

Riley

THE MAN FROM IRON ISLAND WHO TRAINED DIA. AN AURA WIELDER.

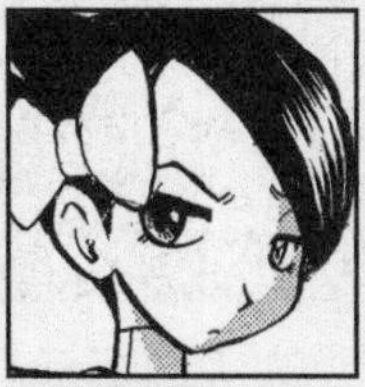

Marley

A MYSTERIOUS GIRL WHO IS HEADED DOWN TO ROUTE 224 WITH A LETTER IN HAND...

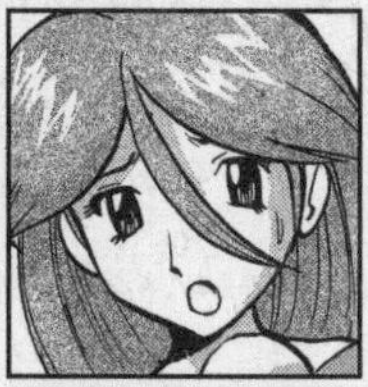

Cheryl

A CALM, GROWN-UP TRAINER WITH A BLISSEY.

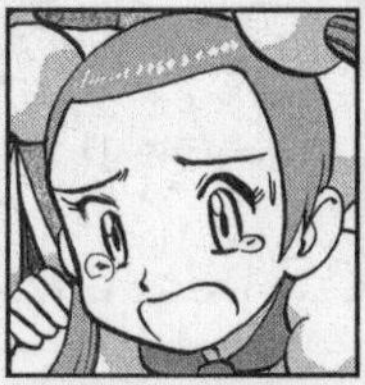

Mira

ONE OF THE BATTLEGROUND TRAINERS. SHE IS UPSET ABOUT BUCK GETTING INJURED IN A RECENT BATTLE.

THE BATTLE AT SPEAR PILLAR HAS ENDED, AND LADY AND HER FRIENDS ARE TRIUMPHANT. HOWEVER, JUST WHEN DIA AND PEARL THINK THEY CAN RELAX, A PORTAL TO A MYSTERIOUS DOMAIN OPENS UP IN FRONT OF THEM AND DIALGA, PALKIA AND EVEN CYRUS ARE DRAGGED INTO THE VOID!

EAGER TO FIND OUT THE WHEREABOUTS OF PAKA AND UJI, LADY'S BODYGUARDS WHO HAVE DISAPPEARED, THE TRAINERS HOPE TO FIGURE OUT THE MEANING OF CHARON'S CRYPTIC COMMENT ABOUT "THE OTHER SIDE OF THIS WORLD." IN ORDER TO GATHER MORE INFORMATION ON IT, DIA AND PEARL HEAD OUT ON THEIR OWN AGAIN IN SEARCH OF THE OTHER LEGENDARY POKÉMON, WHILE LADY HEADS DOWN TO THE BATTLE ZONE LOCATED OUTSIDE OF SINNOH.

JOINED BY INTERNATIONAL POLICE AGENT LOOKER, LADY CHALLENGES THE FIVE BATTLE ARENAS OF THE BATTLE FRONTIER. TEAM GALACTIC COMMANDER CHARON'S SCHEME IS REVEALED AND THE TIDE SEEMS TO TURN AGAINST THE TRAINERS! HEATRAN HAS FALLEN INTO THE HANDS OF THE ENEMY, THE COMMUNICATION DEVICES AT THE BATTLE ZONE ARE BEING JAMMED, AND THE RENEGADE POKÉMON GIRATINA HAS APPEARED AT ETERNA CITY! WHAT NOW...?

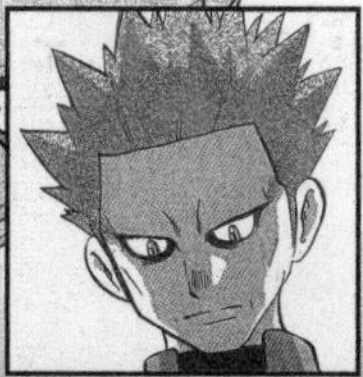

Cyrus

TEAM GALACTIC'S BOSS, WHO WAS DRAGGED INTO A MYSTERIOUS REALM. WHERE IS HE NOW...?

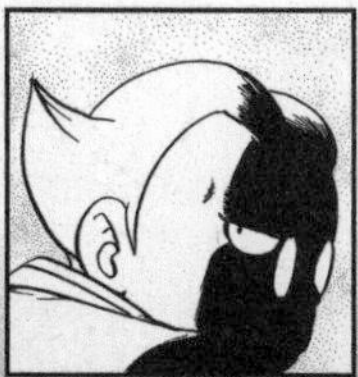

Charon

A TEAM GALACTIC COMMANDER AND SCIENTIST WHO IS PASSIONATE ABOUT HIS LEGENDARY POKÉMON RESEARCH.

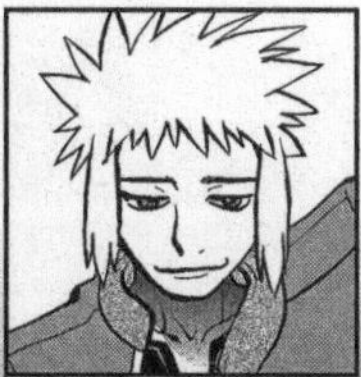

Volkner

ONE OF THE SINNOH GYM LEADERS WHO VISITED FLINT. WHAT WAS HE AFTER...?

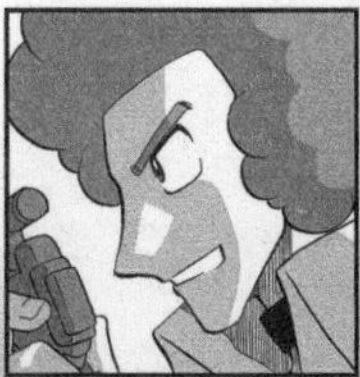

Flint

ONE OF THE SINNOH ELITE FOUR. A CAREFREE FIRE-TYPE POKÉMON EXPERT.

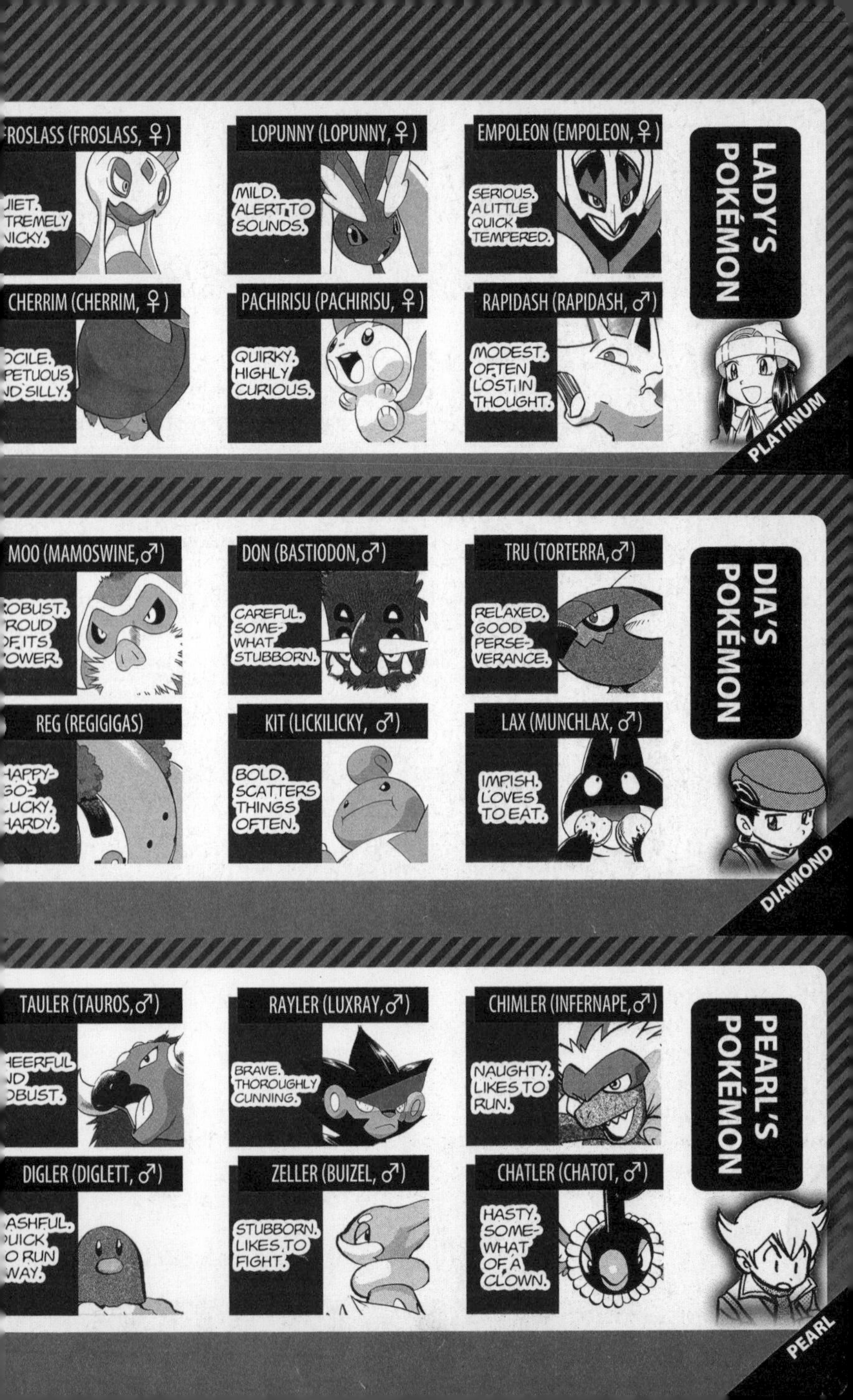
LADY'S POKÉMON
PLATINUM
EMPOLEON (EMPOLEON, ♀)
SERIOUS. A LITTLE QUICK TEMPERED.
LOPUNNY (LOPUNNY, ♀)
MILD. ALERT TO SOUNDS.
FROSLASS (FROSLASS, ♀)
UIET. TREMELY ICKY.
RAPIDASH (RAPIDASH, ♂)
MODEST. OFTEN LOST IN THOUGHT.
PACHIRISU (PACHIRISU, ♀)
QUIRKY. HIGHLY CURIOUS.
CHERRIM (CHERRIM, ♀)
OCILE. PETUOUS ND SILLY.
DIA'S POKÉMON
DIAMOND
TRU (TORTERRA, ♂)
RELAXED. GOOD PERSE-VERANCE.
DON (BASTIODON, ♂)
CAREFUL. SOME-WHAT STUBBORN.
MOO (MAMOSWINE, ♂)
OBUST. ROUD F ITS OWER.
LAX (MUNCHLAX, ♂)
IMPISH. LOVES TO EAT.
KIT (LICKILICKY, ♂)
BOLD. SCATTERS THINGS OFTEN.
REG (REGIGIGAS)
APPY-GO-LUCKY. ARDY.
PEARL'S POKÉMON
PEARL
CHIMLER (INFERNAPE, ♂)
NAUGHTY. LIKES TO RUN.
RAYLER (LUXRAY, ♂)
BRAVE. THOROUGHLY CUNNING.
TAULER (TAUROS, ♂)
HEERFUL D OBUST.
CHATLER (CHATOT, ♂)
HASTY. SOME-WHAT OF A CLOWN.
ZELLER (BUIZEL, ♂)
STUBBORN. LIKES TO FIGHT.
DIGLER (DIGLETT, ♂)
ASHFUL. UICK O RUN WAY.

Pokémon ADVENTURES
Diamond and Pearl PLATINUM

11

CONTENTS

ADVENTURE 94
The Final Dimensional Duel I.................. 14

ADVENTURE 95
The Final Dimensional Duel II 30

ADVENTURE 96
The Final Dimensional Duel III 48

ADVENTURE 97
The Final Dimensional Duel IV 62

ADVENTURE 98
The Final Dimensional Duel V 78

ADVENTURE 99
The Final Dimensional Duel VI 94

ADVENTURE 100
The Final Dimensional Duel VII 115

ADVENTURE 101
The Final Dimensional Duel VIII 128

ADVENTURE 102
The Final Dimensional Duel IX 148

ADVENTURE 103
The Final Dimensional Duel X 164

ADVENTURE 104
The Final Dimensional Duel XI 183

PLATINUM

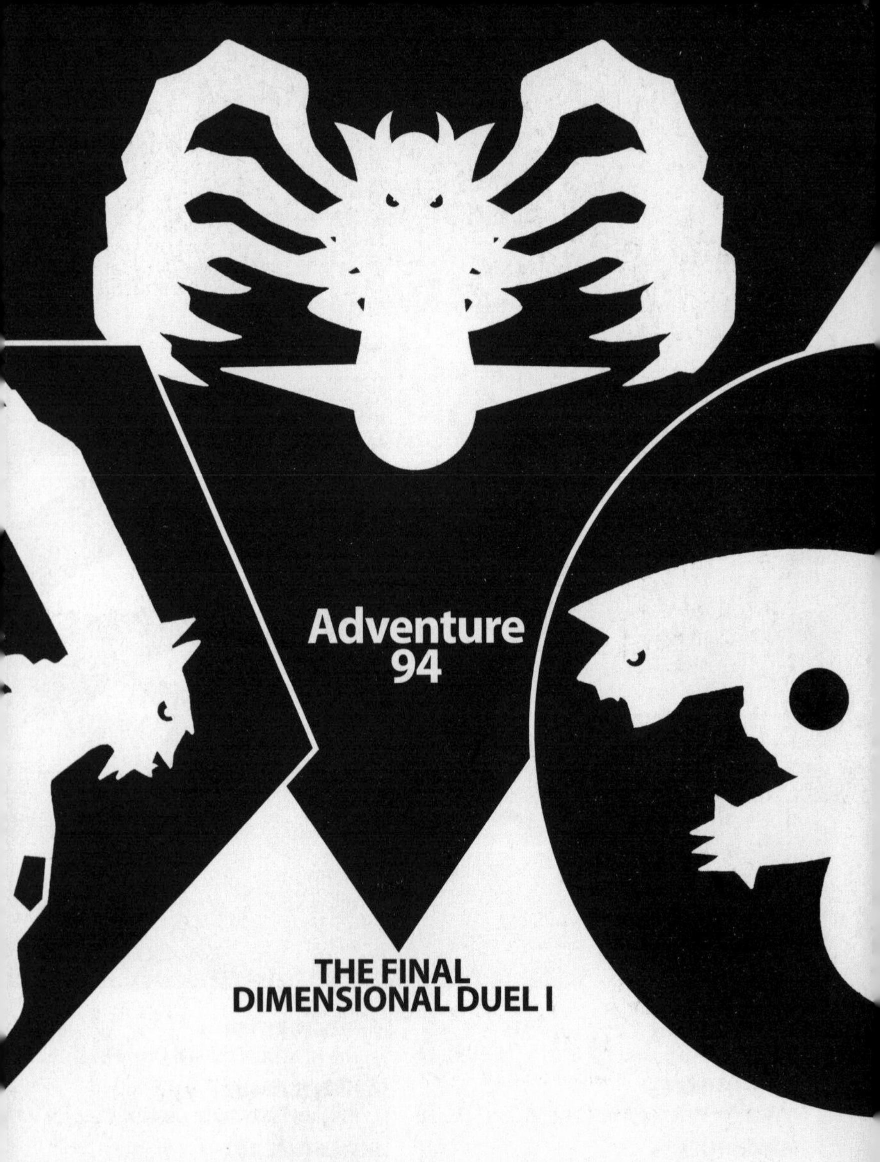

Adventure 94

THE FINAL DIMENSIONAL DUEL I

Pokémon Adventures
The Eighth Chapter

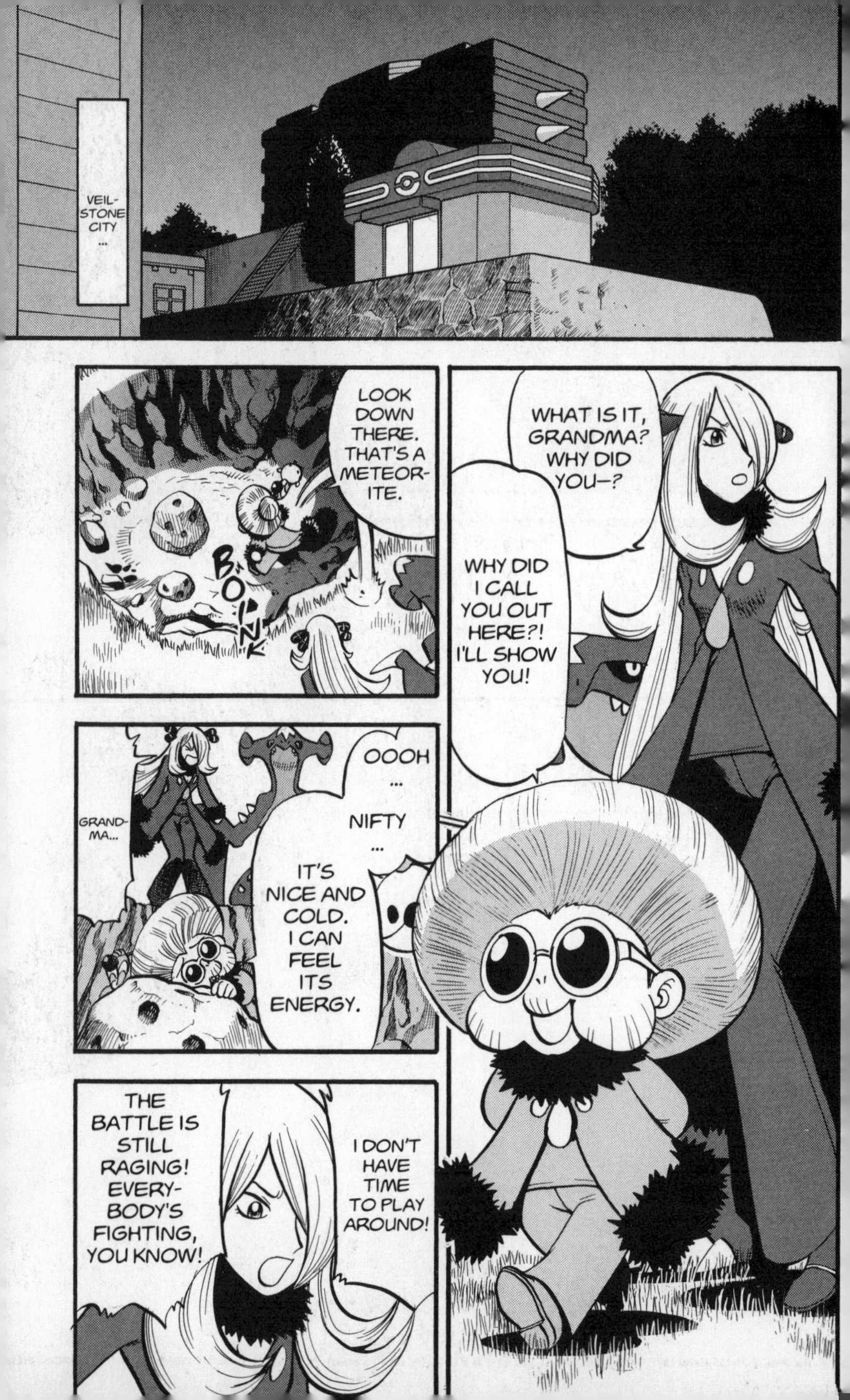
VEIL-STONE CITY ...
WHAT IS IT, GRANDMA? WHY DID YOU–?
WHY DID I CALL YOU OUT HERE?! I'LL SHOW YOU!
LOOK DOWN THERE. THAT'S A METEOR-ITE.
BOINK
OOOH ... NIFTY ... IT'S NICE AND COLD. I CAN FEEL ITS ENERGY.
GRAND-MA...
I DON'T HAVE TIME TO PLAY AROUND!
THE BATTLE IS STILL RAGING! EVERY-BODY'S FIGHTING, YOU KNOW!

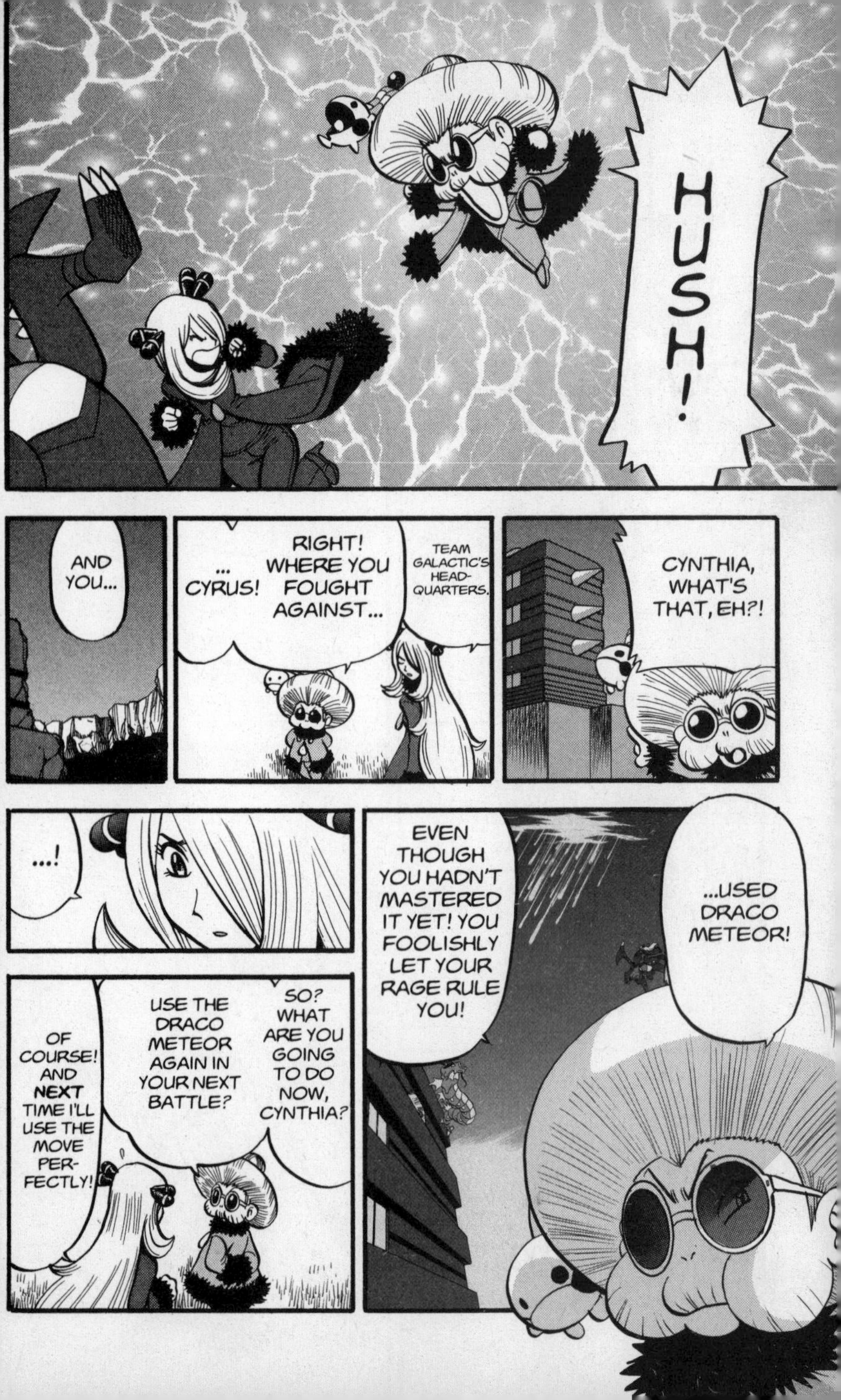
HUSH!
CYNTHIA, WHAT'S THAT, EH?!
TEAM GALACTIC'S HEAD-QUARTERS.
RIGHT! WHERE YOU FOUGHT AGAINST...
... CYRUS!
AND YOU...
...USED DRACO METEOR!
EVEN THOUGH YOU HADN'T MASTERED IT YET! YOU FOOLISHLY LET YOUR RAGE RULE YOU!
...!
SO? WHAT ARE YOU GOING TO DO NOW, CYNTHIA?
USE THE DRACO METEOR AGAIN IN YOUR NEXT BATTLE?
OF COURSE! AND **NEXT** TIME I'LL USE THE MOVE PER-FECTLY!

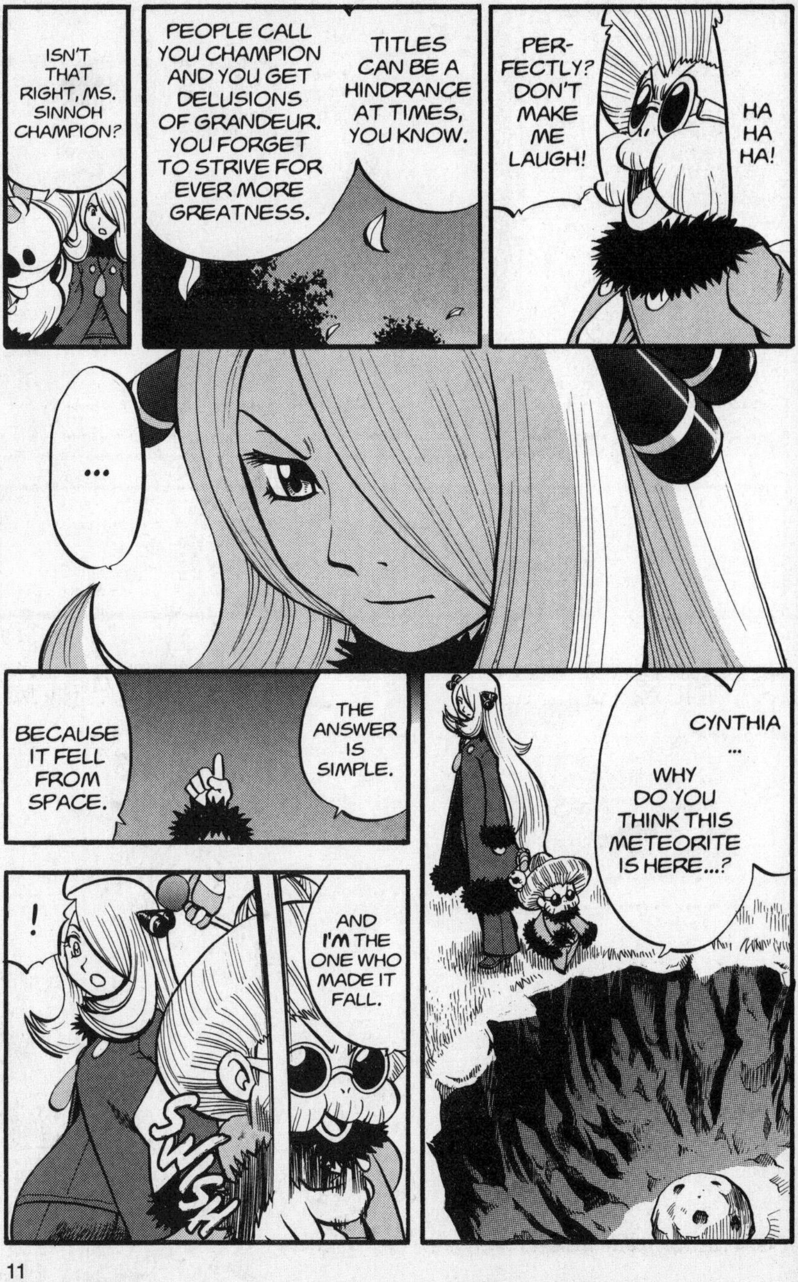
PER-FECTLY? DON'T MAKE ME LAUGH!
HA HA HA!
TITLES CAN BE A HINDRANCE AT TIMES, YOU KNOW.
PEOPLE CALL YOU CHAMPION AND YOU GET DELUSIONS OF GRANDEUR. YOU FORGET TO STRIVE FOR EVER MORE GREATNESS.
ISN'T THAT RIGHT, MS. SINNOH CHAMPION?
...
CYNTHIA ... WHY DO YOU THINK THIS METEORITE IS HERE...?
THE ANSWER IS SIMPLE.
BECAUSE IT FELL FROM SPACE.
AND I'M THE ONE WHO MADE IT FALL.
!
SWISH

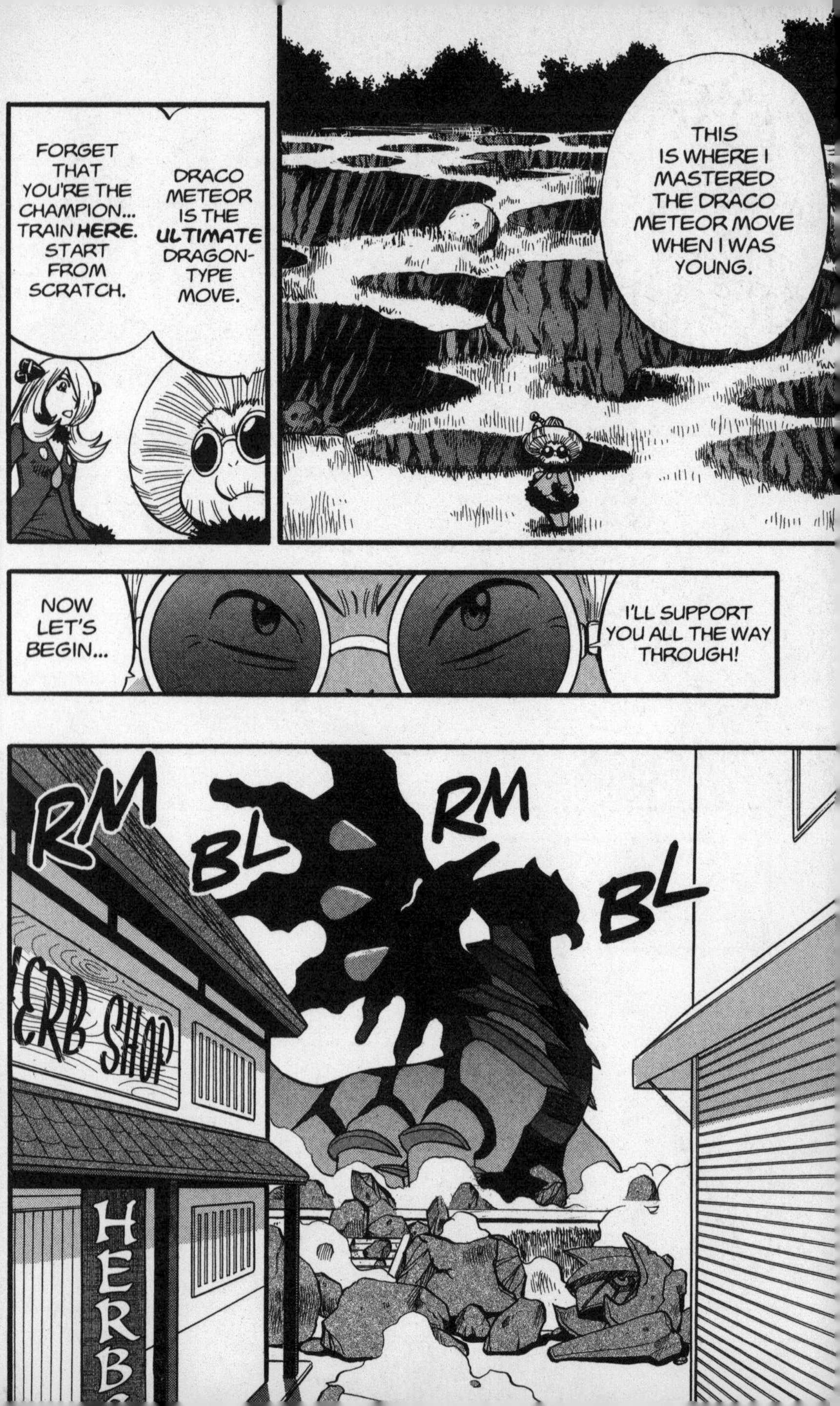
THIS IS WHERE I MASTERED THE DRACO METEOR MOVE WHEN I WAS YOUNG.
DRACO METEOR IS THE ULTIMATE DRAGON-TYPE MOVE.
FORGET THAT YOU'RE THE CHAMPION... TRAIN HERE. START FROM SCRATCH.
I'LL SUPPORT YOU ALL THE WAY THROUGH!
NOW LET'S BEGIN...
BL
RM
BL
RM
ERB SHOP
HERB

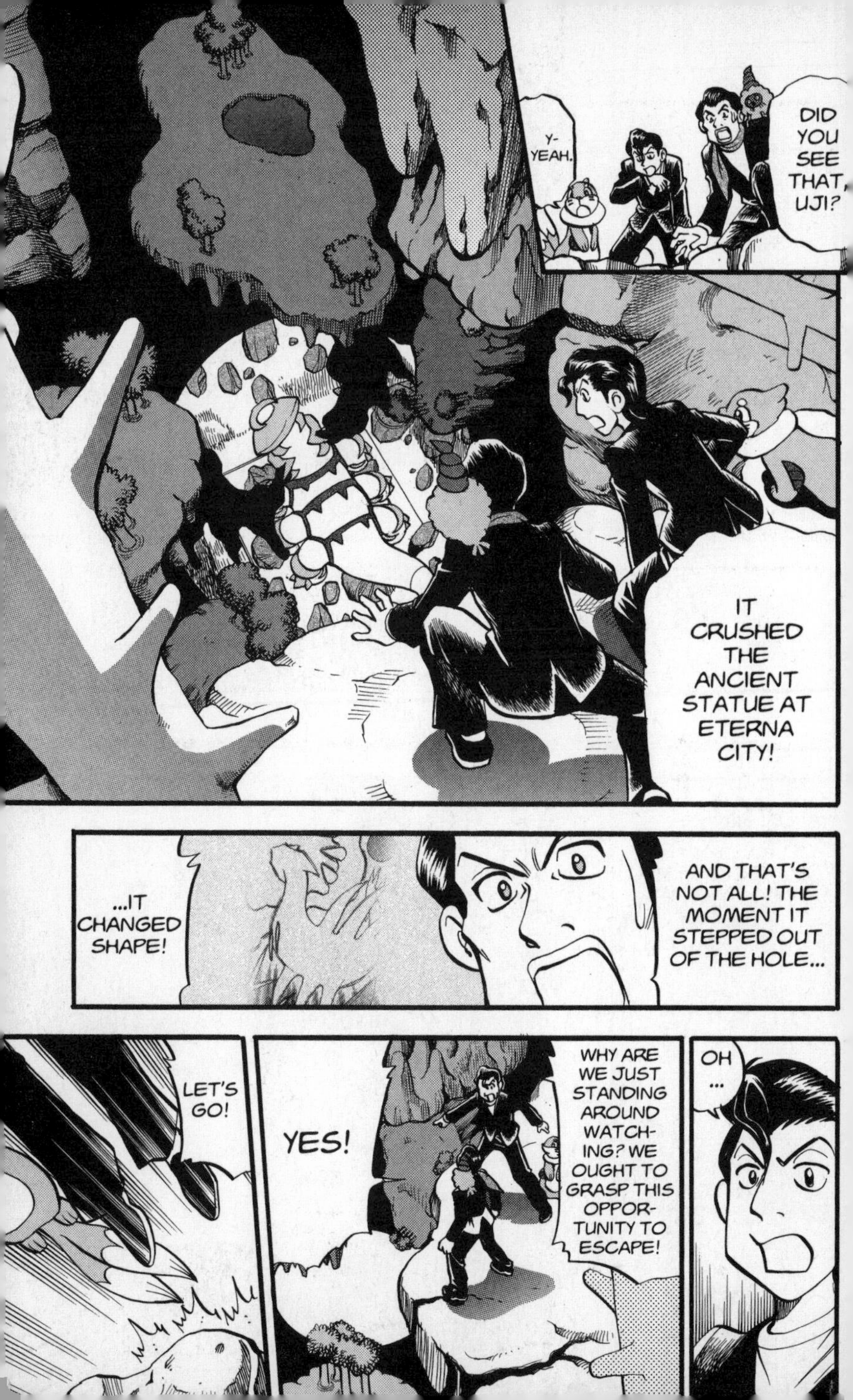
DID YOU SEE THAT, UJI?
Y-YEAH.
IT CRUSHED THE ANCIENT STATUE AT ETERNA CITY!
AND THAT'S NOT ALL! THE MOMENT IT STEPPED OUT OF THE HOLE...
...IT CHANGED SHAPE!
OH ...
WHY ARE WE JUST STANDING AROUND WATCHING? WE OUGHT TO GRASP THIS OPPORTUNITY TO ESCAPE!
YES!
LET'S GO!

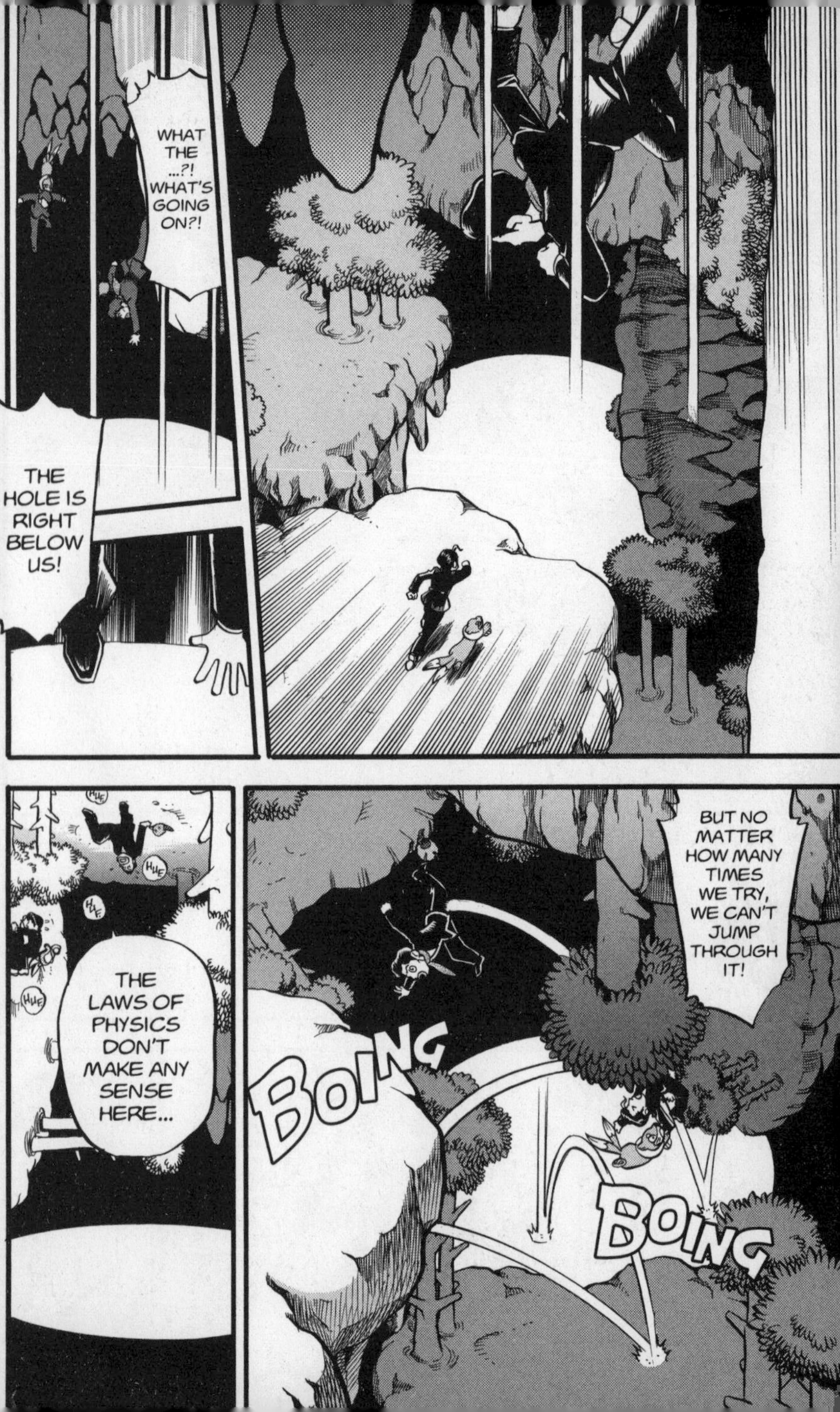
WHAT THE ...?! WHAT'S GOING ON?!
THE HOLE IS RIGHT BELOW US!
BUT NO MATTER HOW MANY TIMES WE TRY, WE CAN'T JUMP THROUGH IT!
BOING
BOING
THE LAWS OF PHYSICS DON'T MAKE ANY SENSE HERE...

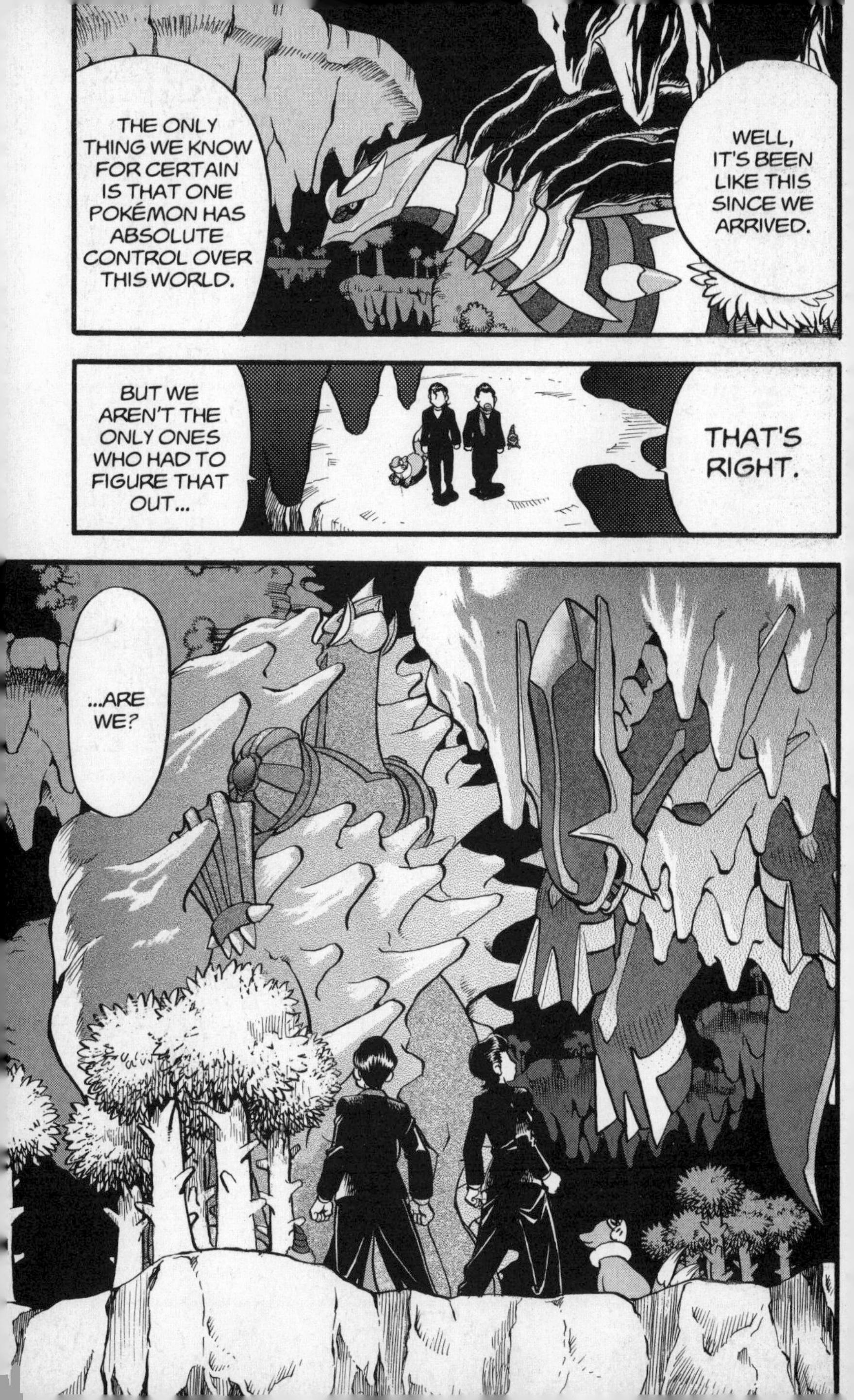
WELL, IT'S BEEN LIKE THIS SINCE WE ARRIVED.
THE ONLY THING WE KNOW FOR CERTAIN IS THAT ONE POKÉMON HAS ABSOLUTE CONTROL OVER THIS WORLD.
THAT'S RIGHT.
BUT WE AREN'T THE ONLY ONES WHO HAD TO FIGURE THAT OUT...
...ARE WE?

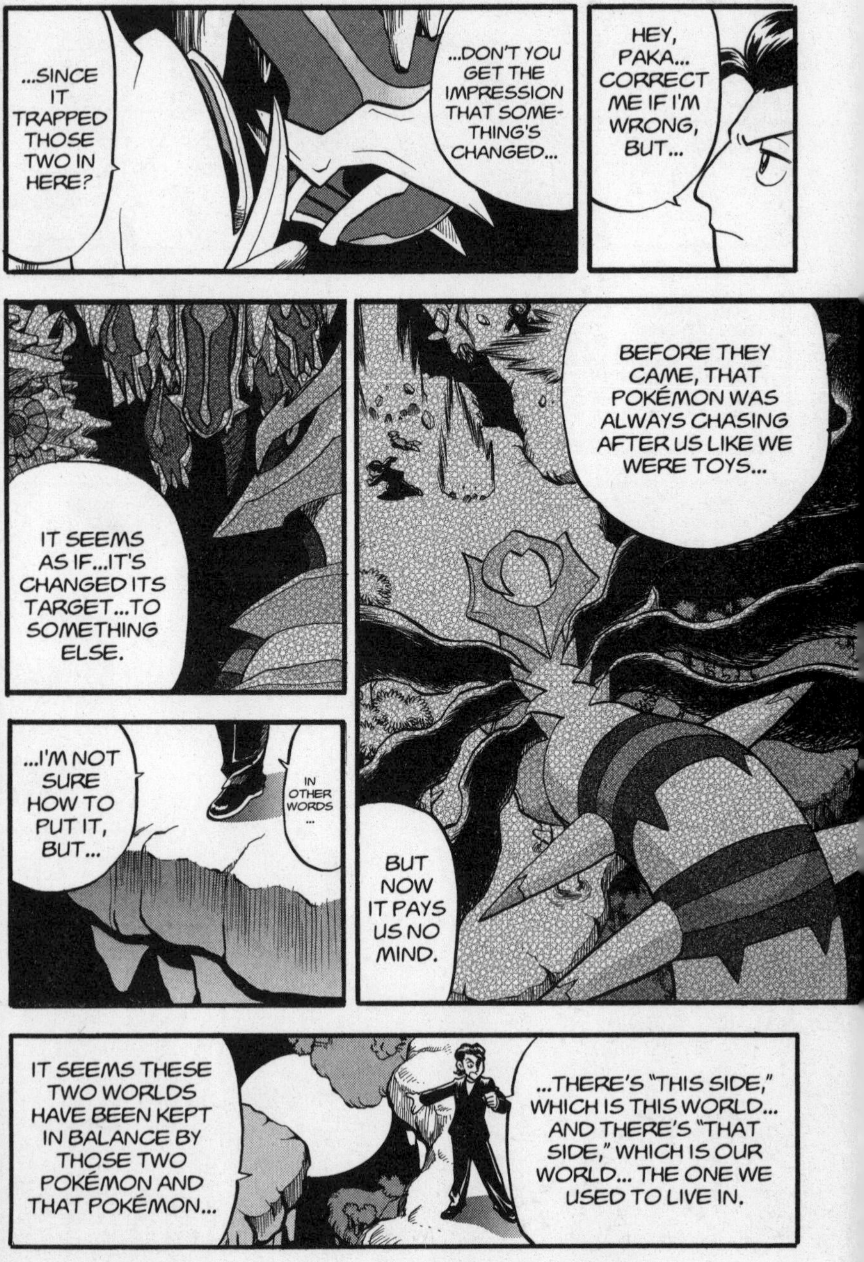
HEY, PAKA... CORRECT ME IF I'M WRONG, BUT...
...DON'T YOU GET THE IMPRESSION THAT SOME-THING'S CHANGED...
...SINCE IT TRAPPED THOSE TWO IN HERE?
BEFORE THEY CAME, THAT POKÉMON WAS ALWAYS CHASING AFTER US LIKE WE WERE TOYS...
BUT NOW IT PAYS US NO MIND.
IT SEEMS AS IF...IT'S CHANGED ITS TARGET...TO SOMETHING ELSE.
IN OTHER WORDS...
...I'M NOT SURE HOW TO PUT IT, BUT...
...THERE'S "THIS SIDE," WHICH IS THIS WORLD... AND THERE'S "THAT SIDE," WHICH IS OUR WORLD... THE ONE WE USED TO LIVE IN.
IT SEEMS THESE TWO WORLDS HAVE BEEN KEPT IN BALANCE BY THOSE TWO POKÉMON AND THAT POKÉMON...

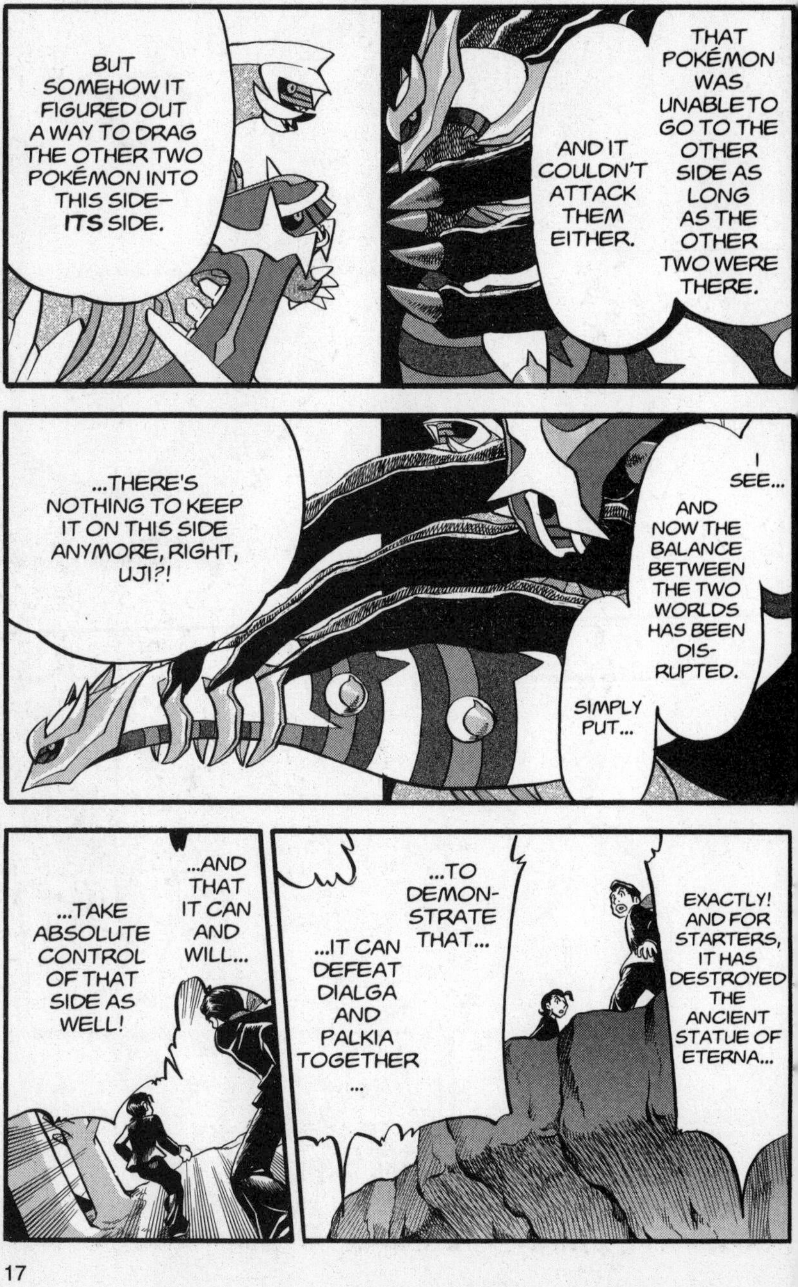
THAT POKÉMON WAS UNABLE TO GO TO THE OTHER SIDE AS LONG AS THE OTHER TWO WERE THERE.
AND IT COULDN'T ATTACK THEM EITHER.
BUT SOMEHOW IT FIGURED OUT A WAY TO DRAG THE OTHER TWO POKÉMON INTO THIS SIDE– **ITS** SIDE.
I SEE...
AND NOW THE BALANCE BETWEEN THE TWO WORLDS HAS BEEN DIS-RUPTED.
SIMPLY PUT...
...THERE'S NOTHING TO KEEP IT ON THIS SIDE ANYMORE, RIGHT, UJI?!
EXACTLY! AND FOR STARTERS, IT HAS DESTROYED THE ANCIENT STATUE OF ETERNA...
...TO DEMON-STRATE THAT...
...IT CAN DEFEAT DIALGA AND PALKIA TOGETHER ...
...AND THAT IT CAN AND WILL...
...TAKE ABSOLUTE CONTROL OF THAT SIDE AS WELL!

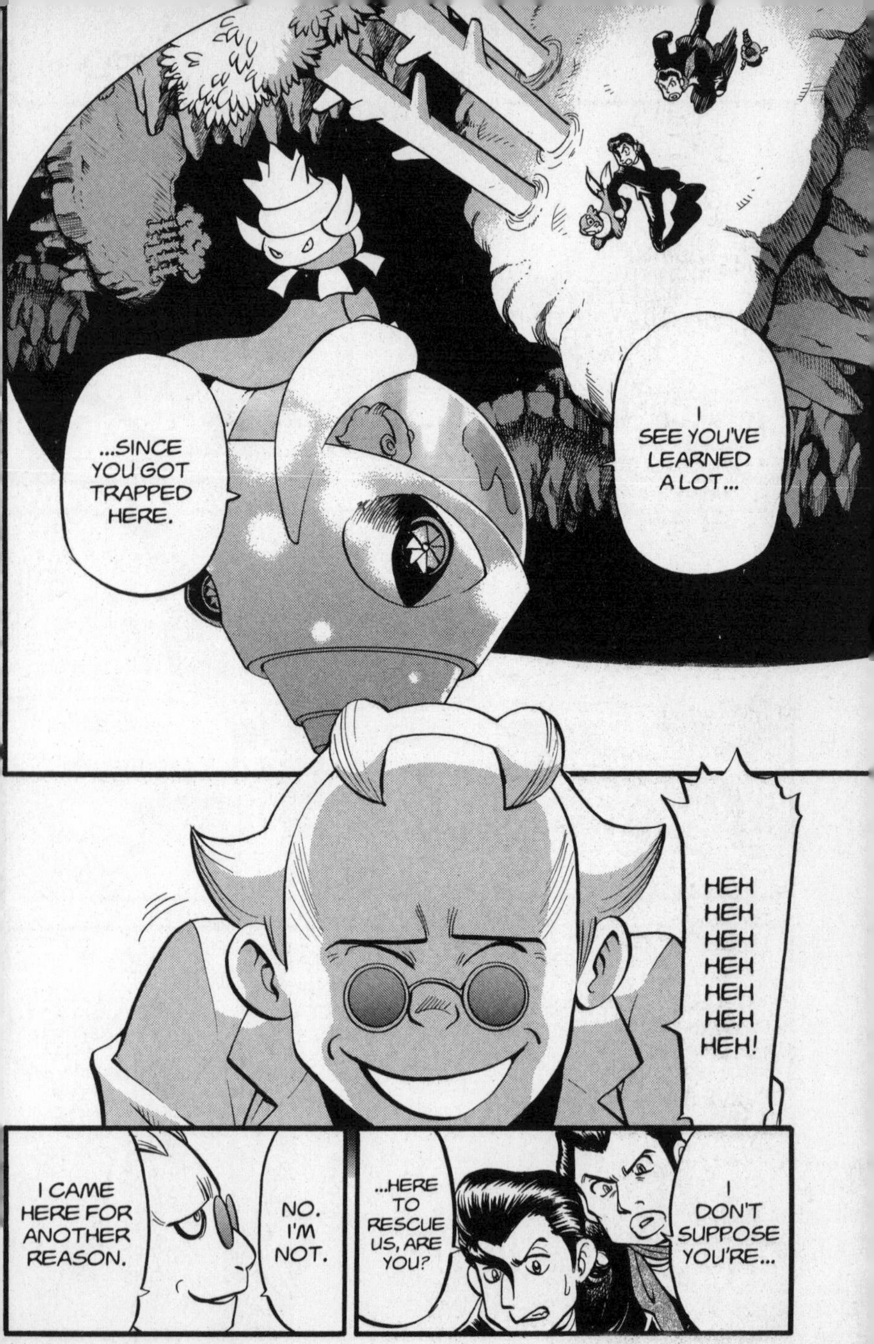
I SEE YOU'VE LEARNED A LOT...
...SINCE YOU GOT TRAPPED HERE.
HEH HEH HEH HEH HEH HEH HEH!
I DON'T SUPPOSE YOU'RE...
...HERE TO RESCUE US, ARE YOU?
NO. I'M NOT.
I CAME HERE FOR ANOTHER REASON.

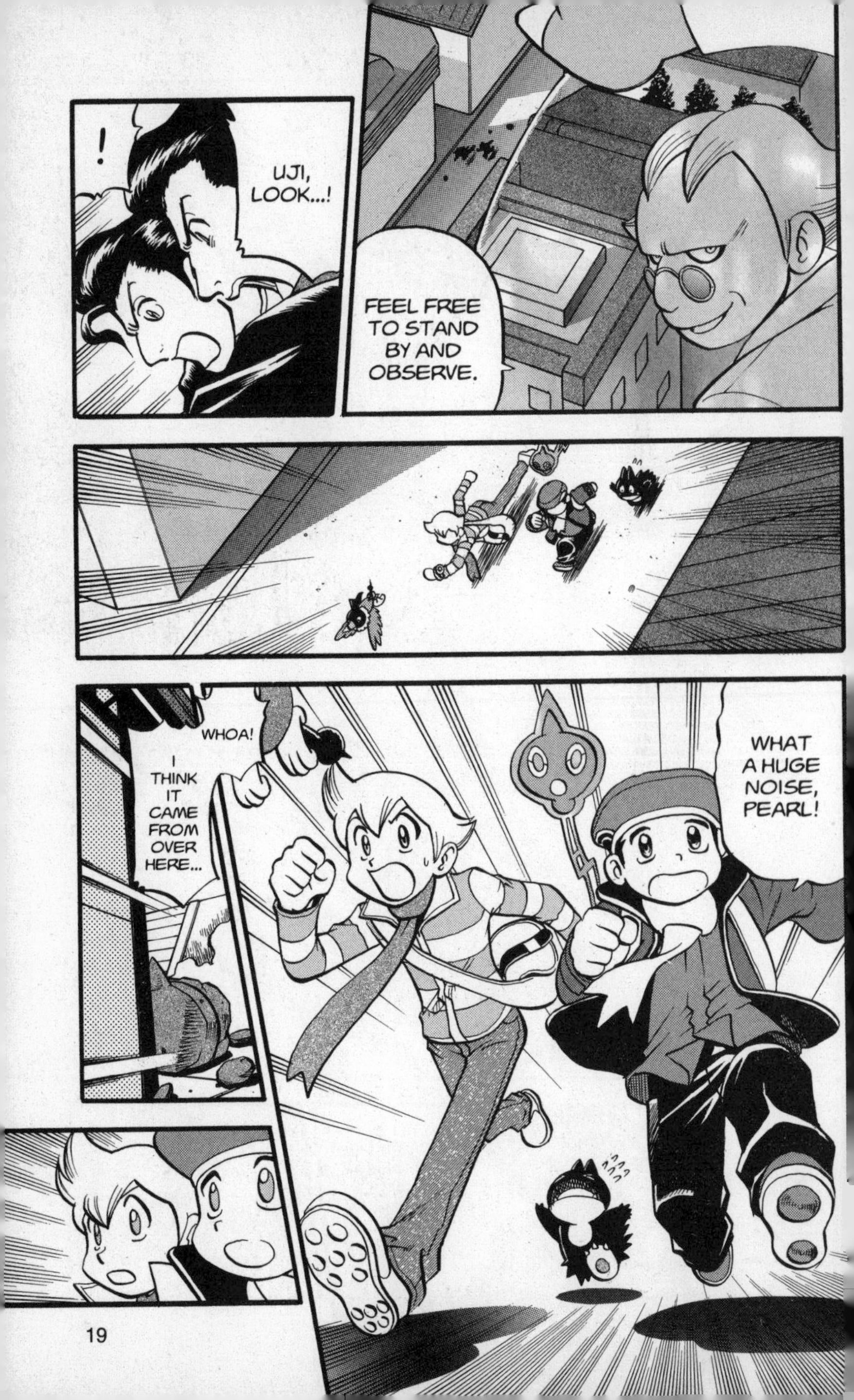
FEEL FREE TO STAND BY AND OBSERVE.
!
UJI, LOOK...!
WHAT A HUGE NOISE, PEARL!
WHOA!
I THINK IT CAME FROM OVER HERE...

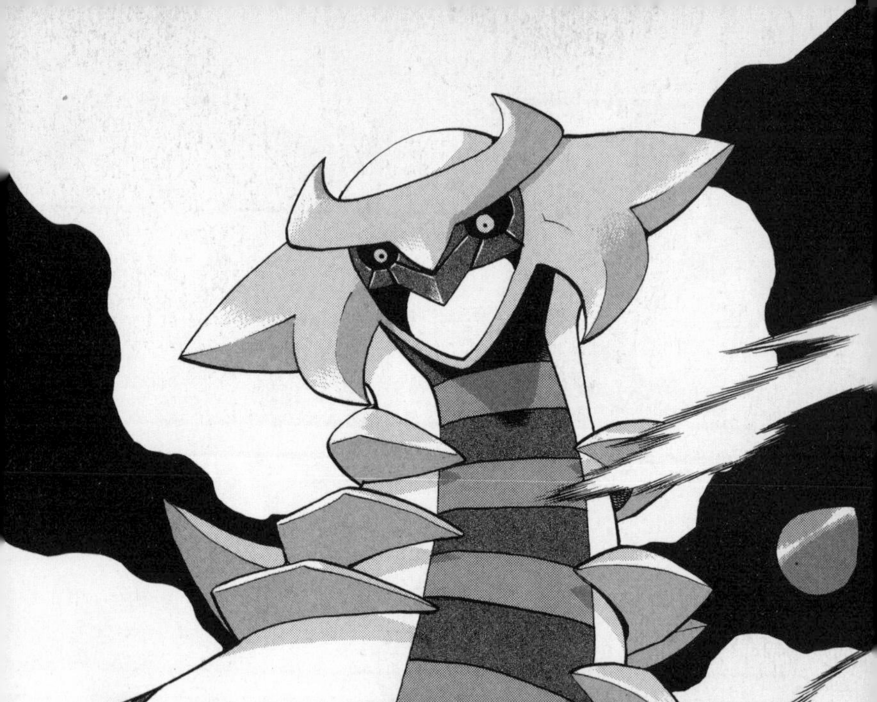

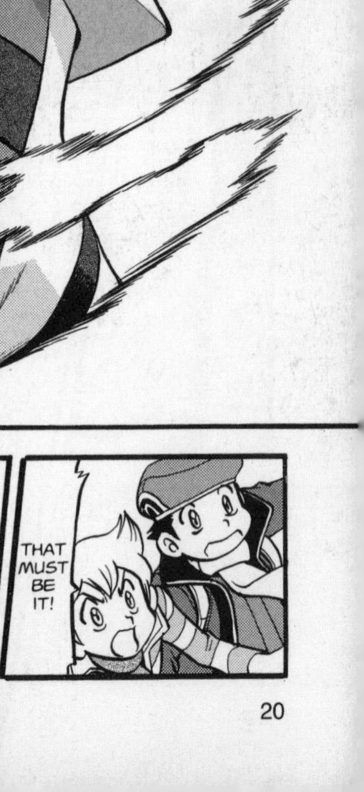
THAT MUST BE IT!

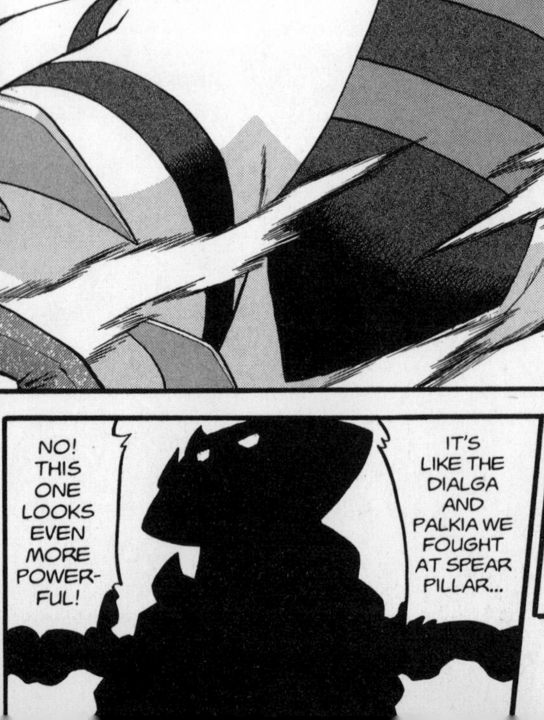
IT'S LIKE THE DIALGA AND PALKIA WE FOUGHT AT SPEAR PILLAR...
NO! THIS ONE LOOKS EVEN MORE POWER-FUL!

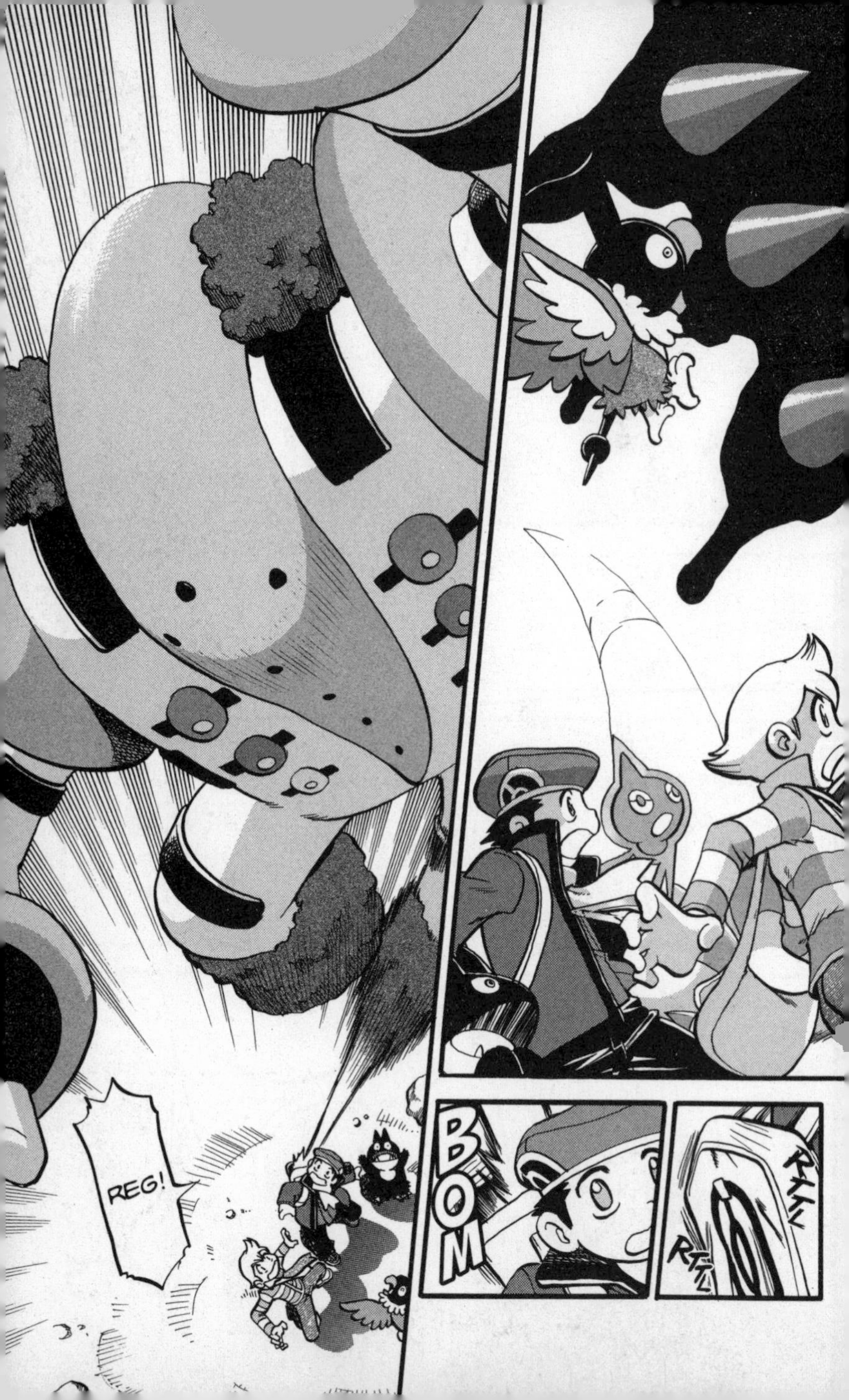
RTTL
RTTL
BOOM
REG!

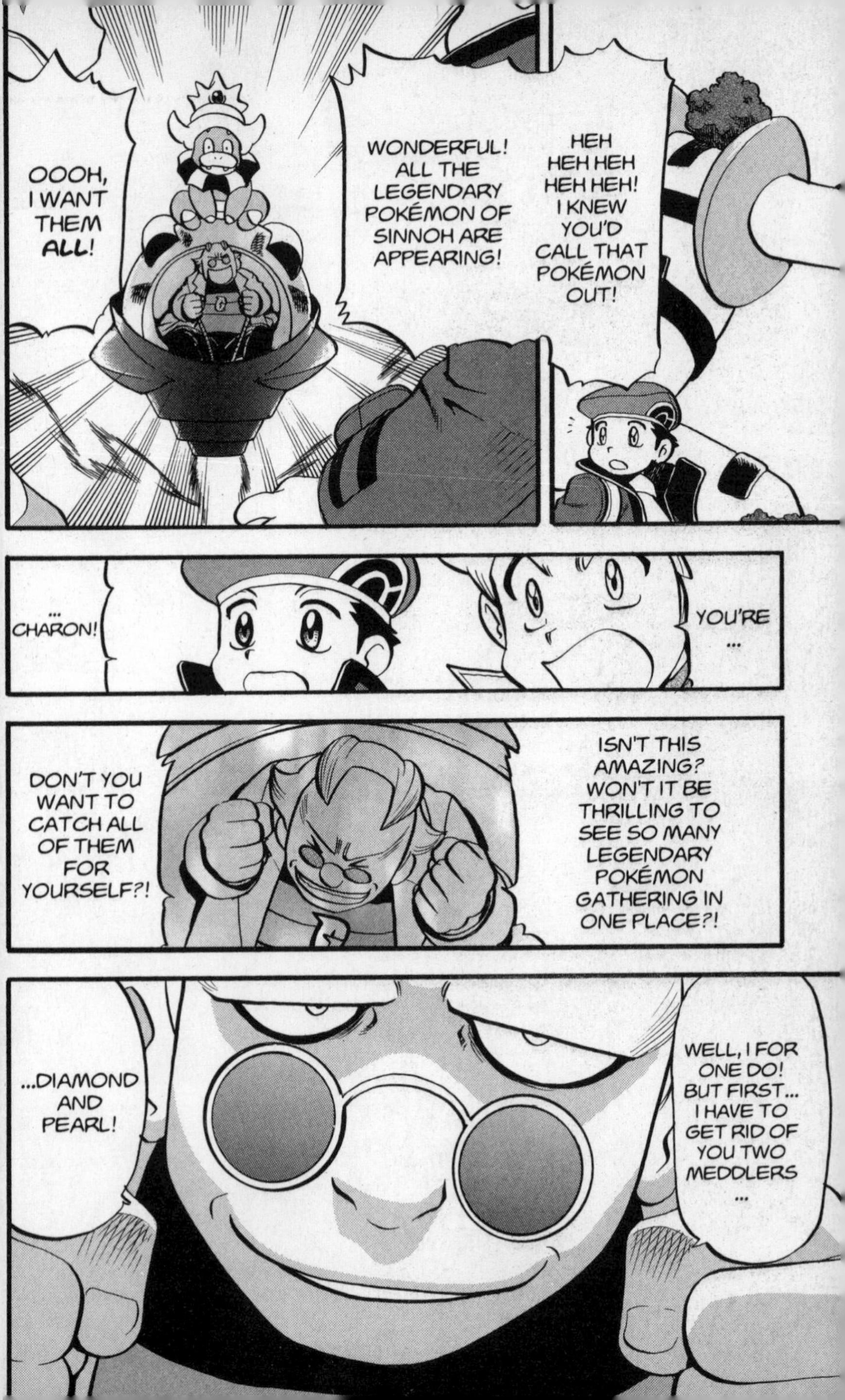
HEH HEH HEH HEH HEH! I KNEW YOU'D CALL THAT POKÉMON OUT!
WONDERFUL! ALL THE LEGENDARY POKÉMON OF SINNOH ARE APPEARING!
OOOH, I WANT THEM **ALL**!
YOU'RE ...
... CHARON!
ISN'T THIS AMAZING? WON'T IT BE THRILLING TO SEE SO MANY LEGENDARY POKÉMON GATHERING IN ONE PLACE?!
DON'T YOU WANT TO CATCH ALL OF THEM FOR YOURSELF?!
WELL, I FOR ONE DO! BUT FIRST... I HAVE TO GET RID OF YOU TWO MEDDLERS ...
...DIAMOND AND PEARL!

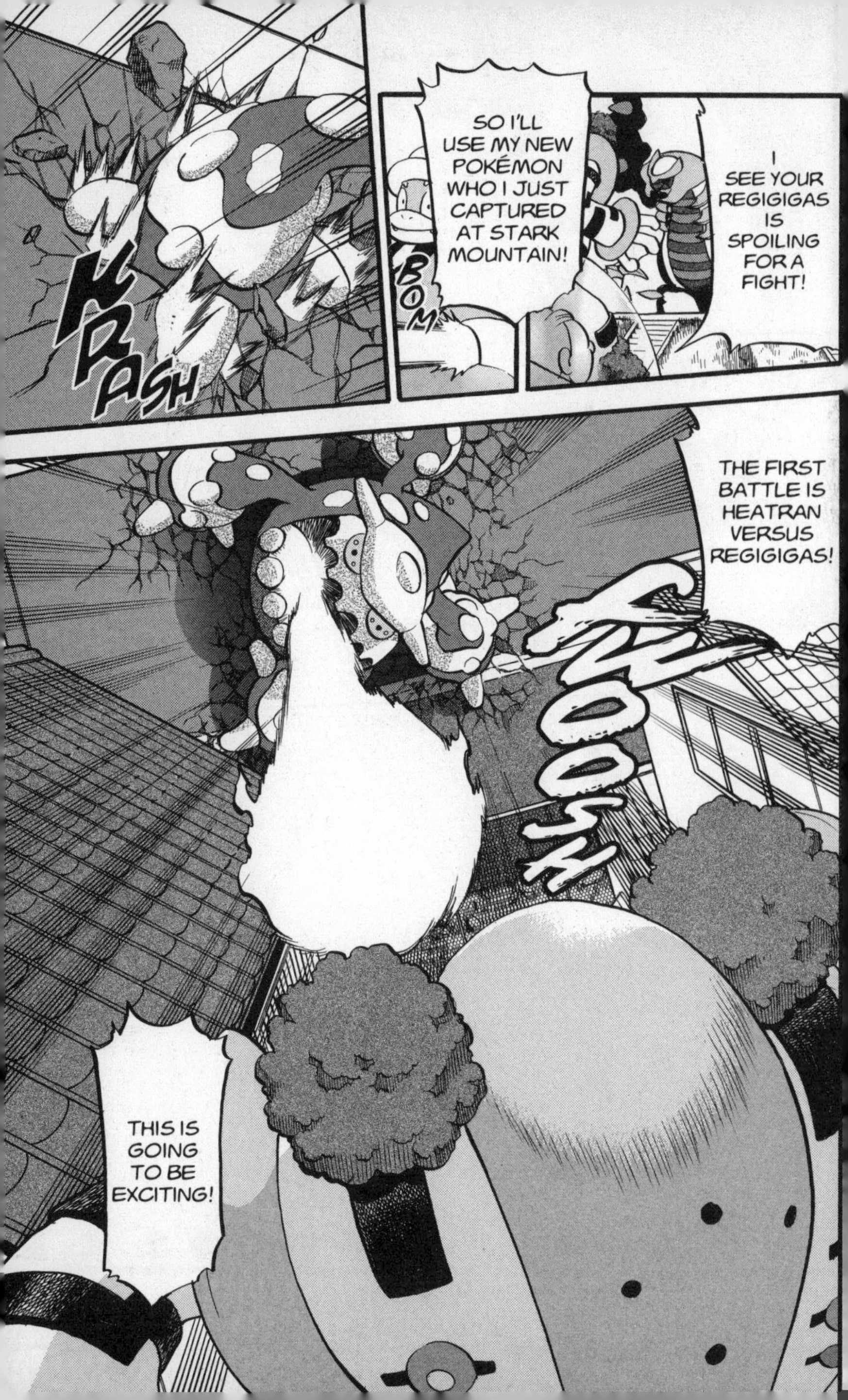
I SEE YOUR REGIGIGAS IS SPOILING FOR A FIGHT!
SO I'LL USE MY NEW POKÉMON WHO I JUST CAPTURED AT STARK MOUNTAIN!
BOOM
KRASH
THE FIRST BATTLE IS HEATRAN VERSUS REGIGIGAS!
WHOOSH
THIS IS GOING TO BE EXCITING!

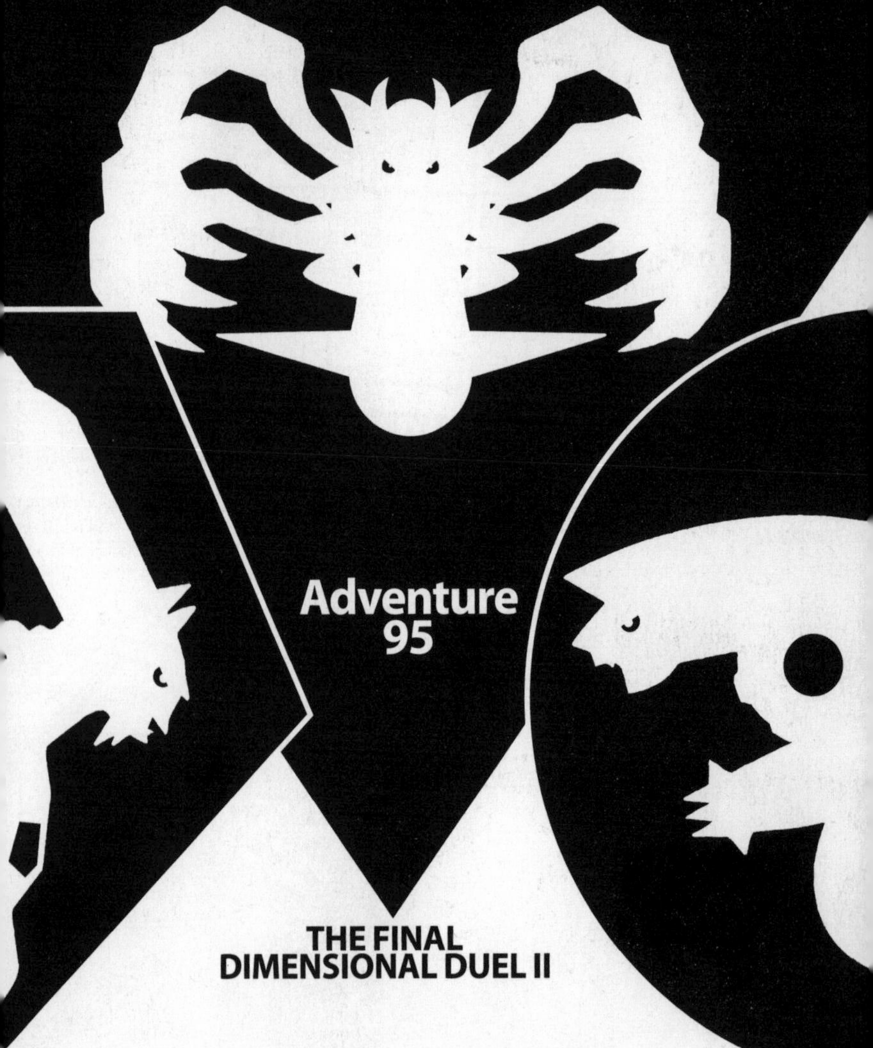

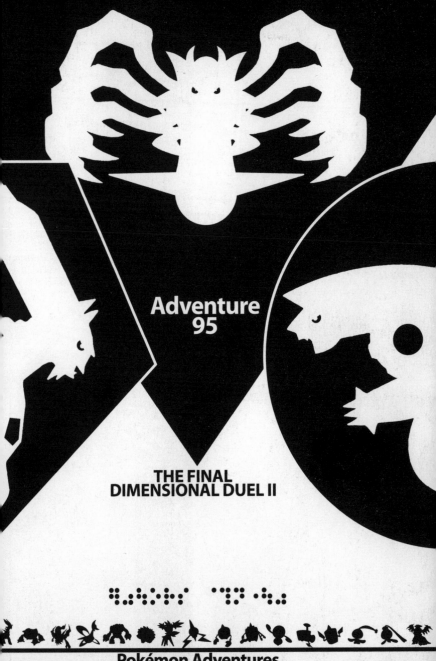

Adventure 95

THE FINAL DIMENSIONAL DUEL II

Pokémon Adventures
The Eighth Chapter

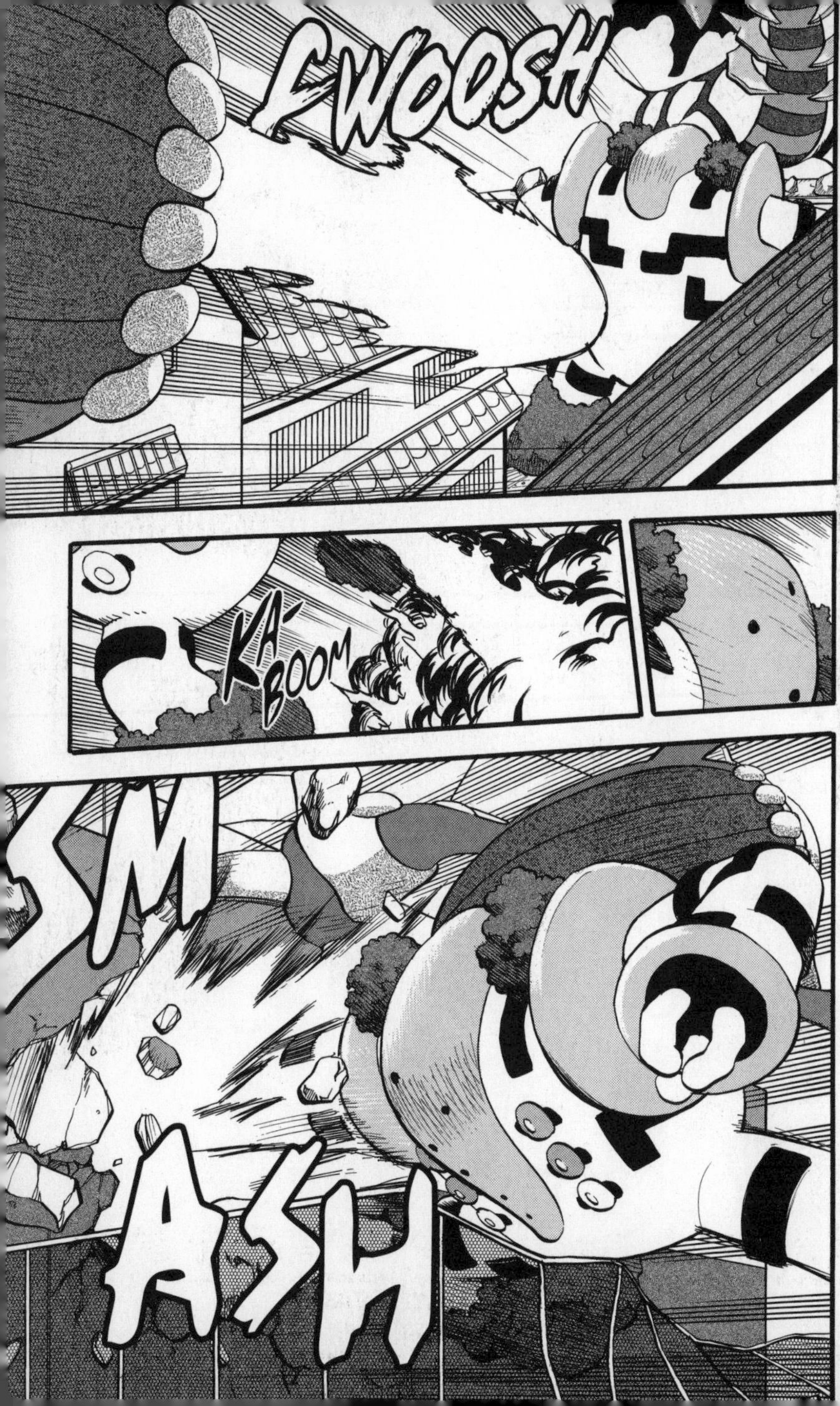
FWOOSH
KA-BOOM
SMASH

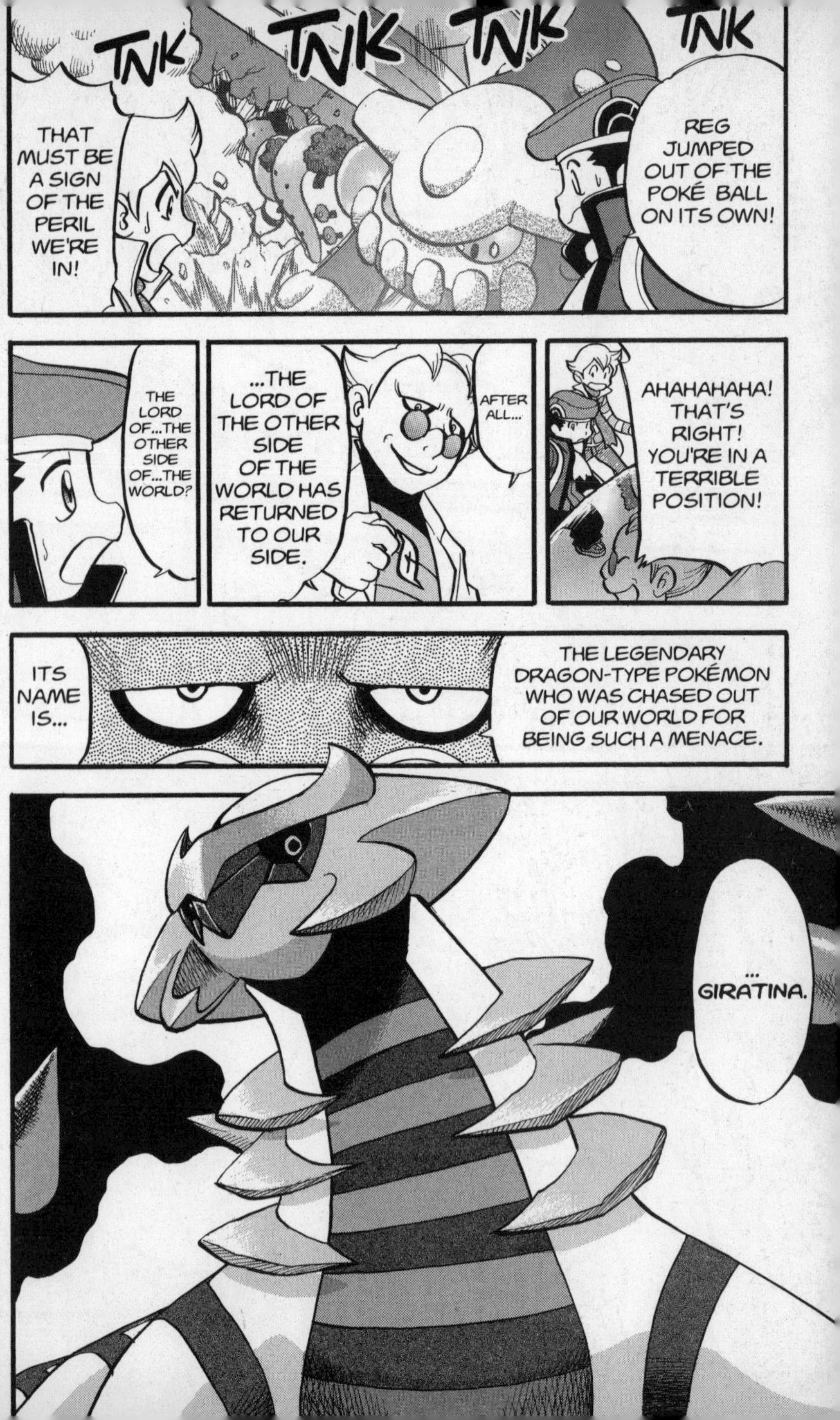
TNK
TNK
TNK
TNK
REG JUMPED OUT OF THE POKÉ BALL ON ITS OWN!
THAT MUST BE A SIGN OF THE PERIL WE'RE IN!
AHAHAHAHA! THAT'S RIGHT! YOU'RE IN A TERRIBLE POSITION!
AFTER ALL...
...THE LORD OF THE OTHER SIDE OF THE WORLD HAS RETURNED TO OUR SIDE.
THE LORD OF...THE OTHER SIDE OF...THE WORLD?
THE LEGENDARY DRAGON-TYPE POKÉMON WHO WAS CHASED OUT OF OUR WORLD FOR BEING SUCH A MENACE.
ITS NAME IS...
...GIRATINA.

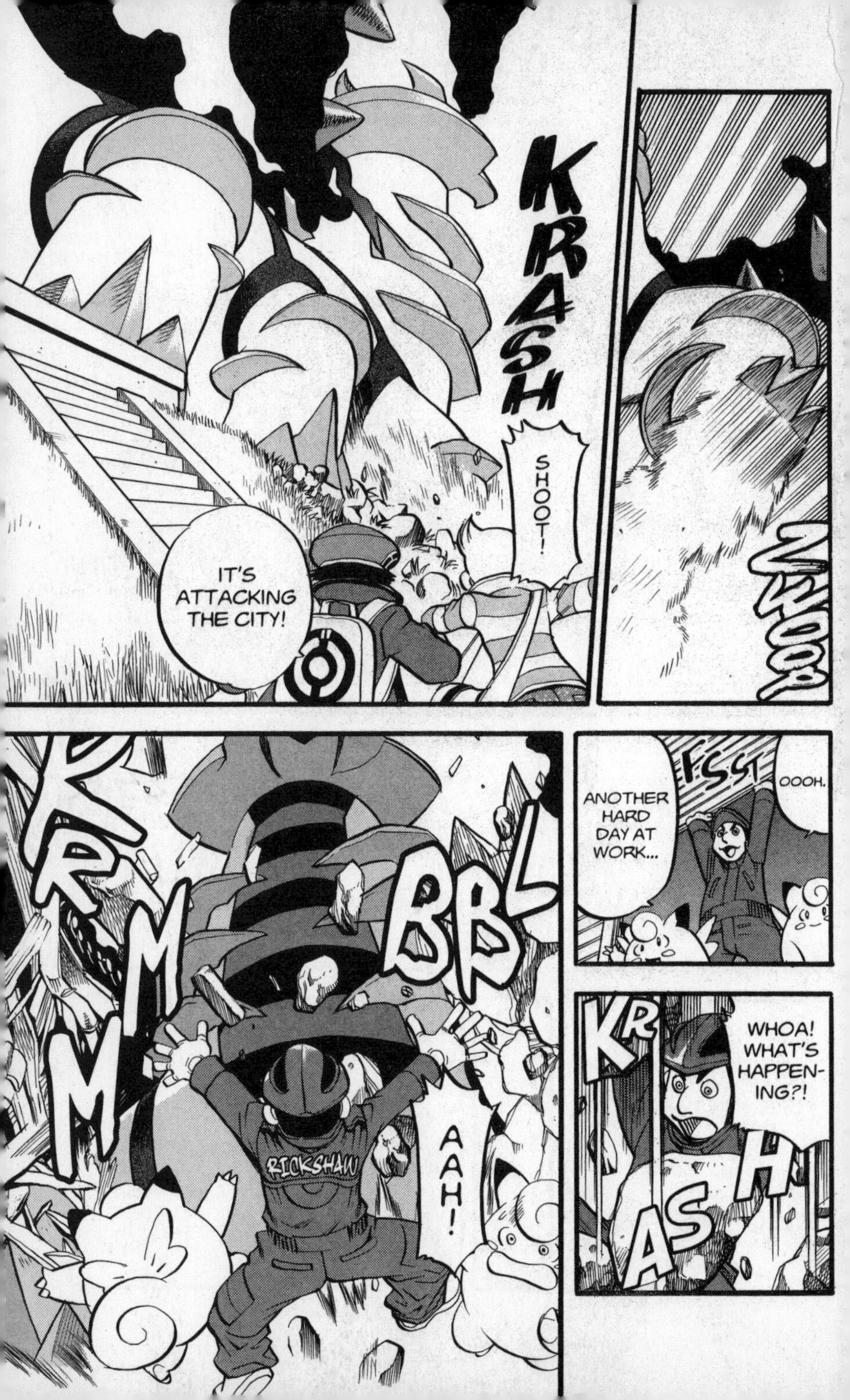
WHOOSH
KRASH
SHOOT!
IT'S ATTACKING THE CITY!
OOOH.
FSST
ANOTHER HARD DAY AT WORK...
WHOA! WHAT'S HAPPEN-ING?!
KRASH
AAH!
RICKSHAW

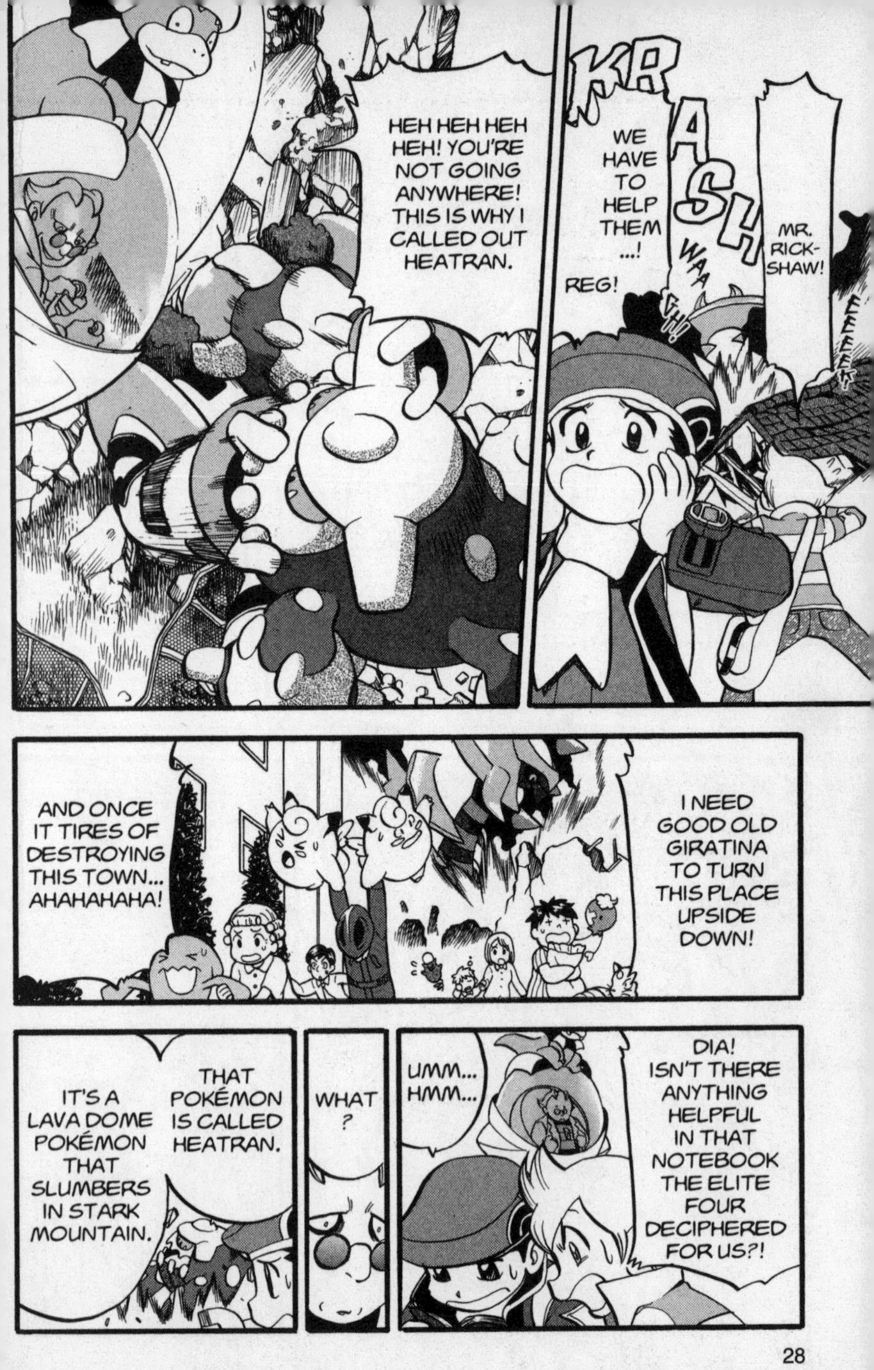
KRASH
MR. RICK-SHAW!
EEEEEK!
WAAAGH!
WE HAVE TO HELP THEM ...!
REG!
HEH HEH HEH HEH! YOU'RE NOT GOING ANYWHERE! THIS IS WHY I CALLED OUT HEATRAN.
I NEED GOOD OLD GIRATINA TO TURN THIS PLACE UPSIDE DOWN!
AND ONCE IT TIRES OF DESTROYING THIS TOWN... AHAHAHAHA!
DIA! ISN'T THERE ANYTHING HELPFUL IN THAT NOTEBOOK THE ELITE FOUR DECIPHERED FOR US?!
UMM... HMM...
WHAT?
THAT POKÉMON IS CALLED HEATRAN.
IT'S A LAVA DOME POKÉMON THAT SLUMBERS IN STARK MOUNTAIN.

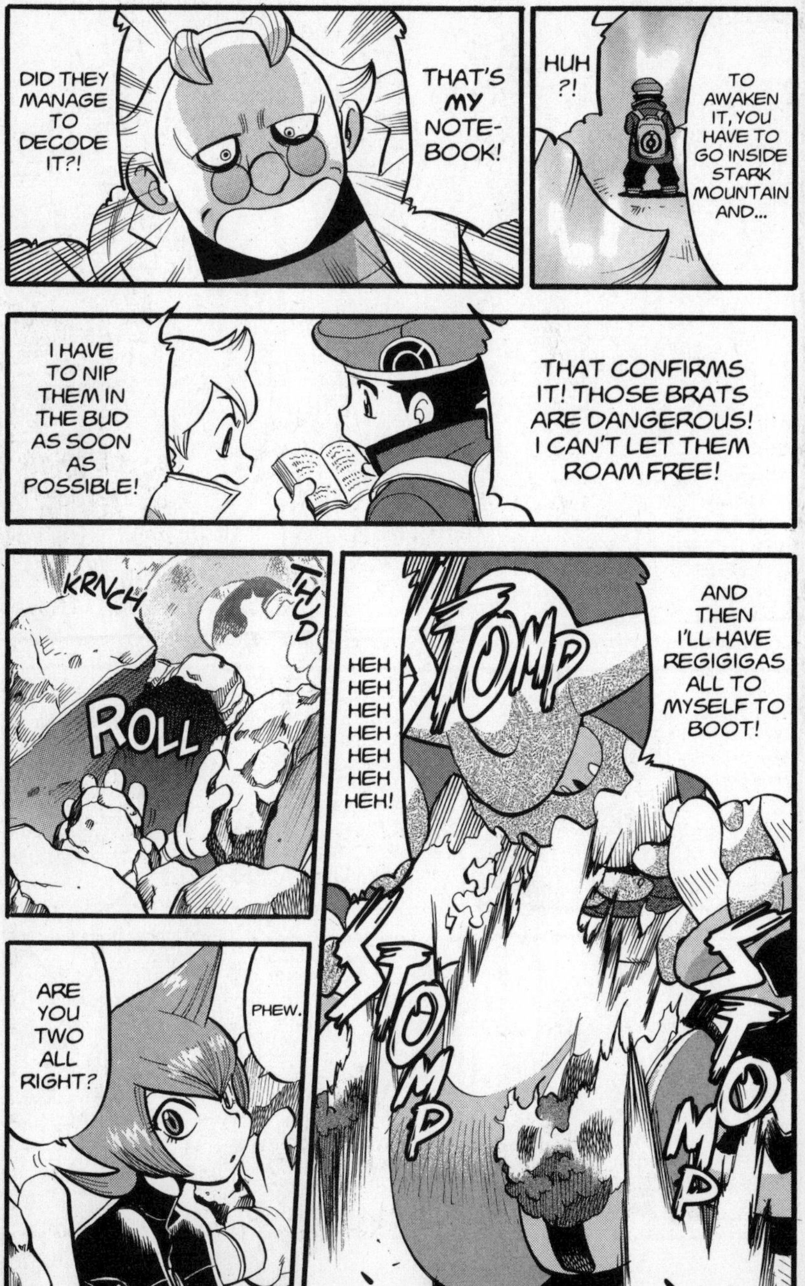
TO AWAKEN IT, YOU HAVE TO GO INSIDE STARK MOUNTAIN AND...
HUH?!
THAT'S MY NOTEBOOK!
DID THEY MANAGE TO DECODE IT?!
THAT CONFIRMS IT! THOSE BRATS ARE DANGEROUS! I CAN'T LET THEM ROAM FREE!
I HAVE TO NIP THEM IN THE BUD AS SOON AS POSSIBLE!
AND THEN I'LL HAVE REGIGIGAS ALL TO MYSELF TO BOOT!
HEH HEH HEH HEH HEH HEH HEH!
STOMP
STOMP
STOMP
THUD
KRNCH
ROLL
PHEW.
ARE YOU TWO ALL RIGHT?

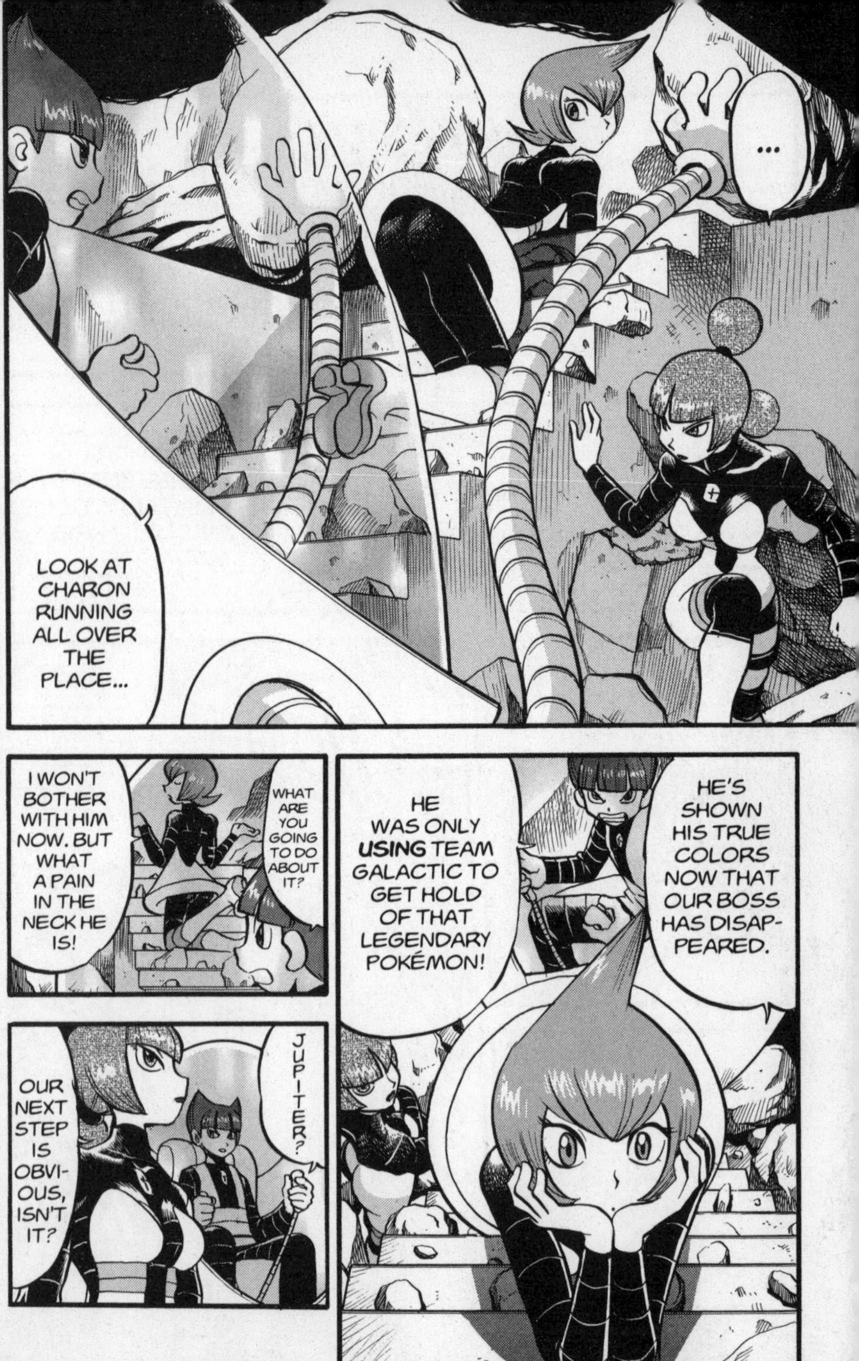
...
LOOK AT CHARON RUNNING ALL OVER THE PLACE...
HE'S SHOWN HIS TRUE COLORS NOW THAT OUR BOSS HAS DISAPPEARED.
HE WAS ONLY **USING** TEAM GALACTIC TO GET HOLD OF THAT LEGENDARY POKÉMON!
WHAT ARE YOU GOING TO DO ABOUT IT?
I WON'T BOTHER WITH HIM NOW. BUT WHAT A PAIN IN THE NECK HE IS!
JUPITER?
OUR NEXT STEP IS OBVIOUS, ISN'T IT?

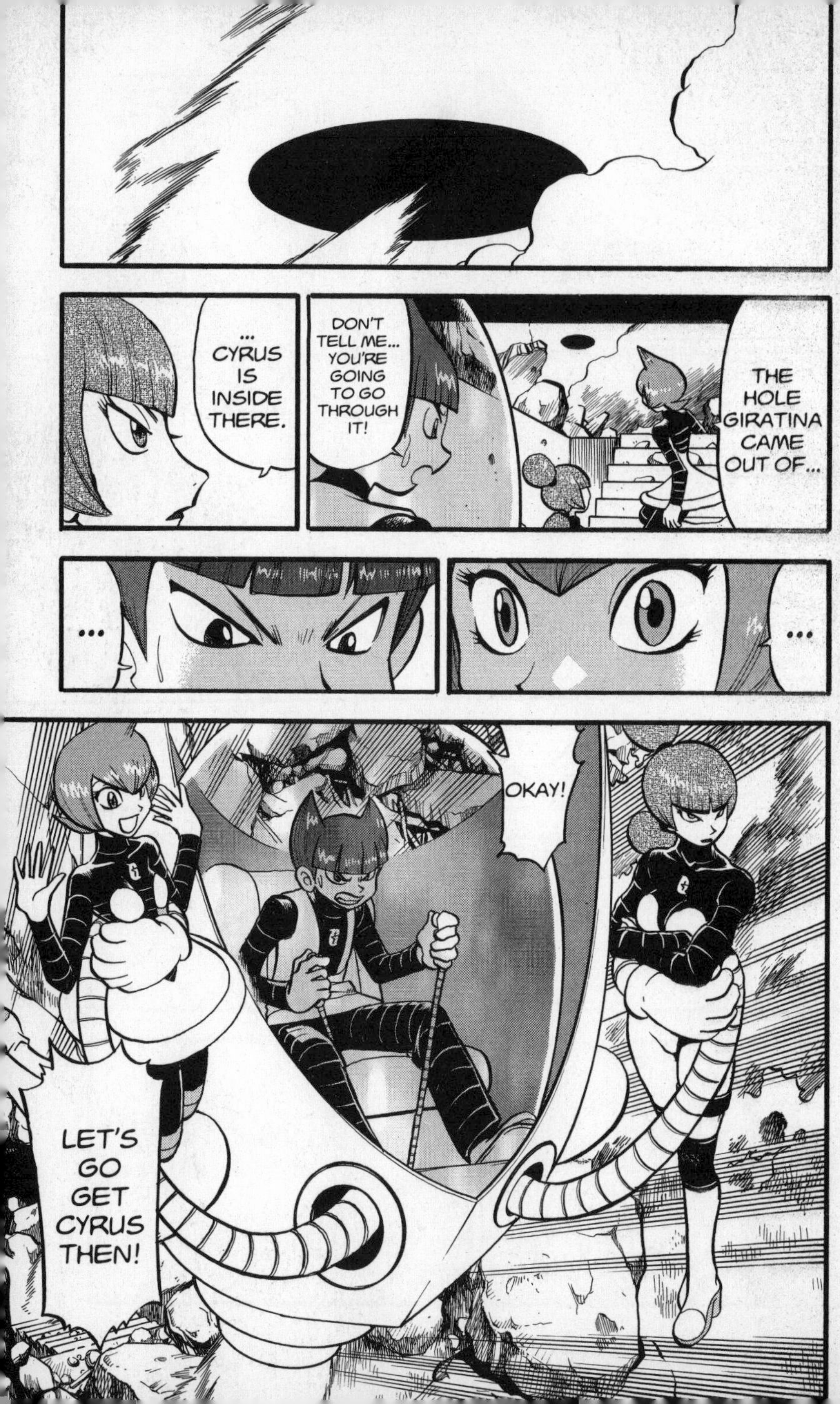
THE HOLE GIRATINA CAME OUT OF...
DON'T TELL ME... YOU'RE GOING TO GO THROUGH IT!
...CYRUS IS INSIDE THERE.
...
...
OKAY!
LET'S GO GET CYRUS THEN!

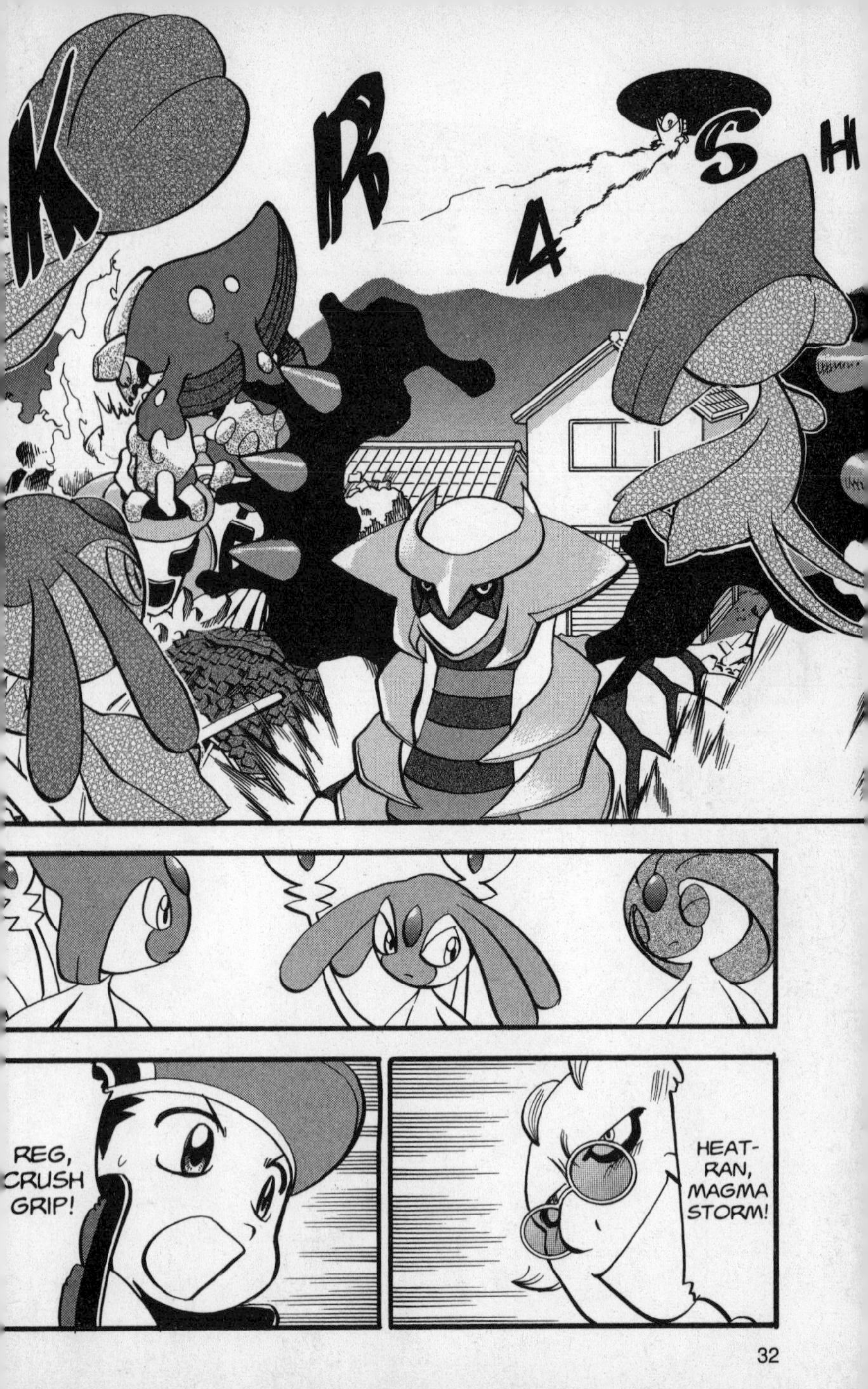
KRASH
HEAT-RAN, MAGMA STORM!
REG, CRUSH GRIP!

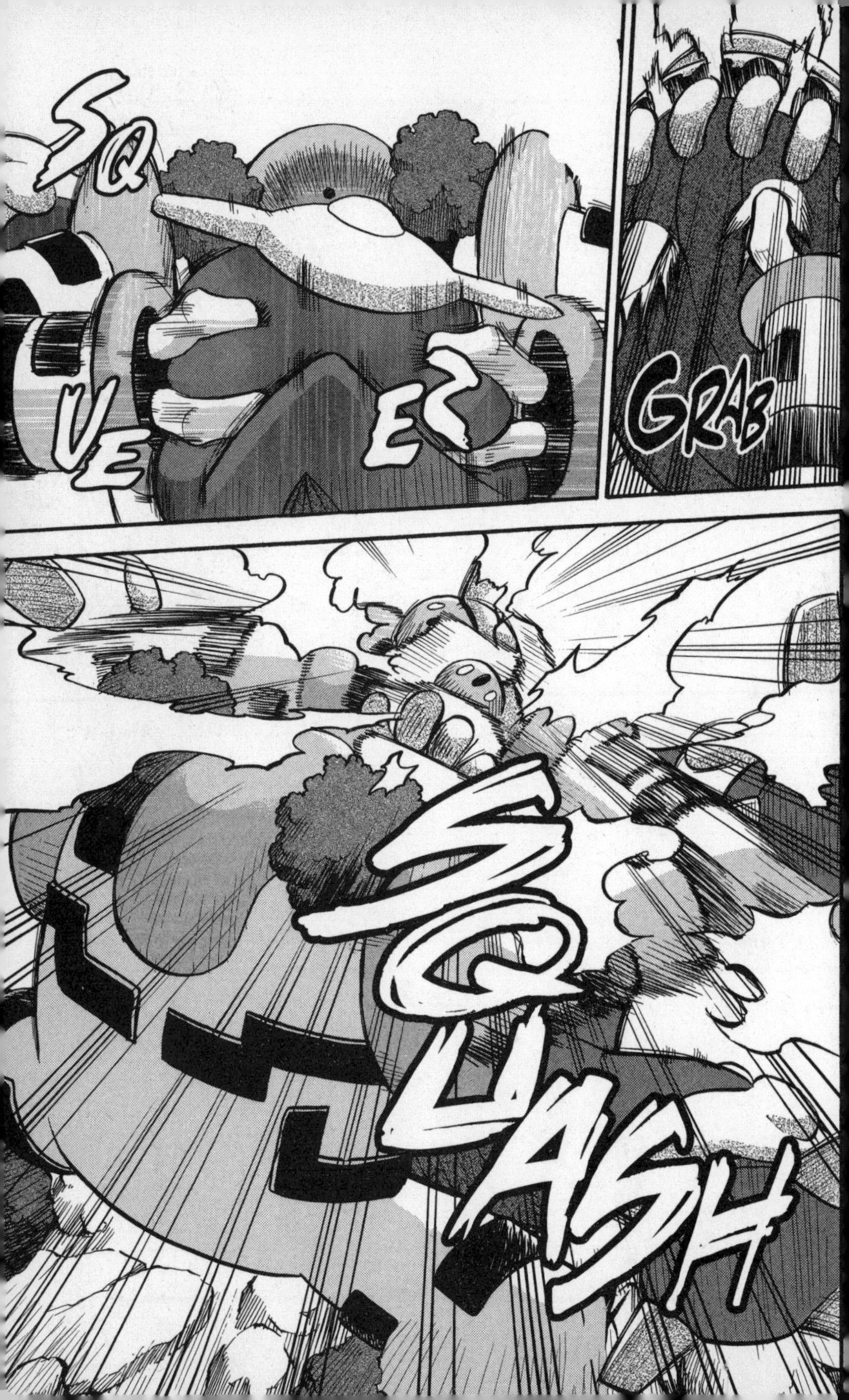
GRAB
SQUEEZE
SQUASH

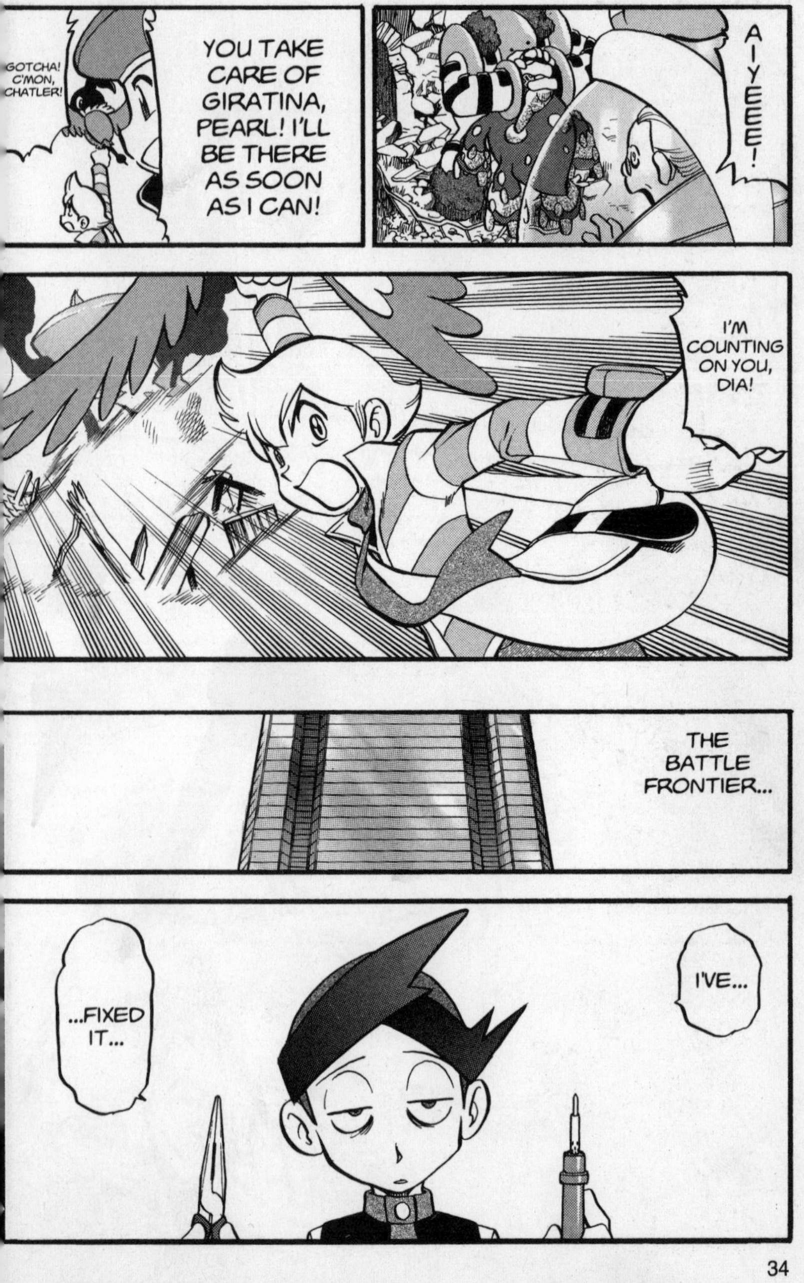
AIYEEE!
YOU TAKE CARE OF GIRATINA, PEARL! I'LL BE THERE AS SOON AS I CAN!
GOTCHA! C'MON, CHATLER!
I'M COUNTING ON YOU, DIA!
THE BATTLE FRONTIER...
I'VE...
...FIXED IT...

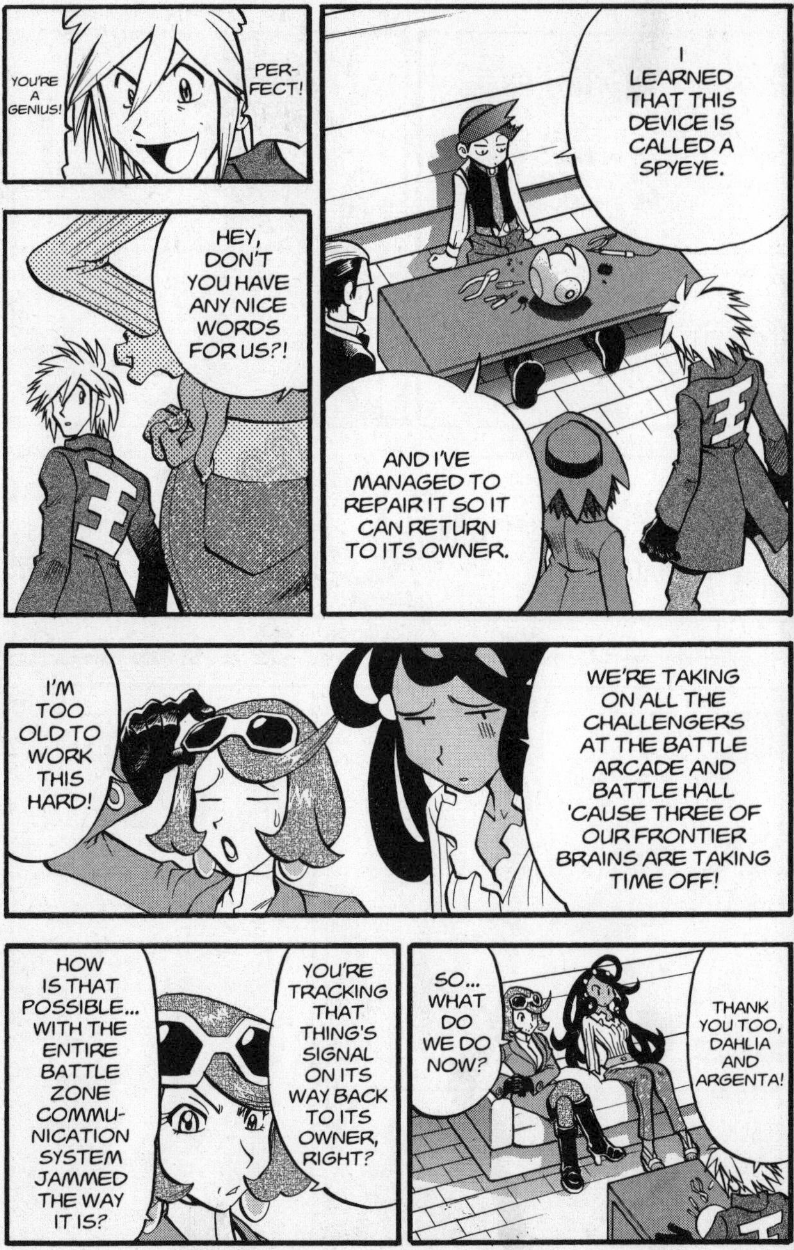
I LEARNED THAT THIS DEVICE IS CALLED A SPYEYE.
AND I'VE MANAGED TO REPAIR IT SO IT CAN RETURN TO ITS OWNER.
PER-FECT!
YOU'RE A GENIUS!
HEY, DON'T YOU HAVE ANY NICE WORDS FOR US?!
WE'RE TAKING ON ALL THE CHALLENGERS AT THE BATTLE ARCADE AND BATTLE HALL 'CAUSE THREE OF OUR FRONTIER BRAINS ARE TAKING TIME OFF!
I'M TOO OLD TO WORK THIS HARD!
THANK YOU TOO, DAHLIA AND ARGENTA!
SO... WHAT DO WE DO NOW?
YOU'RE TRACKING THAT THING'S SIGNAL ON ITS WAY BACK TO ITS OWNER, RIGHT?
HOW IS THAT POSSIBLE... WITH THE ENTIRE BATTLE ZONE COMMUNI-CATION SYSTEM JAMMED THE WAY IT IS?

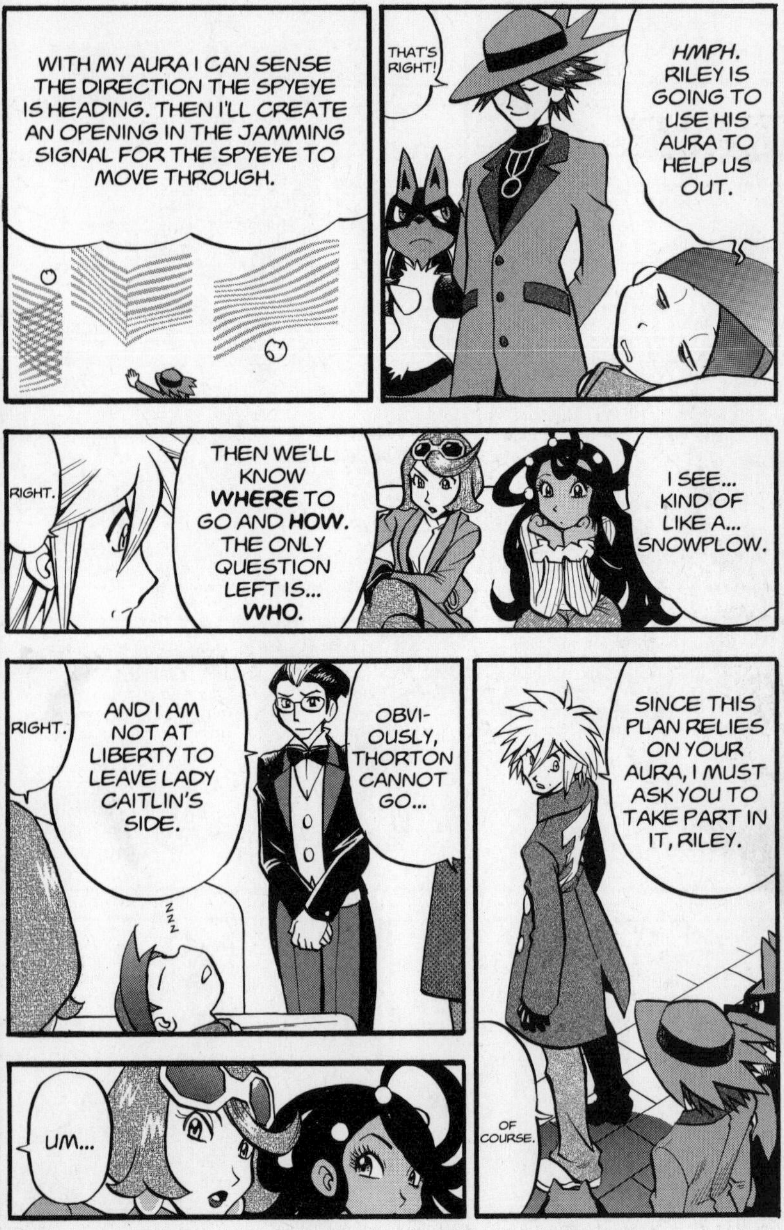
HMPH. RILEY IS GOING TO USE HIS AURA TO HELP US OUT.
THAT'S RIGHT!
WITH MY AURA I CAN SENSE THE DIRECTION THE SPYEYE IS HEADING. THEN I'LL CREATE AN OPENING IN THE JAMMING SIGNAL FOR THE SPYEYE TO MOVE THROUGH.
I SEE... KIND OF LIKE A... SNOWPLOW.
THEN WE'LL KNOW WHERE TO GO AND HOW. THE ONLY QUESTION LEFT IS... WHO.
RIGHT.
SINCE THIS PLAN RELIES ON YOUR AURA, I MUST ASK YOU TO TAKE PART IN IT, RILEY.
OF COURSE.
OBVI-OUSLY, THORTON CANNOT GO...
AND I AM NOT AT LIBERTY TO LEAVE LADY CAITLIN'S SIDE.
RIGHT.
ZZZ
UM...

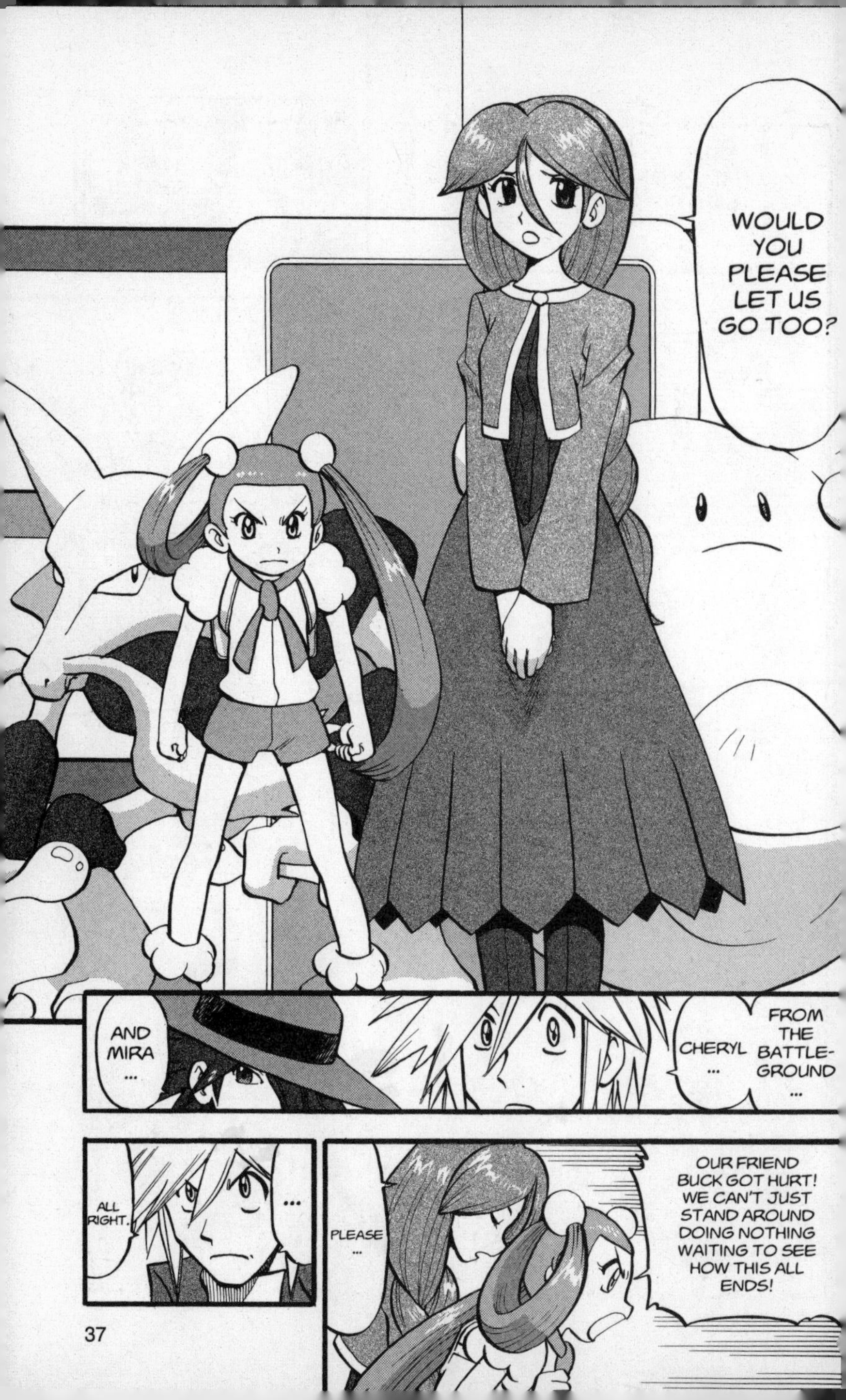
WOULD YOU PLEASE LET US GO TOO?
FROM THE BATTLE-GROUND ...
CHERYL ...
AND MIRA ...
OUR FRIEND BUCK GOT HURT! WE CAN'T JUST STAND AROUND DOING NOTHING WAITING TO SEE HOW THIS ALL ENDS!
PLEASE ...
...
ALL RIGHT.

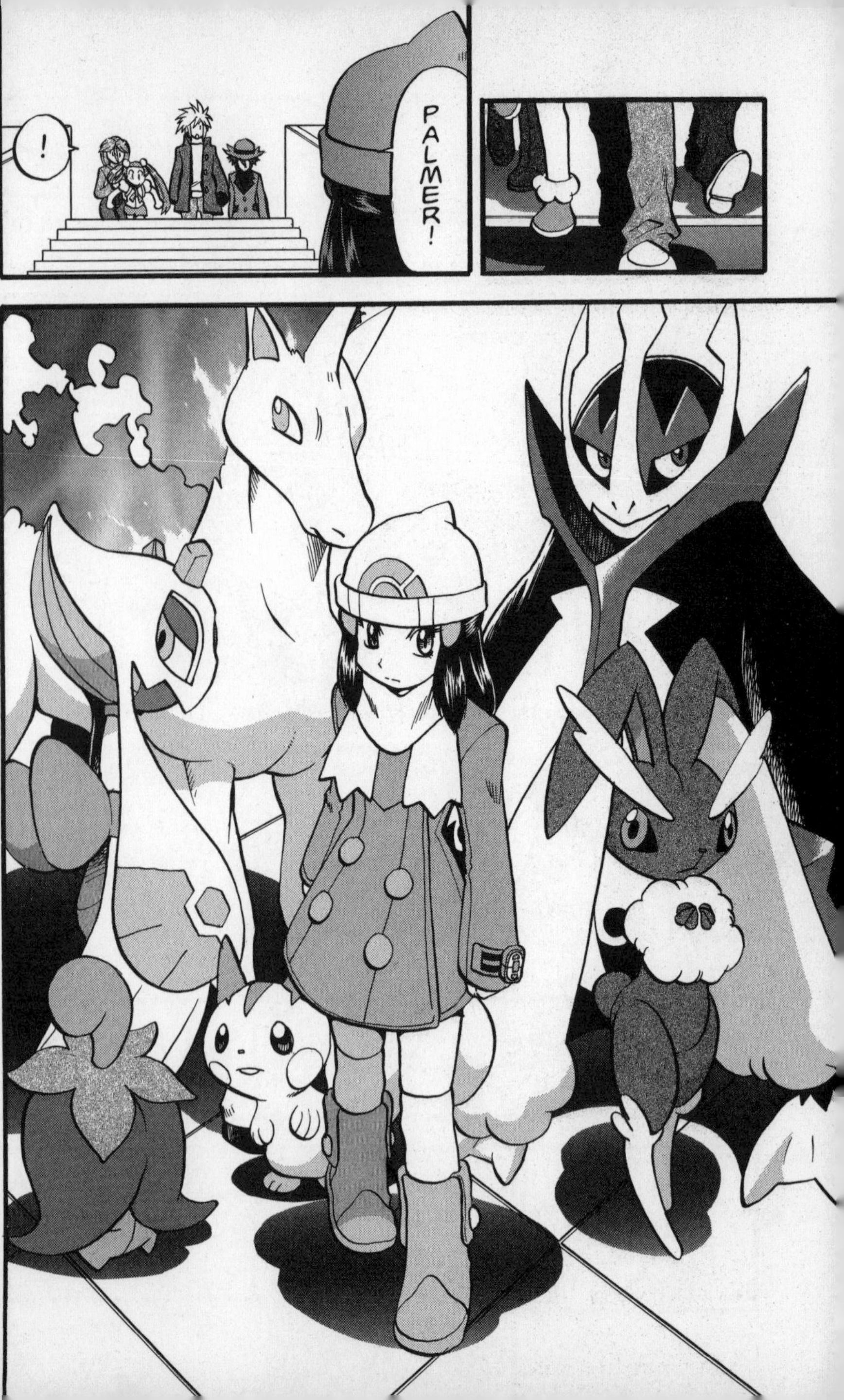
PALMER!
!

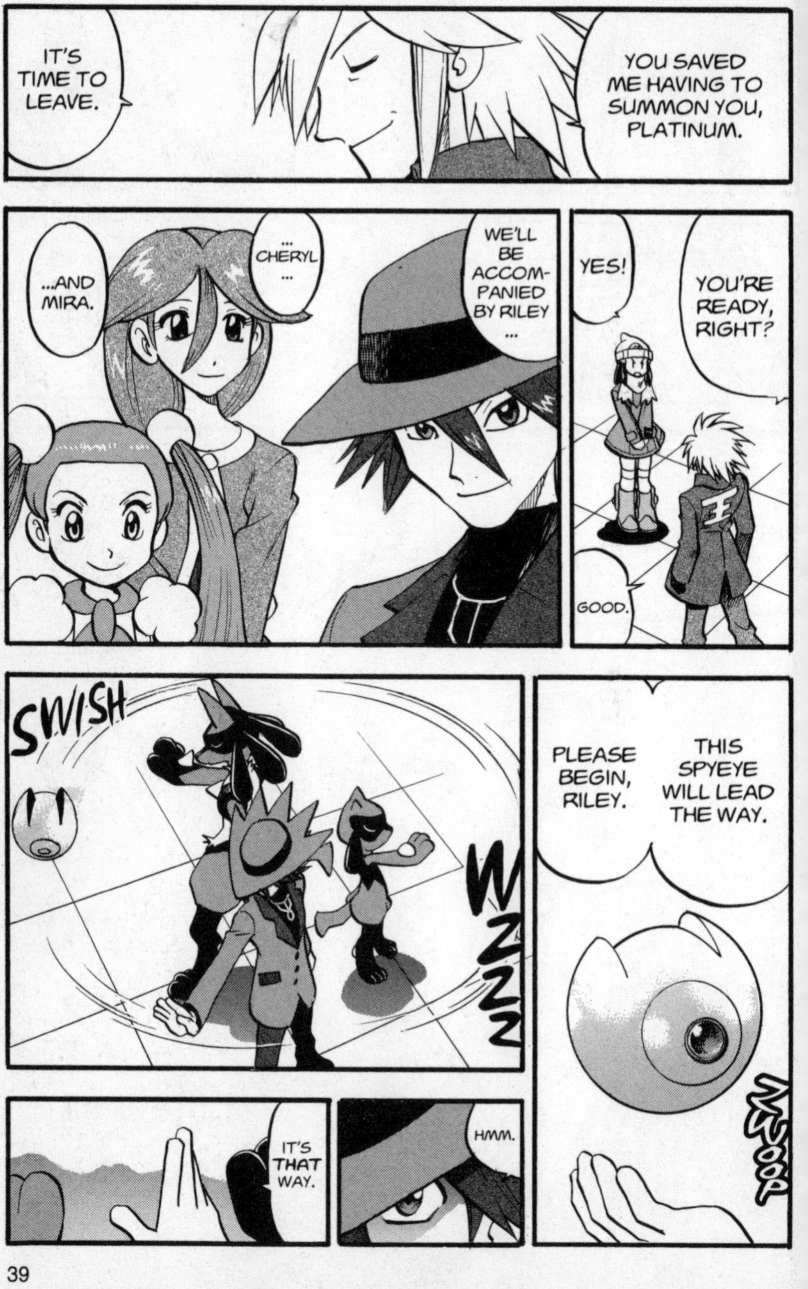

YOU SAVED ME HAVING TO SUMMON YOU, PLATINUM.
IT'S TIME TO LEAVE.
YOU'RE READY, RIGHT?
YES!
GOOD.
WE'LL BE ACCOMPANIED BY RILEY...
...CHERYL...
...AND MIRA.
THIS SPYEYE WILL LEAD THE WAY.
PLEASE BEGIN, RILEY.
ZWOOP
SWISH
WZZZ
HMM.
IT'S THAT WAY.

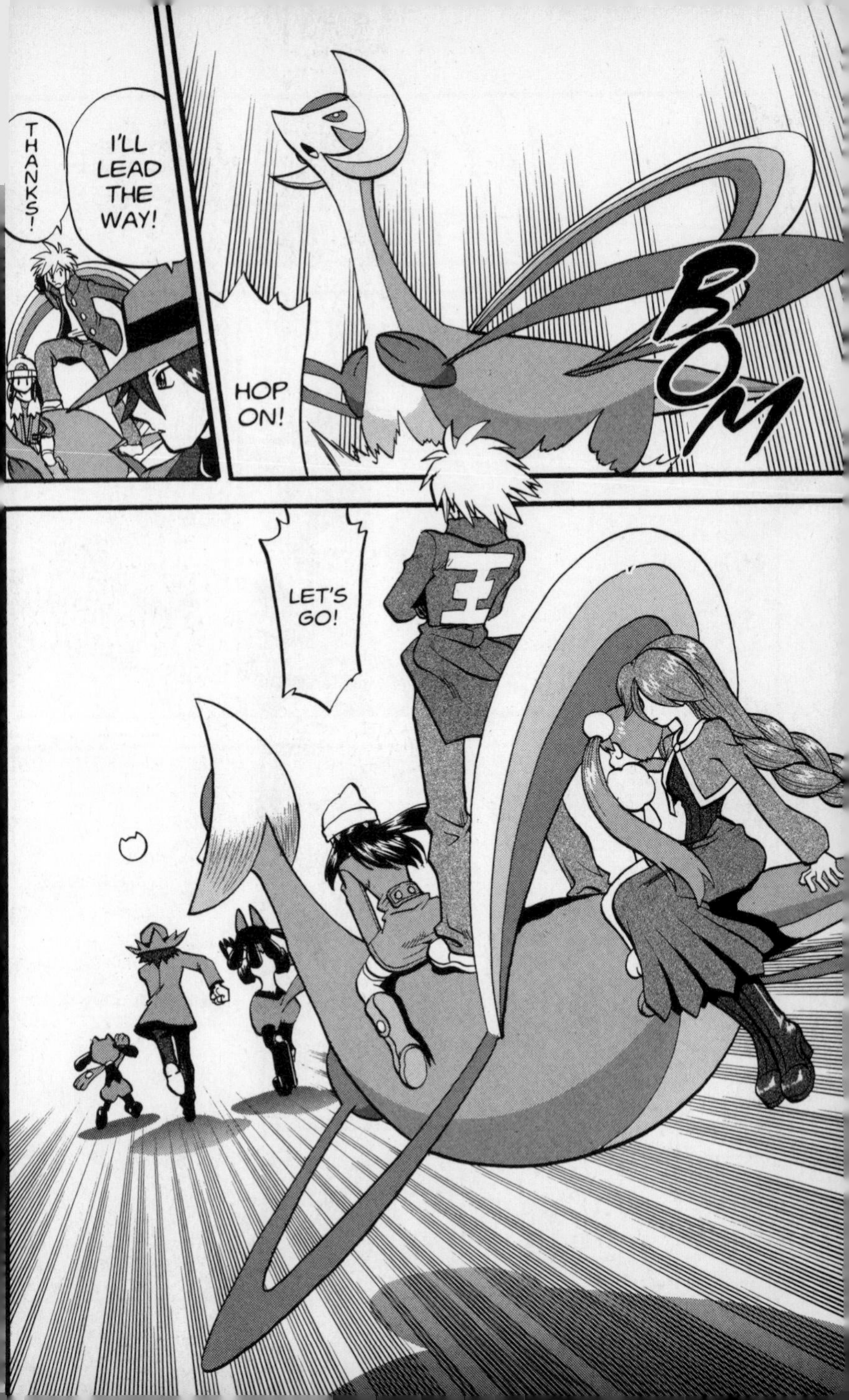
HOP ON!
BOM
I'LL LEAD THE WAY!
THANKS!
LET'S GO!

CHARACTER PROFILE / DIAMOND

DIAMOND

DIAMOND AND HIS CHILDHOOD FRIEND PEARL FORMED A COMEDY DUO IN NURSERY SCHOOL AND HAVE BEEN REHEARSING AND PERFORMING TOGETHER EVER SINCE IN HOPES OF REACHING THE TOP OF THE COMEDY PROFESSION. BUT DUE TO A STRANGE TURN OF EVENTS, THEY ENDED UP ON A JOURNEY THROUGH THE SINNOH REGION AND WERE DRAWN INTO A FIERCE BATTLE AGAINST EVIL TEAM GALACTIC. DIAMOND'S POKÉMON BATTLE SKILLS IMPROVED TREMENDOUSLY AFTER HE MADE UP HIS MIND TO DEDICATE HIMSELF TO PROTECTING HIS TRAVELING COMPANION, LADY. AFTER TRAINING SESSIONS WITH GYM LEADER RILEY ON IRON ISLAND, DIAMOND REALIZED THAT HE EXCELS IN THE USE OF HEAVYWEIGHT POKÉMON IN BATTLE. DIAMOND IS THE FUNNY MAN IN HIS COMEDIC DUO. HIS CURRENT FAVORITE ANIME IS PROTEAM OMEGA.

Hometown: Twinleaf Town

Birthday: April 4th

Age: 12 (As of Adventure 9)

Blood-type: A

Hobbies: Watching robot anime, video gam

Special Skills: Cooking, making Poffin

Award: Next Generation Comedy Grand Pri Special Merit Prize

Family: Mother (Johanna)

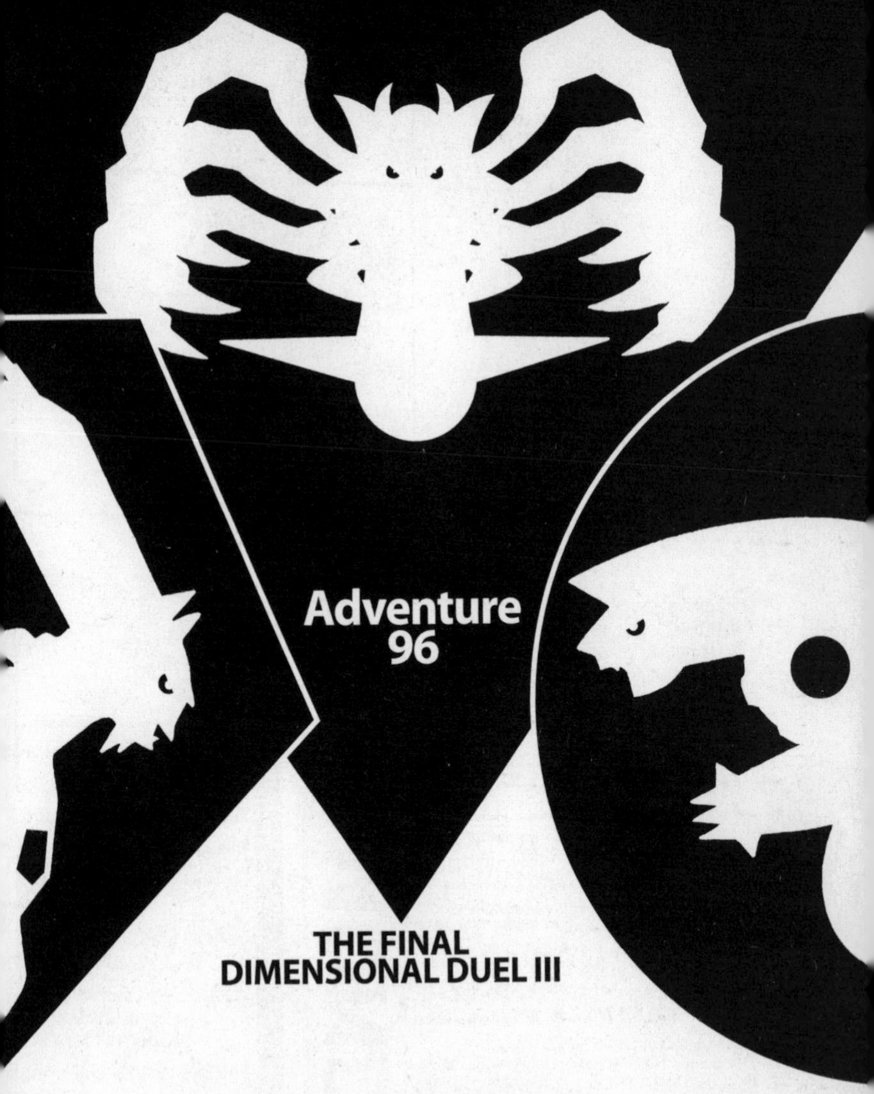

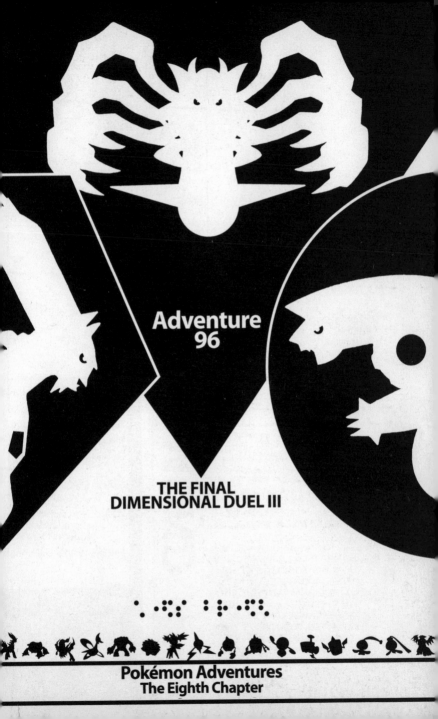

Adventure 96

THE FINAL DIMENSIONAL DUEL III

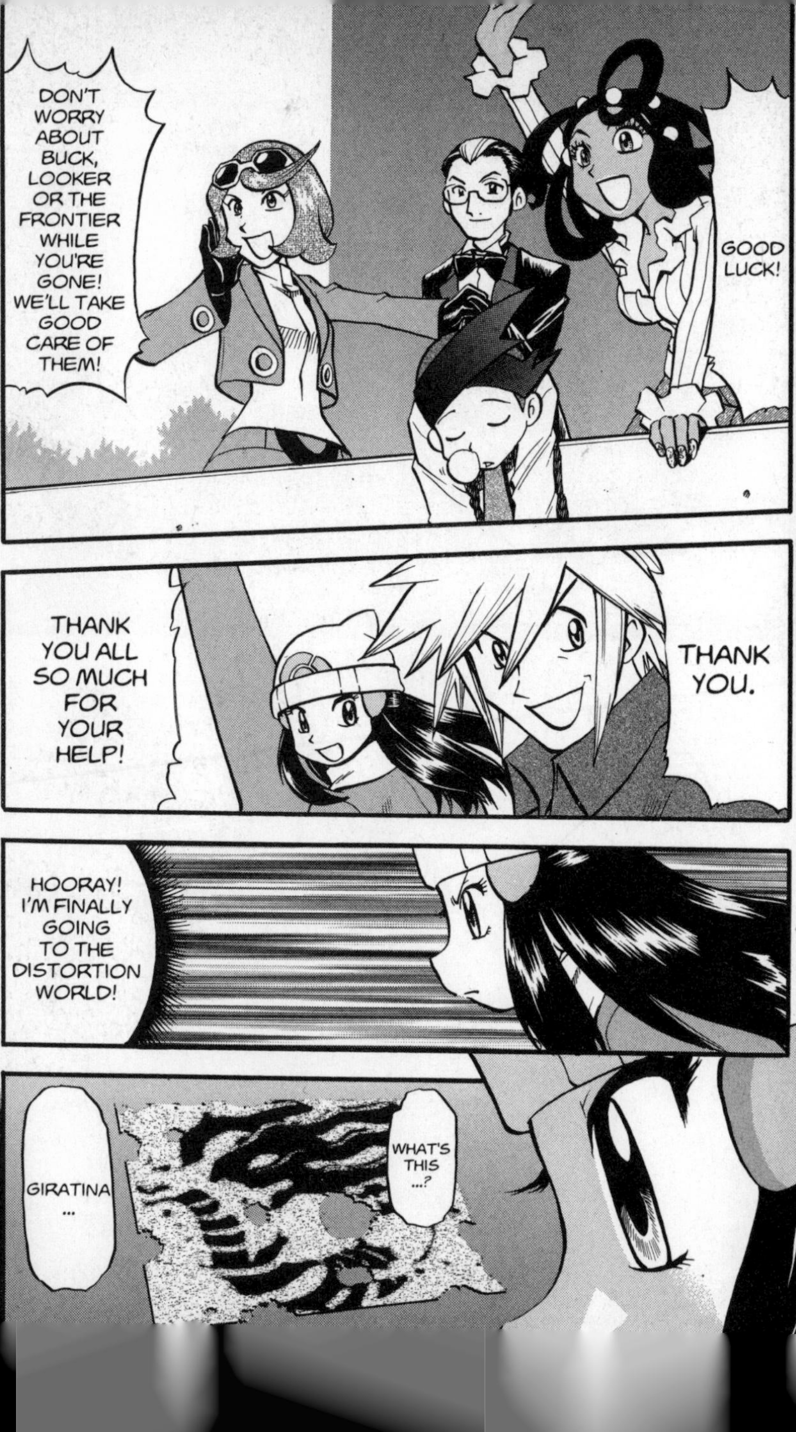
GOOD LUCK!
DON'T WORRY ABOUT BUCK, LOOKER OR THE FRONTIER WHILE YOU'RE GONE! WE'LL TAKE GOOD CARE OF THEM!
THANK YOU.
THANK YOU ALL SO MUCH FOR YOUR HELP!
HOORAY! I'M FINALLY GOING TO THE DISTORTION WORLD!
WHAT'S THIS ...?
GIRATINA ...

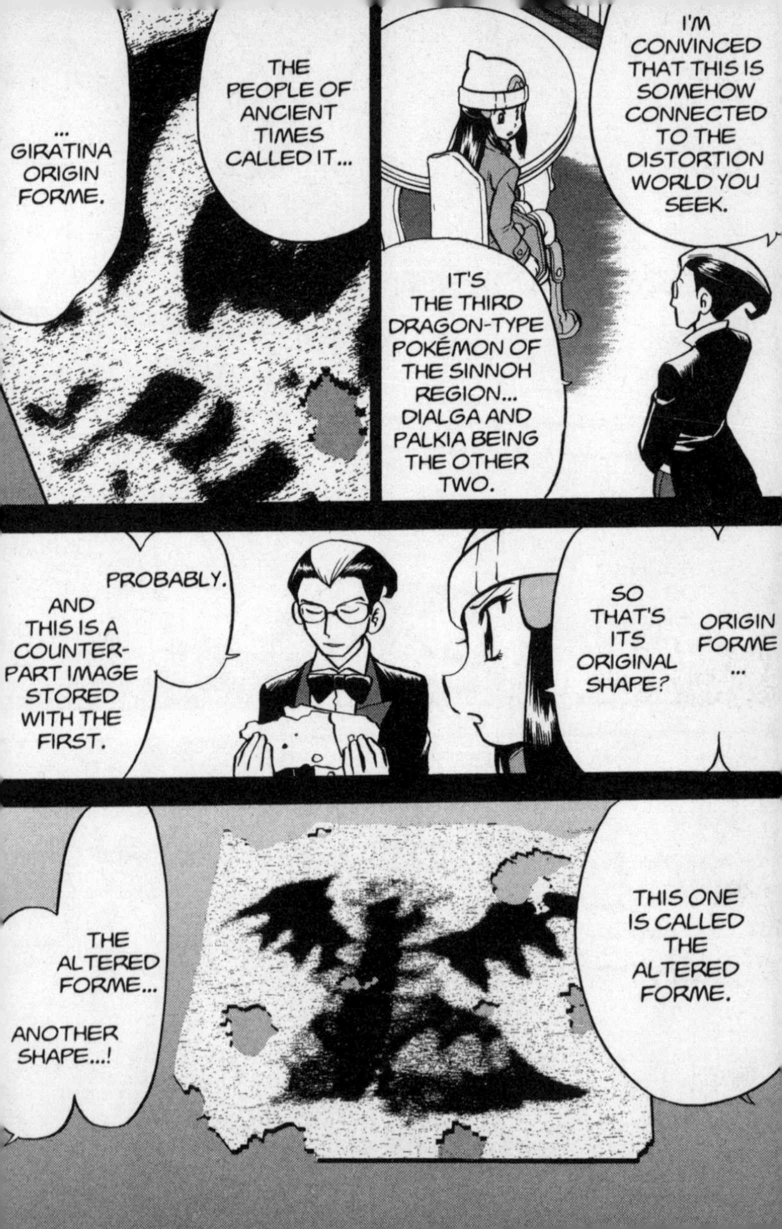
I'M CONVINCED THAT THIS IS SOMEHOW CONNECTED TO THE DISTORTION WORLD YOU SEEK.
IT'S THE THIRD DRAGON-TYPE POKÉMON OF THE SINNOH REGION... DIALGA AND PALKIA BEING THE OTHER TWO.
THE PEOPLE OF ANCIENT TIMES CALLED IT...
... GIRATINA ORIGIN FORME.
ORIGIN FORME ...
SO THAT'S ITS ORIGINAL SHAPE?
PROBABLY.
AND THIS IS A COUNTER-PART IMAGE STORED WITH THE FIRST.
THIS ONE IS CALLED THE ALTERED FORME.
THE ALTERED FORME...
ANOTHER SHAPE...!

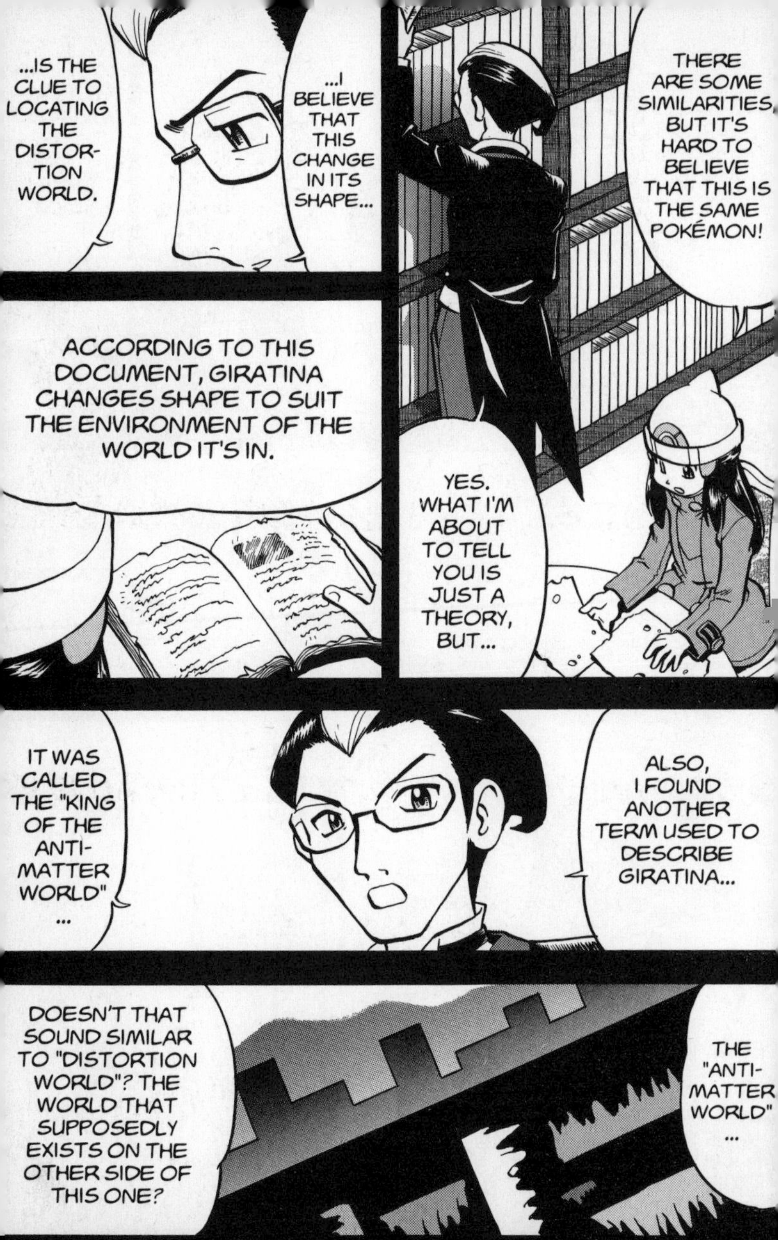
THERE ARE SOME SIMILARITIES, BUT IT'S HARD TO BELIEVE THAT THIS IS THE SAME POKÉMON!
YES. WHAT I'M ABOUT TO TELL YOU IS JUST A THEORY, BUT...
...I BELIEVE THAT THIS CHANGE IN ITS SHAPE...
...IS THE CLUE TO LOCATING THE DISTORTION WORLD.
ACCORDING TO THIS DOCUMENT, GIRATINA CHANGES SHAPE TO SUIT THE ENVIRONMENT OF THE WORLD IT'S IN.
ALSO, I FOUND ANOTHER TERM USED TO DESCRIBE GIRATINA...
IT WAS CALLED THE "KING OF THE ANTI-MATTER WORLD"...
THE "ANTI-MATTER WORLD"...
DOESN'T THAT SOUND SIMILAR TO "DISTORTION WORLD"? THE WORLD THAT SUPPOSEDLY EXISTS ON THE OTHER SIDE OF THIS ONE?

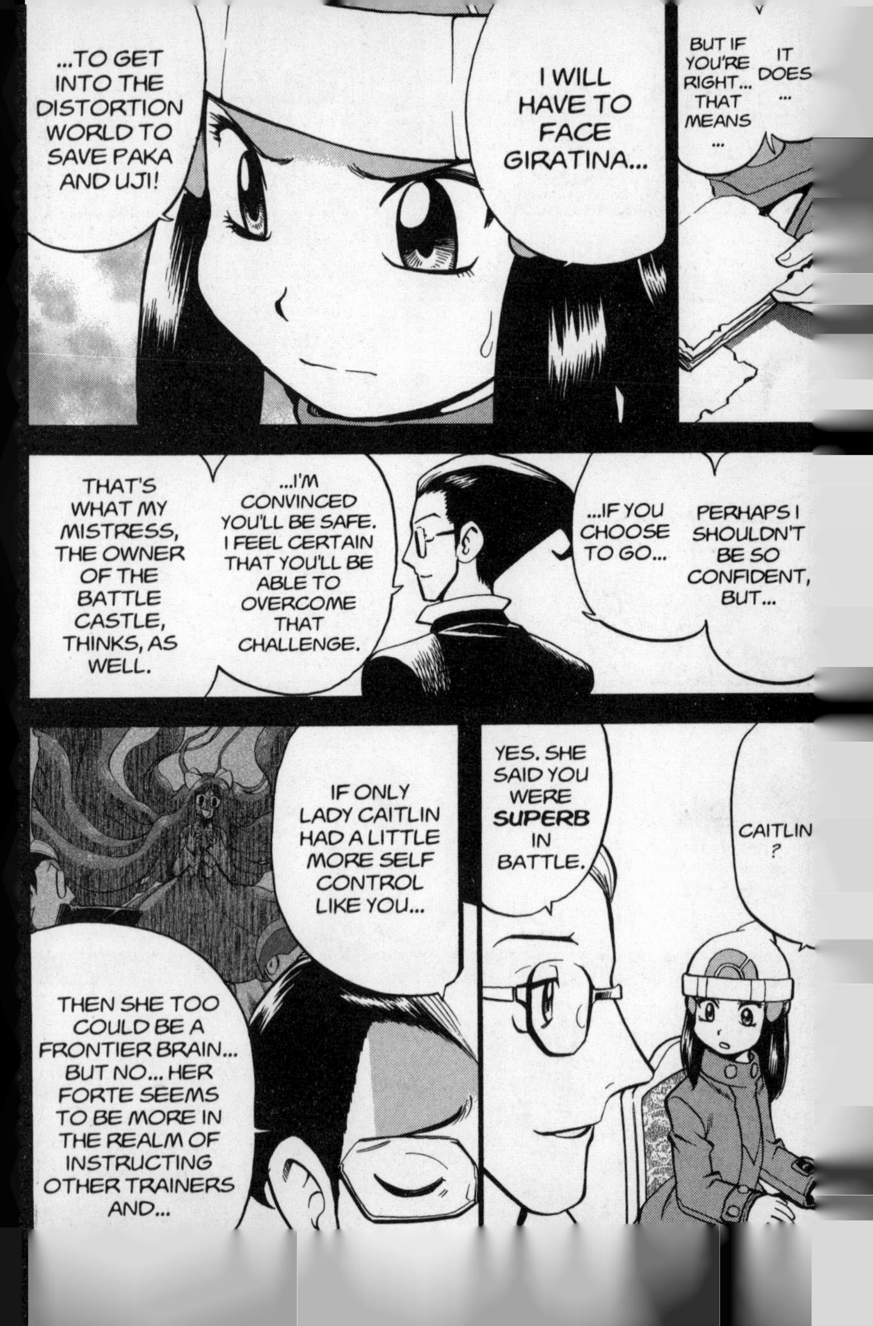
IT DOES...
BUT IF YOU'RE RIGHT... THAT MEANS...
I WILL HAVE TO FACE GIRATINA...
...TO GET INTO THE DISTORTION WORLD TO SAVE PAKA AND UJI!
PERHAPS I SHOULDN'T BE SO CONFIDENT, BUT...
...IF YOU CHOOSE TO GO...
...I'M CONVINCED YOU'LL BE SAFE. I FEEL CERTAIN THAT YOU'LL BE ABLE TO OVERCOME THAT CHALLENGE.
THAT'S WHAT MY MISTRESS, THE OWNER OF THE BATTLE CASTLE, THINKS, AS WELL.
CAITLIN?
YES. SHE SAID YOU WERE **SUPERB** IN BATTLE.
IF ONLY LADY CAITLIN HAD A LITTLE MORE SELF CONTROL LIKE YOU...
THEN SHE TOO COULD BE A FRONTIER BRAIN... BUT NO... HER FORTE SEEMS TO BE MORE IN THE REALM OF INSTRUCTING OTHER TRAINERS AND...

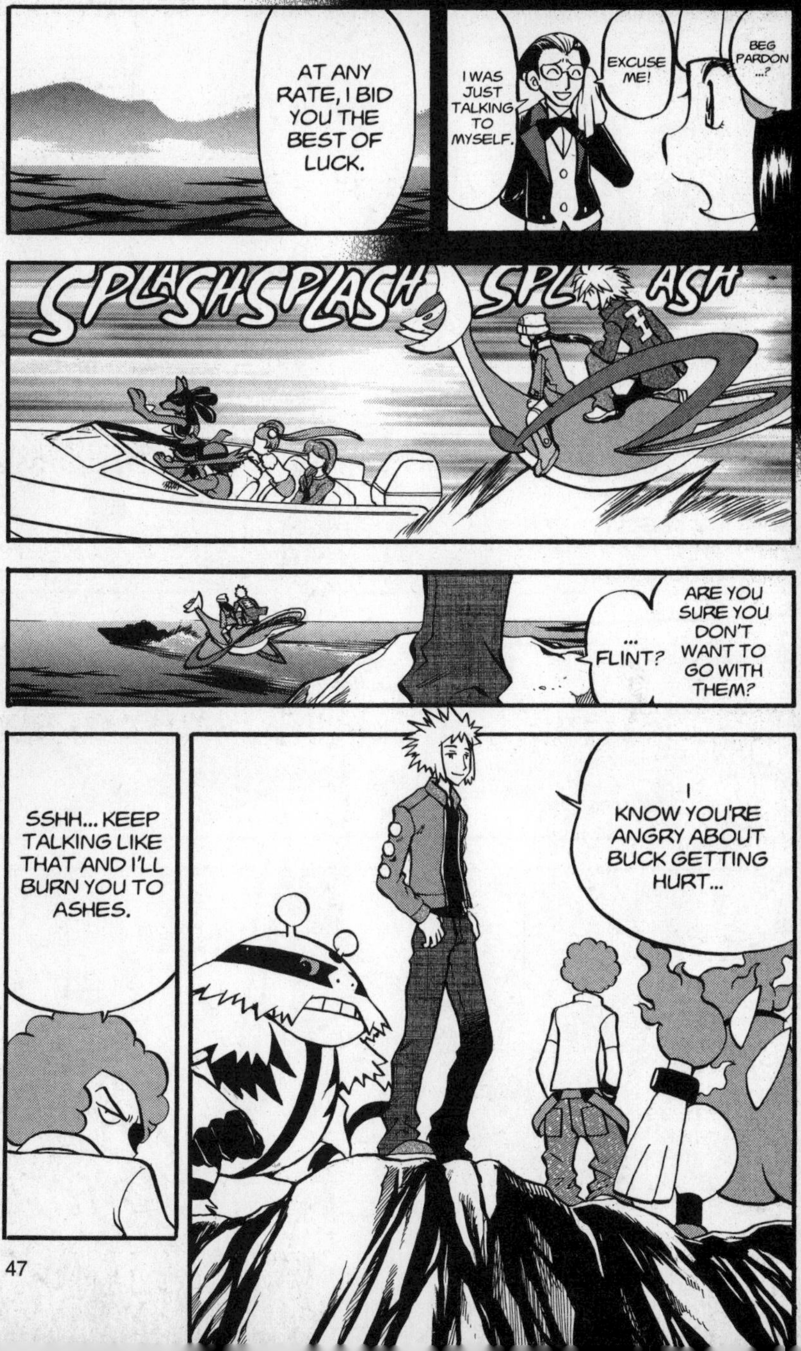
BEG PARDON ...?
EXCUSE ME!
I WAS JUST TALKING TO MYSELF.
AT ANY RATE, I BID YOU THE BEST OF LUCK.
SPLASH SPLASH
SPLASH
... FLINT? ARE YOU SURE YOU DON'T WANT TO GO WITH THEM?
I KNOW YOU'RE ANGRY ABOUT BUCK GETTING HURT...
SSHH... KEEP TALKING LIKE THAT AND I'LL BURN YOU TO ASHES.

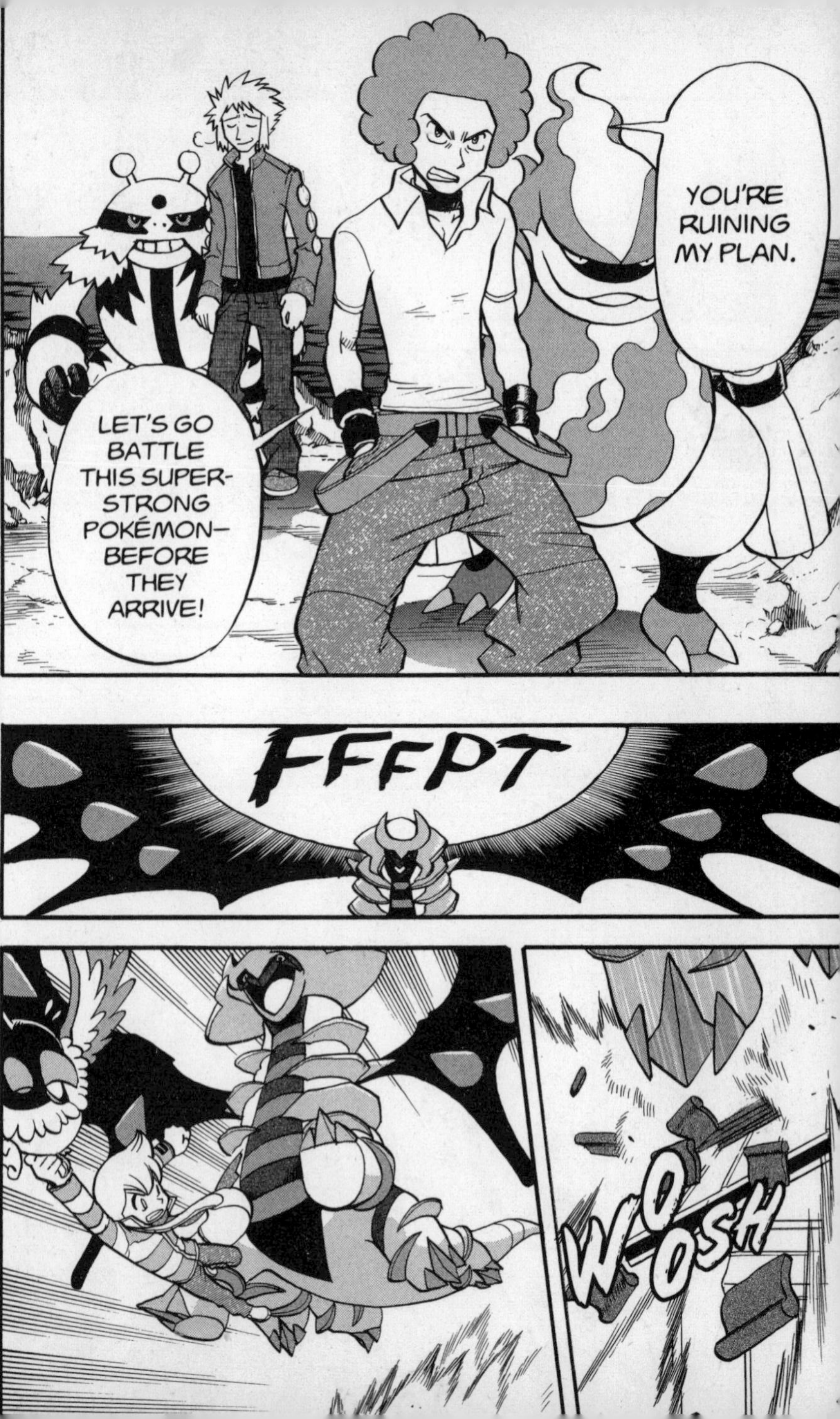
YOU'RE RUINING MY PLAN.
LET'S GO BATTLE THIS SUPER-STRONG POKÉMON—BEFORE THEY ARRIVE!
FFFPT
WOOSH

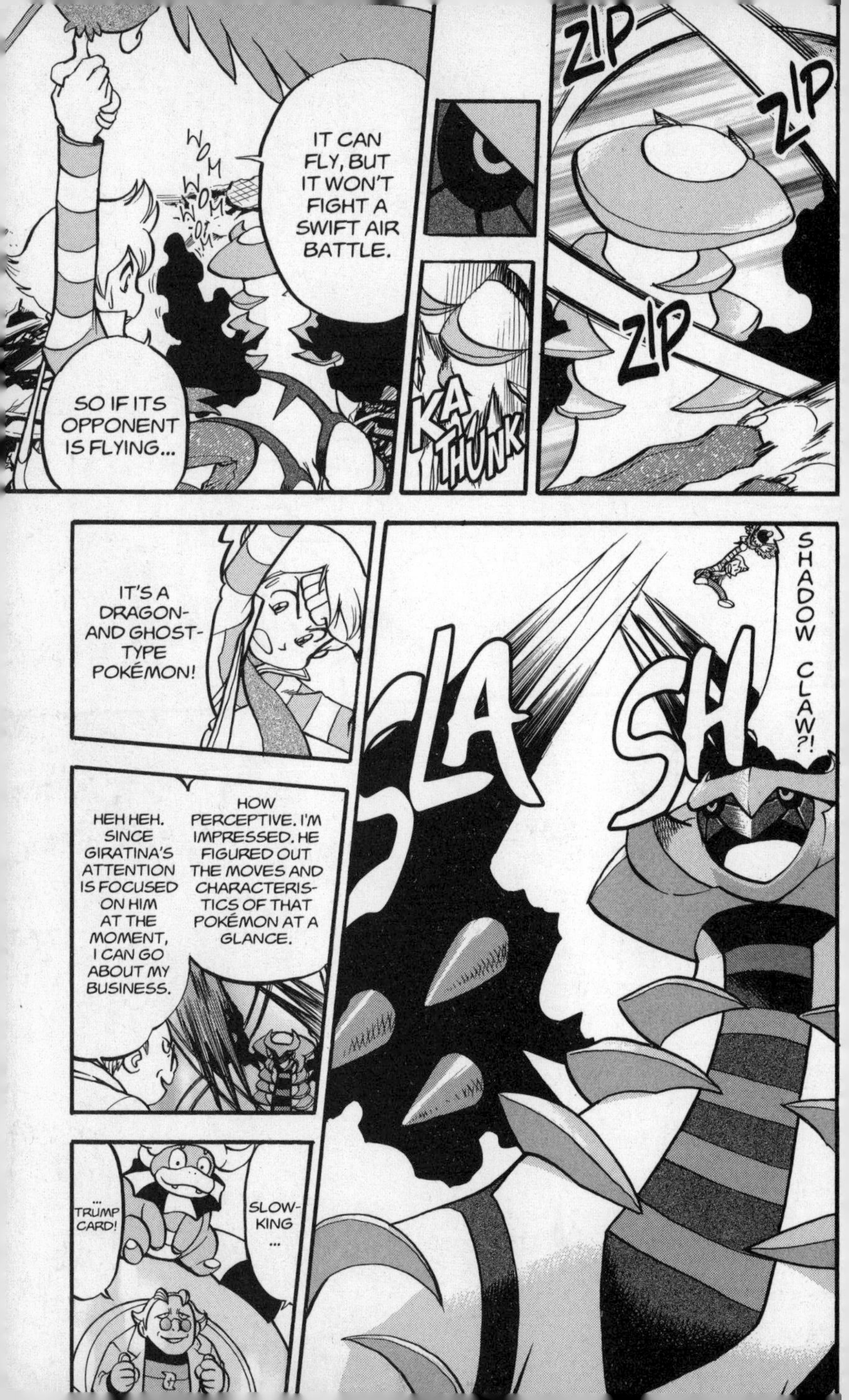
ZIP
ZIP
ZIP
KA THUNK
IT CAN FLY, BUT IT WON'T FIGHT A SWIFT AIR BATTLE.
WOM WOM
SO IF ITS OPPONENT IS FLYING...
SHADOW CLAW?!
SLASH
IT'S A DRAGON- AND GHOST-TYPE POKÉMON!
HOW PERCEPTIVE. I'M IMPRESSED. HE FIGURED OUT THE MOVES AND CHARACTERISTICS OF THAT POKÉMON AT A GLANCE.
HEH HEH. SINCE GIRATINA'S ATTENTION IS FOCUSED ON HIM AT THE MOMENT, I CAN GO ABOUT MY BUSINESS.
SLOWKING...
...TRUMP CARD!

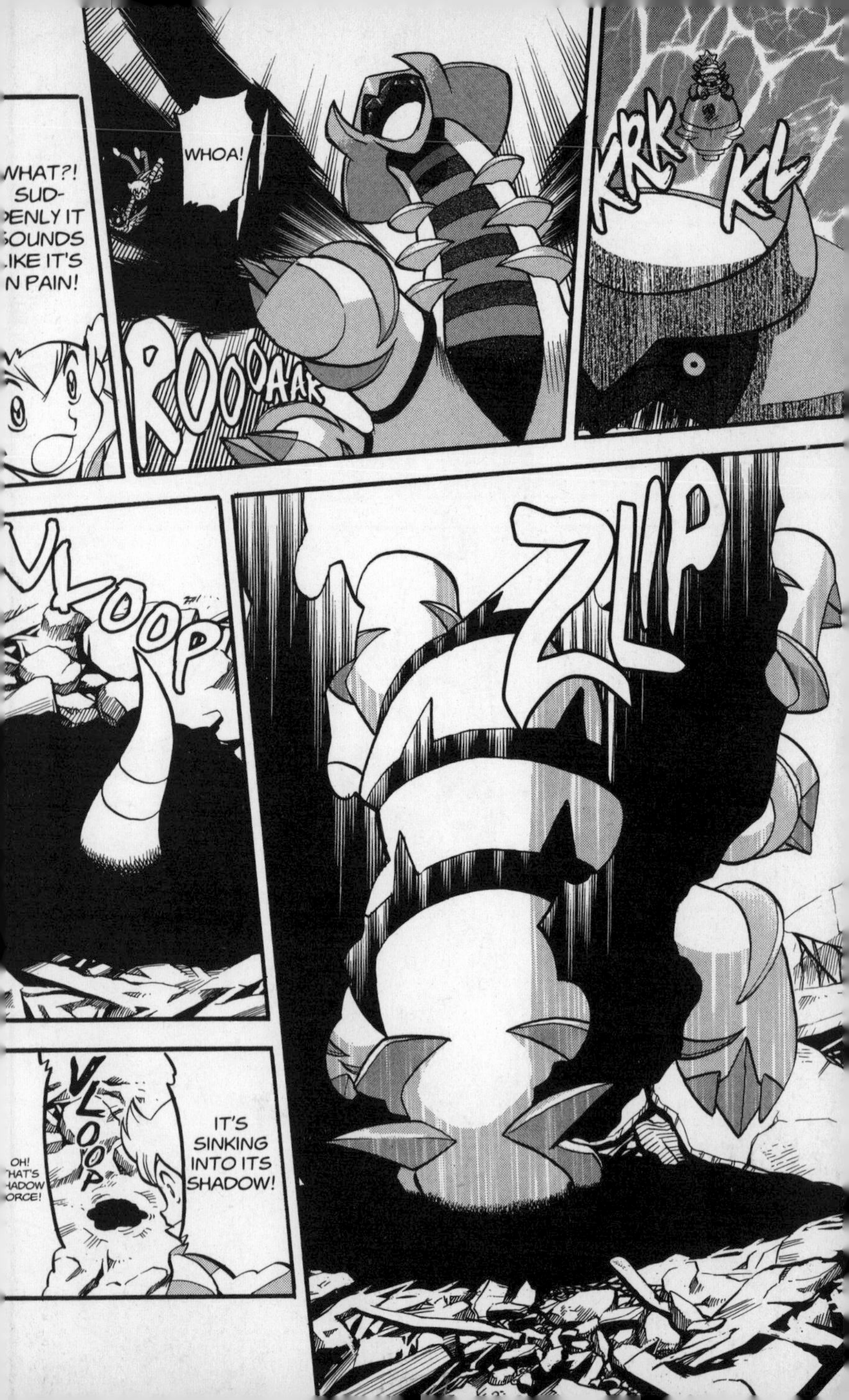
KRK KL
WHOA!
ROOOAAK
WHAT?! SUD-DENLY IT SOUNDS LIKE IT'S IN PAIN!
ZLIP
VVOOP
IT'S SINKING INTO ITS SHADOW!
VLOOOP
OH! THAT'S SHADOW FORCE!

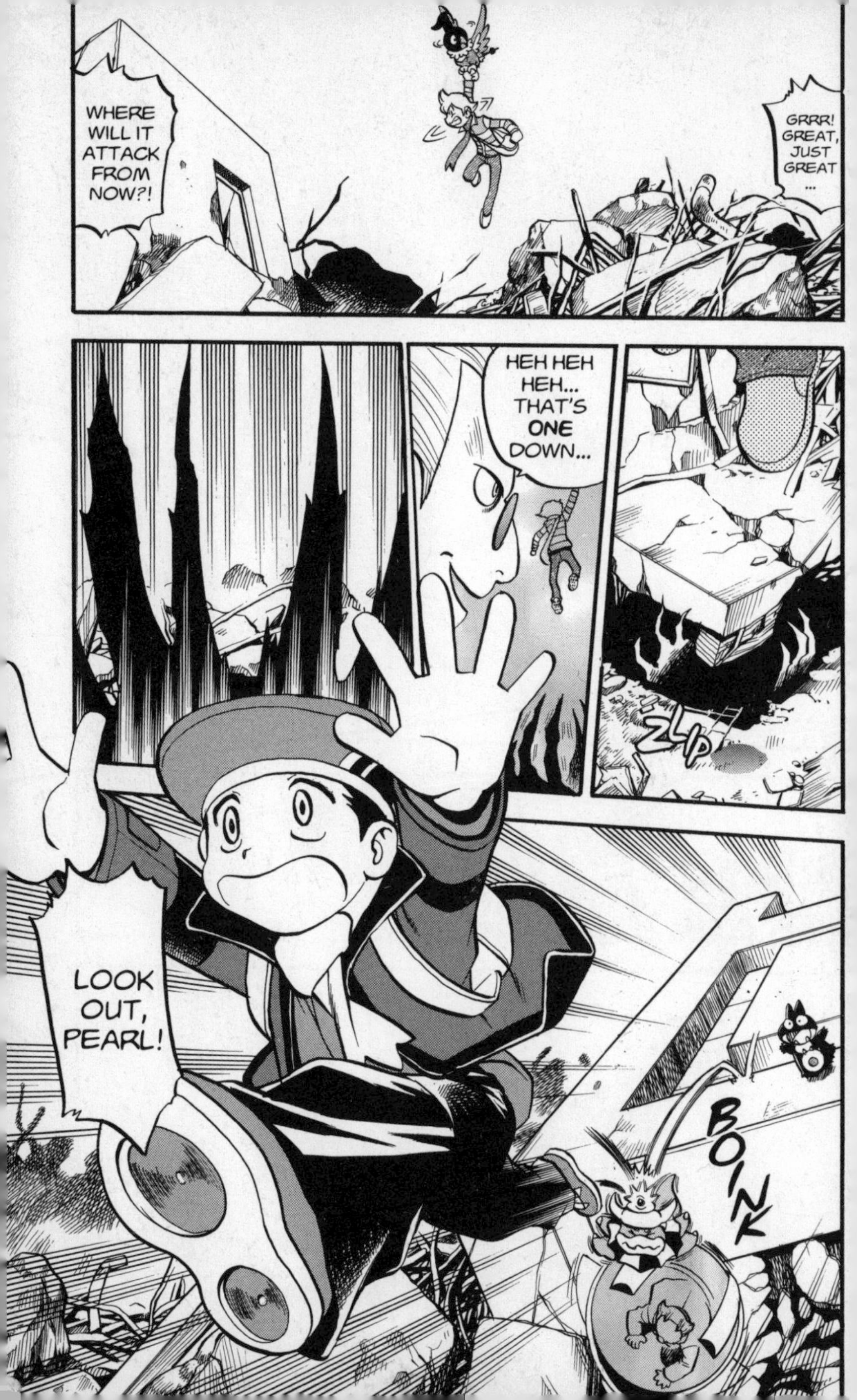
GRRR! GREAT, JUST GREAT...
WHERE WILL IT ATTACK FROM NOW?!
ZIP
HEH HEH HEH... THAT'S ONE DOWN...
LOOK OUT, PEARL!
BOINK

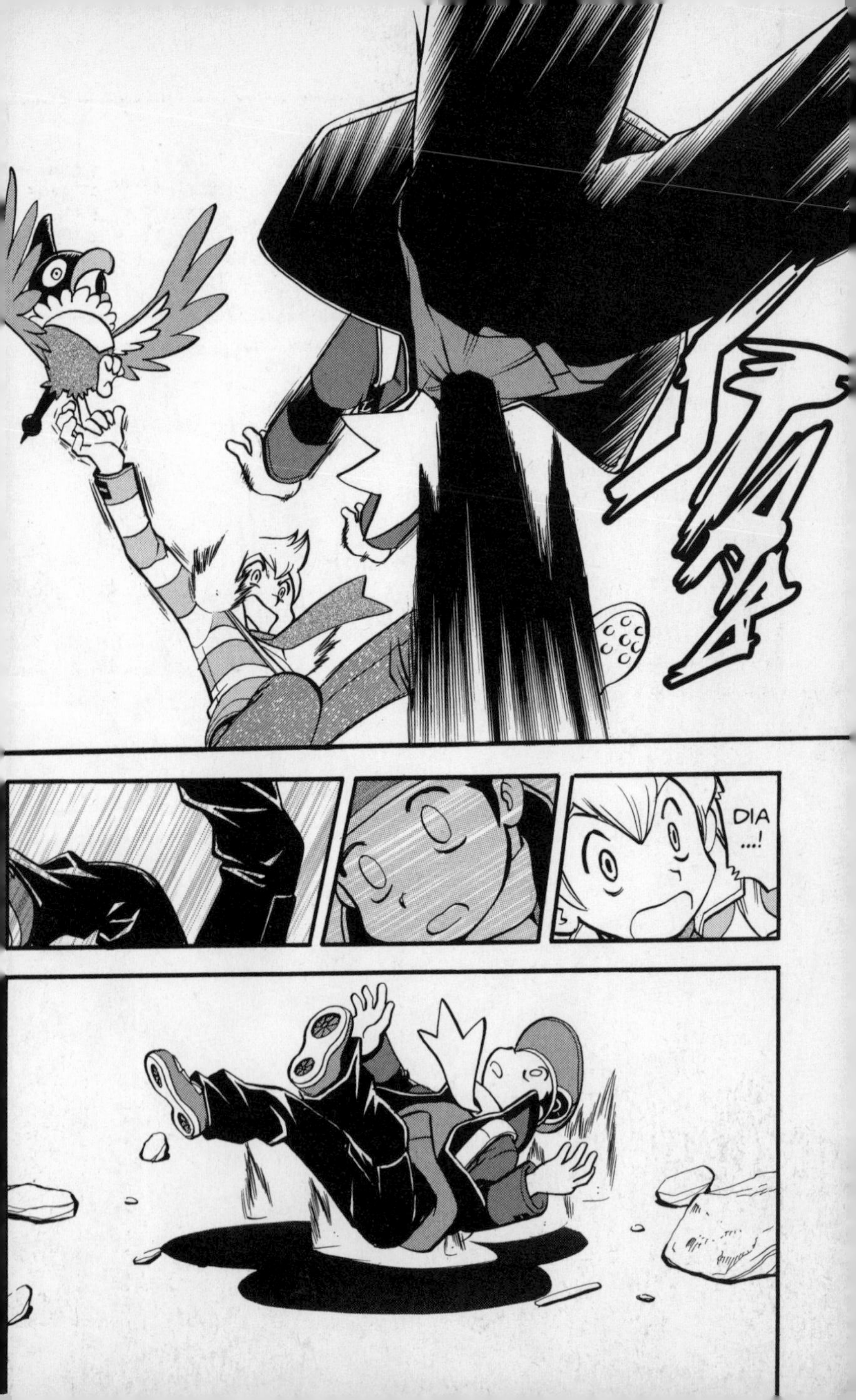
DIA ...!

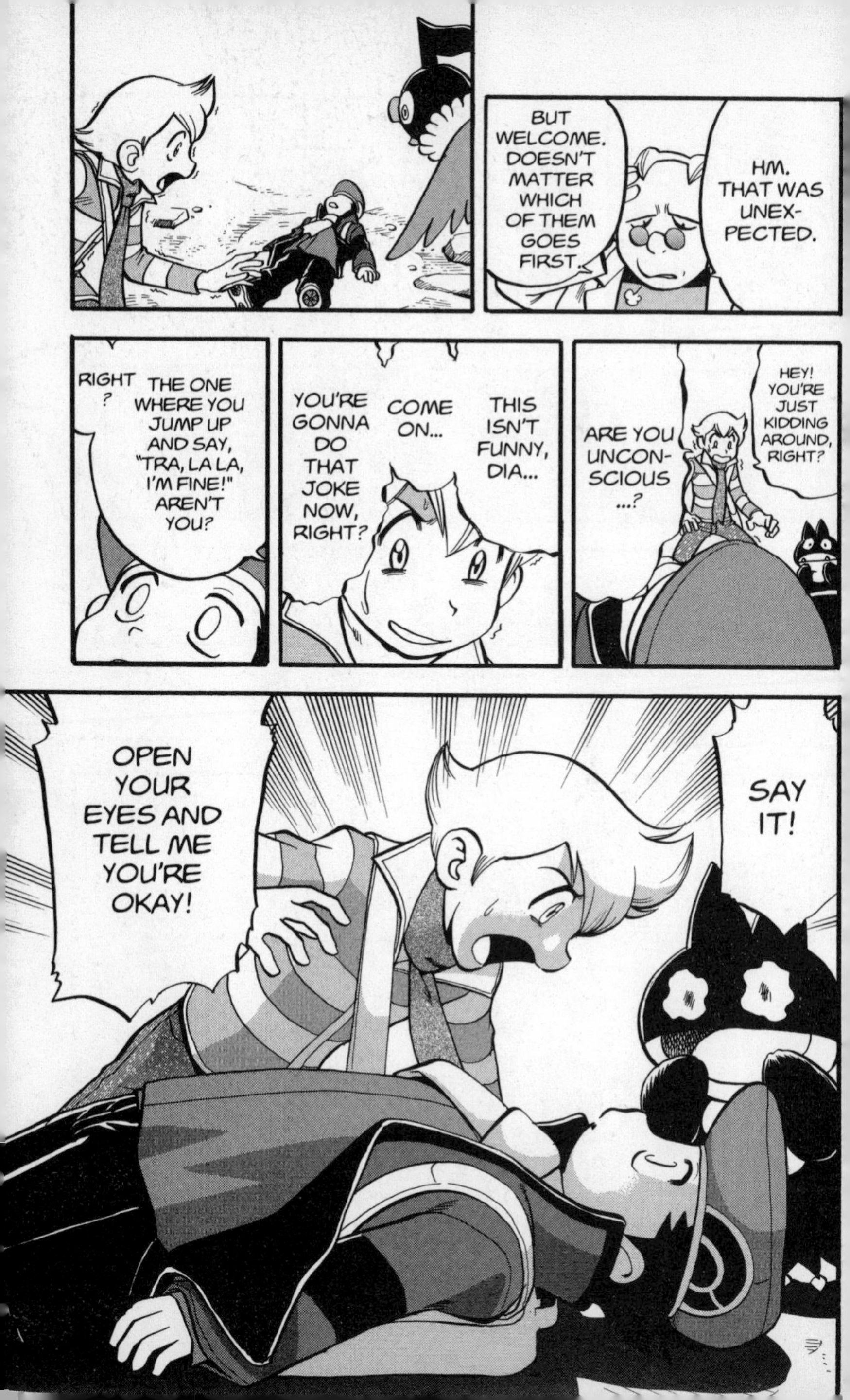
HM. THAT WAS UNEX-PECTED.
BUT WELCOME. DOESN'T MATTER WHICH OF THEM GOES FIRST.
HEY! YOU'RE JUST KIDDING AROUND, RIGHT?
ARE YOU UNCON-SCIOUS ...?
THIS ISN'T FUNNY, DIA...
COME ON...
YOU'RE GONNA DO THAT JOKE NOW, RIGHT?
THE ONE WHERE YOU JUMP UP AND SAY, "TRA, LA LA, I'M FINE!" AREN'T YOU?
RIGHT?
SAY IT!
OPEN YOUR EYES AND TELL ME YOU'RE OKAY!

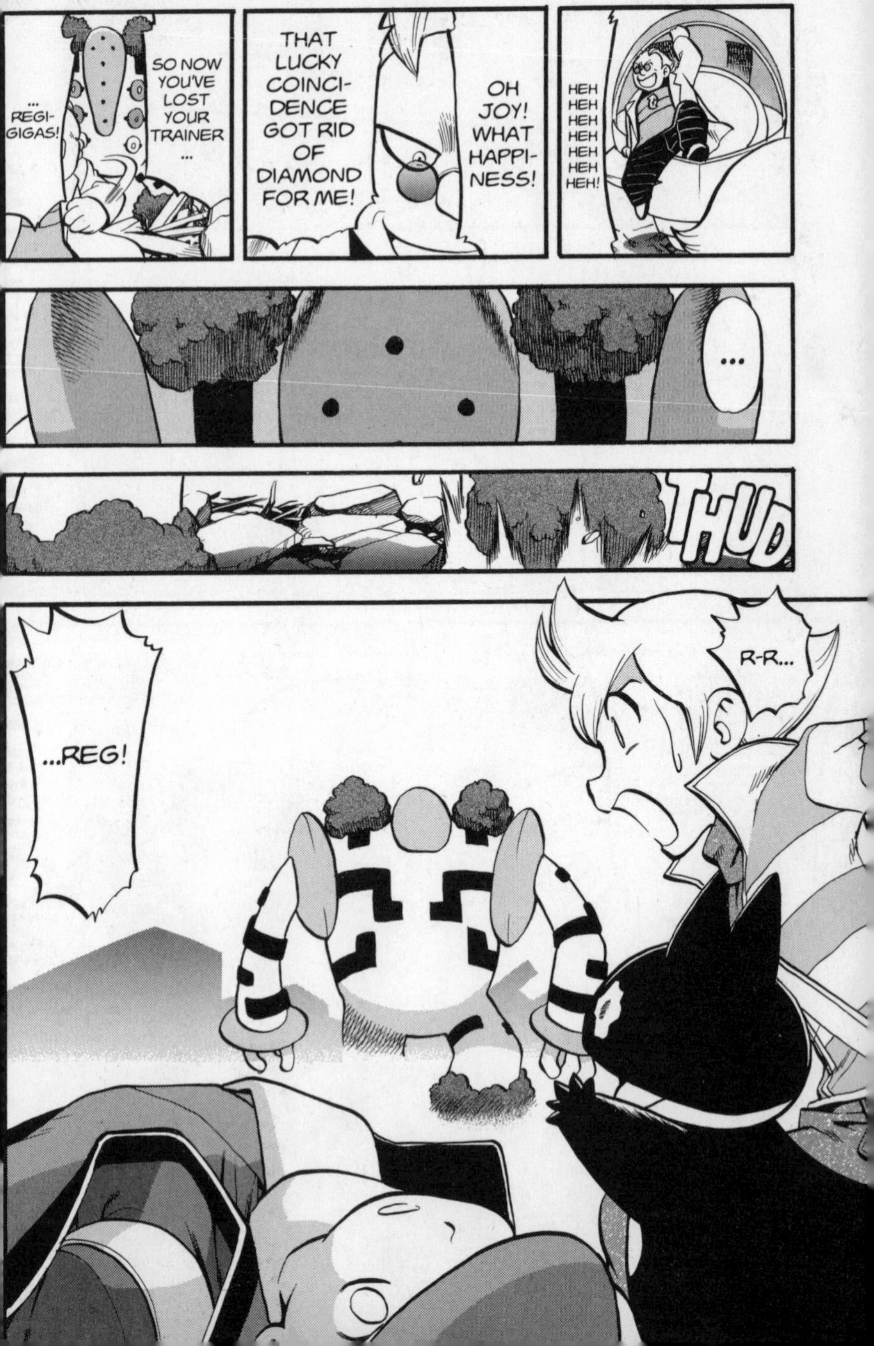
HEH HEH HEH HEH HEH HEH HEH!
OH JOY! WHAT HAPPINESS!
THAT LUCKY COINCIDENCE GOT RID OF DIAMOND FOR ME!
SO NOW YOU'VE LOST YOUR TRAINER ...
... REGIGIGAS!
...
THUD
R-R...
...REG!

 Tru/Torterra ♂

Grass
Ground

LV. 60 (As of Adventure 97)

Ability: Overgrow

Relaxed. Good perseverance.

Tru has learned to increase the speed of its Razor Leaf by controlling the number of leaves it shoots out. It is a very dependable Pokémon.

Lax/Munchlax ♂

Normal

LV. 56 (As of Adventure 97)

Ability: Pickup

Impish. Loves to eat.

Like Dia, Lax loves to chow down. Lax has been with Dia from before he set out on his journey. Dia hatched its egg.

Don/Bastiodon ♂

Rock
Steel

LV. 49 (As of Adventure 97)

Ability: Sturdy

Careful. Somewhat stubborn.

Don was originally Byron's Pokémon, but it took a liking to Dia and joined his team. It literally shields the team from enemy attacks.

POKEMON ON TEAM DIAMOND 1

Pokémon Stats

TEAM DIAMOND

TEAM DIAMOND 1

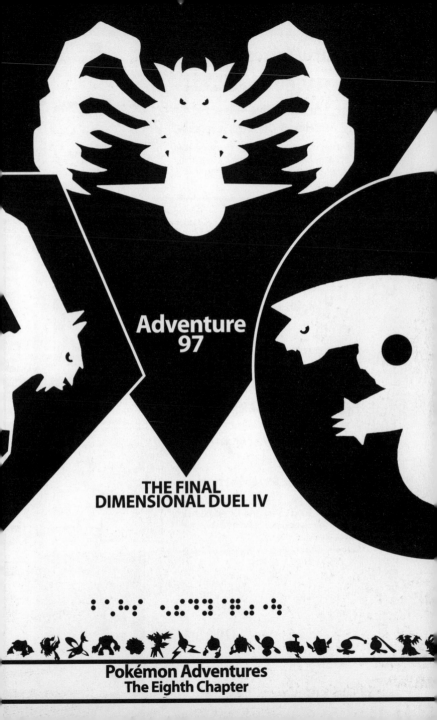

Adventure
97

THE FINAL
DIMENSIONAL DUEL IV

Pokémon Adventures
The Eighth Chapter

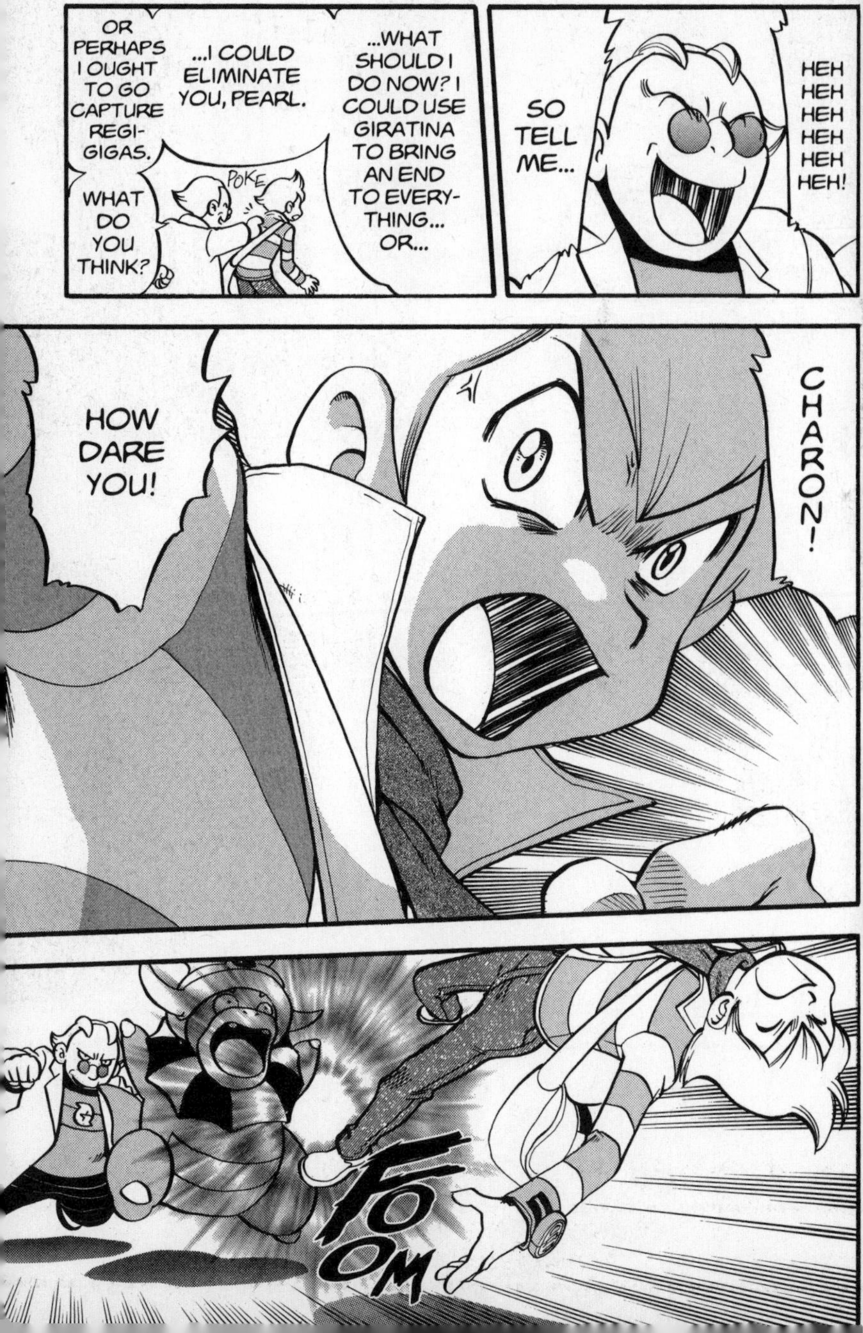
HEH HEH HEH HEH HEH HEH!
SO TELL ME...
...WHAT SHOULD I DO NOW? I COULD USE GIRATINA TO BRING AN END TO EVERYTHING... OR...
...I COULD ELIMINATE YOU, PEARL.
OR PERHAPS I OUGHT TO GO CAPTURE REGI-GIGAS.
WHAT DO YOU THINK?
POKE
CHARON!
HOW DARE YOU!
FOOM

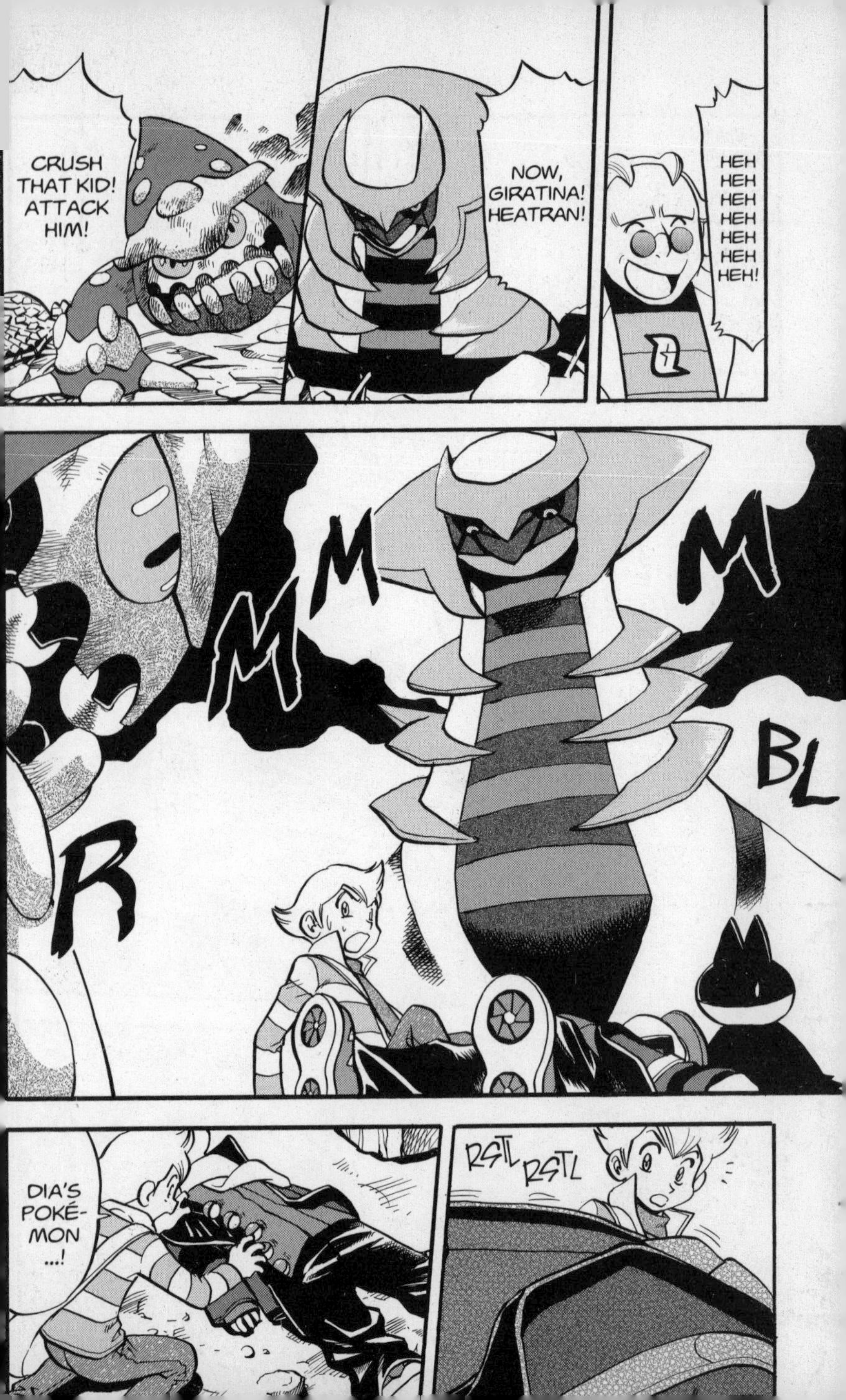
HEH HEH HEH HEH HEH HEH HEH!
NOW, GIRATINA! HEATRAN!
CRUSH THAT KID! ATTACK HIM!
RMMMBL
RSTL RSTL
DIA'S POKÉMON ...!

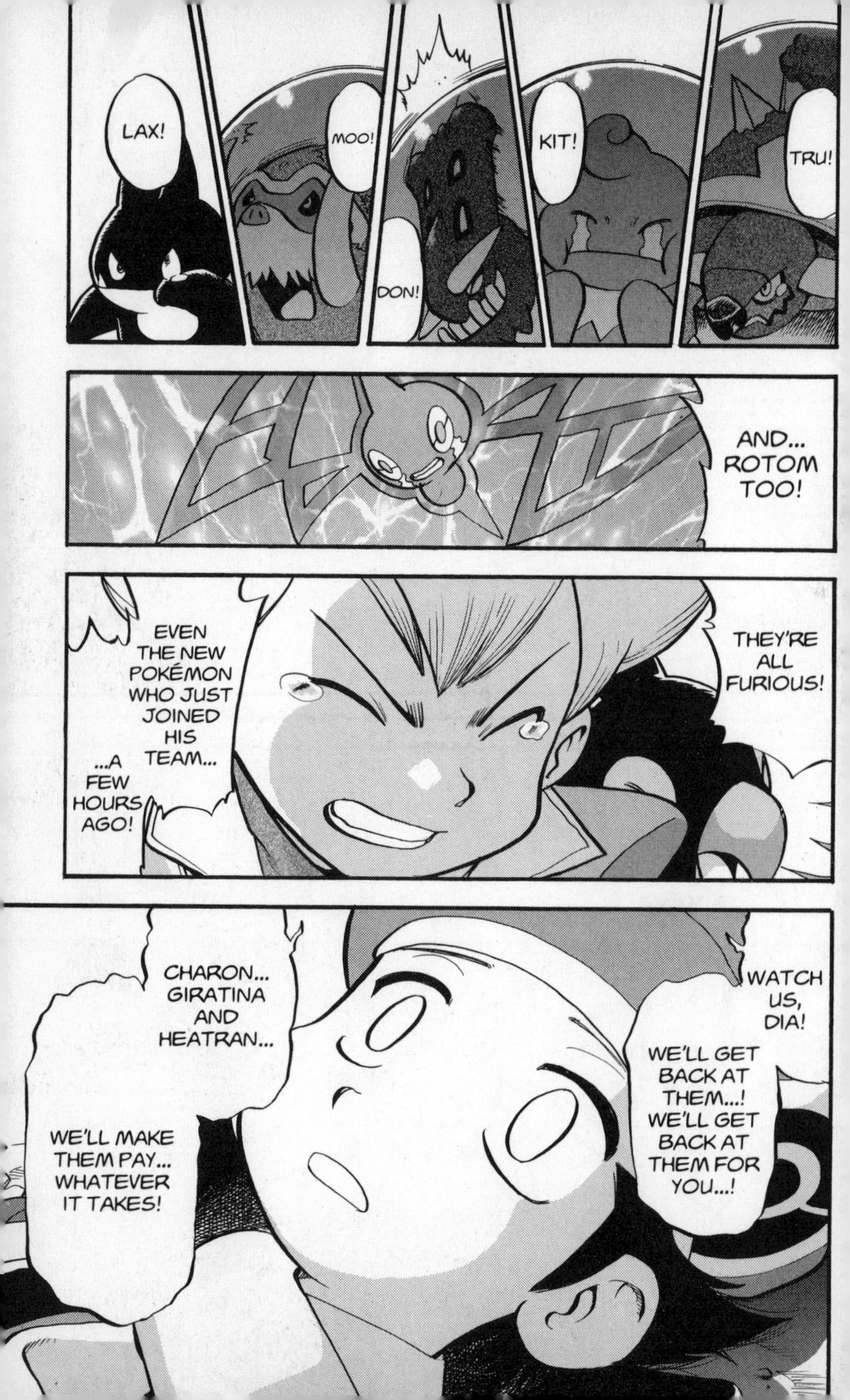
TRU!
KIT!
DON!
MOO!
LAX!
AND... ROTOM TOO!
THEY'RE ALL FURIOUS!
EVEN THE NEW POKÉMON WHO JUST JOINED HIS TEAM...
...A FEW HOURS AGO!
WATCH US, DIA!
WE'LL GET BACK AT THEM...! WE'LL GET BACK AT THEM FOR YOU...!
CHARON... GIRATINA AND HEATRAN...
WE'LL MAKE THEM PAY... WHATEVER IT TAKES!

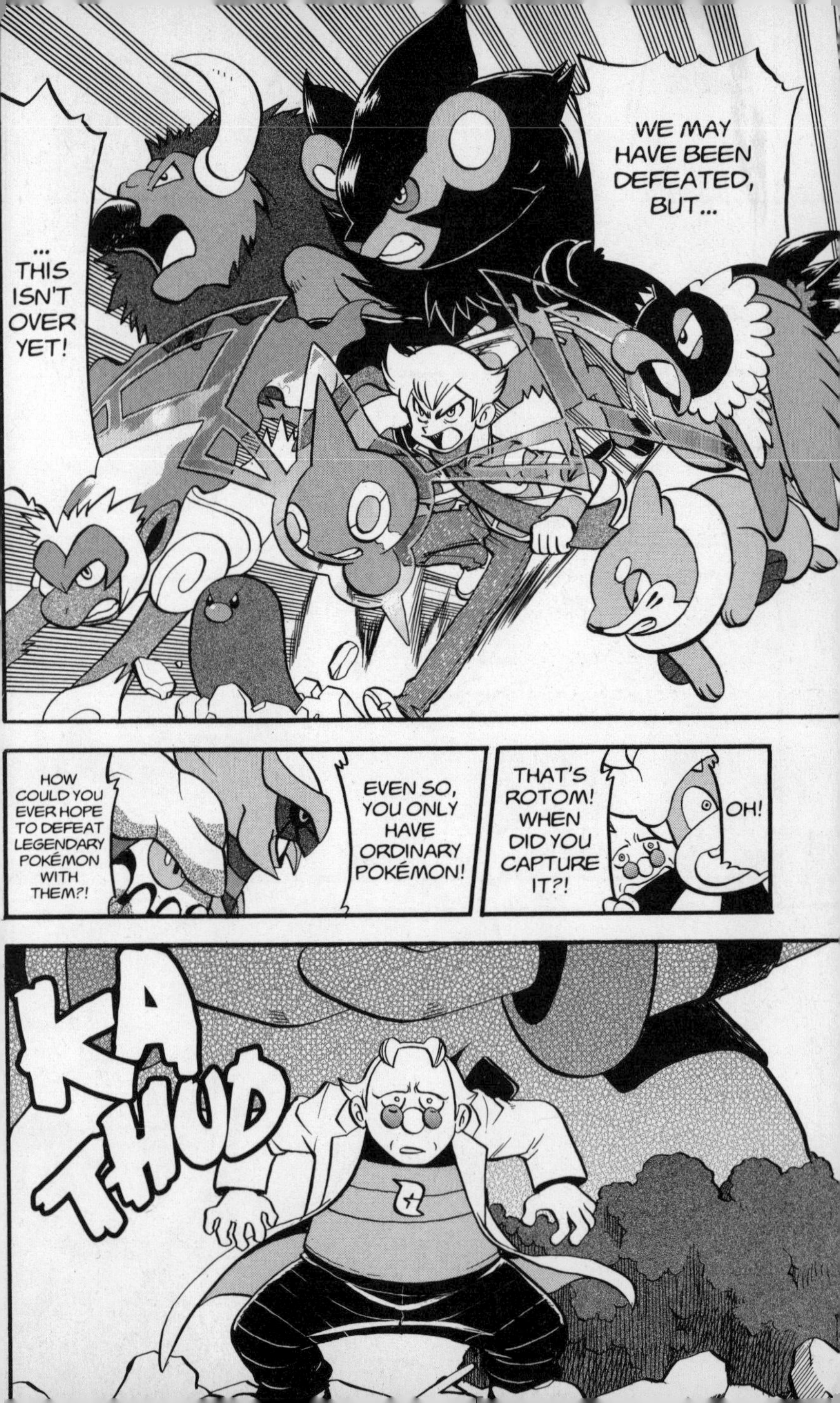
WE MAY HAVE BEEN DEFEATED, BUT...
... THIS ISN'T OVER YET!
OH!
THAT'S ROTOM! WHEN DID YOU CAPTURE IT?!
EVEN SO, YOU ONLY HAVE ORDINARY POKÉMON!
HOW COULD YOU EVER HOPE TO DEFEAT LEGENDARY POKÉMON WITH THEM?!
KA THUD

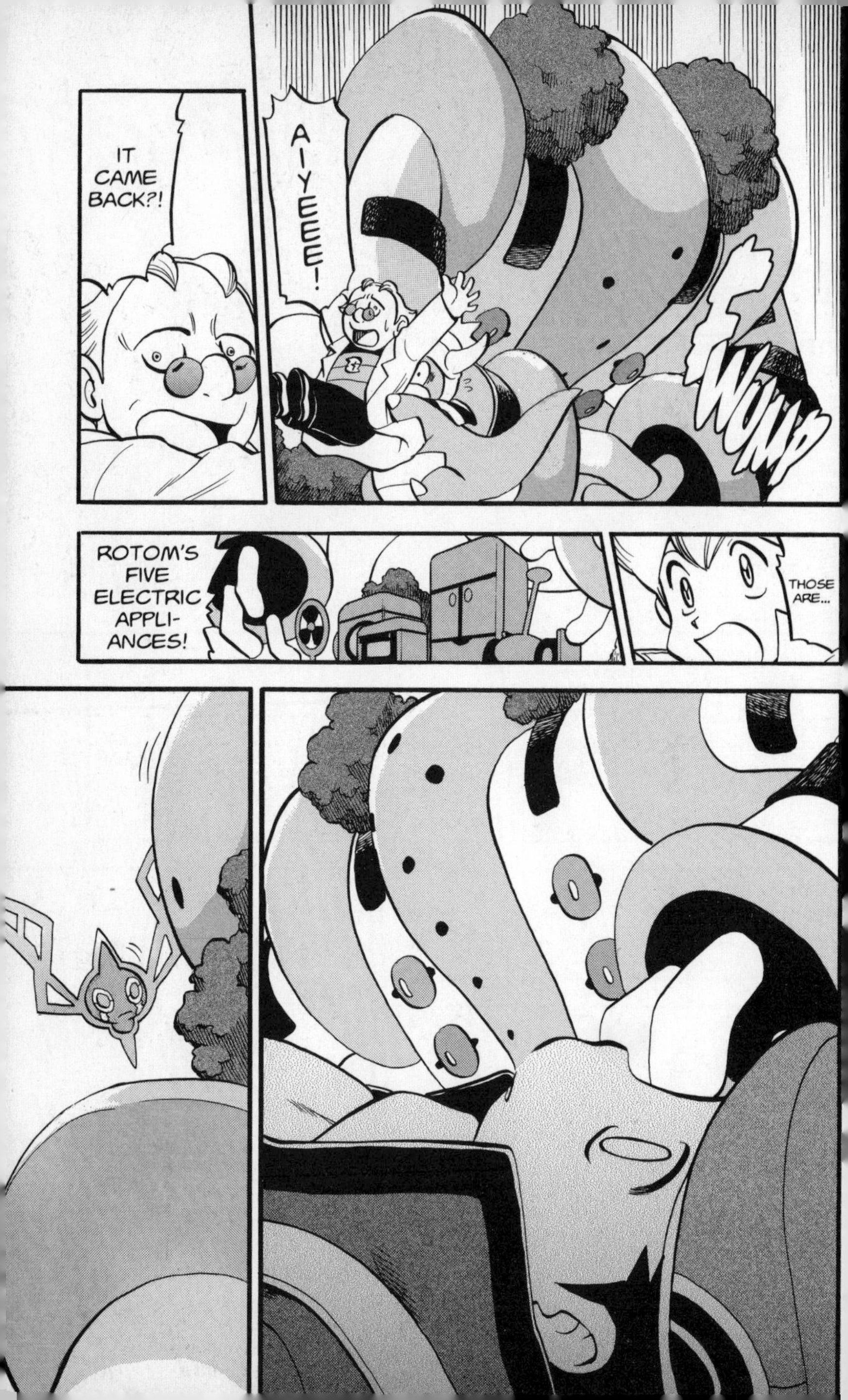
AIYEEE!
WOMP
IT CAME BACK?!
THOSE ARE...
ROTOM'S FIVE ELECTRIC APPLI-ANCES!

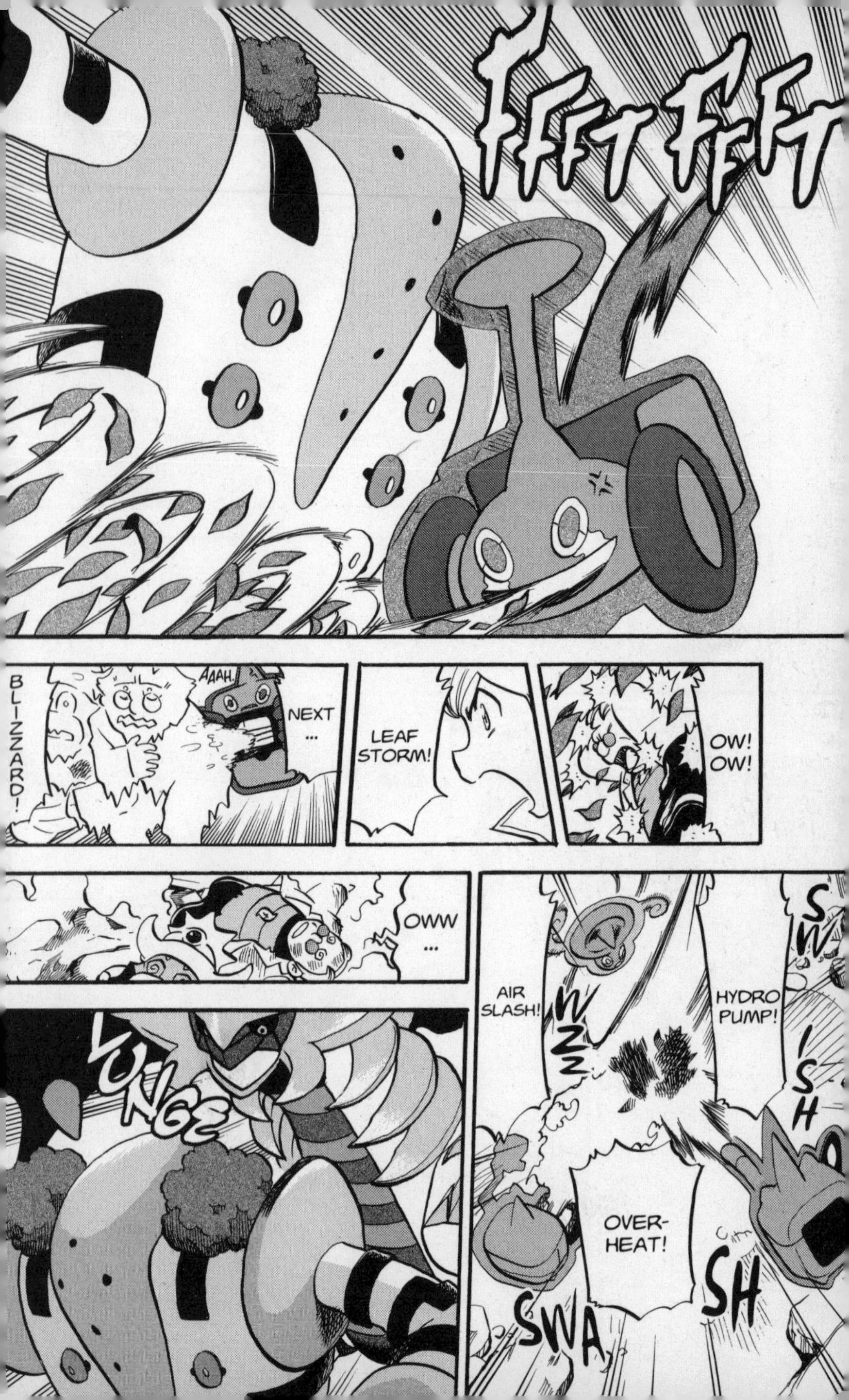
FFFT FFFT
OW! OW!
LEAF STORM!
NEXT ...
AAAH.
BLIZZARD!
SW
ISH
HYDRO PUMP!
AIR SLASH!
WZZ
OVER-HEAT!
SH
SWA
OWW ...
LUNGE

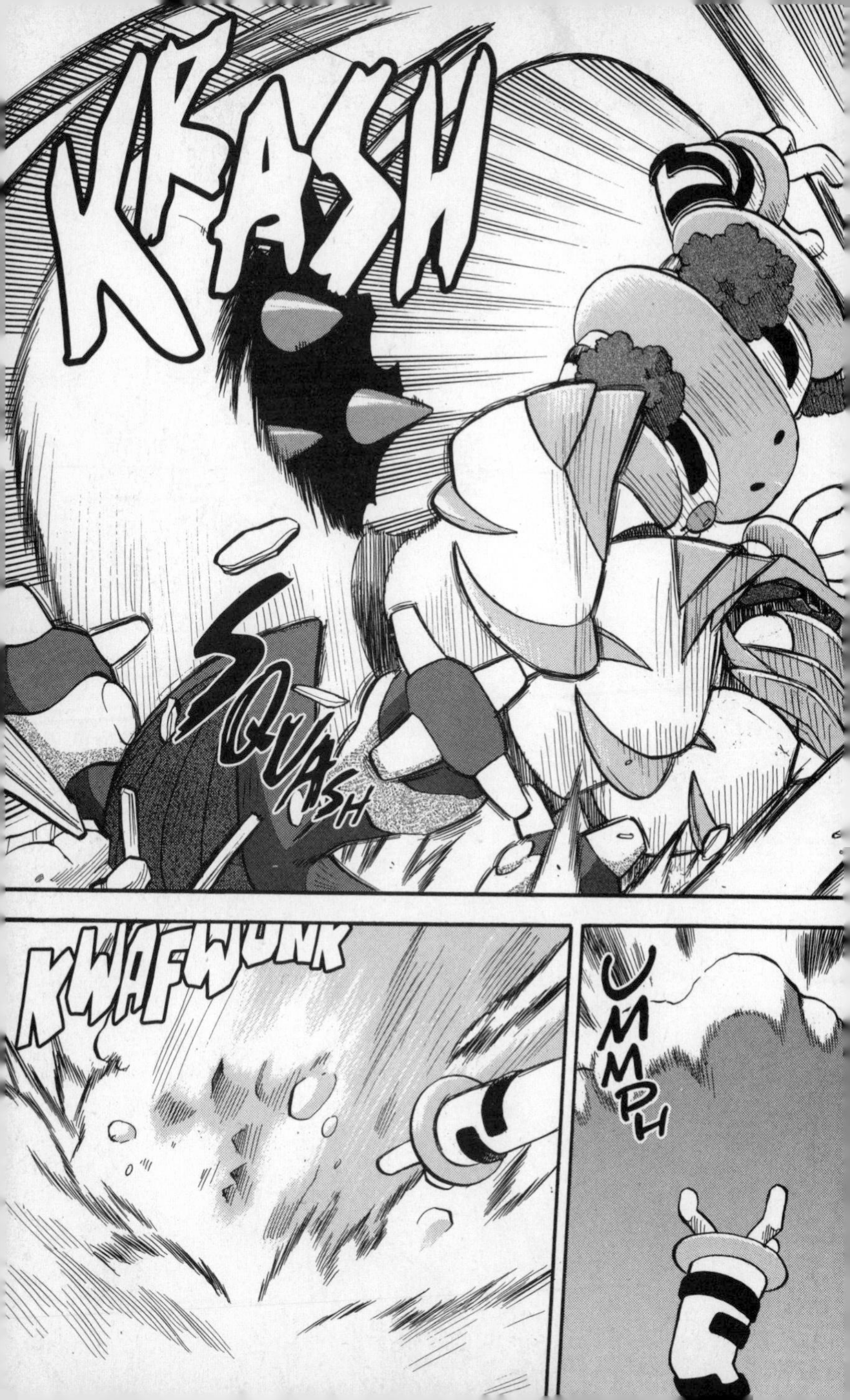
KRASH
SQUASH
UMMPH
KWAFWONK

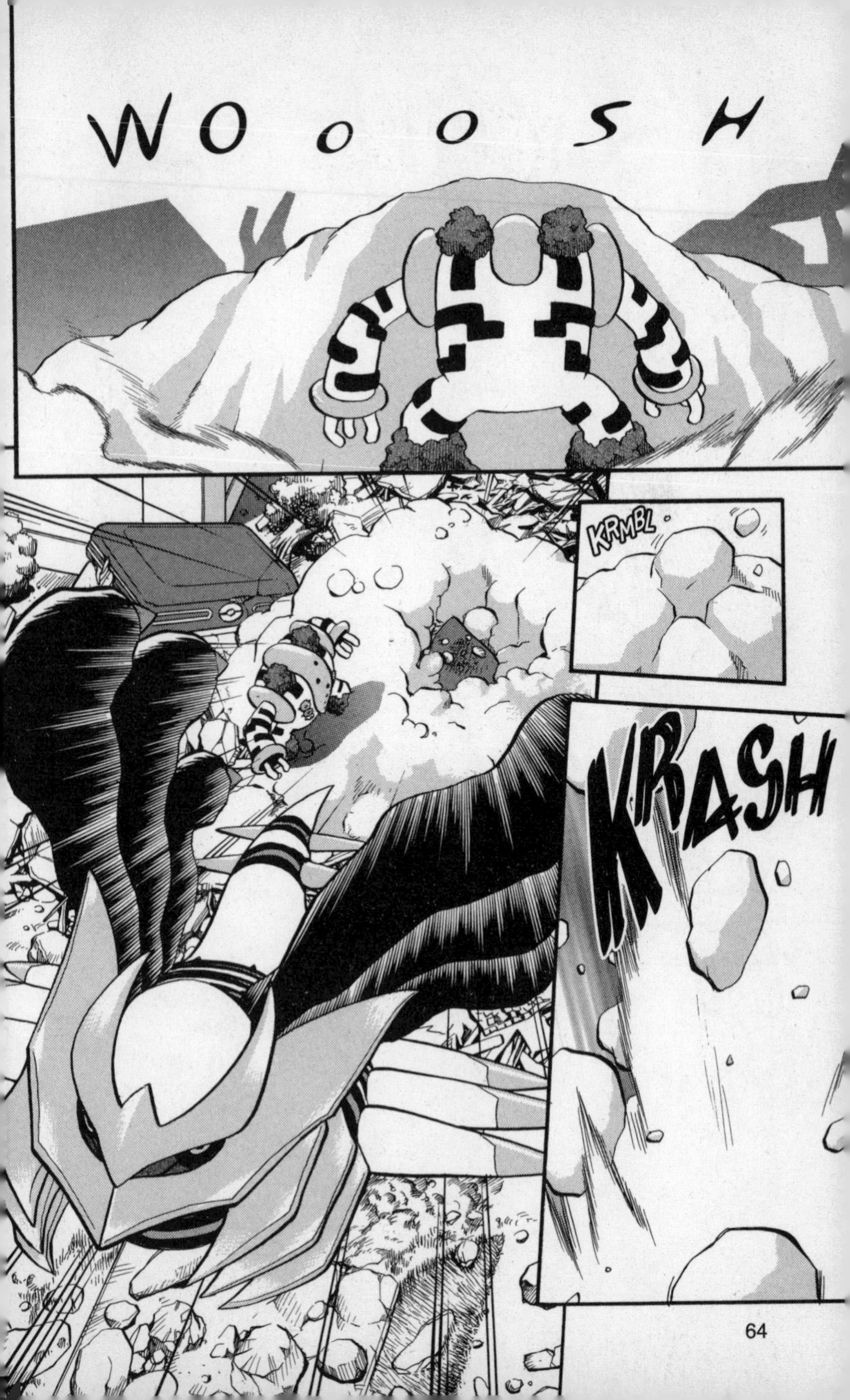
WOOOSH
KRMBL
KRASH

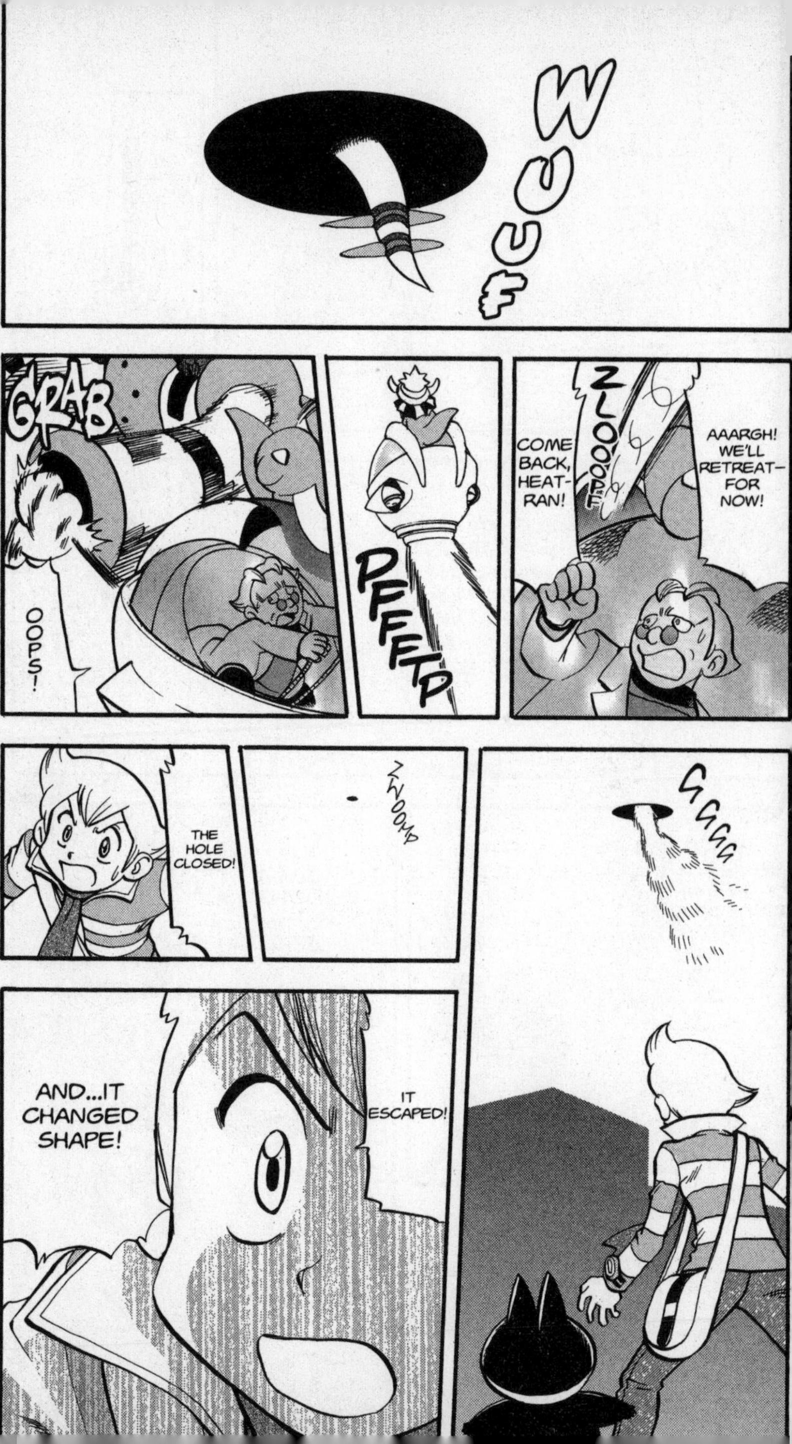
FUUW
AAARGH! WE'LL RETREAT—FOR NOW!
ZLOOOOOP
COME BACK, HEAT-RAN!
PFFFTP
GRAB
OOPS!
GGGG
ZWOOMP
THE HOLE CLOSED!
IT ESCAPED!
AND...IT CHANGED SHAPE!

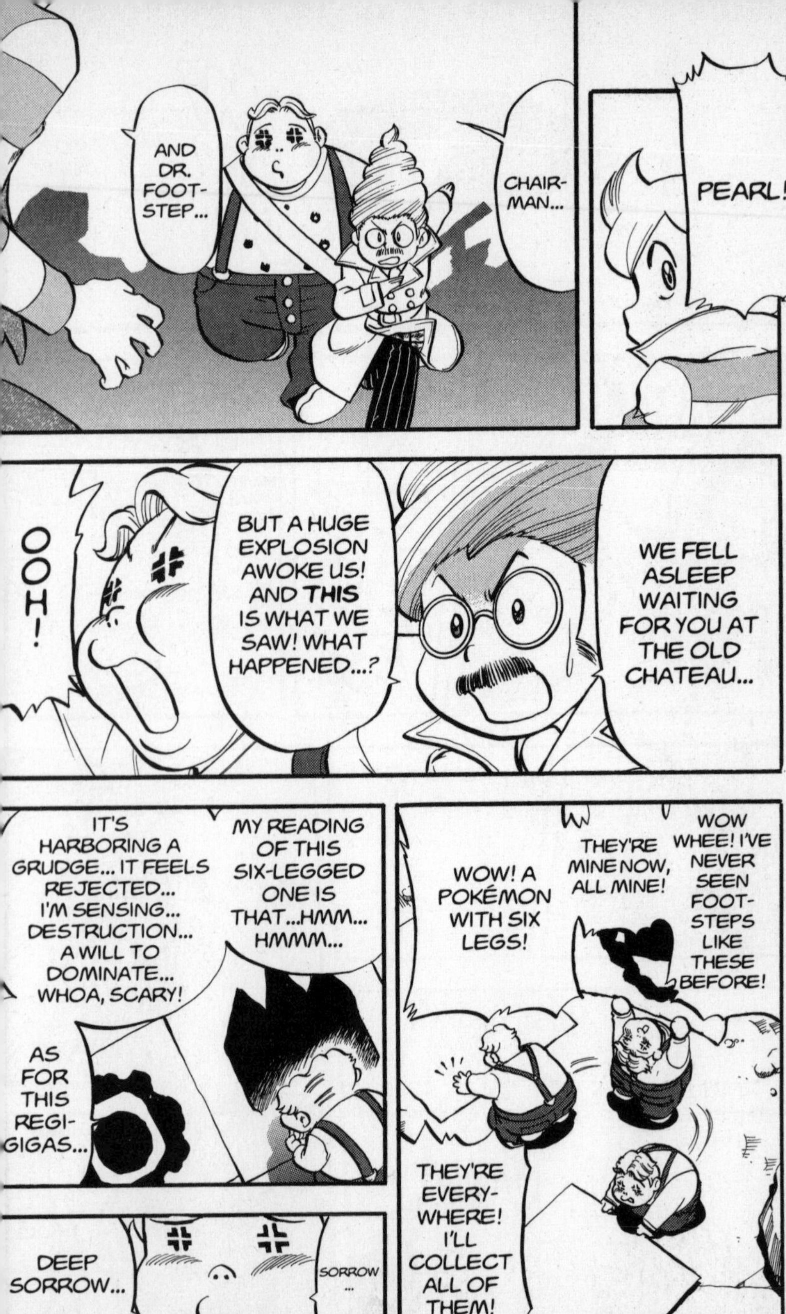
PEARL!
CHAIR-MAN...
AND DR. FOOT-STEP...
WE FELL ASLEEP WAITING FOR YOU AT THE OLD CHATEAU...
BUT A HUGE EXPLOSION AWOKE US! AND **THIS** IS WHAT WE SAW! WHAT HAPPENED...?
OOH!
WOW WHEE! I'VE NEVER SEEN FOOT-STEPS LIKE THESE BEFORE!
THEY'RE MINE NOW, ALL MINE!
WOW! A POKÉMON WITH SIX LEGS!
THEY'RE EVERY-WHERE! I'LL COLLECT ALL OF THEM!
MY READING OF THIS SIX-LEGGED ONE IS THAT...HMM... HMMM...
IT'S HARBORING A GRUDGE... IT FEELS REJECTED... I'M SENSING... DESTRUCTION... A WILL TO DOMINATE... WHOA, SCARY!
AS FOR THIS REGI-GIGAS...
SORROW...
DEEP SORROW...

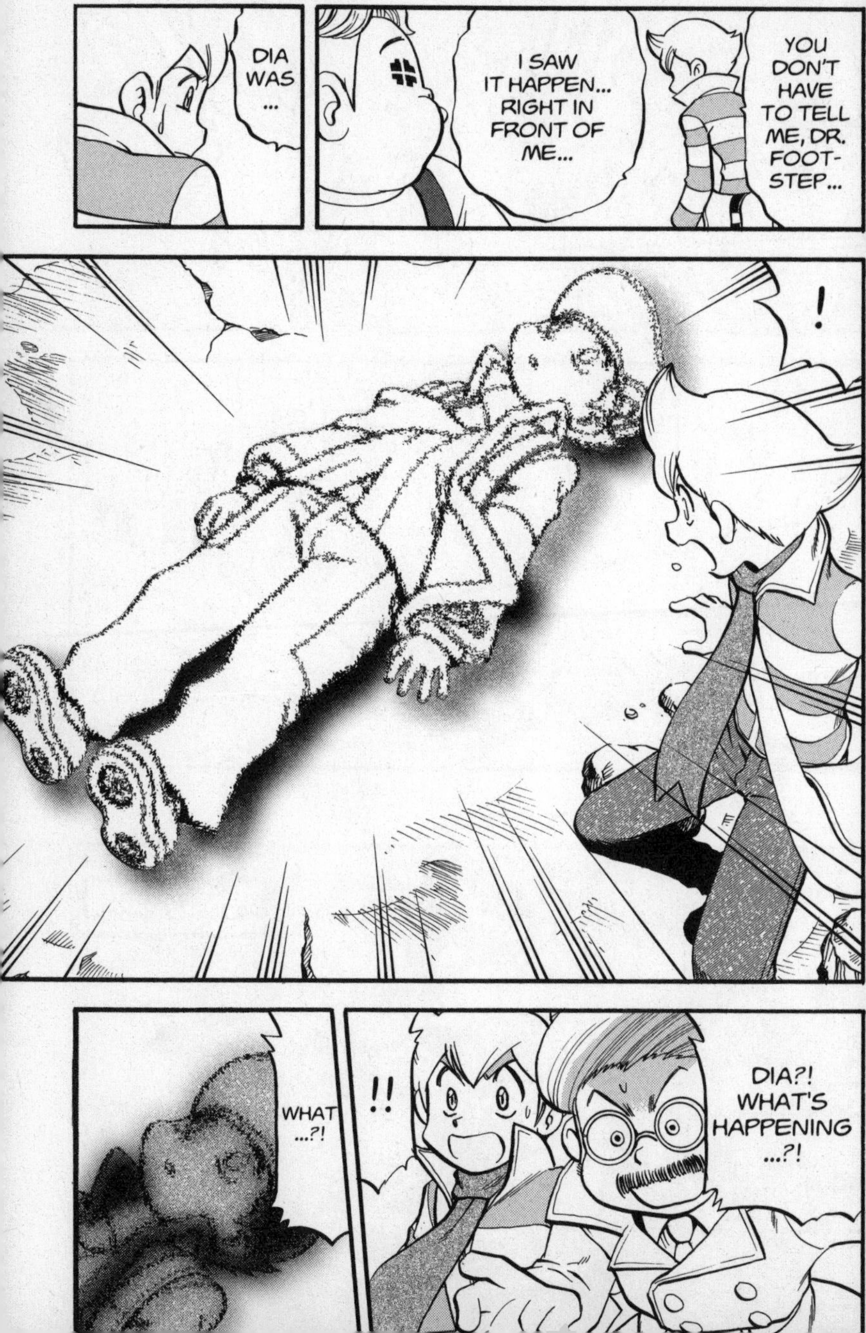
YOU DON'T HAVE TO TELL ME, DR. FOOT-STEP...
I SAW IT HAPPEN... RIGHT IN FRONT OF ME...
DIA WAS ...
!
DIA?! WHAT'S HAPPENING ...?!
!!
WHAT ...?!

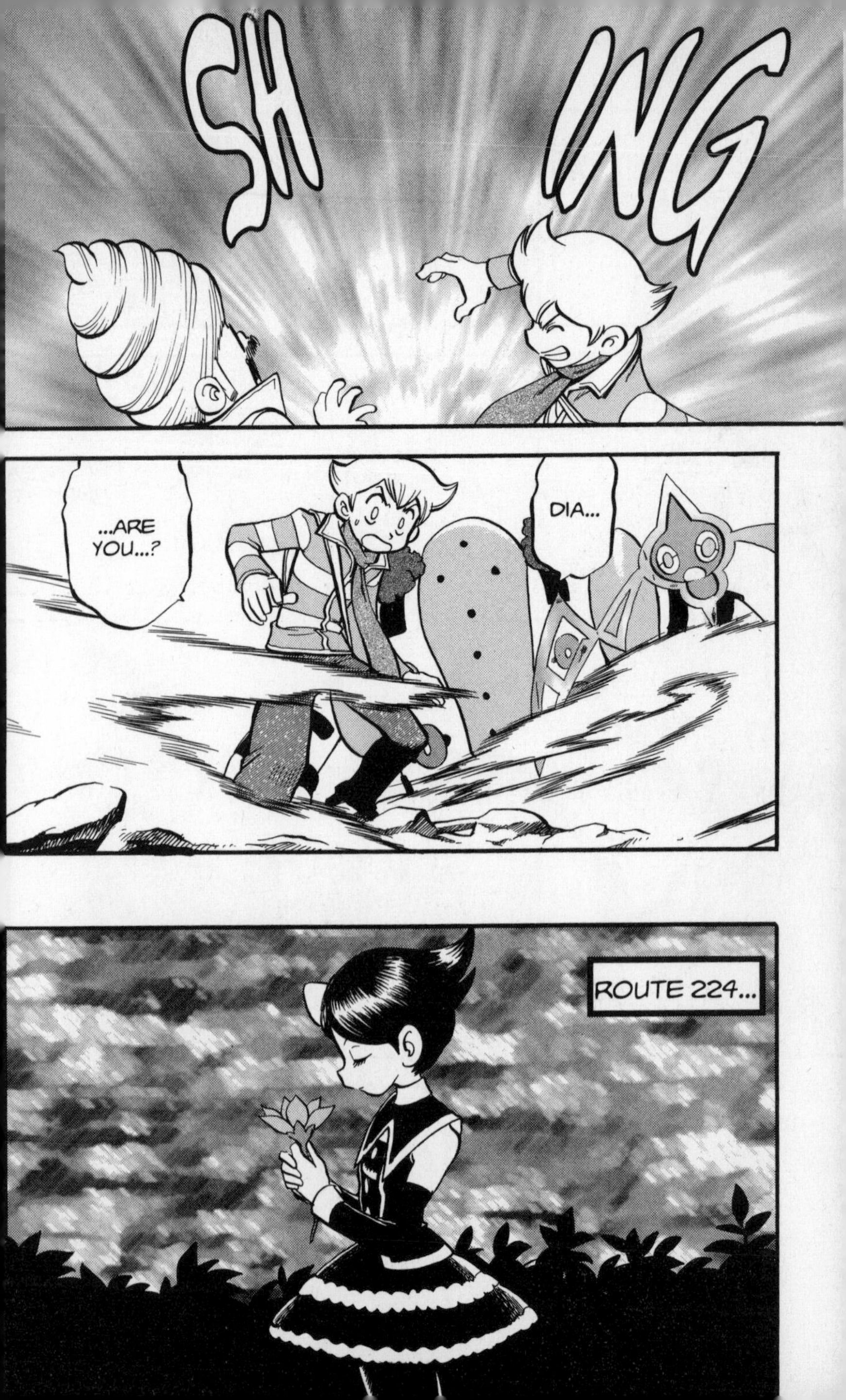
SH ING
DIA...
...ARE YOU...?
ROUTE 224...

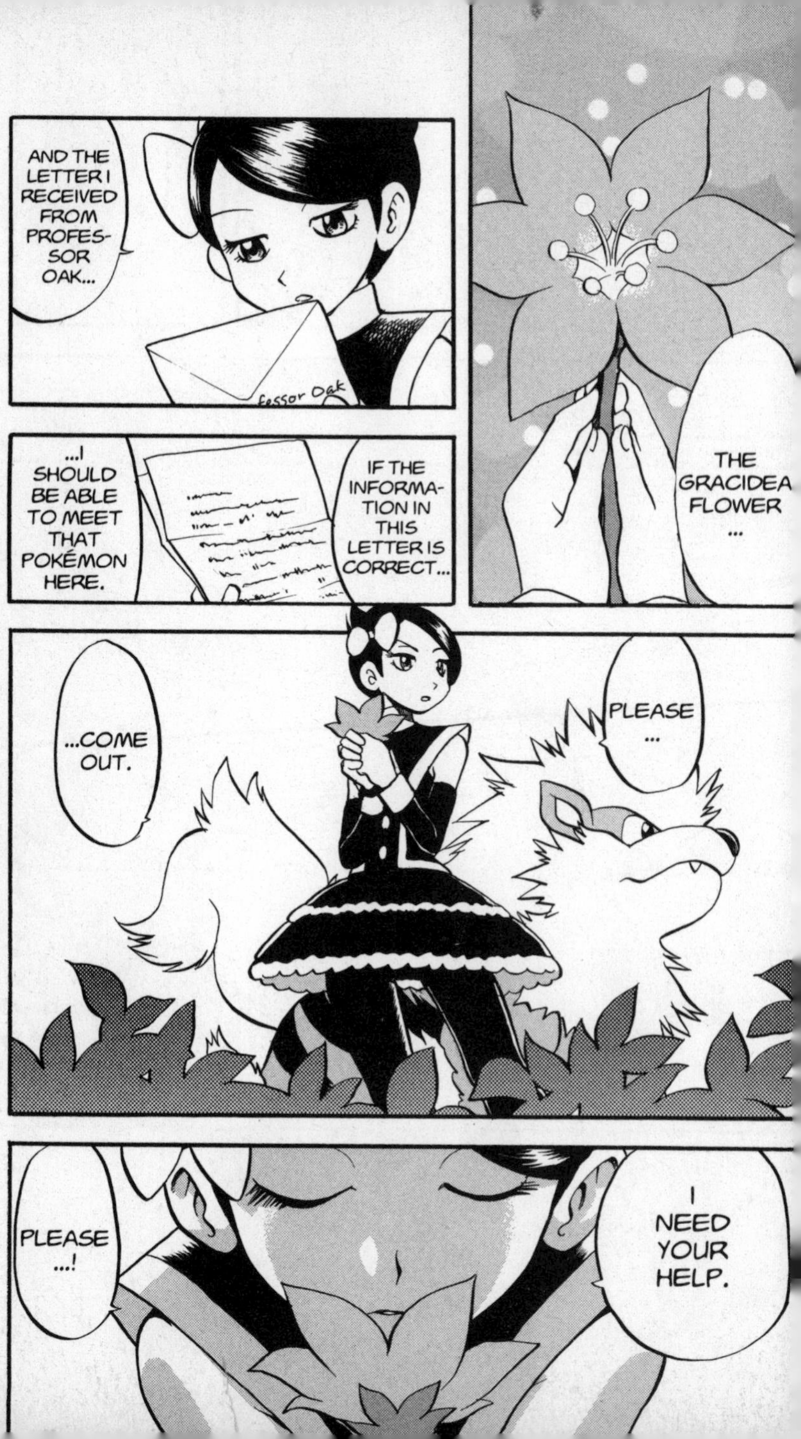
THE GRACIDEA FLOWER ...
AND THE LETTER I RECEIVED FROM PROFESSOR OAK...
fessor Oak
IF THE INFORMATION IN THIS LETTER IS CORRECT...
...I SHOULD BE ABLE TO MEET THAT POKÉMON HERE.
PLEASE ...
...COME OUT.
I NEED YOUR HELP.
PLEASE ...!

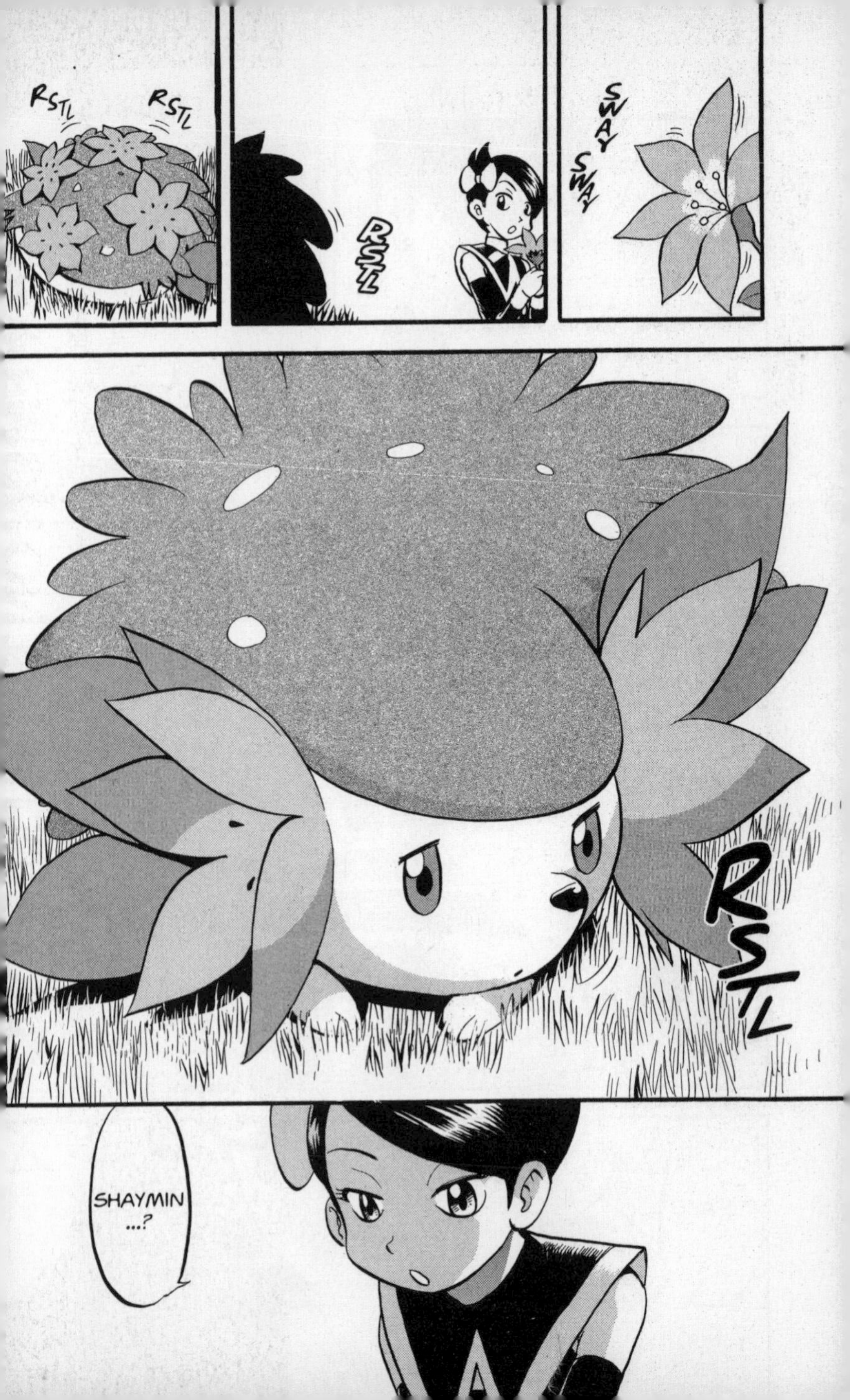
SWAY SWAY
RSTL
RSTL
RSTL
RSTL
SHAYMIN ...?

Kit/Lickilicky ♂

LV. 53 (As of Adventure 97)

Ability: Own Tempo

Bold. Scatters things often.

Kit has successfully saved Dia from many dangerous situations using its long tongue, which has earned it the nickname "Swift Giant"!

Moo/Mamoswine ♂

Ice
Ground

LV. 65 (As of Adventure 97)

Ability: Thick Fat

Robust. Proud of its power.

Moo was a huge help during the battle at the Spear Pillar on Mt. Coronet. It uses powerful Ice-type moves like Ice Fang and Blizzard.

Reg (Regigigas)

Normal

LV. 75 (As of Adventure 97)

Ability: Slow Start

Happy-go-lucky. Hardy.

One of the Legendary Pokémon waiting to be "awakened." It seems to have chosen to participate in this battle...but why?!

Pokémon Stats

TEAM DIAMOND

TEAM DIAMOND 2

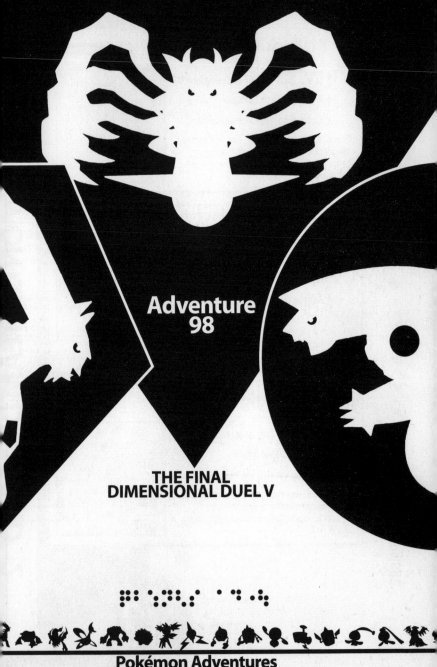

Adventure
98

THE FINAL
DIMENSIONAL DUEL V

Pokémon Adventures
The Eighth Chapter

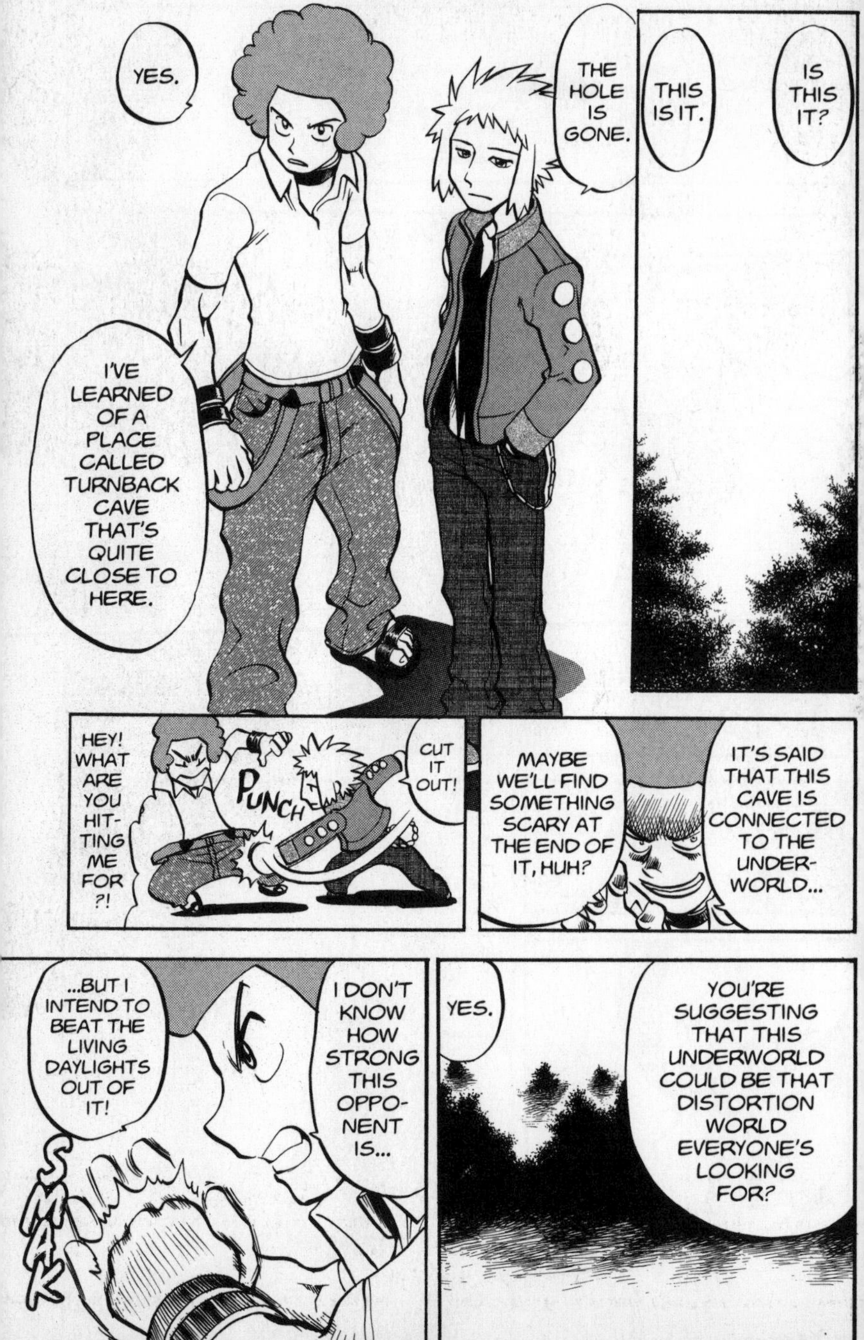
IS THIS IT?
THIS IS IT.
THE HOLE IS GONE.
YES.
I'VE LEARNED OF A PLACE CALLED TURNBACK CAVE THAT'S QUITE CLOSE TO HERE.
IT'S SAID THAT THIS CAVE IS CONNECTED TO THE UNDER-WORLD...
MAYBE WE'LL FIND SOMETHING SCARY AT THE END OF IT, HUH?
CUT IT OUT!
PUNCH
HEY! WHAT ARE YOU HIT-TING ME FOR?!
YOU'RE SUGGESTING THAT THIS UNDERWORLD COULD BE THAT DISTORTION WORLD EVERYONE'S LOOKING FOR?
YES.
I DON'T KNOW HOW STRONG THIS OPPO-NENT IS...
...BUT I INTEND TO BEAT THE LIVING DAYLIGHTS OUT OF IT!
SMAK

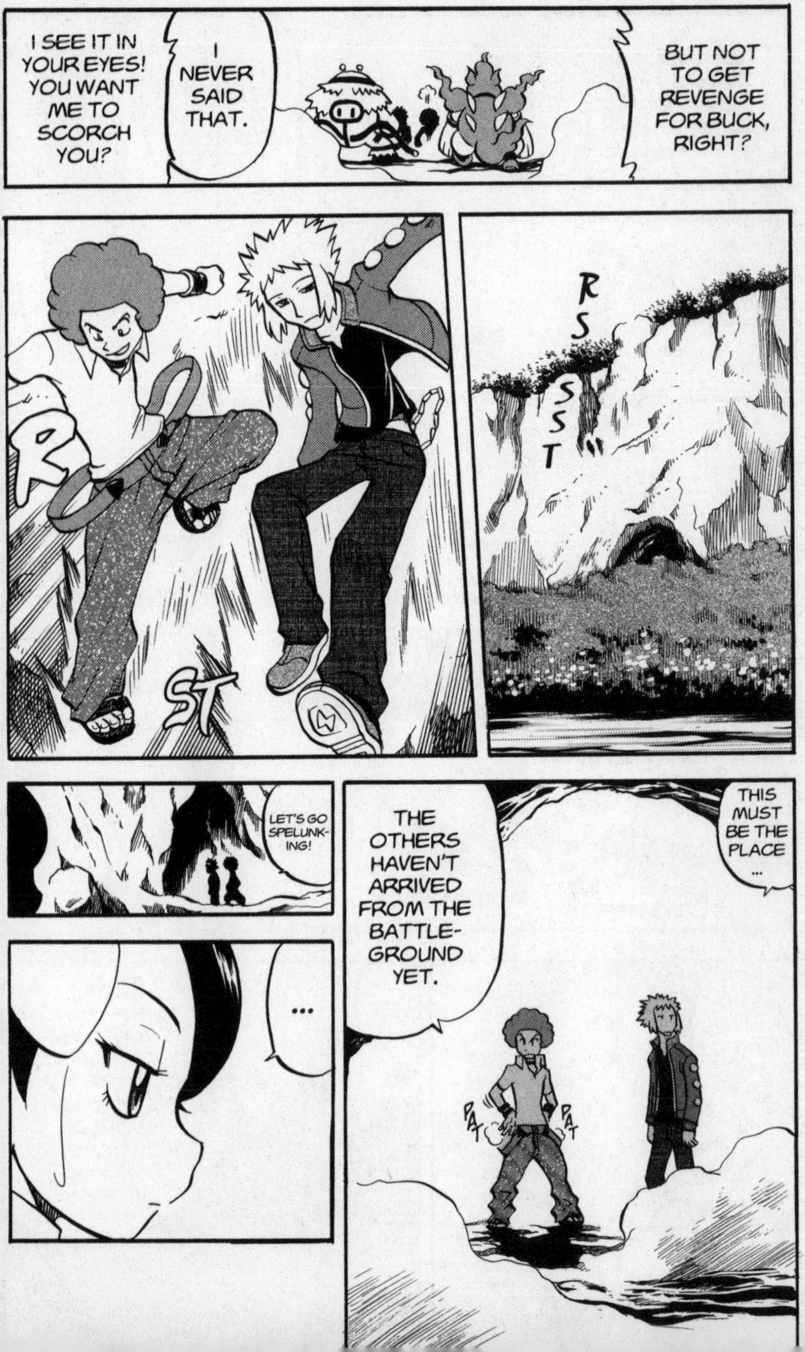
BUT NOT TO GET REVENGE FOR BUCK, RIGHT?
I NEVER SAID THAT.
I SEE IT IN YOUR EYES! YOU WANT ME TO SCORCH YOU?
RSSST
R
ST
THIS MUST BE THE PLACE...
THE OTHERS HAVEN'T ARRIVED FROM THE BATTLEGROUND YET.
PAT
PAT
LET'S GO SPELUNKING!
...

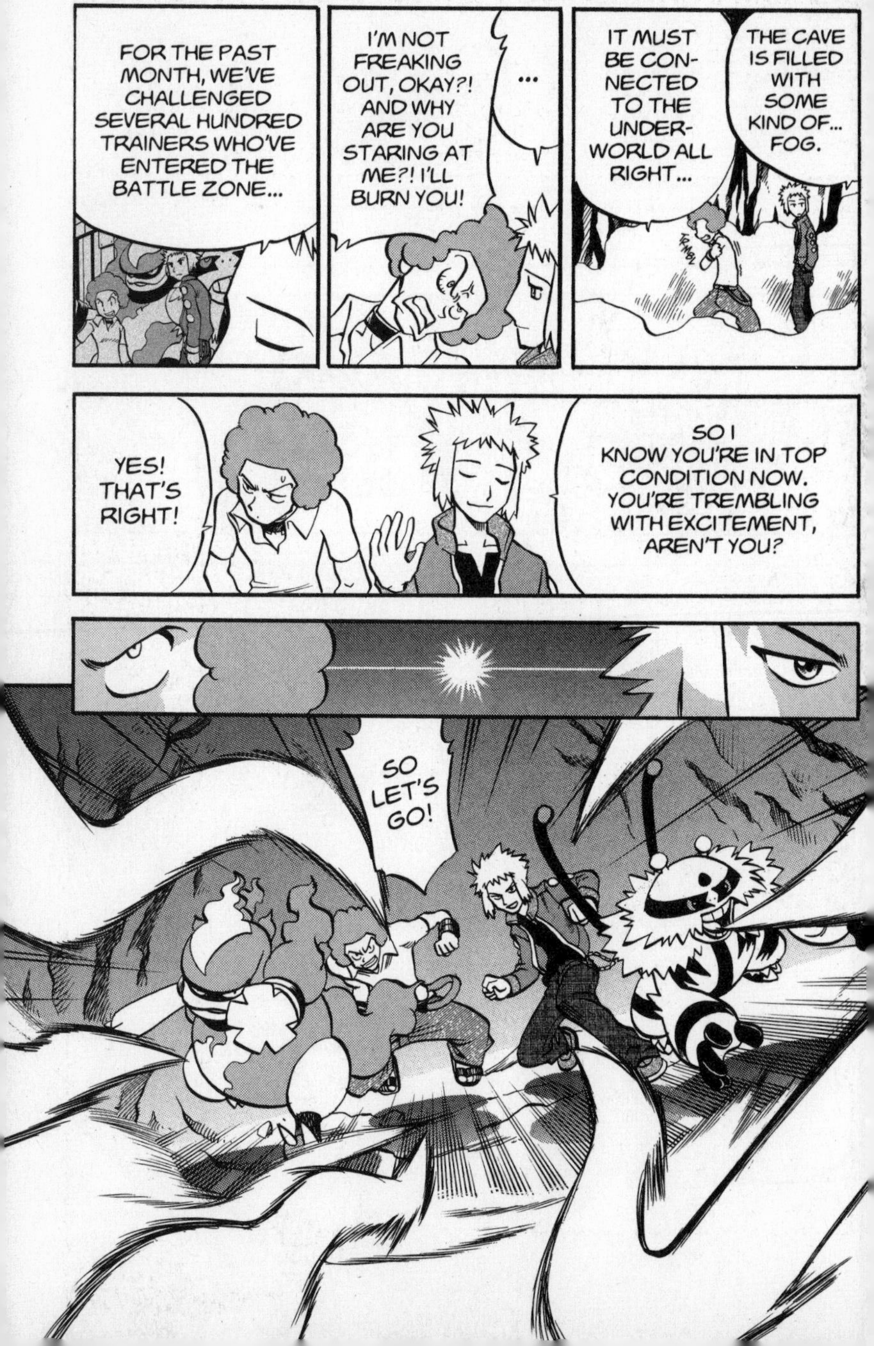
THE CAVE IS FILLED WITH SOME KIND OF... FOG.
IT MUST BE CONNECTED TO THE UNDERWORLD ALL RIGHT...
...
I'M NOT FREAKING OUT, OKAY?! AND WHY ARE YOU STARING AT ME?! I'LL BURN YOU!
FOR THE PAST MONTH, WE'VE CHALLENGED SEVERAL HUNDRED TRAINERS WHO'VE ENTERED THE BATTLE ZONE...
SO I KNOW YOU'RE IN TOP CONDITION NOW. YOU'RE TREMBLING WITH EXCITEMENT, AREN'T YOU?
YES! THAT'S RIGHT!
SO LET'S GO!

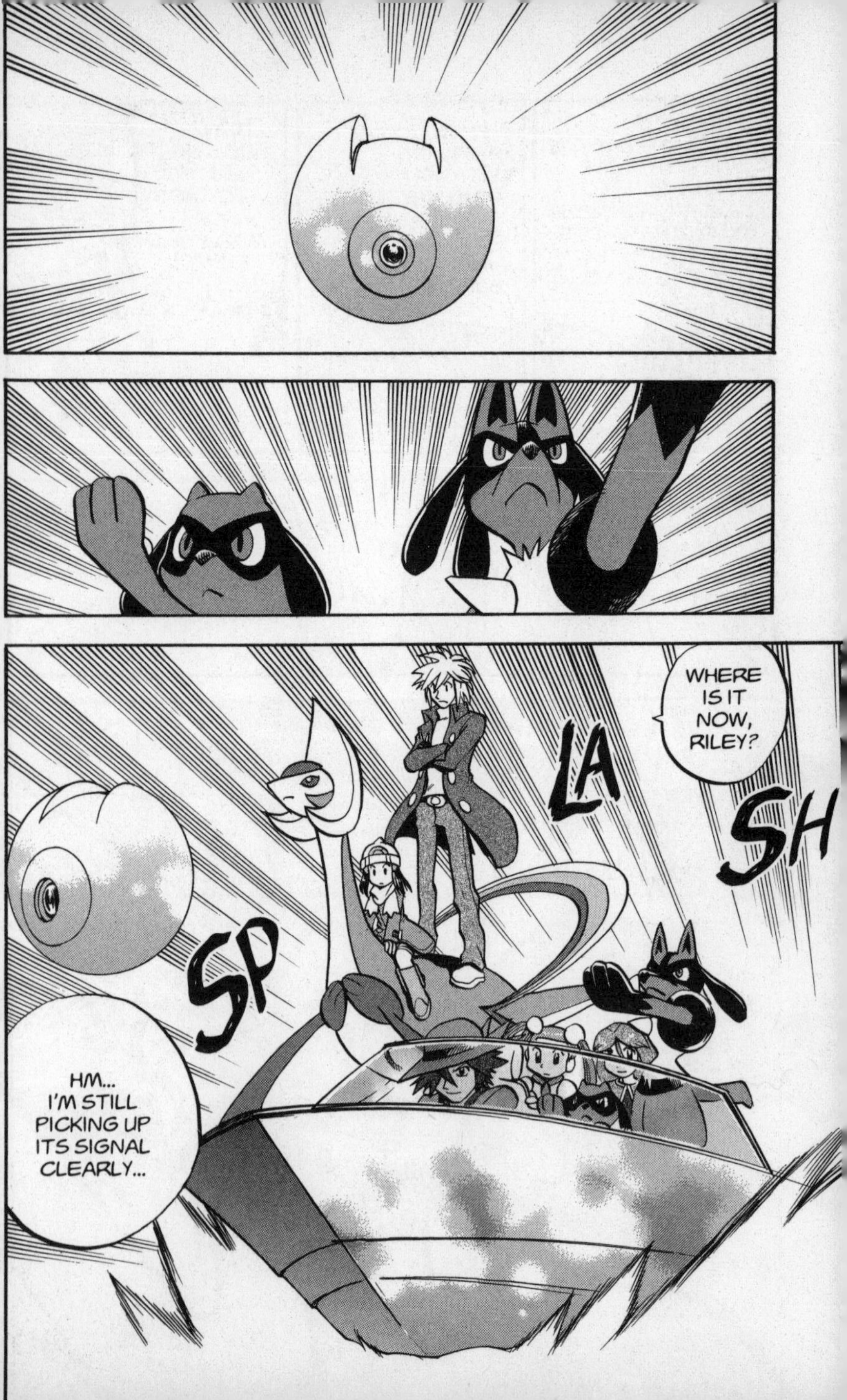
WHERE IS IT NOW, RILEY?
SP LA SH
HM... I'M STILL PICKING UP ITS SIGNAL CLEARLY...

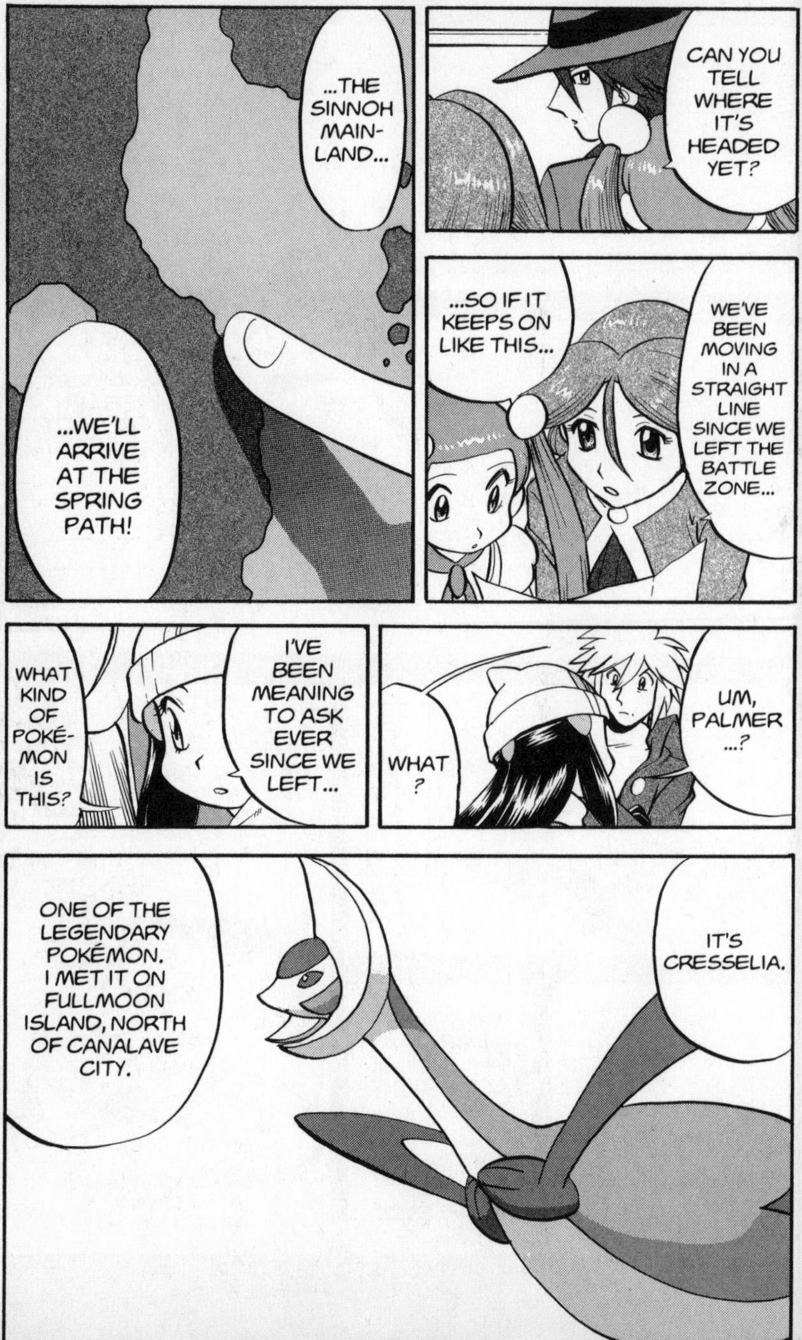
CAN YOU TELL WHERE IT'S HEADED YET?
WE'VE BEEN MOVING IN A STRAIGHT LINE SINCE WE LEFT THE BATTLE ZONE...
...SO IF IT KEEPS ON LIKE THIS...
...THE SINNOH MAIN-LAND...
...WE'LL ARRIVE AT THE SPRING PATH!
UM, PALMER ...?
WHAT ?
I'VE BEEN MEANING TO ASK EVER SINCE WE LEFT...
WHAT KIND OF POKÉ-MON IS THIS?
IT'S CRESSELIA.
ONE OF THE LEGENDARY POKÉMON. I MET IT ON FULLMOON ISLAND, NORTH OF CANALAVE CITY.

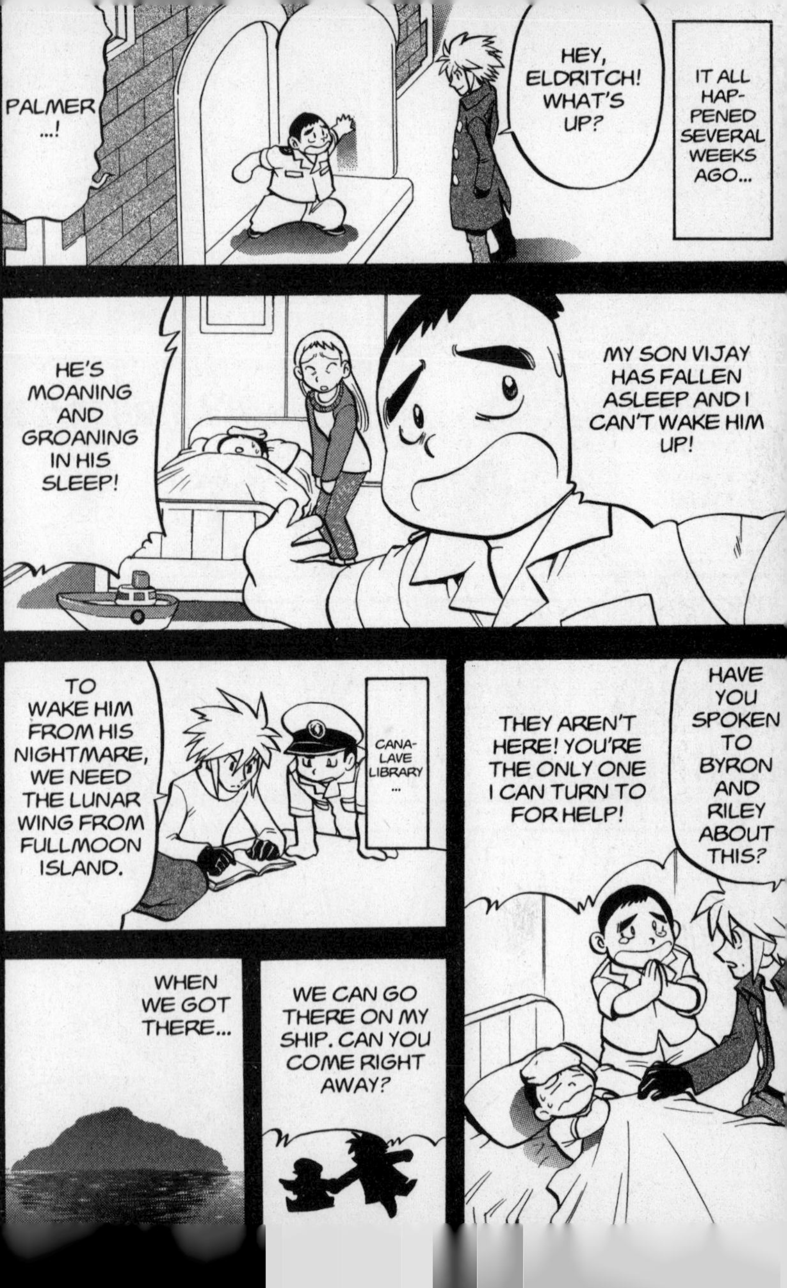
IT ALL HAP-PENED SEVERAL WEEKS AGO...
HEY, ELDRITCH! WHAT'S UP?
PALMER ...!
MY SON VIJAY HAS FALLEN ASLEEP AND I CAN'T WAKE HIM UP!
HE'S MOANING AND GROANING IN HIS SLEEP!
HAVE YOU SPOKEN TO BYRON AND RILEY ABOUT THIS?
THEY AREN'T HERE! YOU'RE THE ONLY ONE I CAN TURN TO FOR HELP!
CANA-LAVE LIBRARY ...
TO WAKE HIM FROM HIS NIGHTMARE, WE NEED THE LUNAR WING FROM FULLMOON ISLAND.
WE CAN GO THERE ON MY SHIP. CAN YOU COME RIGHT AWAY?
WHEN WE GOT THERE...

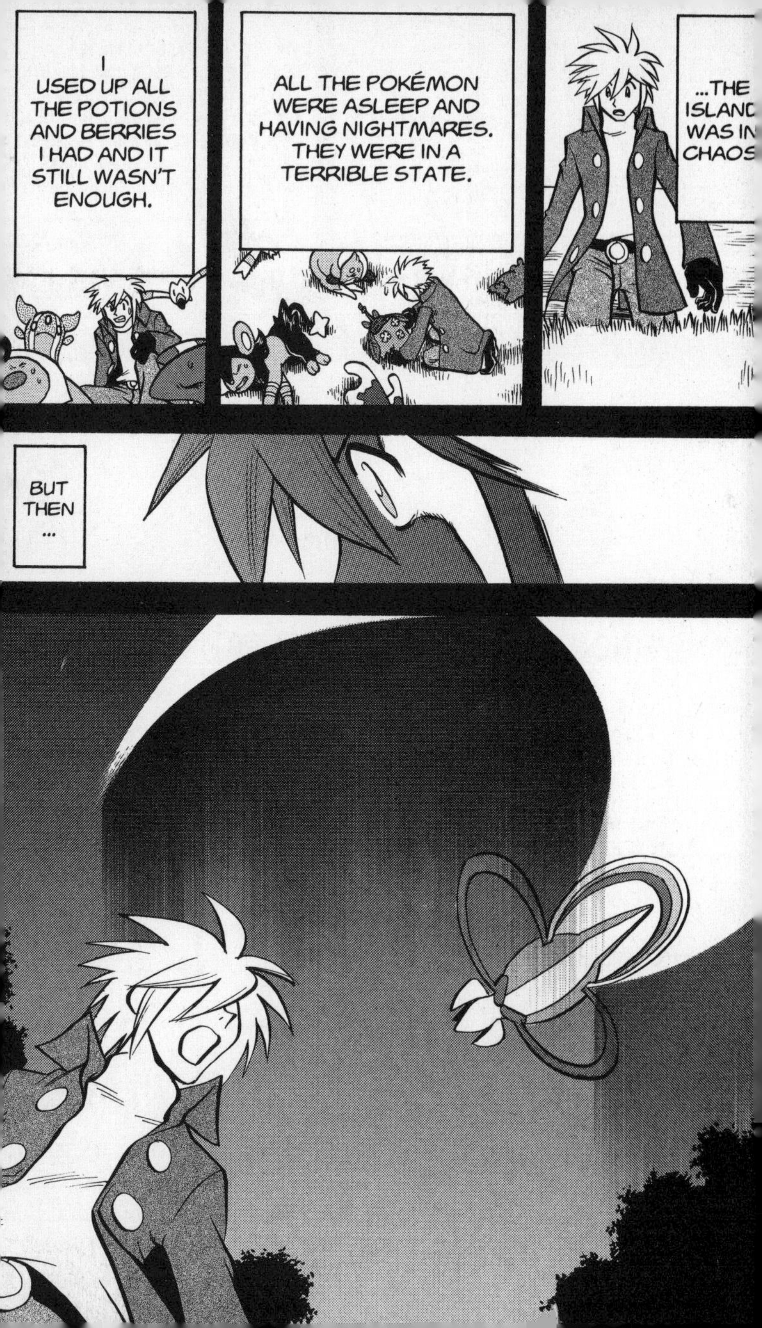
...THE ISLAN WAS IN CHAOS
ALL THE POKÉMON WERE ASLEEP AND HAVING NIGHTMARES. THEY WERE IN A TERRIBLE STATE.
I USED UP ALL THE POTIONS AND BERRIES I HAD AND IT STILL WASN'T ENOUGH.
BUT THEN ...

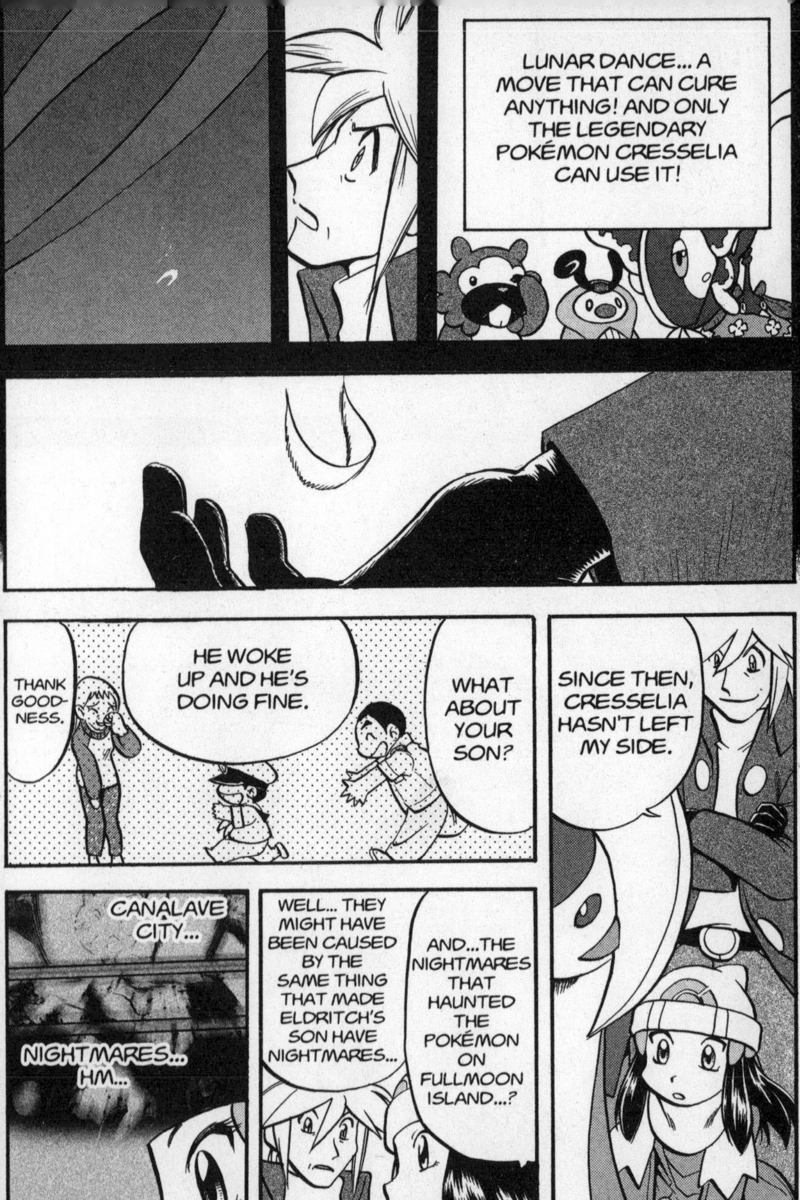
LUNAR DANCE... A MOVE THAT CAN CURE ANYTHING! AND ONLY THE LEGENDARY POKéMON CRESSELIA CAN USE IT!
SINCE THEN, CRESSELIA HASN'T LEFT MY SIDE.
WHAT ABOUT YOUR SON?
HE WOKE UP AND HE'S DOING FINE.
THANK GOODNESS.
AND...THE NIGHTMARES THAT HAUNTED THE POKéMON ON FULLMOON ISLAND...?
WELL... THEY MIGHT HAVE BEEN CAUSED BY THE SAME THING THAT MADE ELDRITCH'S SON HAVE NIGHTMARES...
CANALAVE CITY...
NIGHTMARES... HM...

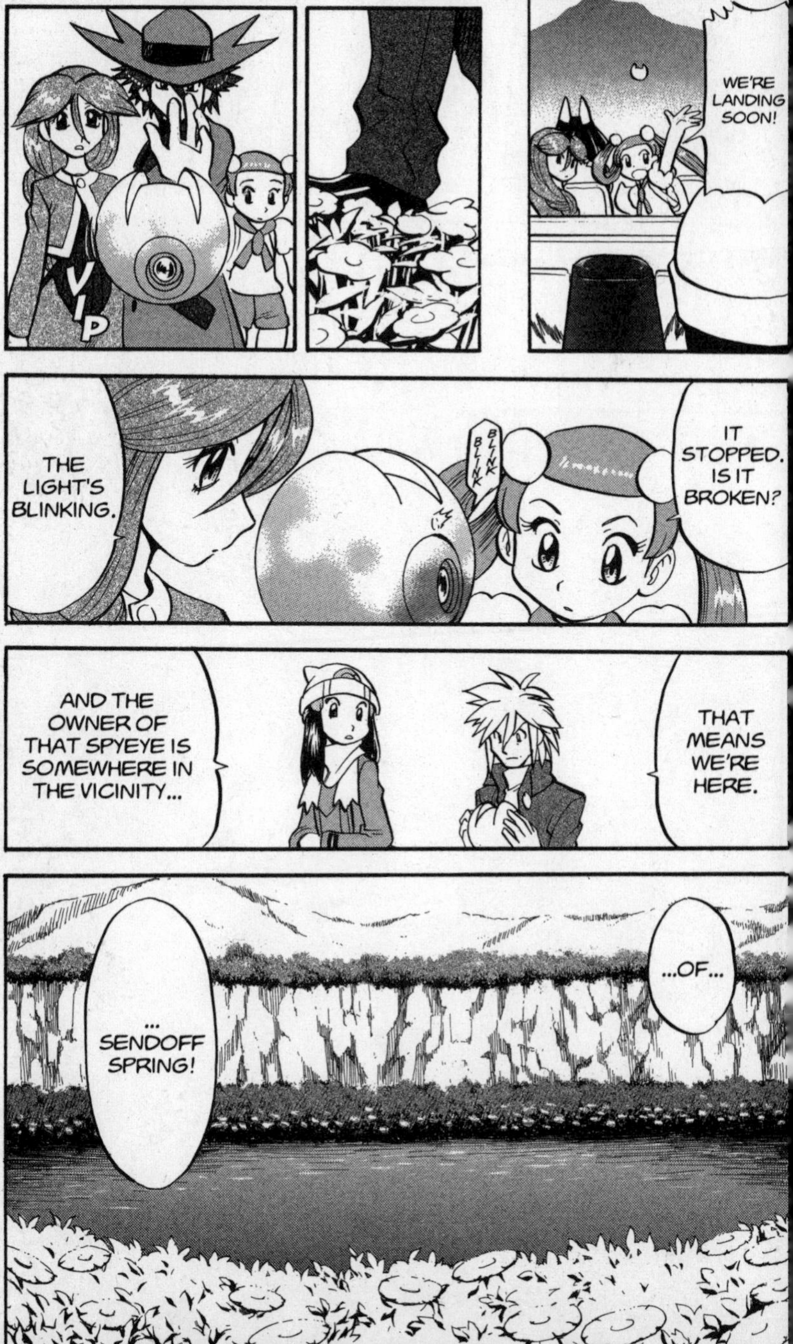
WE'RE LANDING SOON!
VIP
IT STOPPED. IS IT BROKEN?
BLINK BLINK
THE LIGHT'S BLINKING.
THAT MEANS WE'RE HERE.
AND THE OWNER OF THAT SPYEYE IS SOMEWHERE IN THE VICINITY...
...OF...
... SENDOFF SPRING!

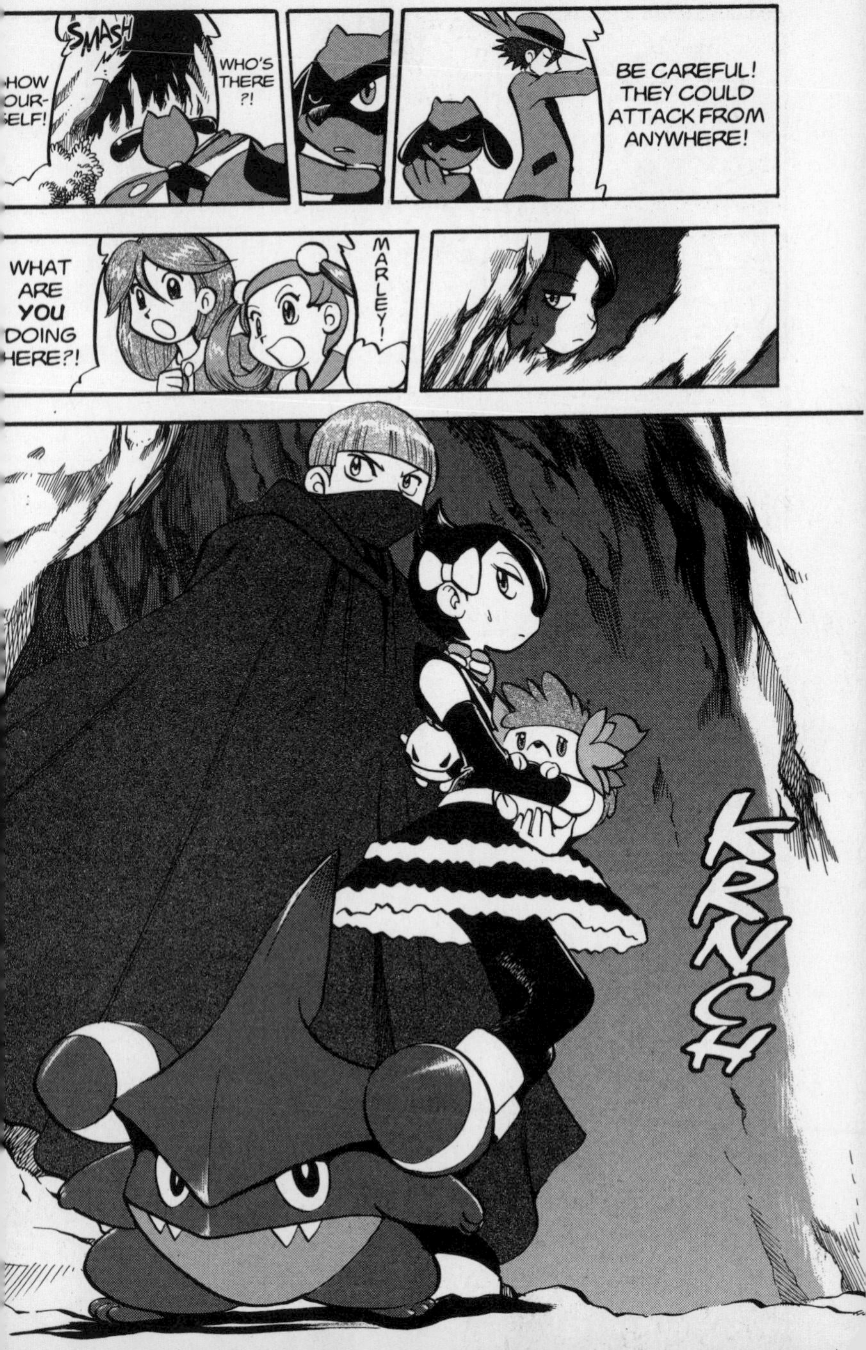
BE CAREFUL! THEY COULD ATTACK FROM ANYWHERE!
WHO'S THERE ?!
SMASH
HOW OUR-ELF!
MARLEY!
WHAT ARE YOU DOING HERE?!
KRNCH

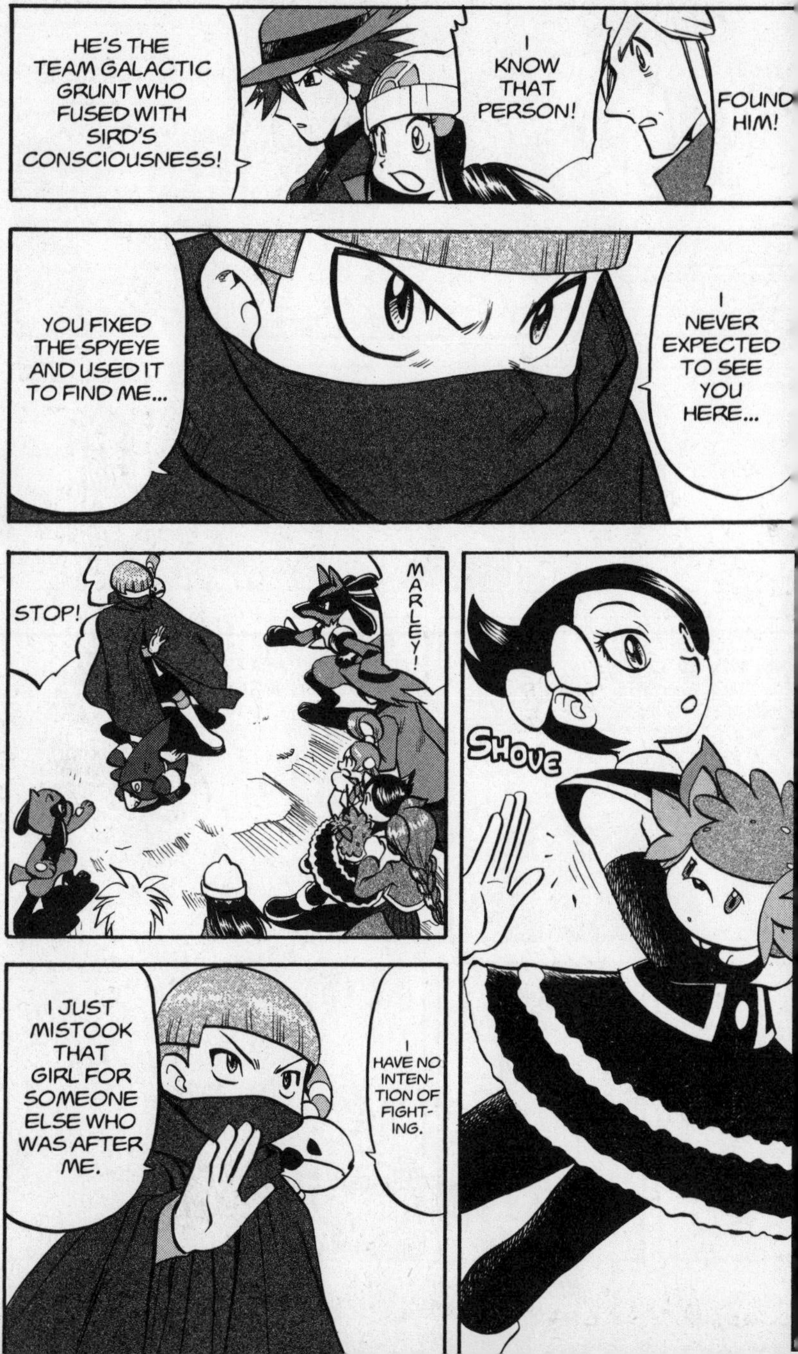
FOUND HIM!
I KNOW THAT PERSON!
HE'S THE TEAM GALACTIC GRUNT WHO FUSED WITH SIRD'S CONSCIOUSNESS!
I NEVER EXPECTED TO SEE YOU HERE...
YOU FIXED THE SPYEYE AND USED IT TO FIND ME...
SHOVE
MARLEY!
STOP!
I HAVE NO INTENTION OF FIGHTING.
I JUST MISTOOK THAT GIRL FOR SOMEONE ELSE WHO WAS AFTER ME.

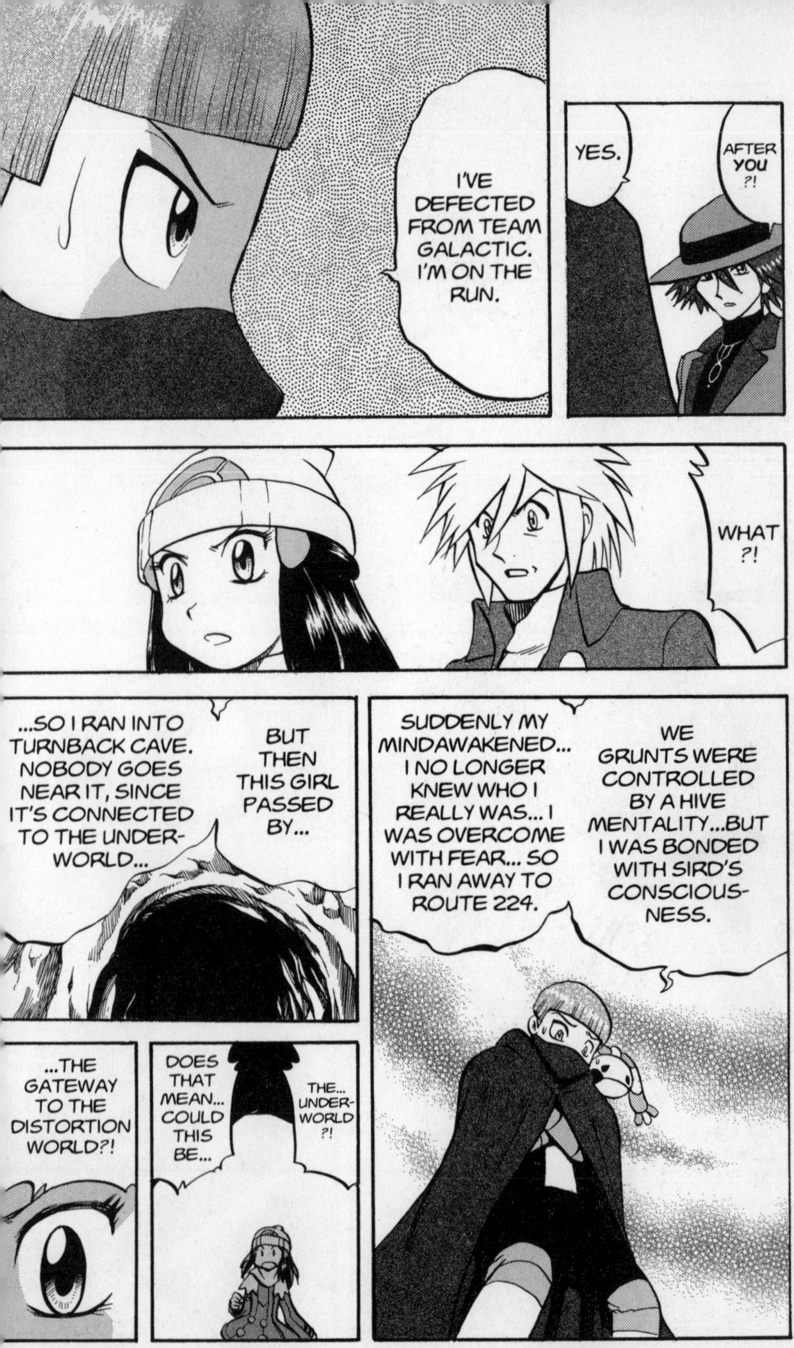
AFTER YOU?!
YES.
I'VE DEFECTED FROM TEAM GALACTIC. I'M ON THE RUN.
WHAT?!
WE GRUNTS WERE CONTROLLED BY A HIVE MENTALITY...BUT I WAS BONDED WITH SIRD'S CONSCIOUS-NESS.
SUDDENLY MY MINDAWAKENED... I NO LONGER KNEW WHO I REALLY WAS... I WAS OVERCOME WITH FEAR... SO I RAN AWAY TO ROUTE 224.
BUT THEN THIS GIRL PASSED BY...
...SO I RAN INTO TURNBACK CAVE. NOBODY GOES NEAR IT, SINCE IT'S CONNECTED TO THE UNDER-WORLD...
THE... UNDER-WORLD?!
DOES THAT MEAN... COULD THIS BE...
...THE GATEWAY TO THE DISTORTION WORLD?!

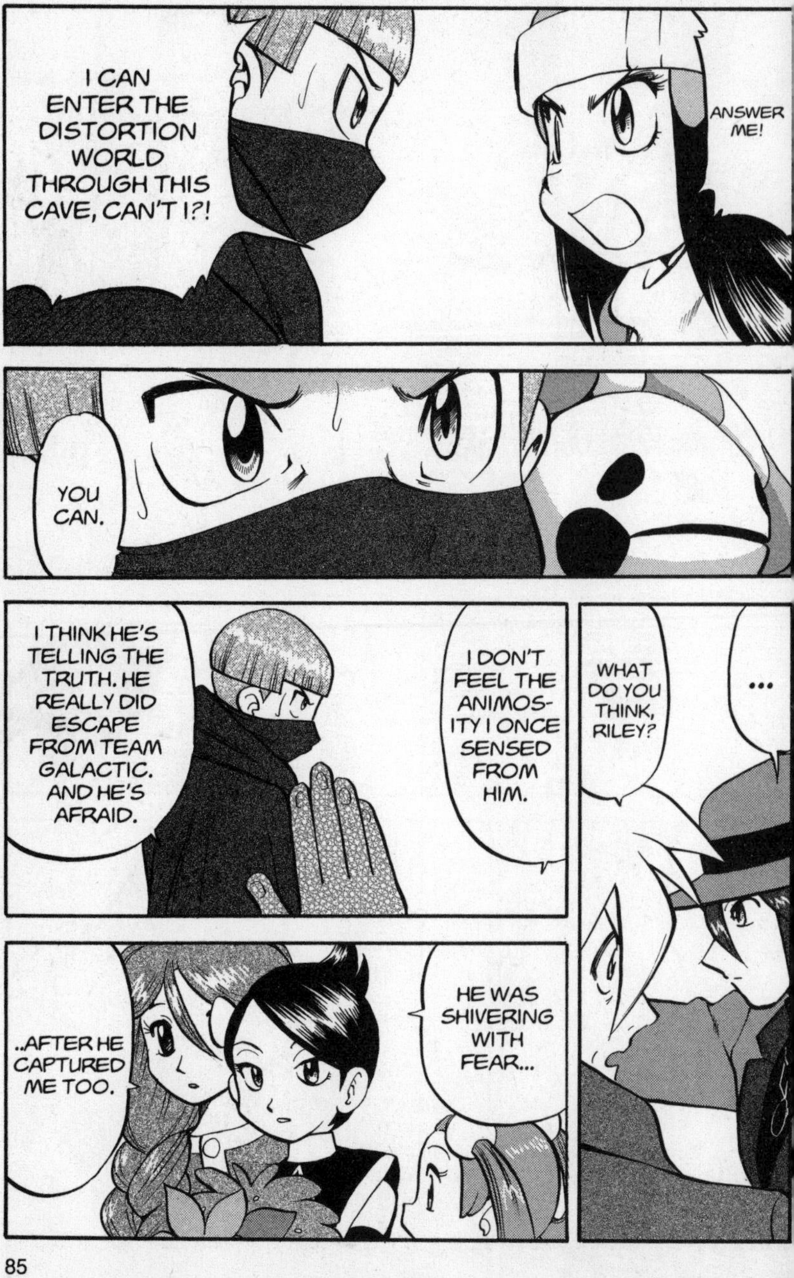
ANSWER ME!
I CAN ENTER THE DISTORTION WORLD THROUGH THIS CAVE, CAN'T I?!
YOU CAN.
...
WHAT DO YOU THINK, RILEY?
I DON'T FEEL THE ANIMOS-ITY I ONCE SENSED FROM HIM.
I THINK HE'S TELLING THE TRUTH. HE REALLY DID ESCAPE FROM TEAM GALACTIC. AND HE'S AFRAID.
HE WAS SHIVERING WITH FEAR...
..AFTER HE CAPTURED ME TOO.

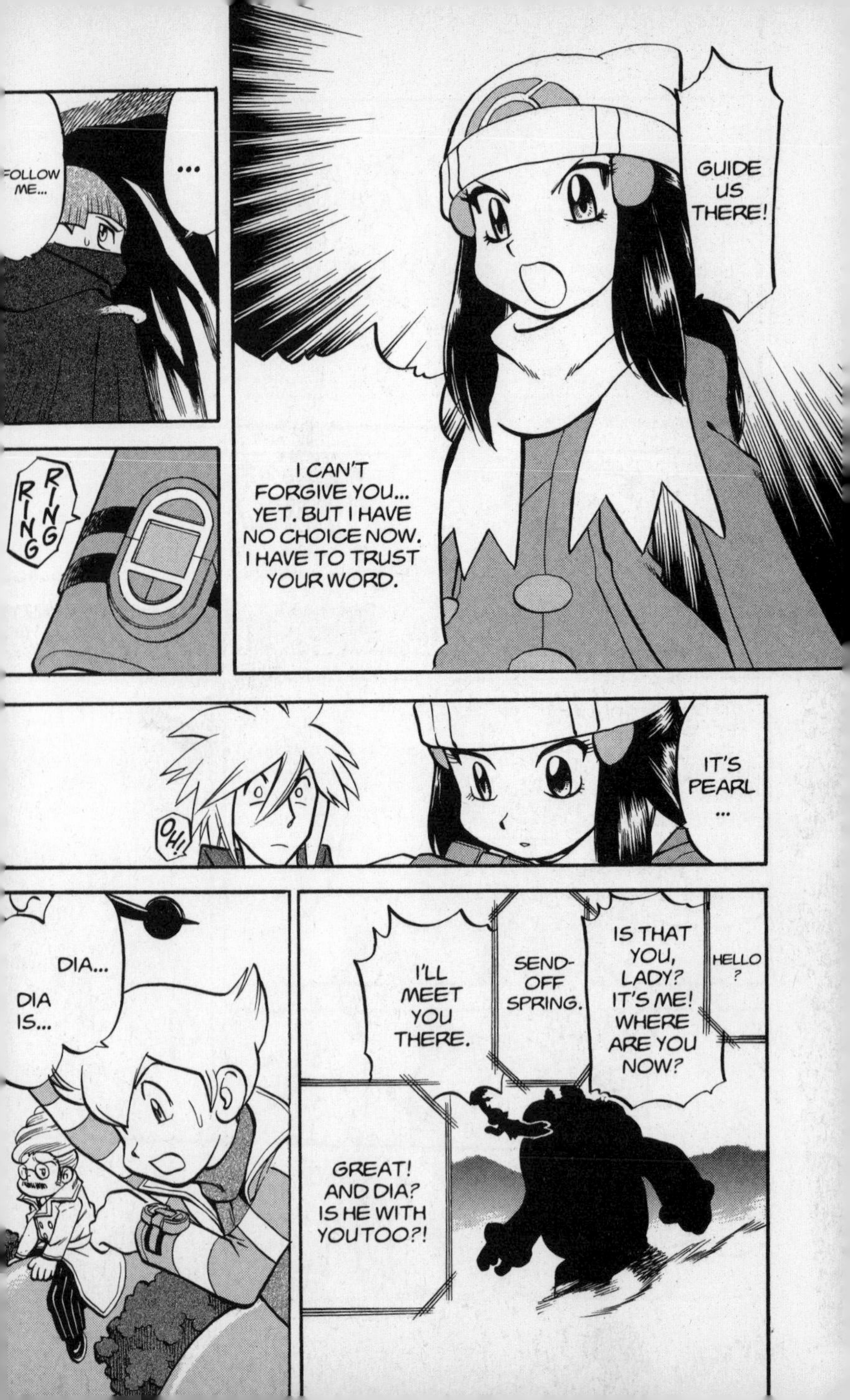
GUIDE US THERE!
I CAN'T FORGIVE YOU... YET. BUT I HAVE NO CHOICE NOW. I HAVE TO TRUST YOUR WORD.
...
FOLLOW ME...
RING RING
IT'S PEARL ...
OH!
HELLO?
IS THAT YOU, LADY? IT'S ME! WHERE ARE YOU NOW?
SEND-OFF SPRING.
I'LL MEET YOU THERE.
GREAT! AND DIA? IS HE WITH YOU TOO?!
DIA...
DIA IS...

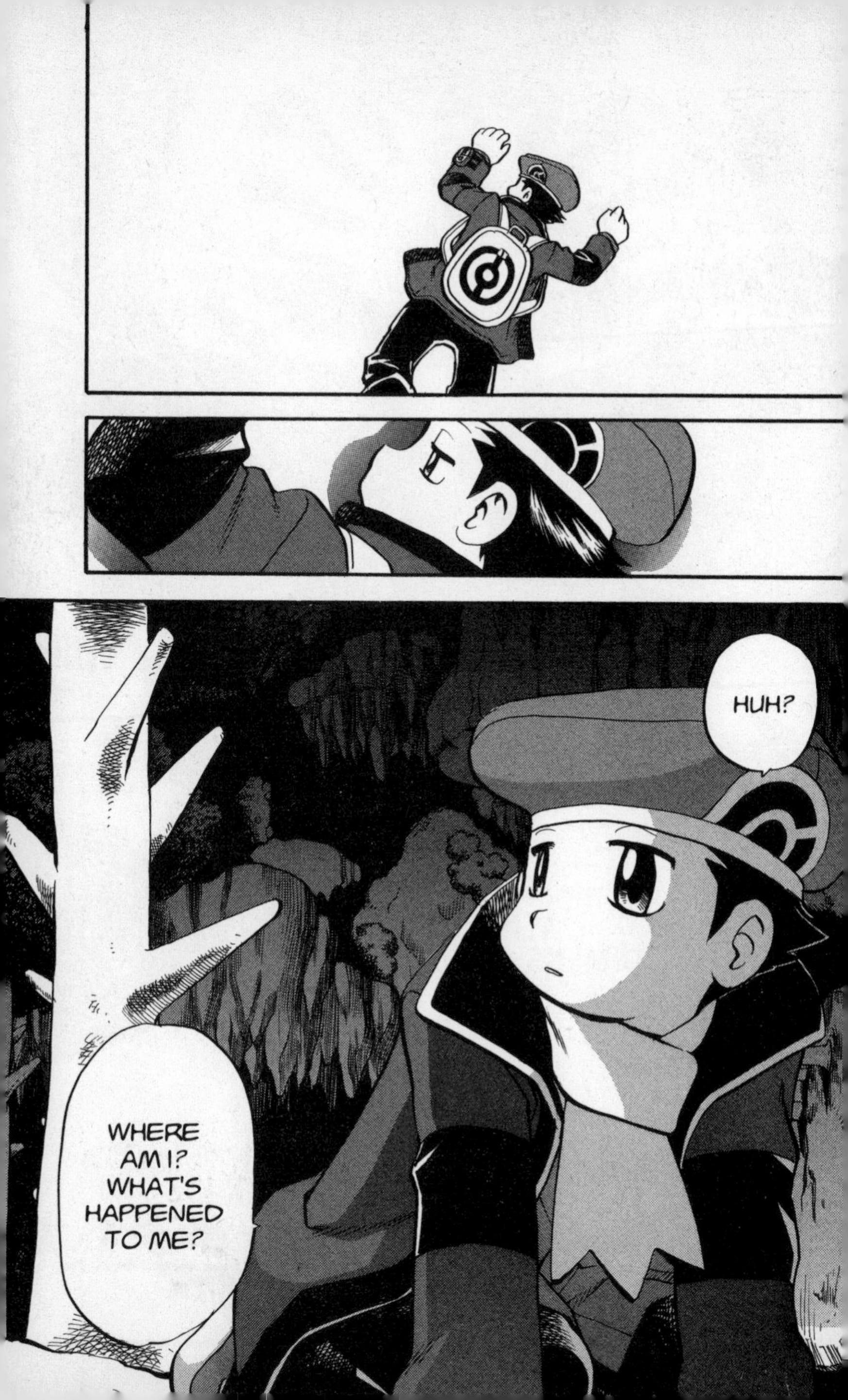
HUH?
WHERE AM I? WHAT'S HAPPENED TO ME?

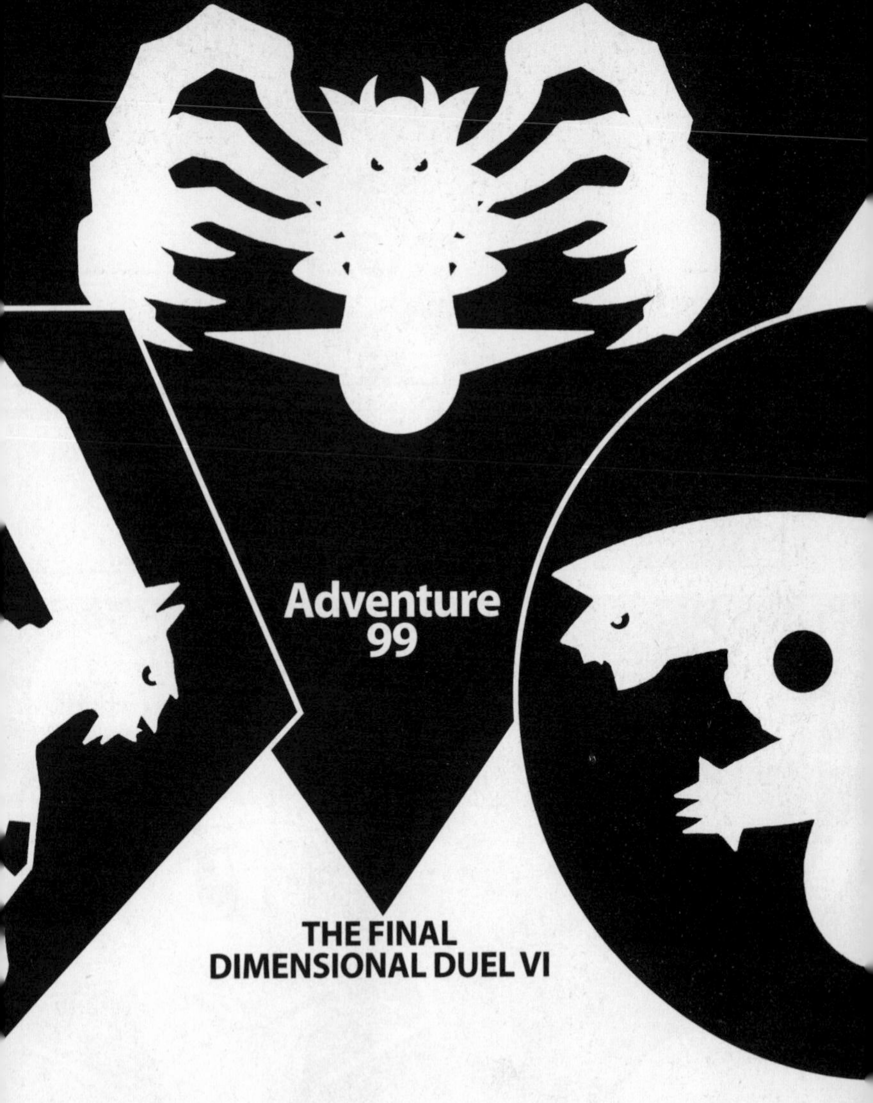

Adventure 99

THE FINAL DIMENSIONAL DUEL VI

Pokémon Adventures
The Eighth Chapter

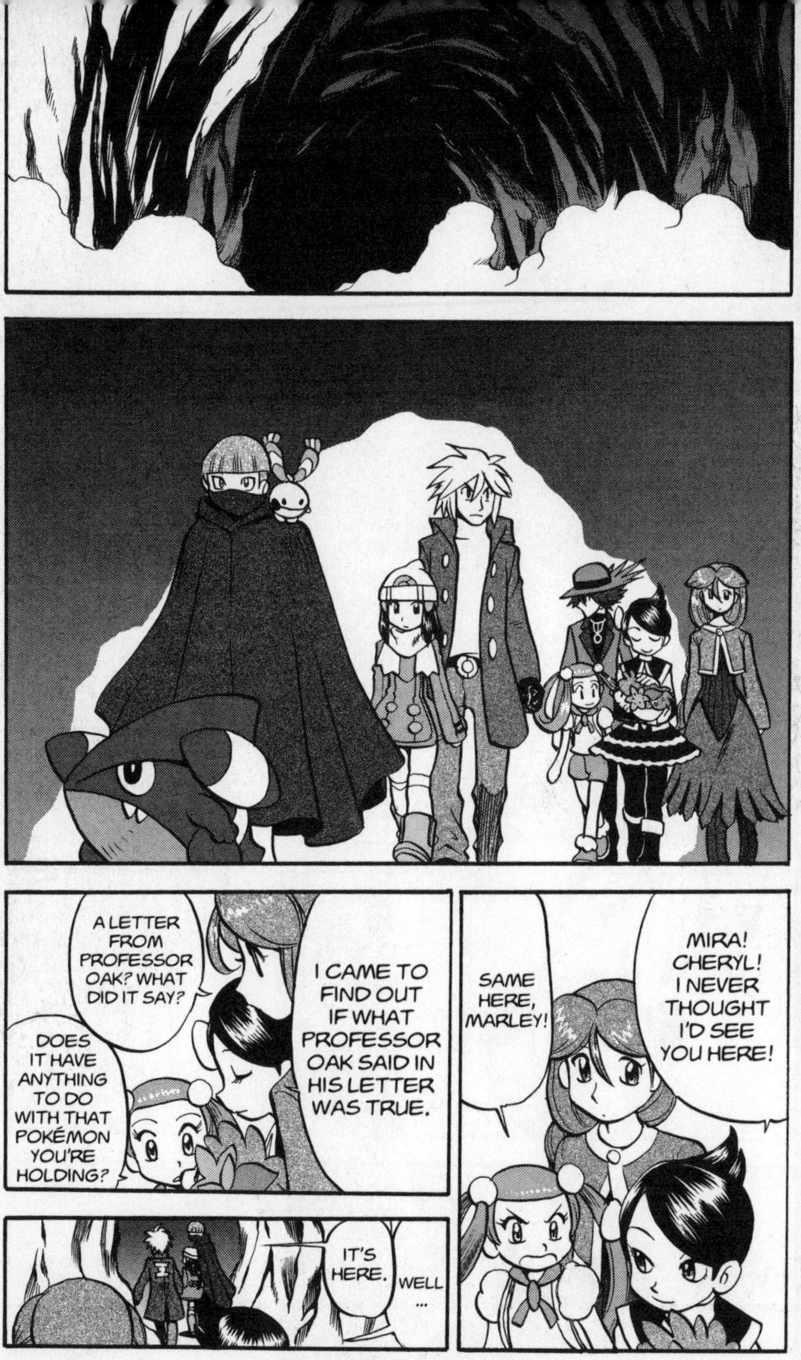

MIRA! CHERYL! I NEVER THOUGHT I'D SEE YOU HERE!
SAME HERE, MARLEY!
I CAME TO FIND OUT IF WHAT PROFESSOR OAK SAID IN HIS LETTER WAS TRUE.
A LETTER FROM PROFESSOR OAK? WHAT DID IT SAY?
DOES IT HAVE ANYTHING TO DO WITH THAT POKÉMON YOU'RE HOLDING?
WELL ...
IT'S HERE.

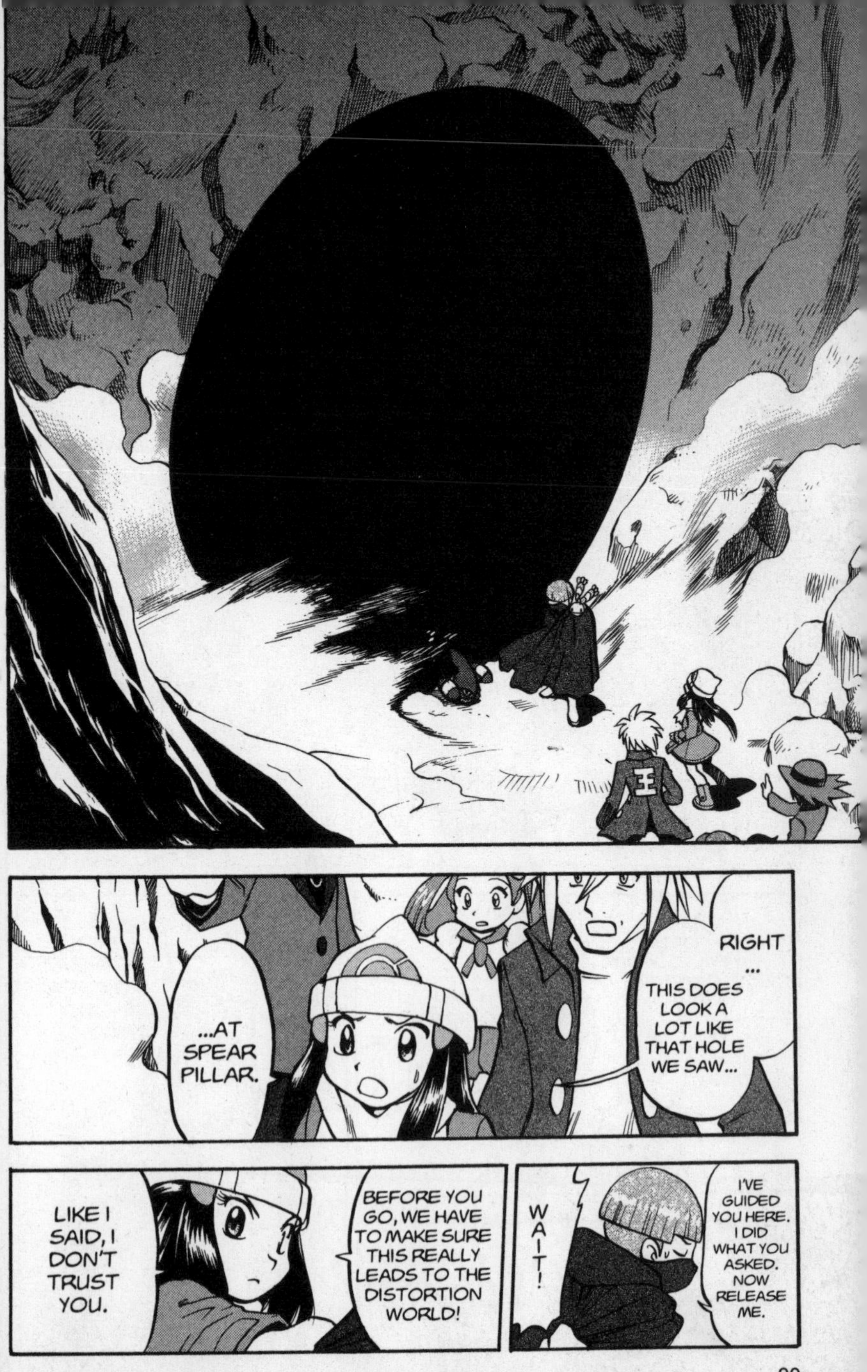
RIGHT... THIS DOES LOOK A LOT LIKE THAT HOLE WE SAW...
...AT SPEAR PILLAR.
I'VE GUIDED YOU HERE. I DID WHAT YOU ASKED. NOW RELEASE ME.
WAIT!
BEFORE YOU GO, WE HAVE TO MAKE SURE THIS REALLY LEADS TO THE DISTORTION WORLD!
LIKE I SAID, I DON'T TRUST YOU.

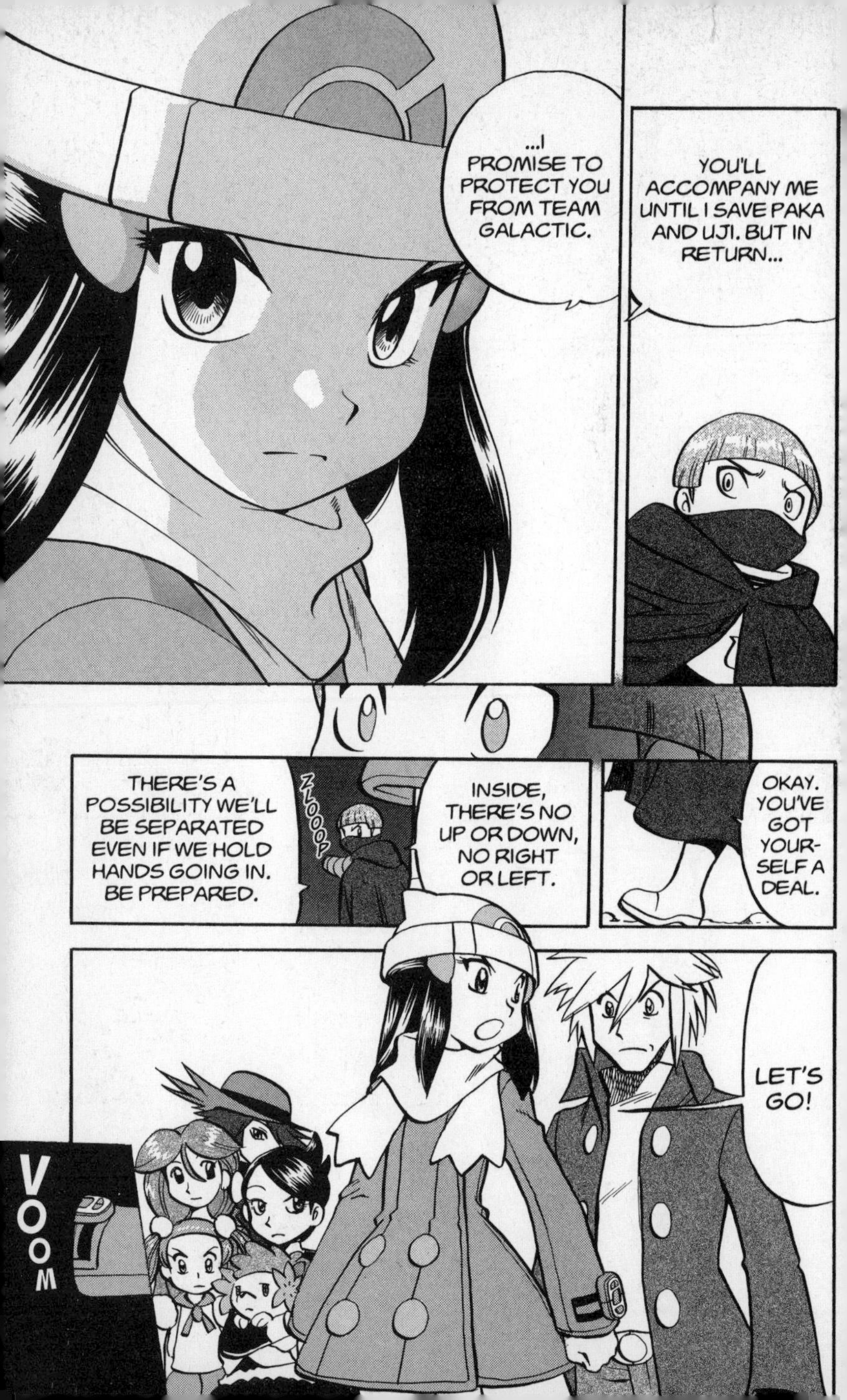

YOU'LL ACCOMPANY ME UNTIL I SAVE PAKA AND UJI. BUT IN RETURN...
...I PROMISE TO PROTECT YOU FROM TEAM GALACTIC.
OKAY. YOU'VE GOT YOUR-SELF A DEAL.
INSIDE, THERE'S NO UP OR DOWN, NO RIGHT OR LEFT.
ZLOOOP
THERE'S A POSSIBILITY WE'LL BE SEPARATED EVEN IF WE HOLD HANDS GOING IN. BE PREPARED.
LET'S GO!
VOOM

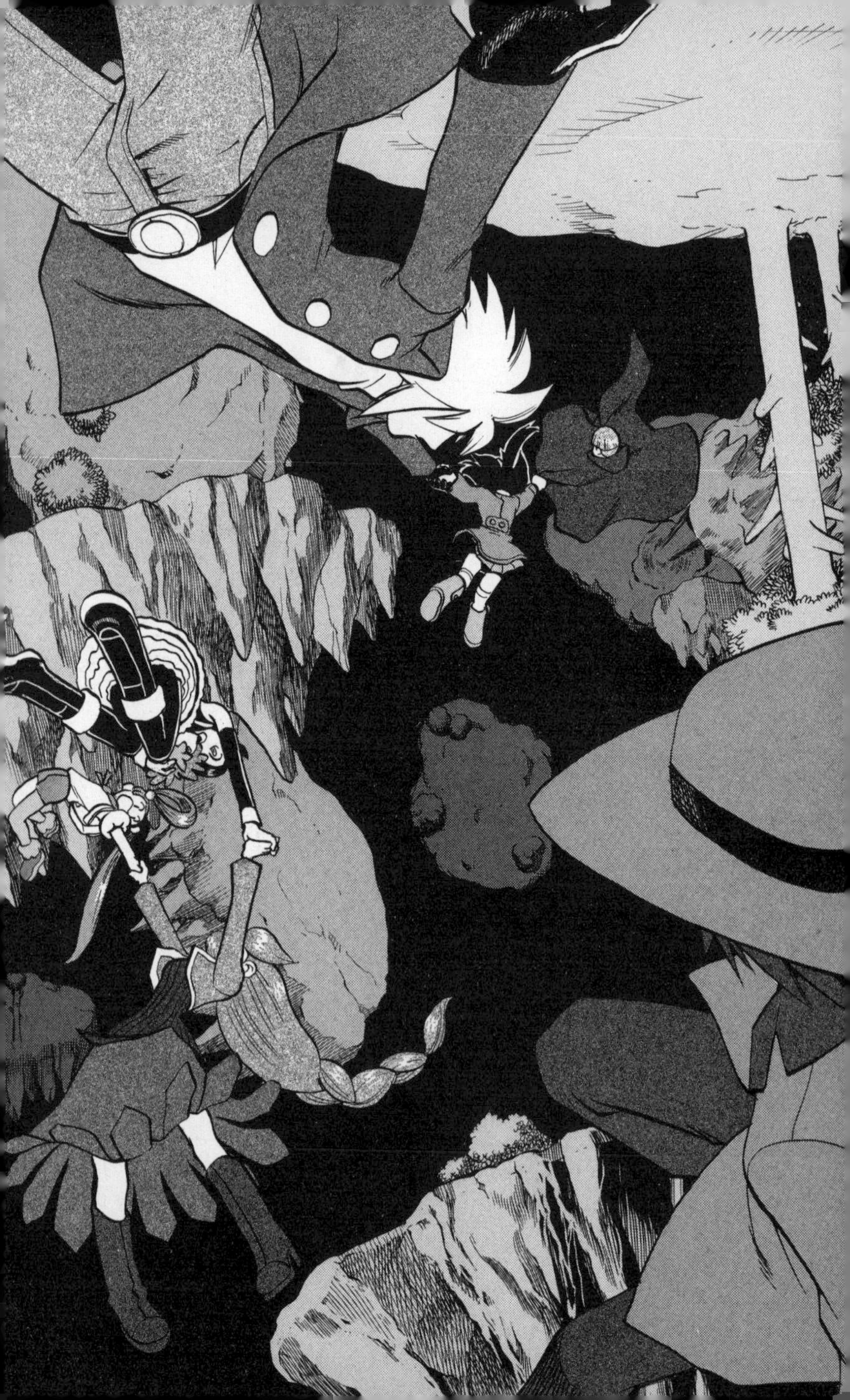

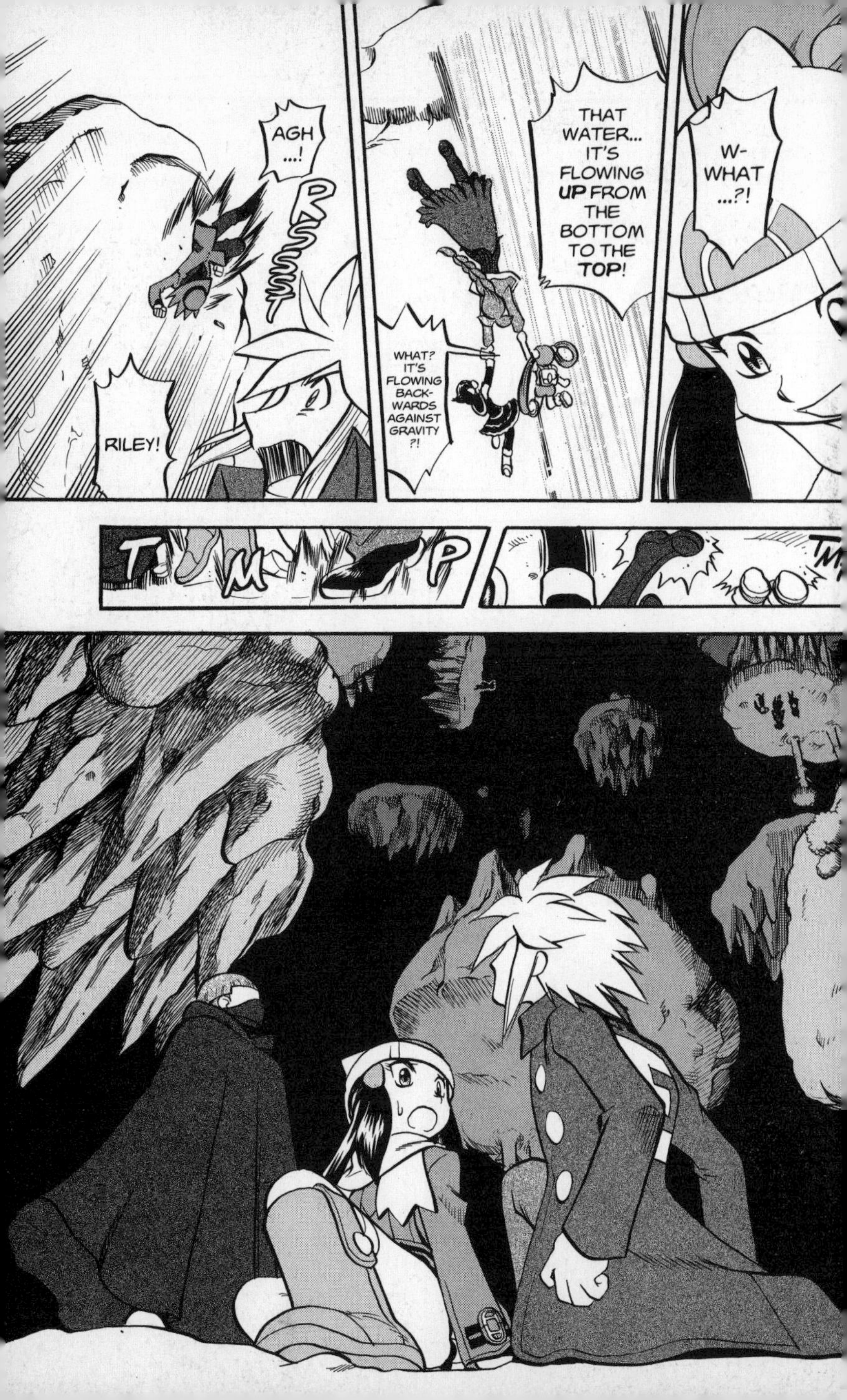
W-WHAT ...?!
THAT WATER... IT'S FLOWING UP FROM THE BOTTOM TO THE TOP!
WHAT? IT'S FLOWING BACKWARDS AGAINST GRAVITY ?!
AGH ...!
RSSSST
RILEY!
TMP

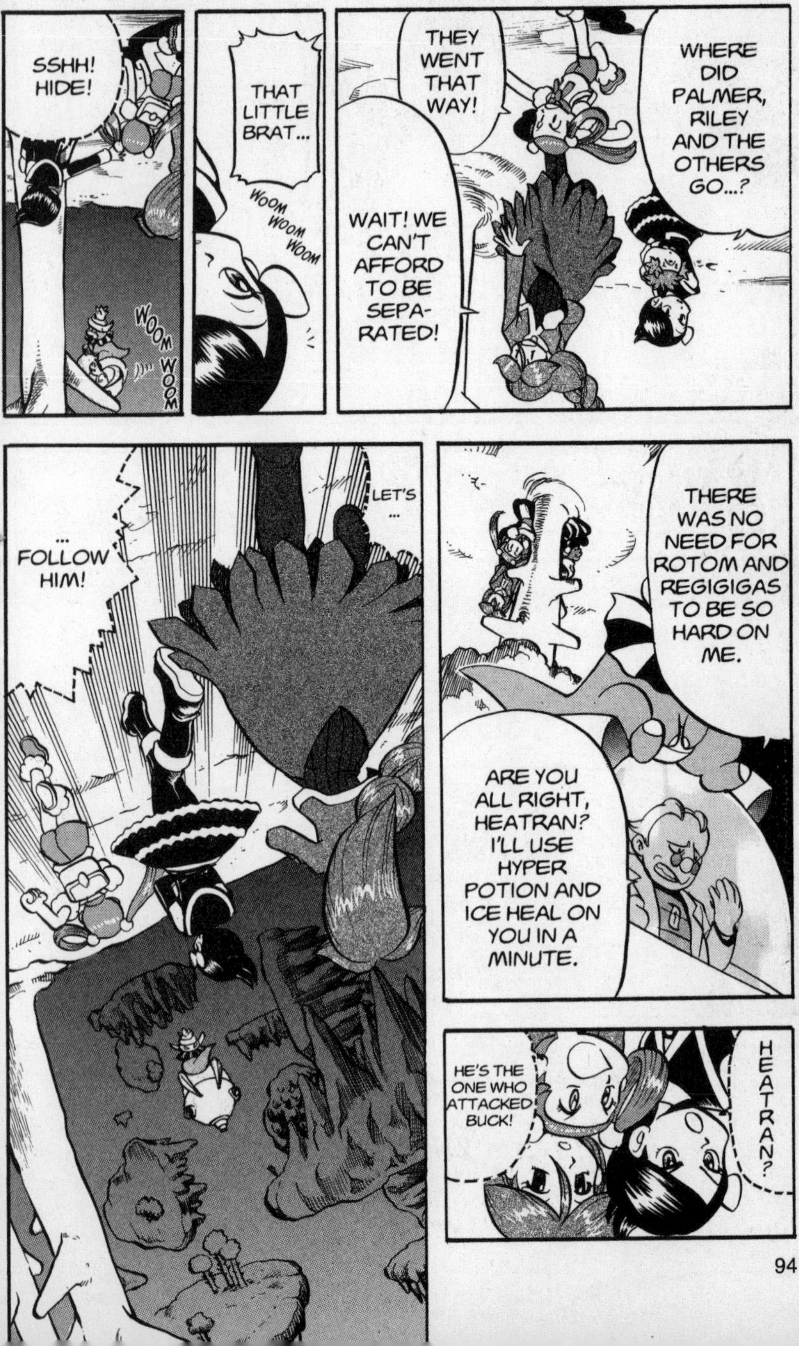
WHERE DID PALMER, RILEY AND THE OTHERS GO...?
THEY WENT THAT WAY!
WAIT! WE CAN'T AFFORD TO BE SEPA-RATED!
THAT LITTLE BRAT...
WOOM WOOM WOOM
SSHH! HIDE!
WOOM WOOM
THERE WAS NO NEED FOR ROTOM AND REGIGIGAS TO BE SO HARD ON ME.
ARE YOU ALL RIGHT, HEATRAN? I'LL USE HYPER POTION AND ICE HEAL ON YOU IN A MINUTE.
HEATRAN?
HE'S THE ONE WHO ATTACKED BUCK!
LET'S...
...FOLLOW HIM!

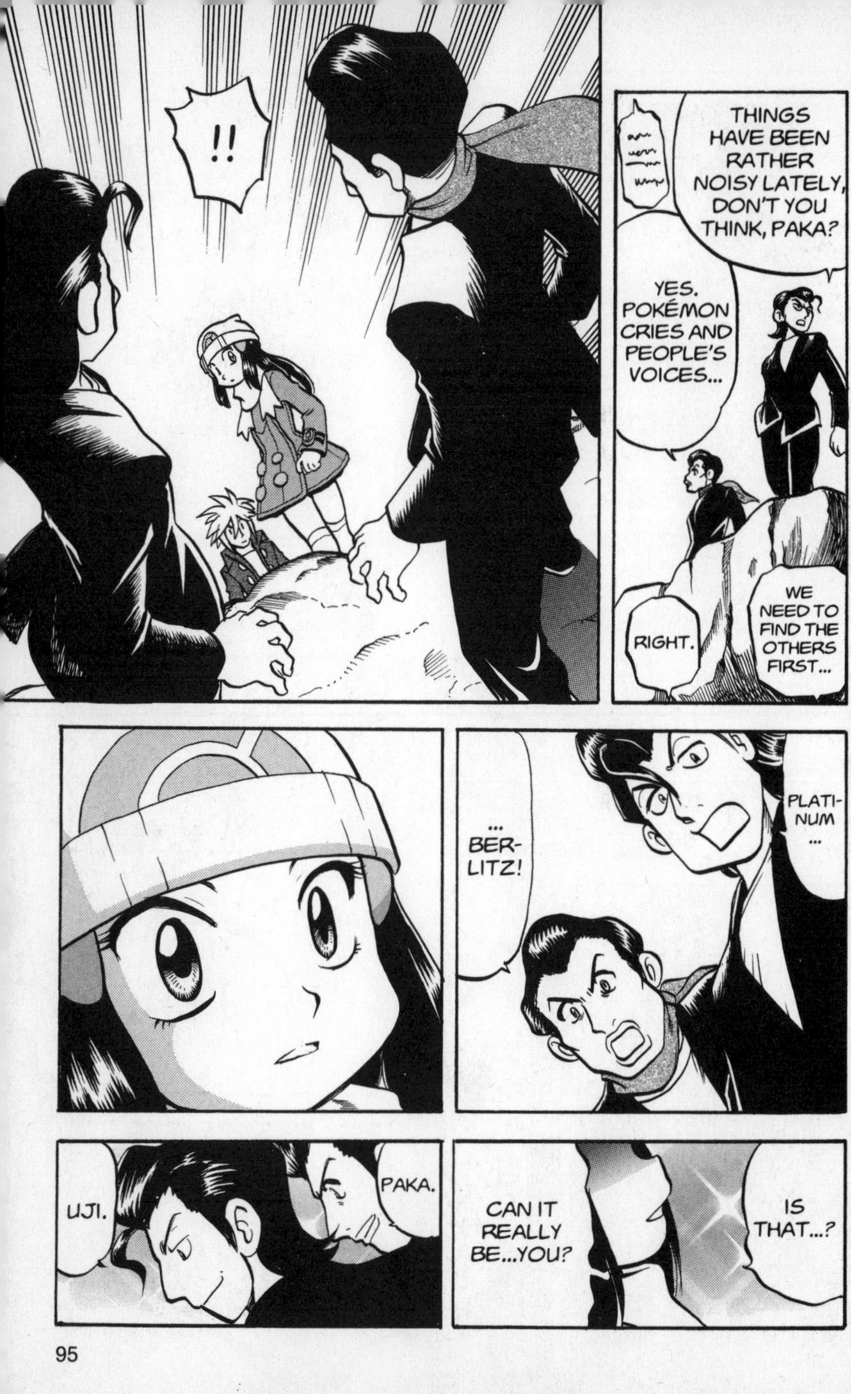
THINGS HAVE BEEN RATHER NOISY LATELY, DON'T YOU THINK, PAKA?
YES. POKÉMON CRIES AND PEOPLE'S VOICES...
WE NEED TO FIND THE OTHERS FIRST...
RIGHT.
!!
PLATINUM...
...BERLITZ!
IS THAT...?
CAN IT REALLY BE...YOU?
PAKA.
UJI.

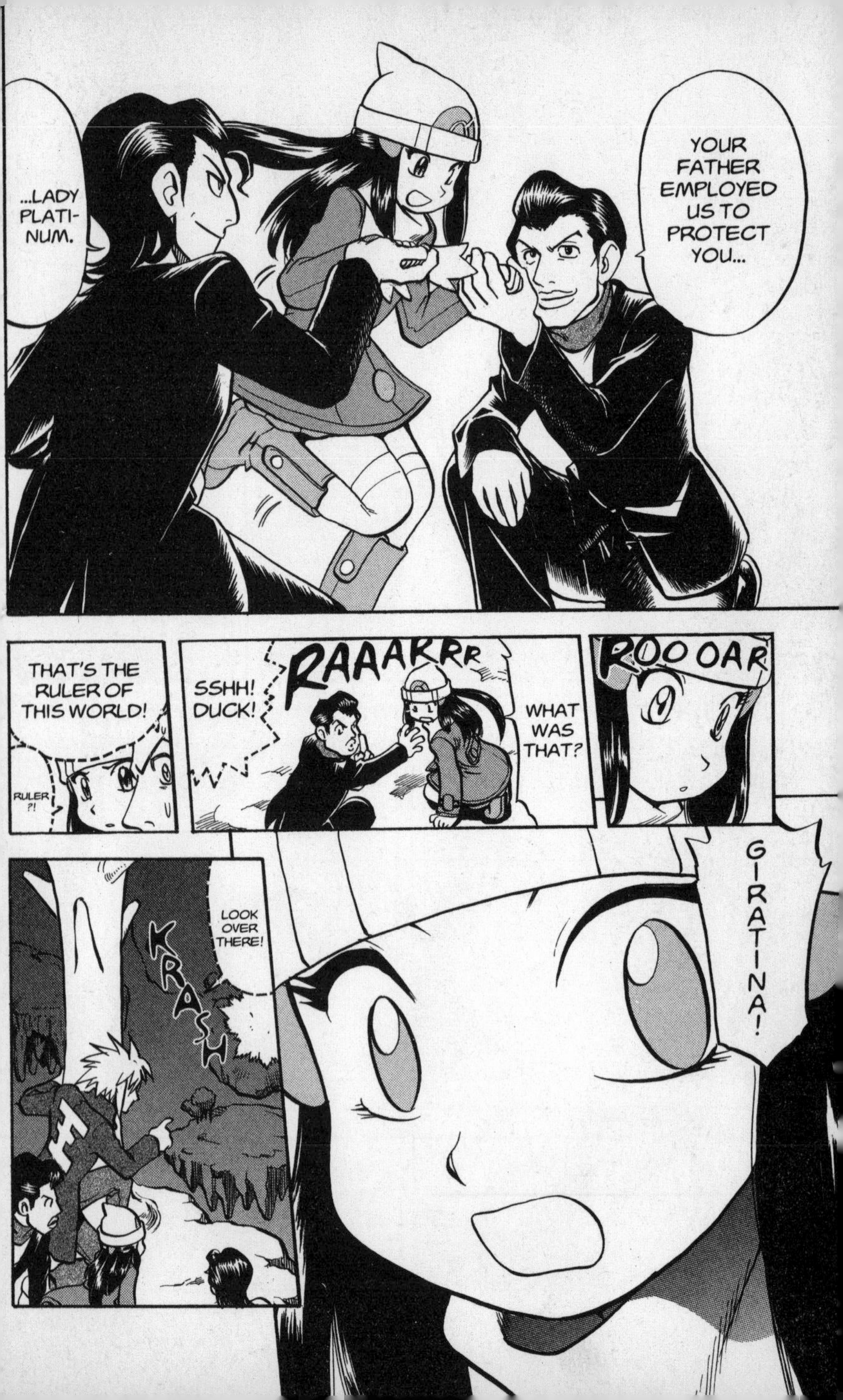
YOUR FATHER EMPLOYED US TO PROTECT YOU...
...LADY PLATINUM.
ROOOAR
RAAARRR
WHAT WAS THAT?
SSHH! DUCK!
THAT'S THE RULER OF THIS WORLD!
RULER?!
GIRATINA!
LOOK OVER THERE!
KRASH

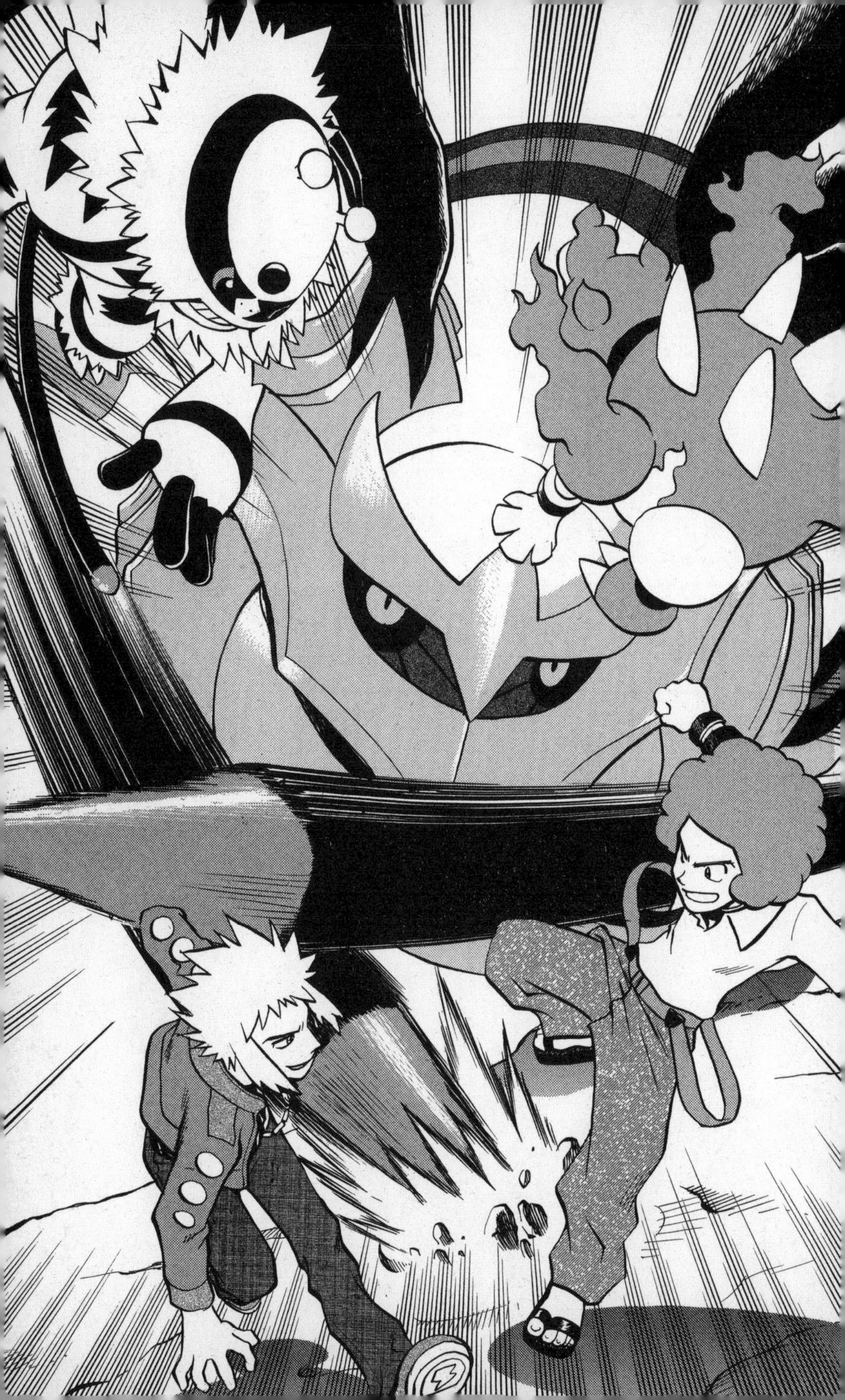

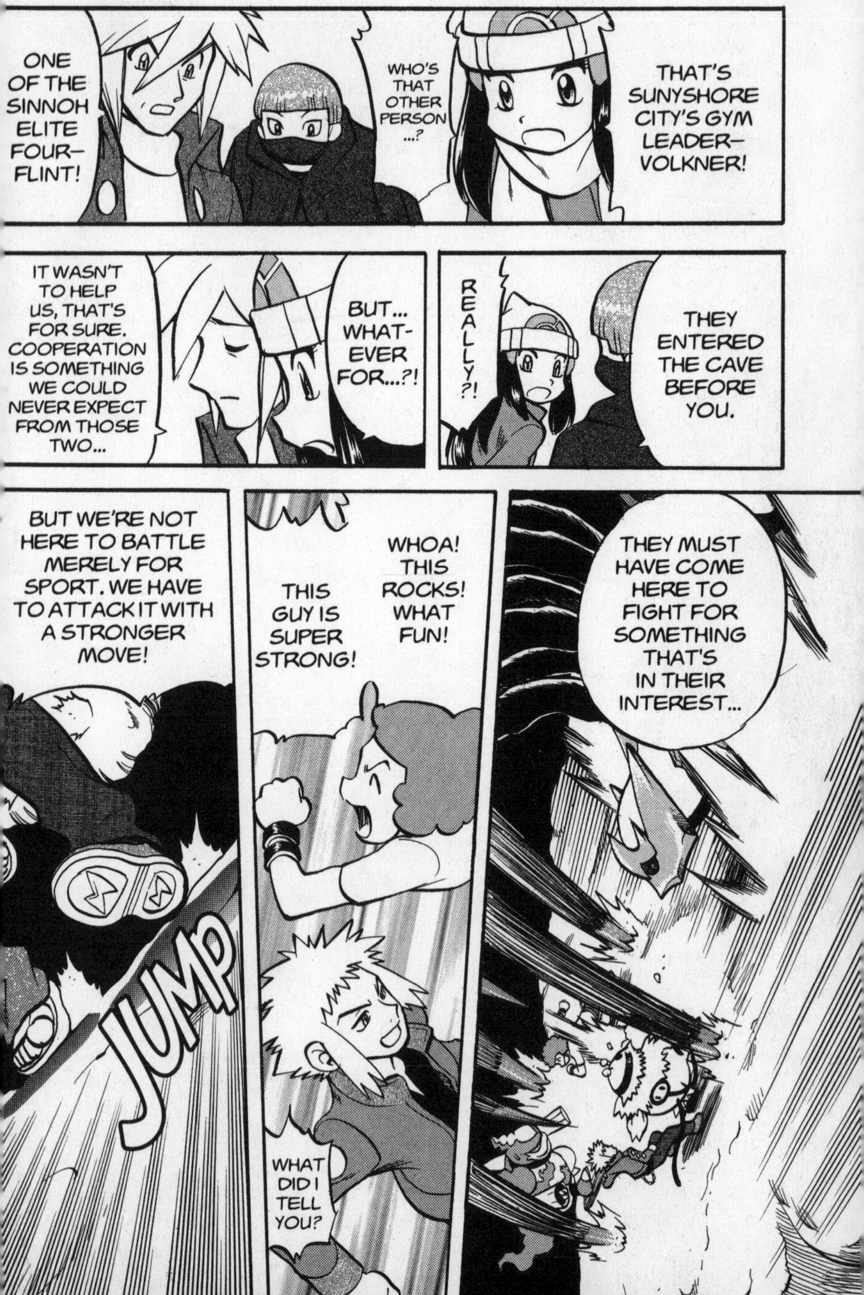
THAT'S SUNYSHORE CITY'S GYM LEADER—VOLKNER!
WHO'S THAT OTHER PERSON...?
ONE OF THE SINNOH ELITE FOUR—FLINT!
THEY ENTERED THE CAVE BEFORE YOU.
REALLY?!
BUT... WHATEVER FOR...?!
IT WASN'T TO HELP US, THAT'S FOR SURE. COOPERATION IS SOMETHING WE COULD NEVER EXPECT FROM THOSE TWO...
THEY MUST HAVE COME HERE TO FIGHT FOR SOMETHING THAT'S IN THEIR INTEREST...
WHOA! THIS ROCKS! WHAT FUN!
THIS GUY IS SUPER STRONG!
WHAT DID I TELL YOU?
BUT WE'RE NOT HERE TO BATTLE MERELY FOR SPORT. WE HAVE TO ATTACK IT WITH A STRONGER MOVE!
JUMP

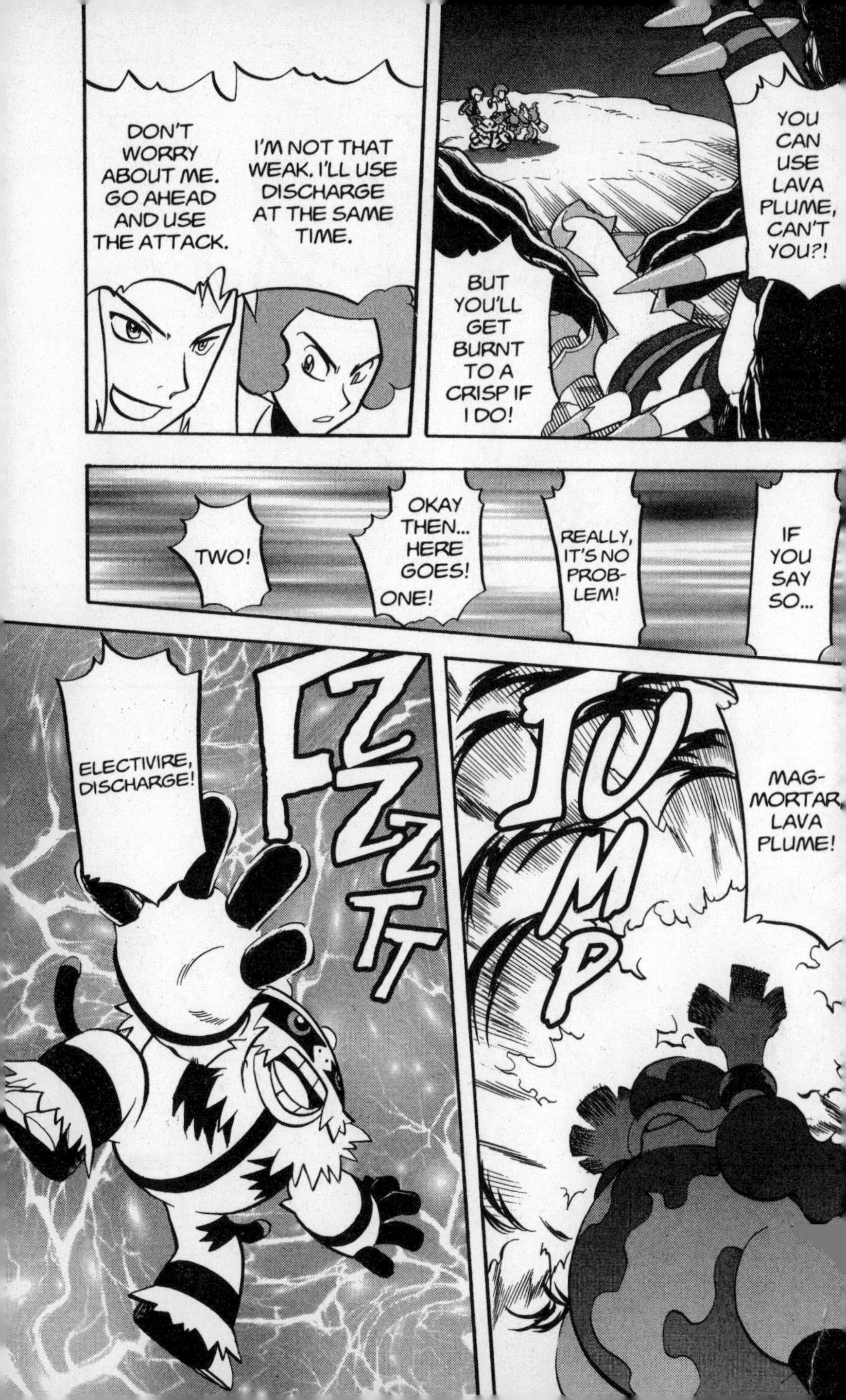
YOU CAN USE LAVA PLUME, CAN'T YOU?!
BUT YOU'LL GET BURNT TO A CRISP IF I DO!
I'M NOT THAT WEAK. I'LL USE DISCHARGE AT THE SAME TIME.
DON'T WORRY ABOUT ME. GO AHEAD AND USE THE ATTACK.
IF YOU SAY SO...
REALLY, IT'S NO PROB-LEM!
OKAY THEN... HERE GOES!
ONE!
TWO!
MAG-MORTAR, LAVA PLUME!
TOMP
ZZZTT
ELECTIVIRE, DISCHARGE!

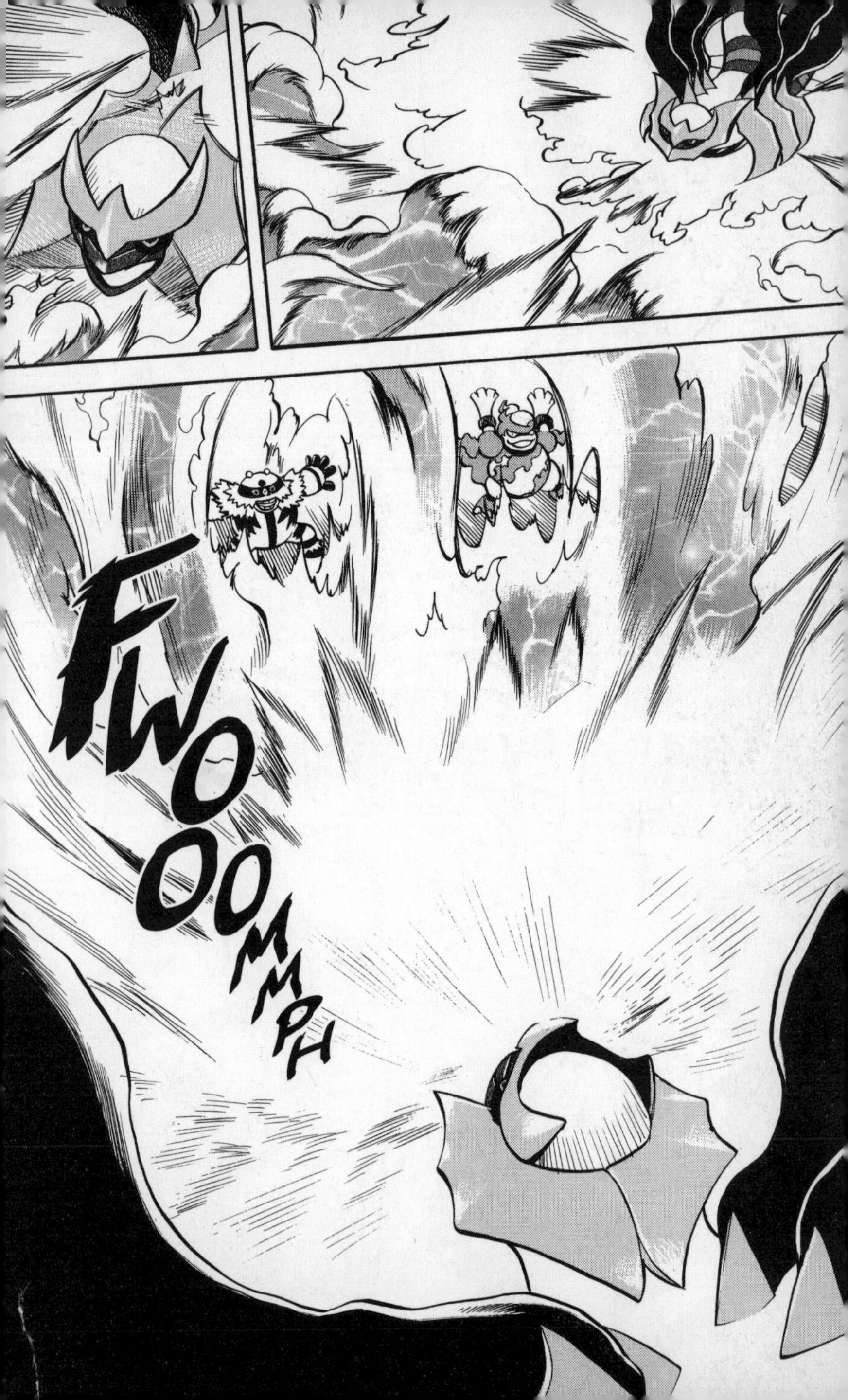
FWOOOMMPH

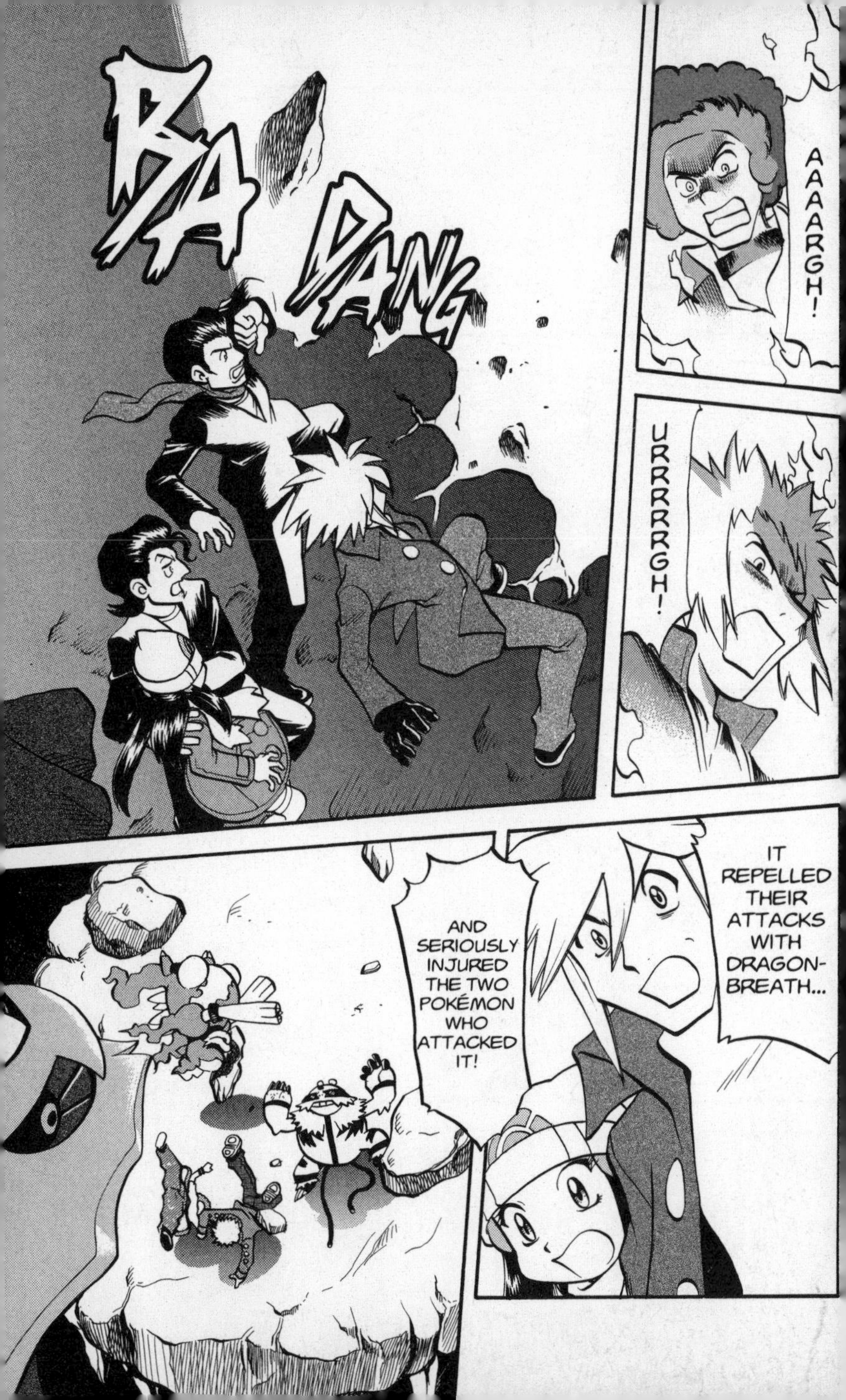
AAAARGH!
URRRRRGH!
BA DANG
IT REPELLED THEIR ATTACKS WITH DRAGON-BREATH...
AND SERIOUSLY INJURED THE TWO POKÉMON WHO ATTACKED IT!

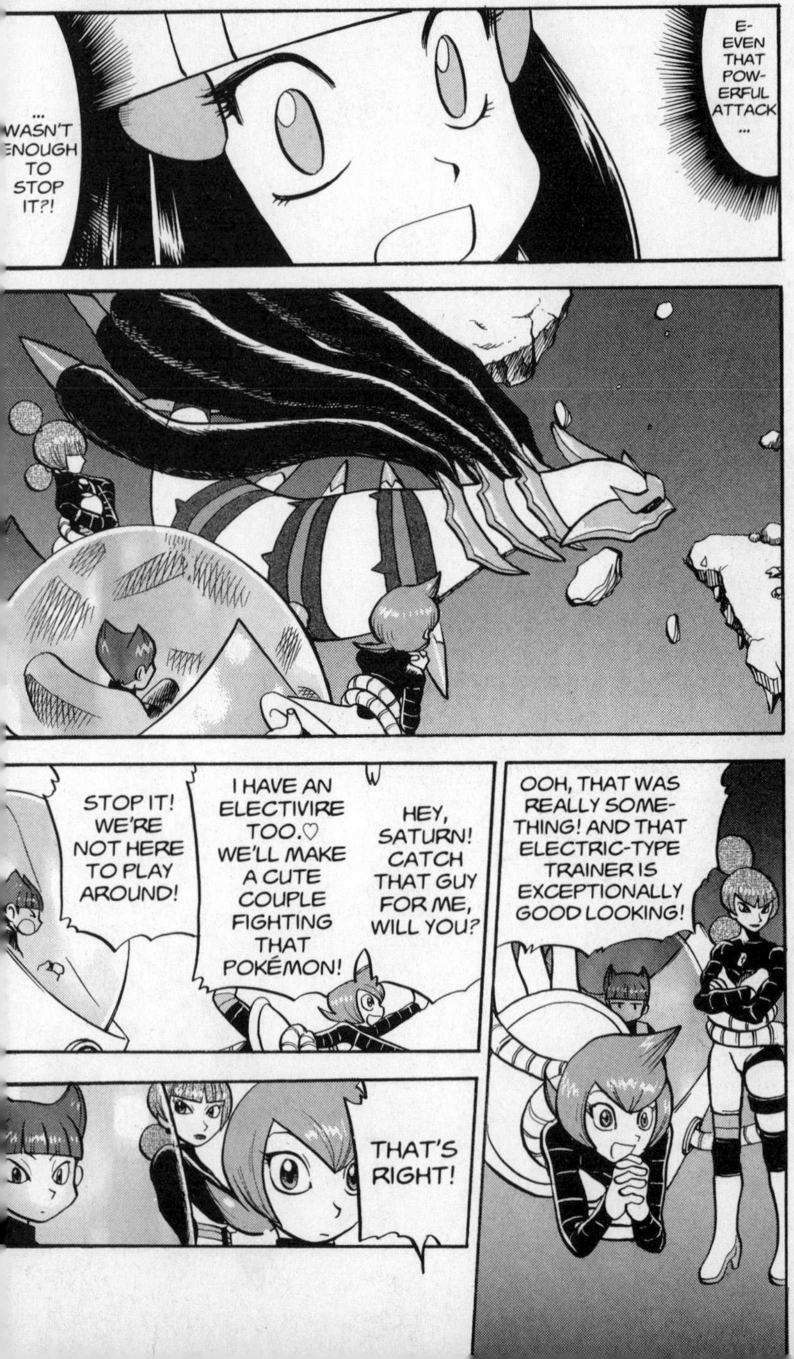
E- EVEN THAT POWERFUL ATTACK...
...WASN'T ENOUGH TO STOP IT?!
OOH, THAT WAS REALLY SOMETHING! AND THAT ELECTRIC-TYPE TRAINER IS EXCEPTIONALLY GOOD LOOKING!
HEY, SATURN! CATCH THAT GUY FOR ME, WILL YOU?
I HAVE AN ELECTIVIRE TOO.♡ WE'LL MAKE A CUTE COUPLE FIGHTING THAT POKÉMON!
STOP IT! WE'RE NOT HERE TO PLAY AROUND!
THAT'S RIGHT!

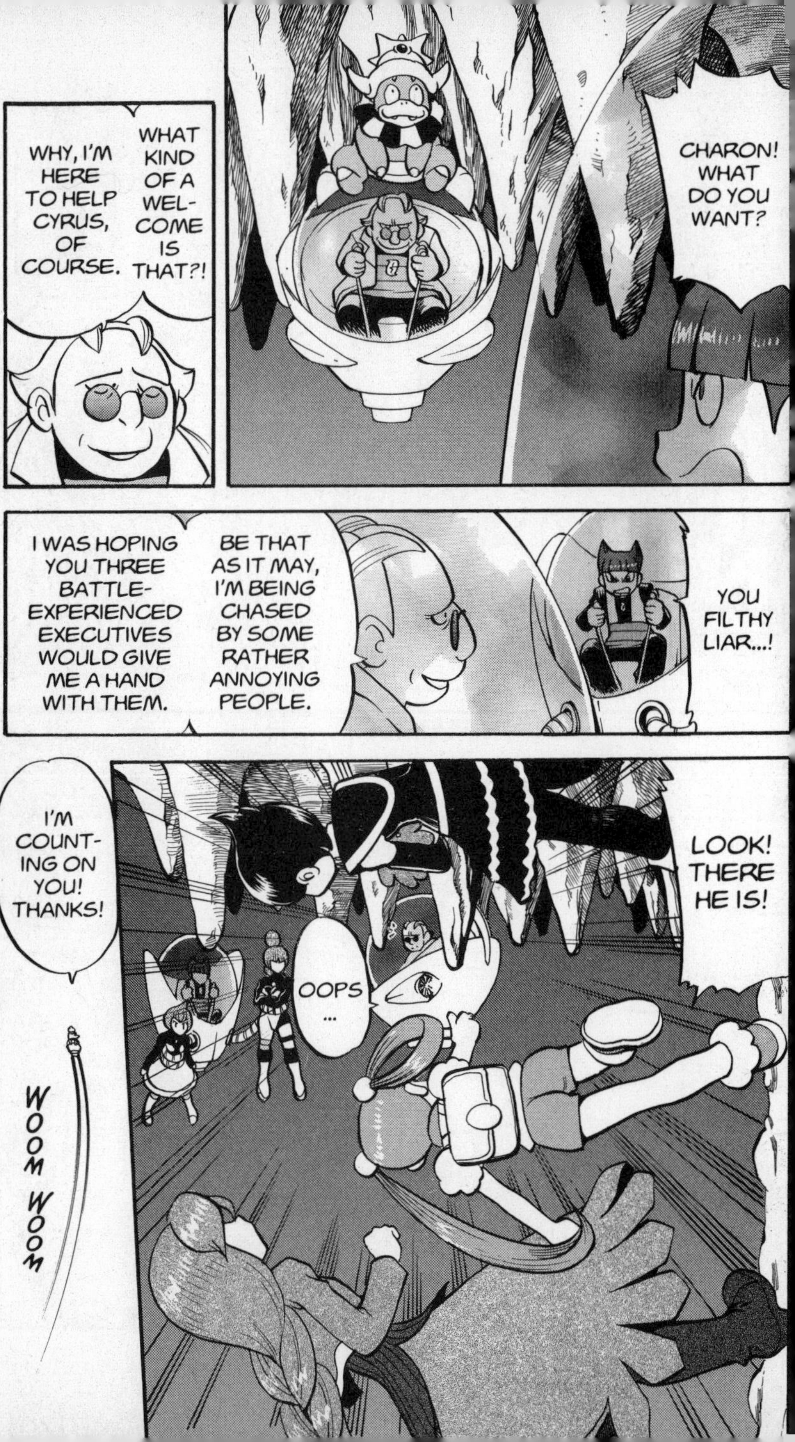
CHARON! WHAT DO YOU WANT?
WHAT KIND OF A WEL-COME IS THAT?!
WHY, I'M HERE TO HELP CYRUS, OF COURSE.
YOU FILTHY LIAR...!
BE THAT AS IT MAY, I'M BEING CHASED BY SOME RATHER ANNOYING PEOPLE.
I WAS HOPING YOU THREE BATTLE-EXPERIENCED EXECUTIVES WOULD GIVE ME A HAND WITH THEM.
LOOK! THERE HE IS!
OOPS...
I'M COUNT-ING ON YOU! THANKS!
WOOM WOOM

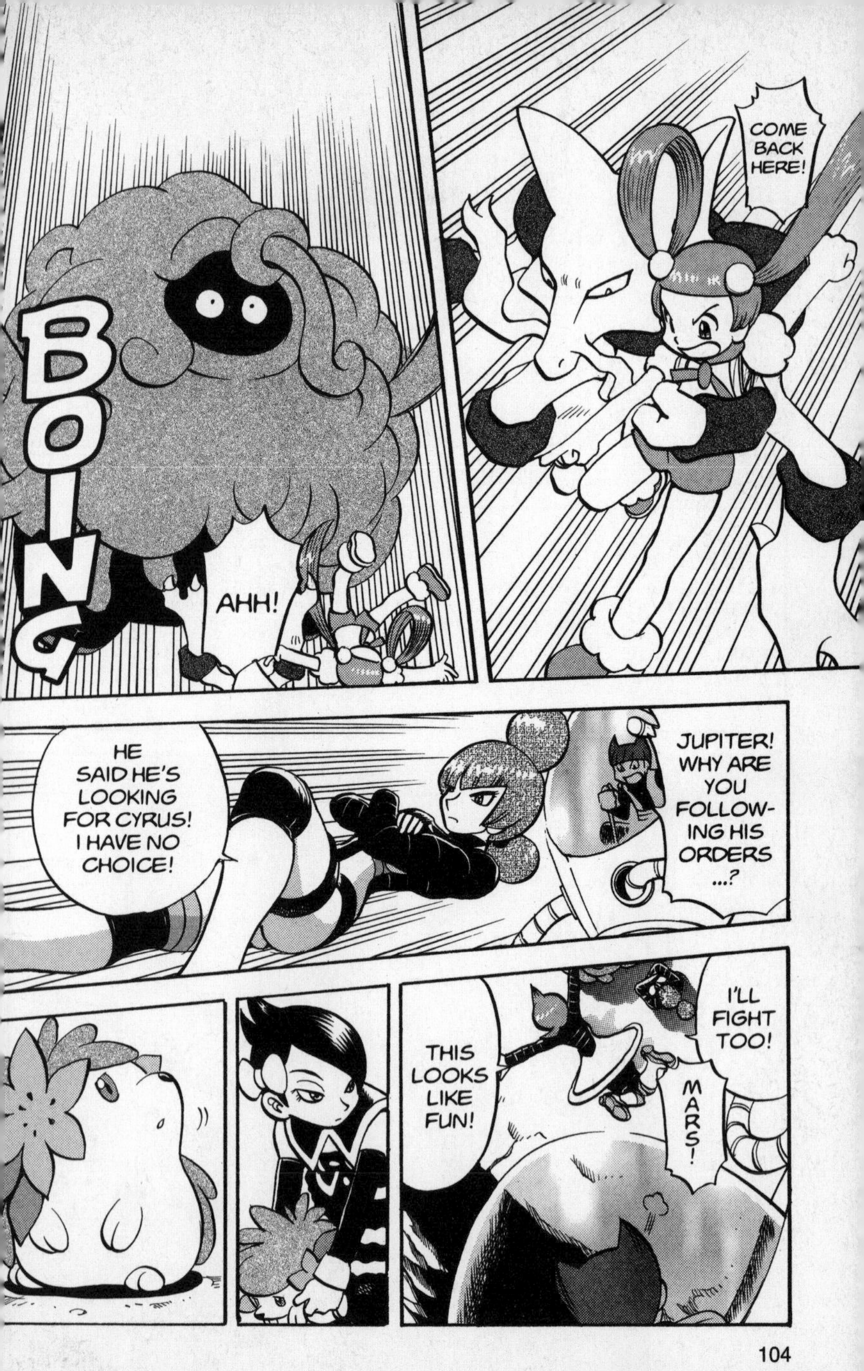
COME BACK HERE!
BOING
AHH!
JUPITER! WHY ARE YOU FOLLOWING HIS ORDERS ...?
HE SAID HE'S LOOKING FOR CYRUS! I HAVE NO CHOICE!
I'LL FIGHT TOO!
MARS!
THIS LOOKS LIKE FUN!

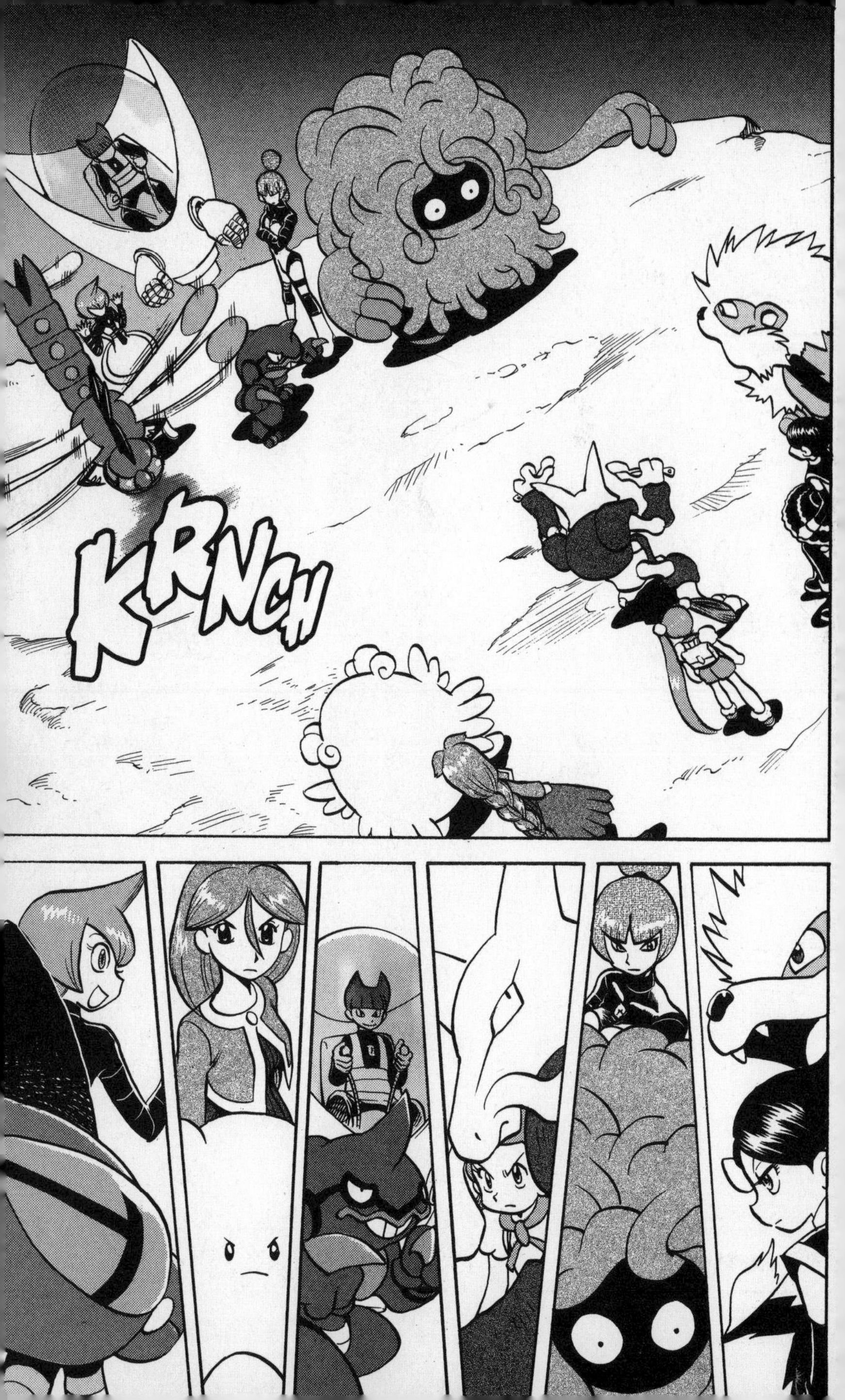
KRNCH

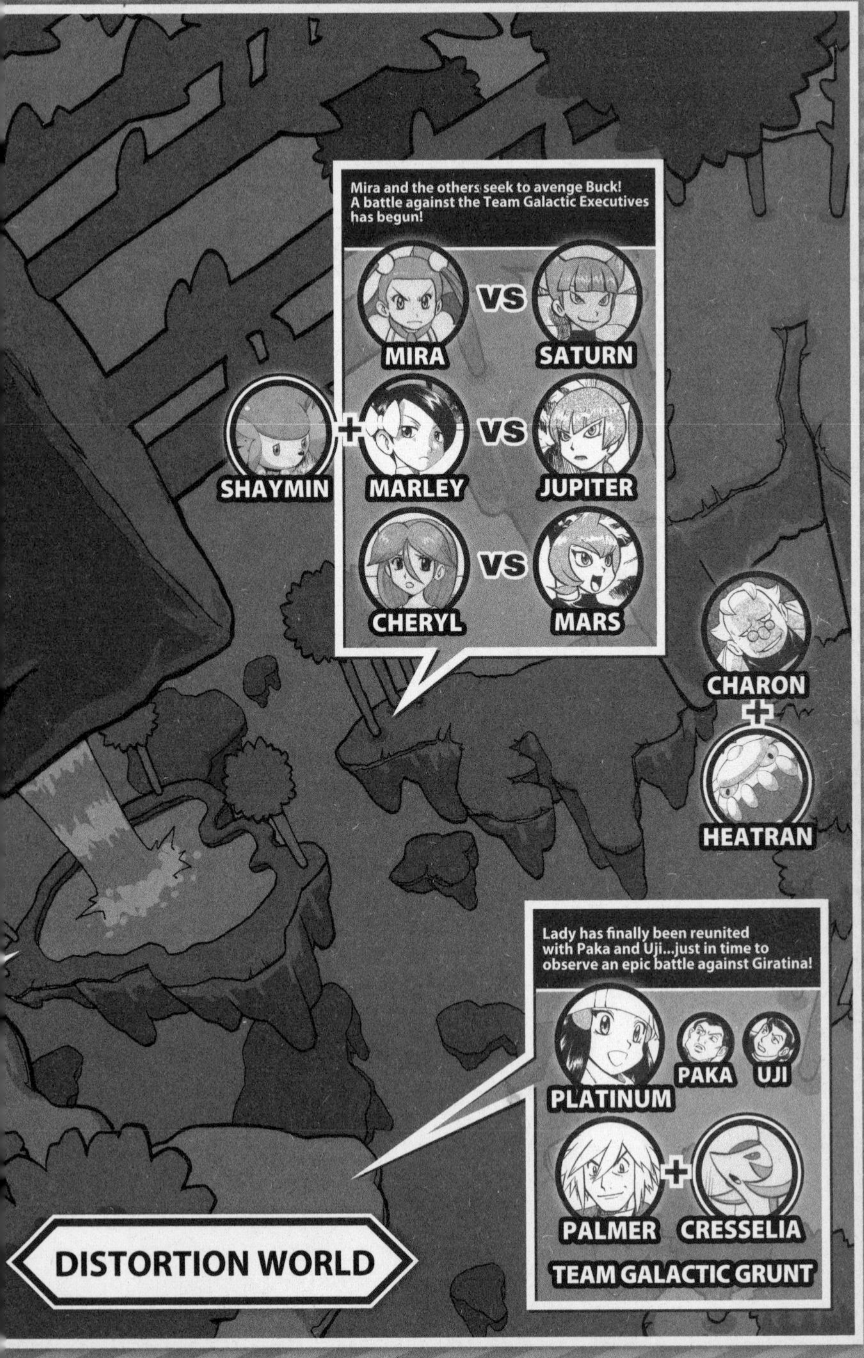

Mira and the others seek to avenge Buck! A battle against the Team Galactic Executives has begun!
MIRA
VS
SATURN
SHAYMIN
MARLEY
VS
JUPITER
CHERYL
VS
MARS
CHARON
HEATRAN
Lady has finally been reunited with Paka and Uji...just in time to observe an epic battle against Giratina!
PLATINUM
PAKA
UJI
PALMER
CRESSELIA
TEAM GALACTIC GRUNT
DISTORTION WORLD

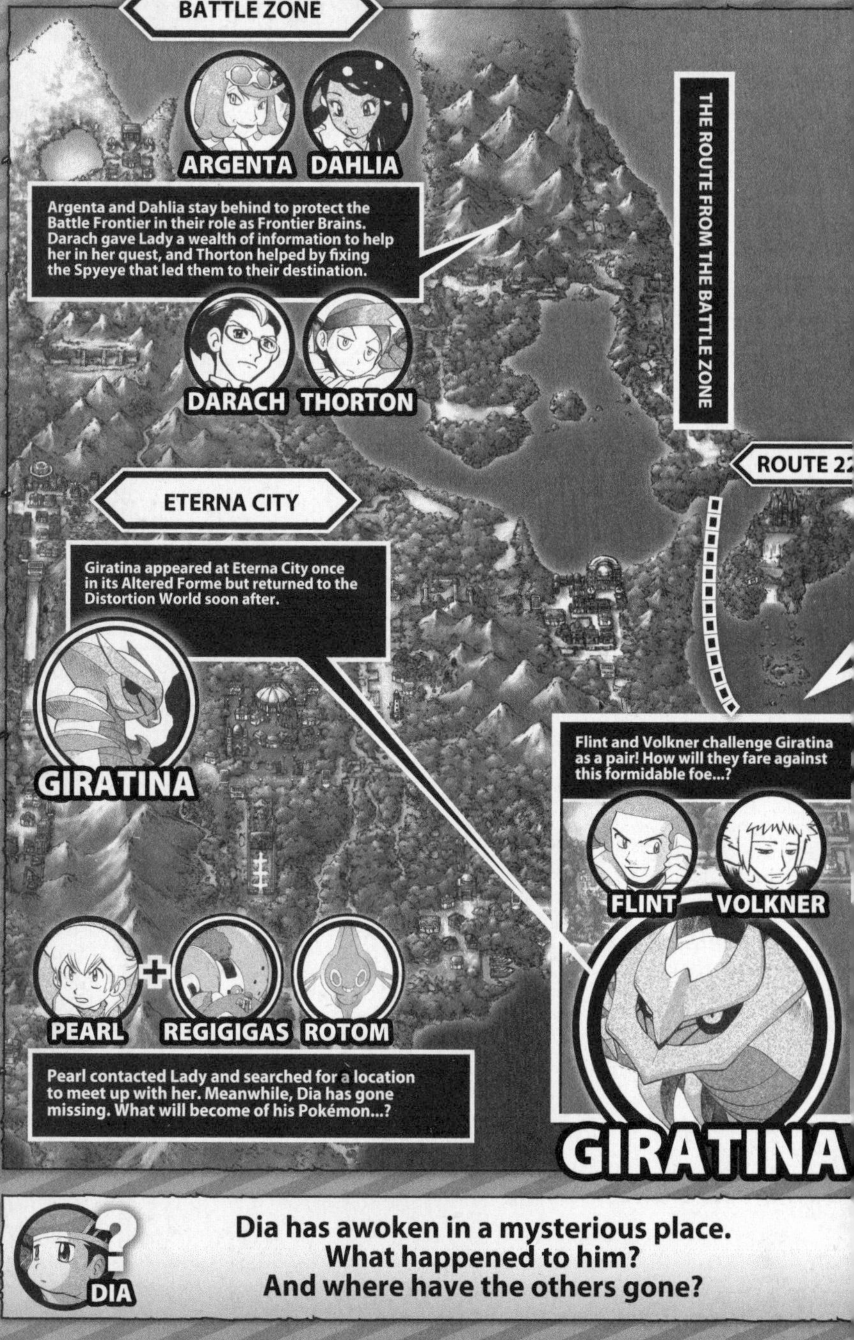
BATTLE ZONE
ARGENTA
DAHLIA
Argenta and Dahlia stay behind to protect the Battle Frontier in their role as Frontier Brains. Darach gave Lady a wealth of information to help her in her quest, and Thorton helped by fixing the Spyeye that led them to their destination.
DARACH
THORTON
THE ROUTE FROM THE BATTLE ZONE
ROUTE 22
ETERNA CITY
Giratina appeared at Eterna City once in its Altered Forme but returned to the Distortion World soon after.
GIRATINA
Flint and Volkner challenge Giratina as a pair! How will they fare against this formidable foe...?
FLINT
VOLKNER
PEARL
REGIGIGAS
ROTOM
Pearl contacted Lady and searched for a location to meet up with her. Meanwhile, Dia has gone missing. What will become of his Pokémon...?
GIRATINA
DIA
Dia has awoken in a mysterious place.
What happened to him?
And where have the others gone?

CHARACTER PROFILE

PEARL

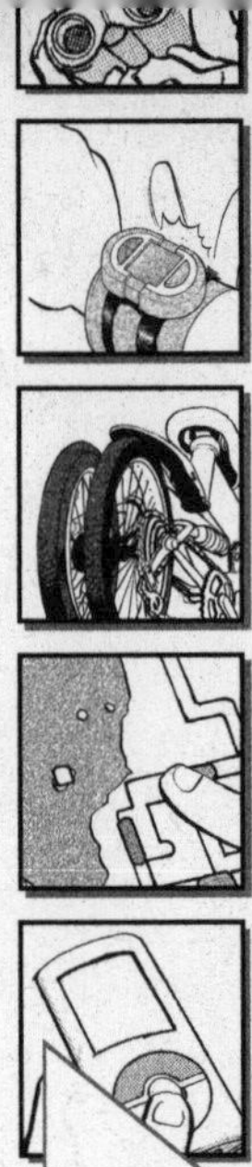

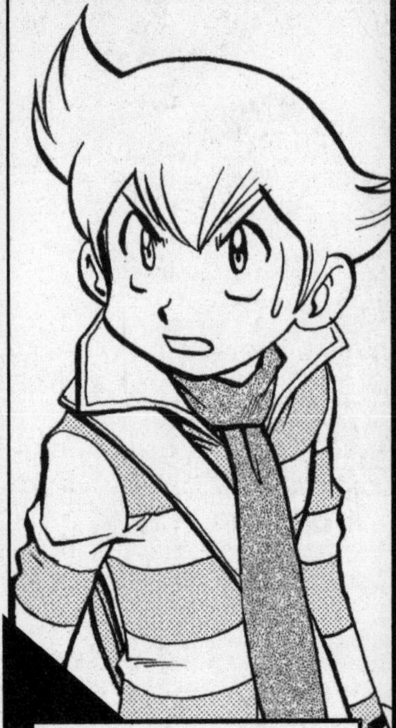

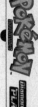

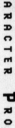

PEARL

THE SON OF TOWER TYCOON PALMER. SEPARATED FROM HIS FATHER SINCE HE WAS YOUNG, PEARL HAS NEVERTHELESS INHERITED HIS FATHER'S BATTLE SKILLS. PEARL DEMONSTRATED EXCELLENT LEADERSHIP AT THE BEGINNING OF THE TRIO'S JOURNEY. HE HAS IMPROVED HIS BATTLE SKILLS EVEN MORE BY TRAINING WITH CRASHER WAKE. PEARL IS ADEPT AT USING FAST POKÉMON TO BAFFLE HIS OPPONENTS. HE IS THE STRAIGHT MAN IN HIS COMEDIC DUO, AND HAS BEEN DIA'S COMEDY PARTNER SINCE NURSERY SCHOOL. THE TWO HAVE GREAT COMEDIC CHEMISTRY.

Hometown: Twinleaf Town

Birthday: June 6th

Age: 12 (As of Adventure 99)

Blood-type: B

Special Skills: Developing comedy routines, foretelling a Pokémon's next move by analyzing its body language.

Award: Next Generation Comedy Grand Prix Special Merit Prize

Family: Father (Palmer)

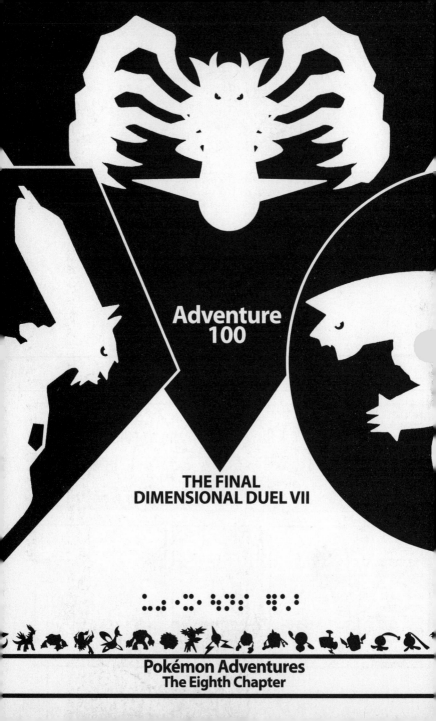

Adventure 100

THE FINAL
DIMENSIONAL DUEL VII

Pokémon Adventures
The Eighth Chapter

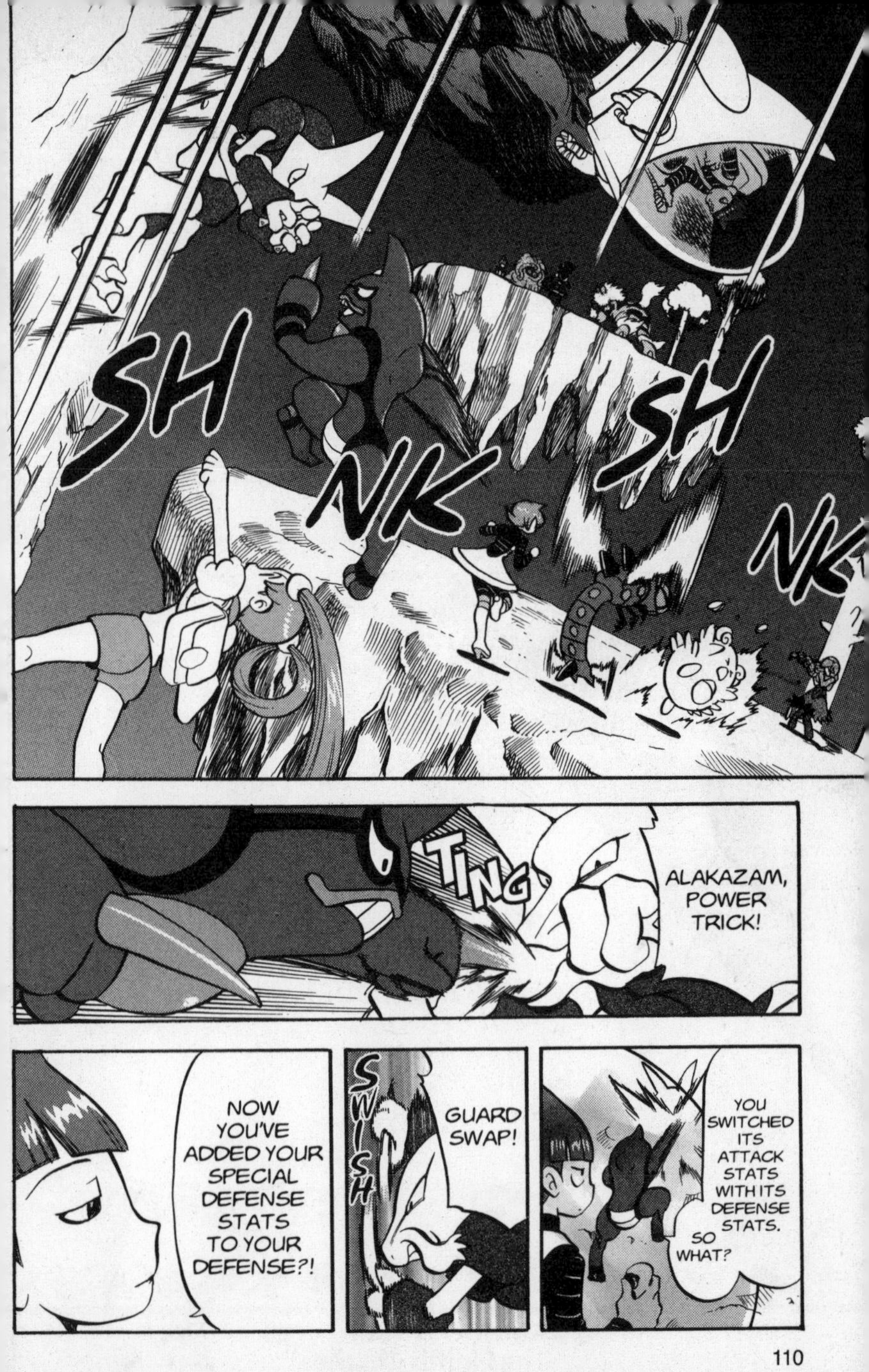
SH NK
SH NK
TING
ALAKAZAM, POWER TRICK!
YOU SWITCHED ITS ATTACK STATS WITH ITS DEFENSE STATS.
SO WHAT?
GUARD SWAP!
SWISH
NOW YOU'VE ADDED YOUR SPECIAL DEFENSE STATS TO YOUR DEFENSE?!

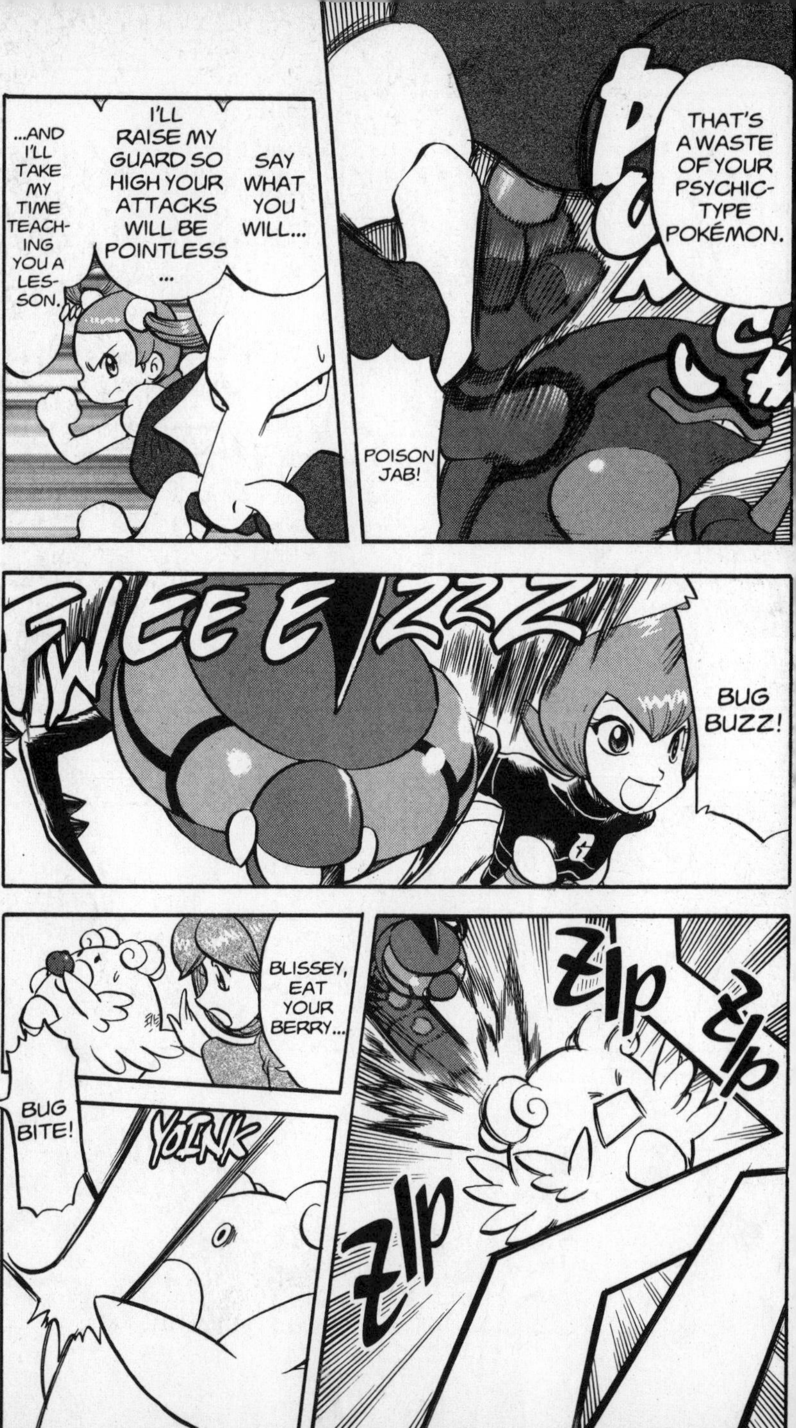
THAT'S A WASTE OF YOUR PSYCHIC-TYPE POKÉMON.
POISON JAB!
SAY WHAT YOU WILL...
I'LL RAISE MY GUARD SO HIGH YOUR ATTACKS WILL BE POINTLESS...
...AND I'LL TAKE MY TIME TEACHING YOU A LES-SON.
FWEEEZZZ
BUG BUZZ!
ZIP
ZIP
ZIP
BLISSEY, EAT YOUR BERRY...
BUG BITE!
YOINK

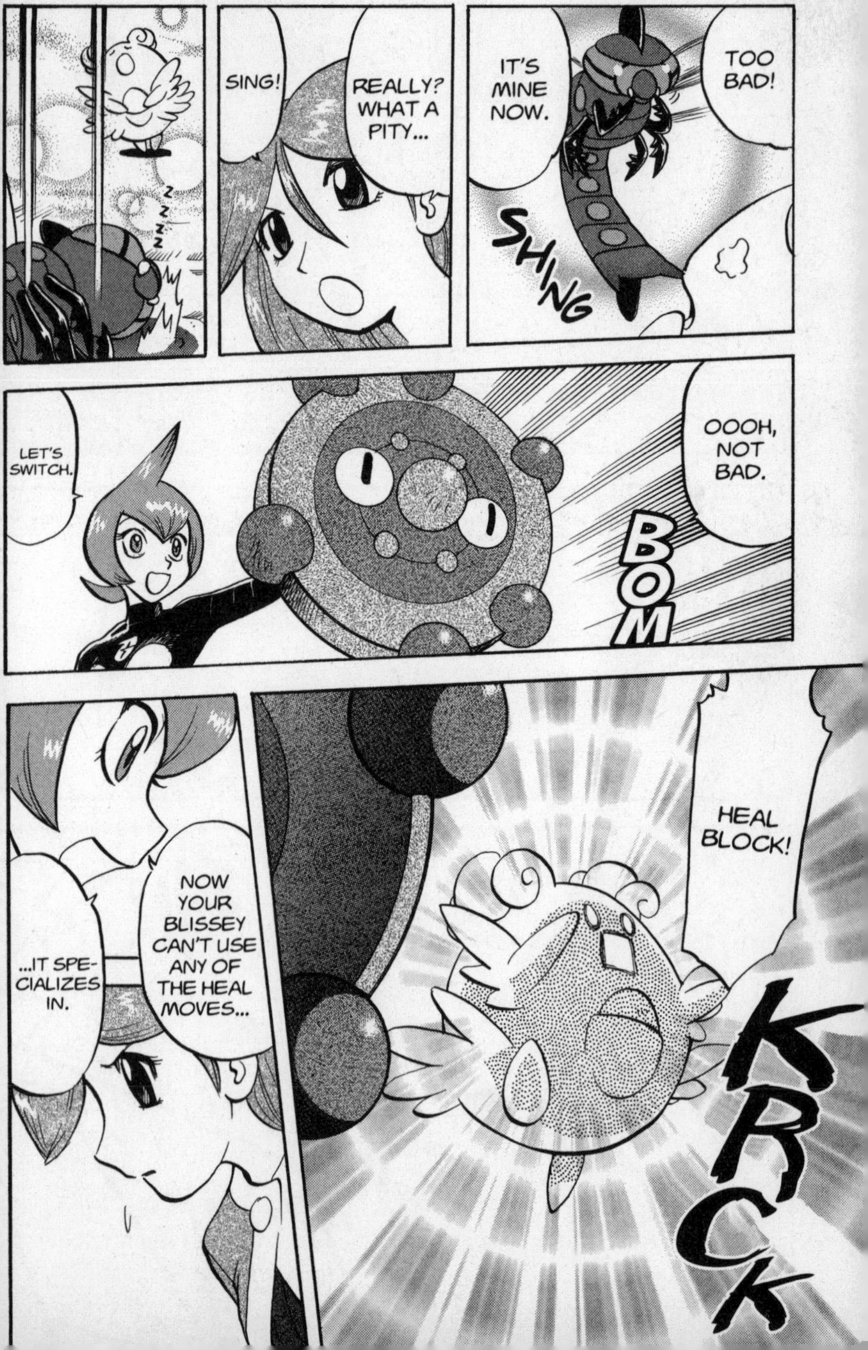
TOO BAD!
IT'S MINE NOW.
SHING
REALLY? WHAT A PITY...
SING!
ZZZZZ
OOOH, NOT BAD.
BOM
LET'S SWITCH.
HEAL BLOCK!
KRCK
NOW YOUR BLISSEY CAN'T USE ANY OF THE HEAL MOVES...
...IT SPE-CIALIZES IN.

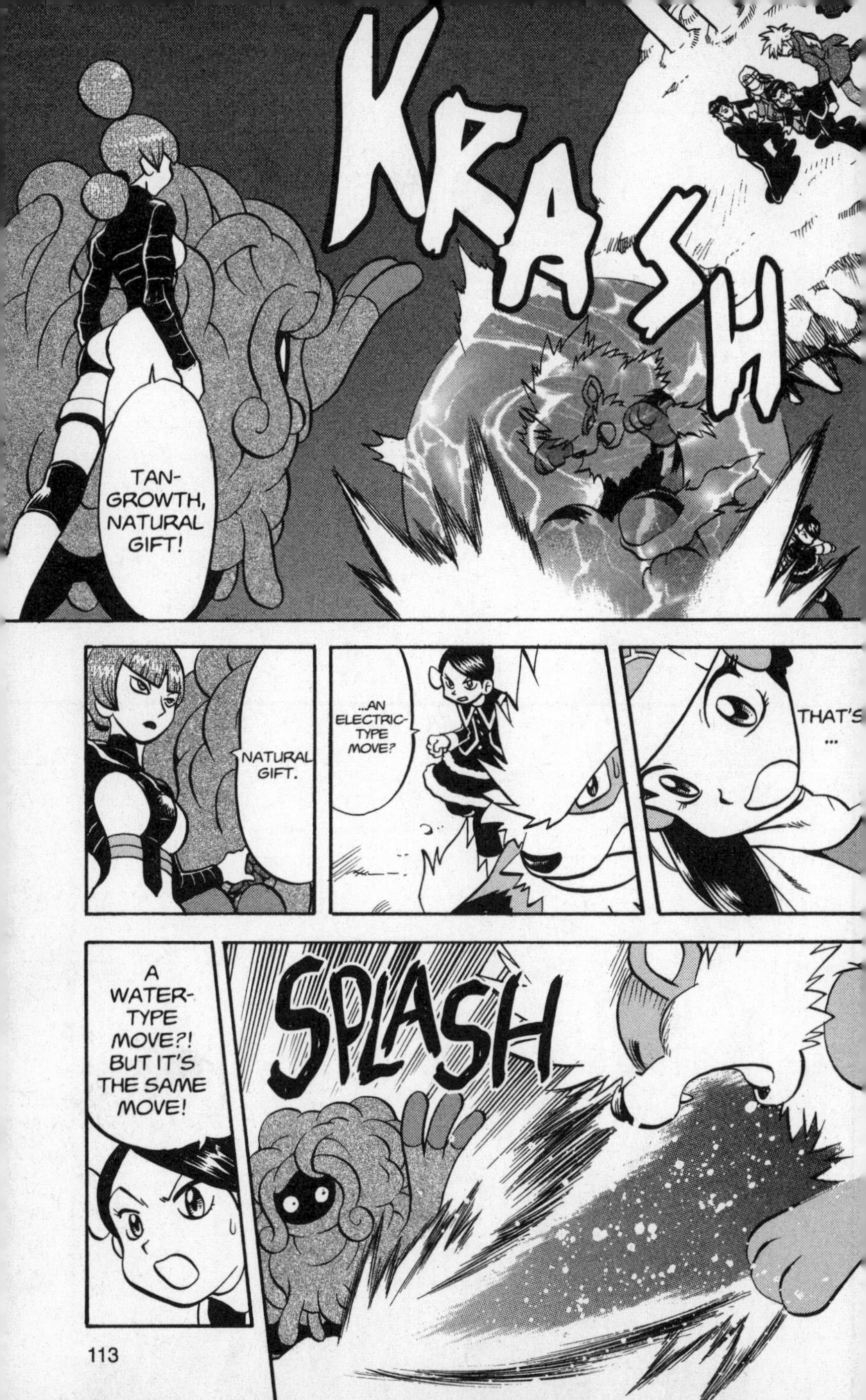
KRASH
TAN-GROWTH, NATURAL GIFT!
THAT'S ...
...AN ELECTRIC-TYPE MOVE?
NATURAL GIFT.
SPLASH
A WATER-TYPE MOVE?! BUT IT'S THE SAME MOVE!

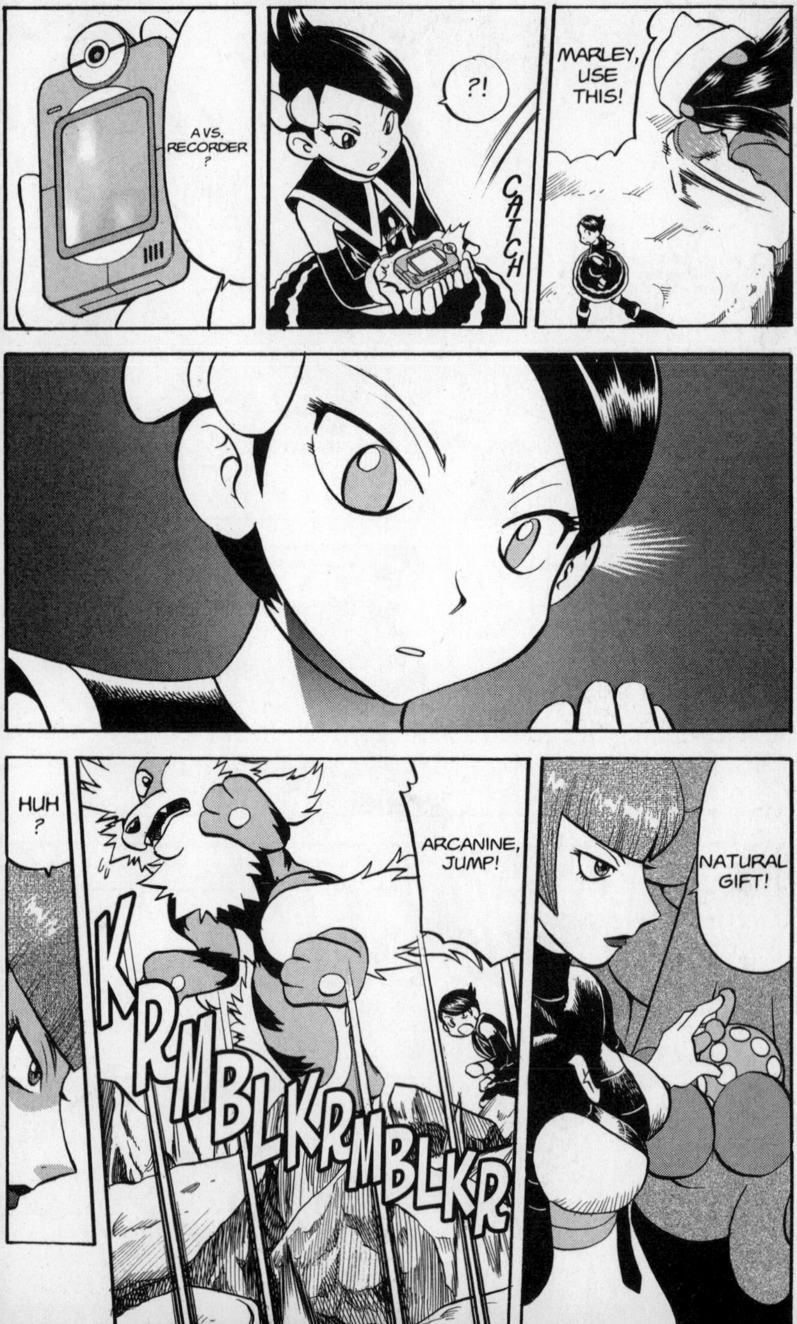
MARLEY, USE THIS!
?!
CATCH
A VS. RECORDER ?
NATURAL GIFT!
ARCANINE, JUMP!
KRMBLKRMBLKR
HUH ?

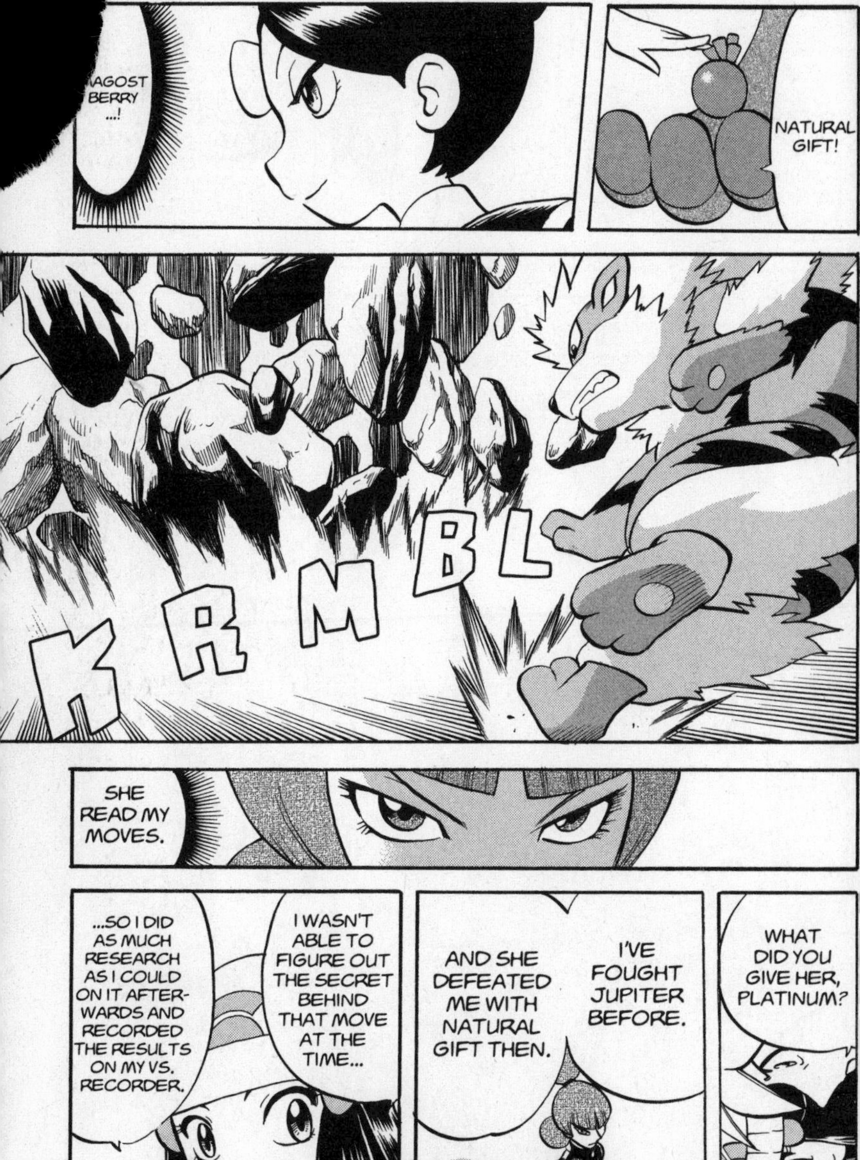
NATURAL GIFT!
AGOST BERRY ...!
KRMBL
SHE READ MY MOVES.
WHAT DID YOU GIVE HER, PLATINUM?
I'VE FOUGHT JUPITER BEFORE.
AND SHE DEFEATED ME WITH NATURAL GIFT THEN.
I WASN'T ABLE TO FIGURE OUT THE SECRET BEHIND THAT MOVE AT THE TIME...
...SO I DID AS MUCH RESEARCH AS I COULD ON IT AFTER-WARDS AND RECORDED THE RESULTS ON MY VS. RECORDER.

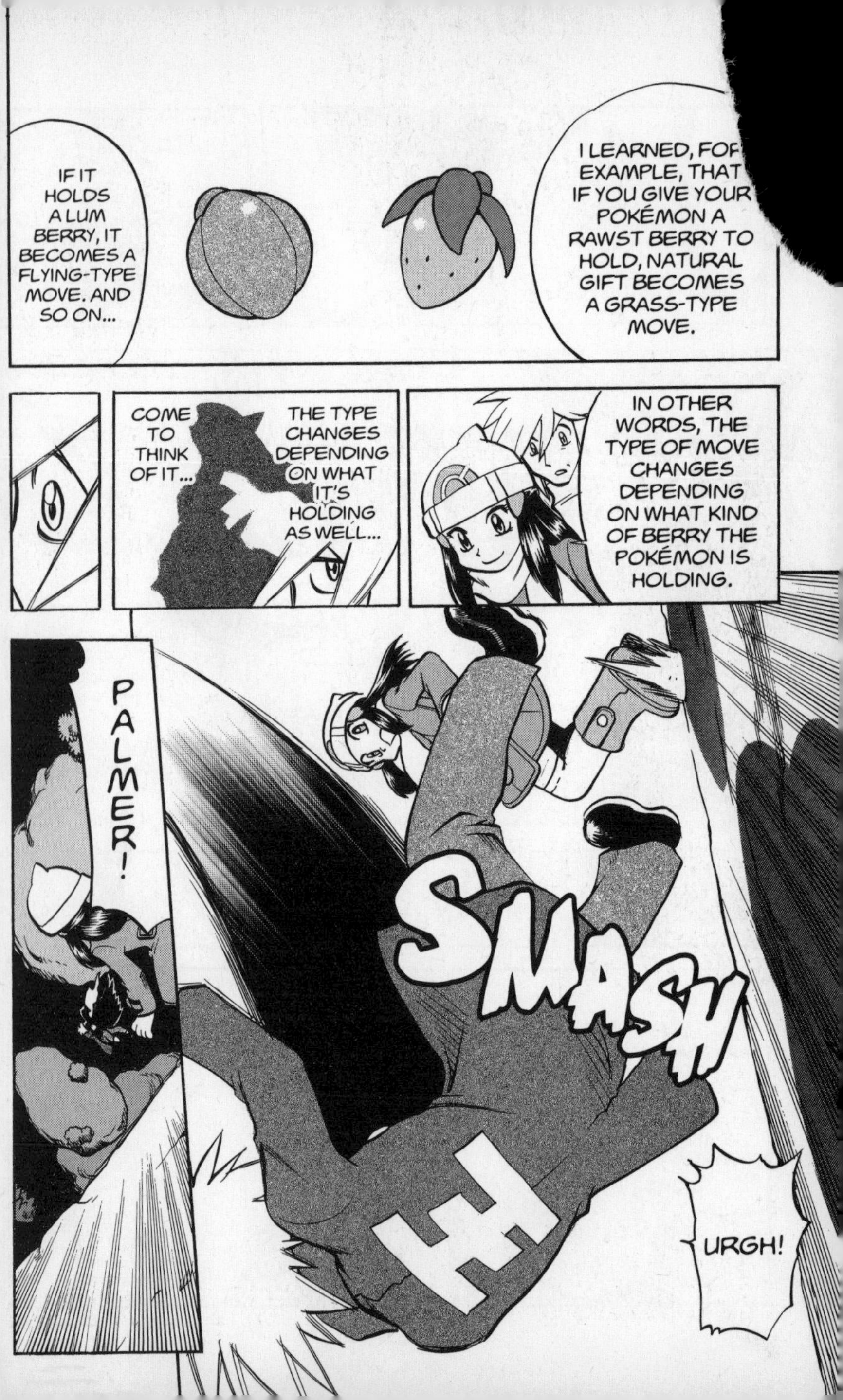
I LEARNED, FOR EXAMPLE, THAT IF YOU GIVE YOUR POKÉMON A RAWST BERRY TO HOLD, NATURAL GIFT BECOMES A GRASS-TYPE MOVE.
IF IT HOLDS A LUM BERRY, IT BECOMES A FLYING-TYPE MOVE. AND SO ON...
IN OTHER WORDS, THE TYPE OF MOVE CHANGES DEPENDING ON WHAT KIND OF BERRY THE POKÉMON IS HOLDING.
THE TYPE CHANGES DEPENDING ON WHAT IT'S HOLDING AS WELL...
COME TO THINK OF IT...
PALMER!
SMASH
URGH!

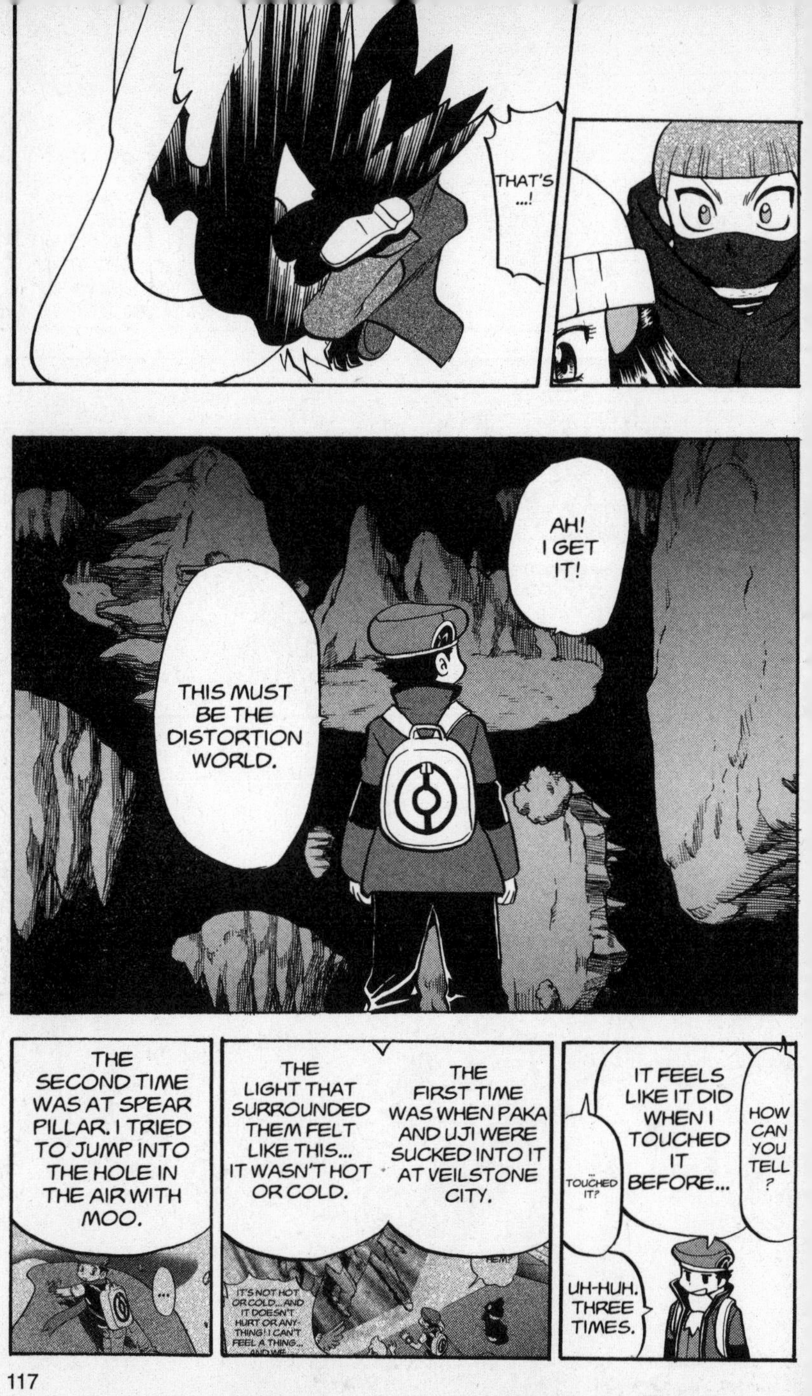
THAT'S ...!
AH! I GET IT!
THIS MUST BE THE DISTORTION WORLD.
HOW CAN YOU TELL?
IT FEELS LIKE IT DID WHEN I TOUCHED IT BEFORE...
...TOUCHED IT?
UH-HUH. THREE TIMES.
THE FIRST TIME WAS WHEN PAKA AND UJI WERE SUCKED INTO IT AT VEILSTONE CITY.
THE LIGHT THAT SURROUNDED THEM FELT LIKE THIS... IT WASN'T HOT OR COLD.
IT'S NOT HOT OR COLD... AND IT DOESN'T HURT OR ANYTHING! I CAN'T FEEL A THING...
THE SECOND TIME WAS AT SPEAR PILLAR. I TRIED TO JUMP INTO THE HOLE IN THE AIR WITH MOO.
...

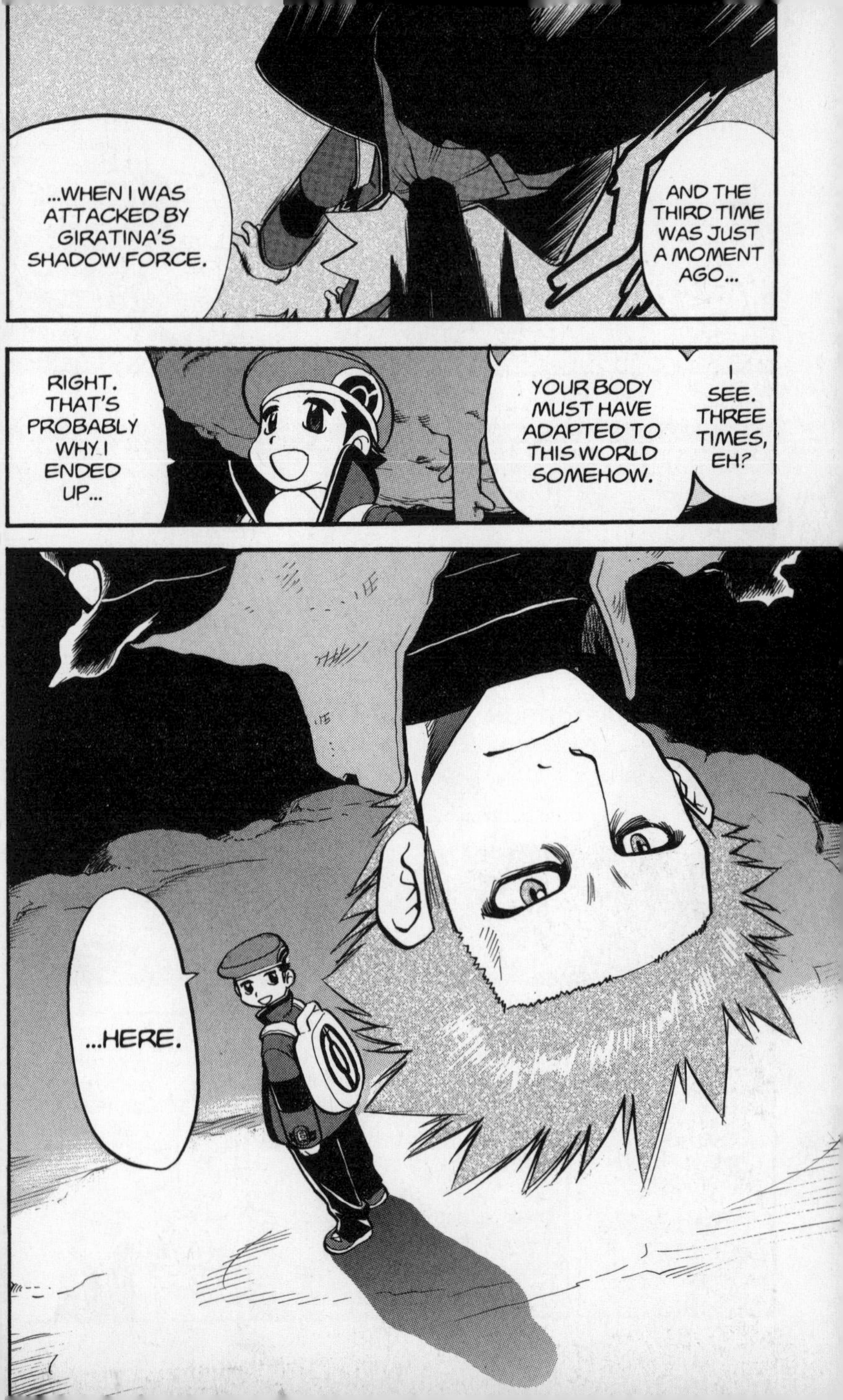
...WHEN I WAS ATTACKED BY GIRATINA'S SHADOW FORCE.
AND THE THIRD TIME WAS JUST A MOMENT AGO...
I SEE. THREE TIMES, EH?
YOUR BODY MUST HAVE ADAPTED TO THIS WORLD SOMEHOW.
RIGHT. THAT'S PROBABLY WHY I ENDED UP...
...HERE.

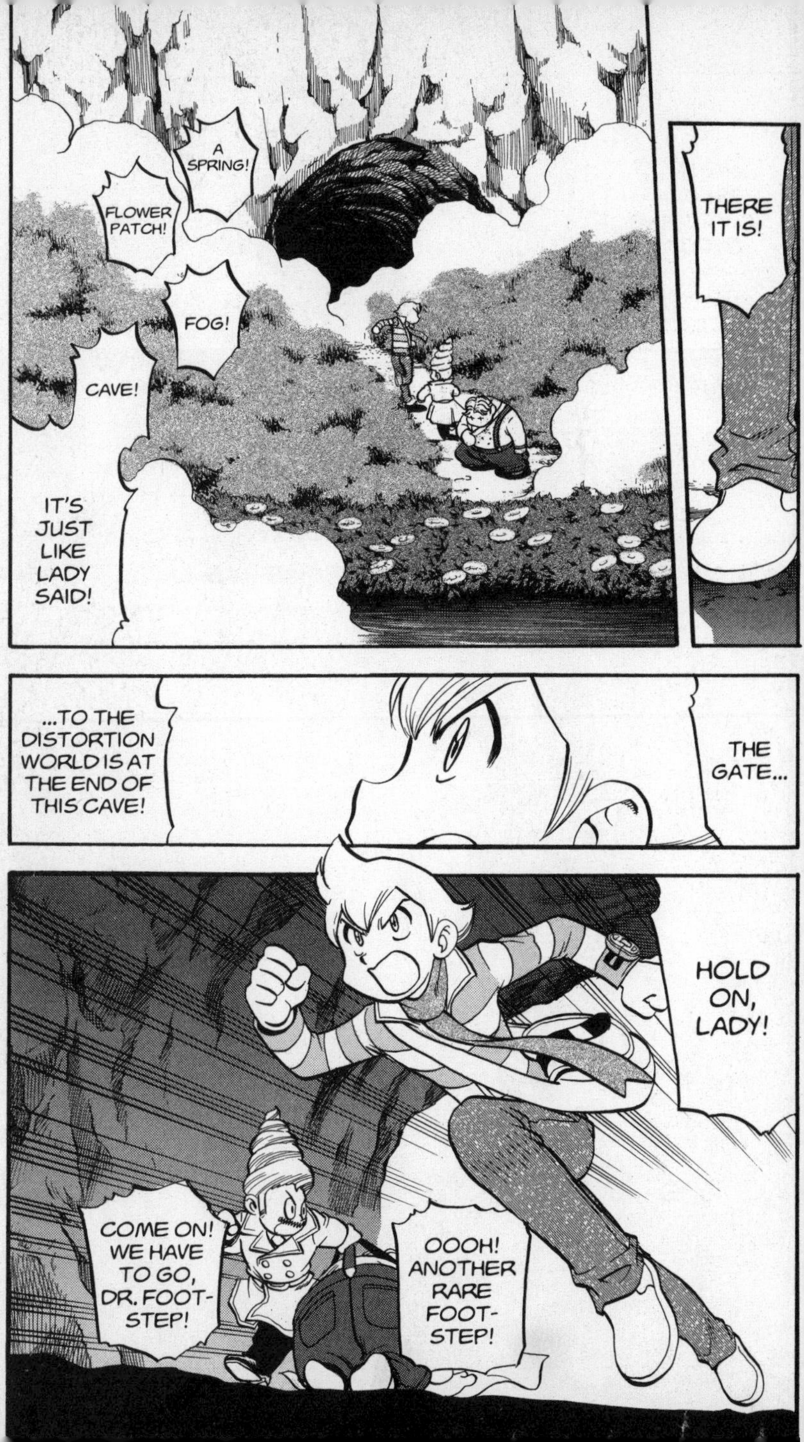
THERE IT IS!
A SPRING!
FLOWER PATCH!
FOG!
CAVE!
IT'S JUST LIKE LADY SAID!
THE GATE...
...TO THE DISTORTION WORLD IS AT THE END OF THIS CAVE!
HOLD ON, LADY!
OOOH! ANOTHER RARE FOOT-STEP!
COME ON! WE HAVE TO GO, DR. FOOT-STEP!

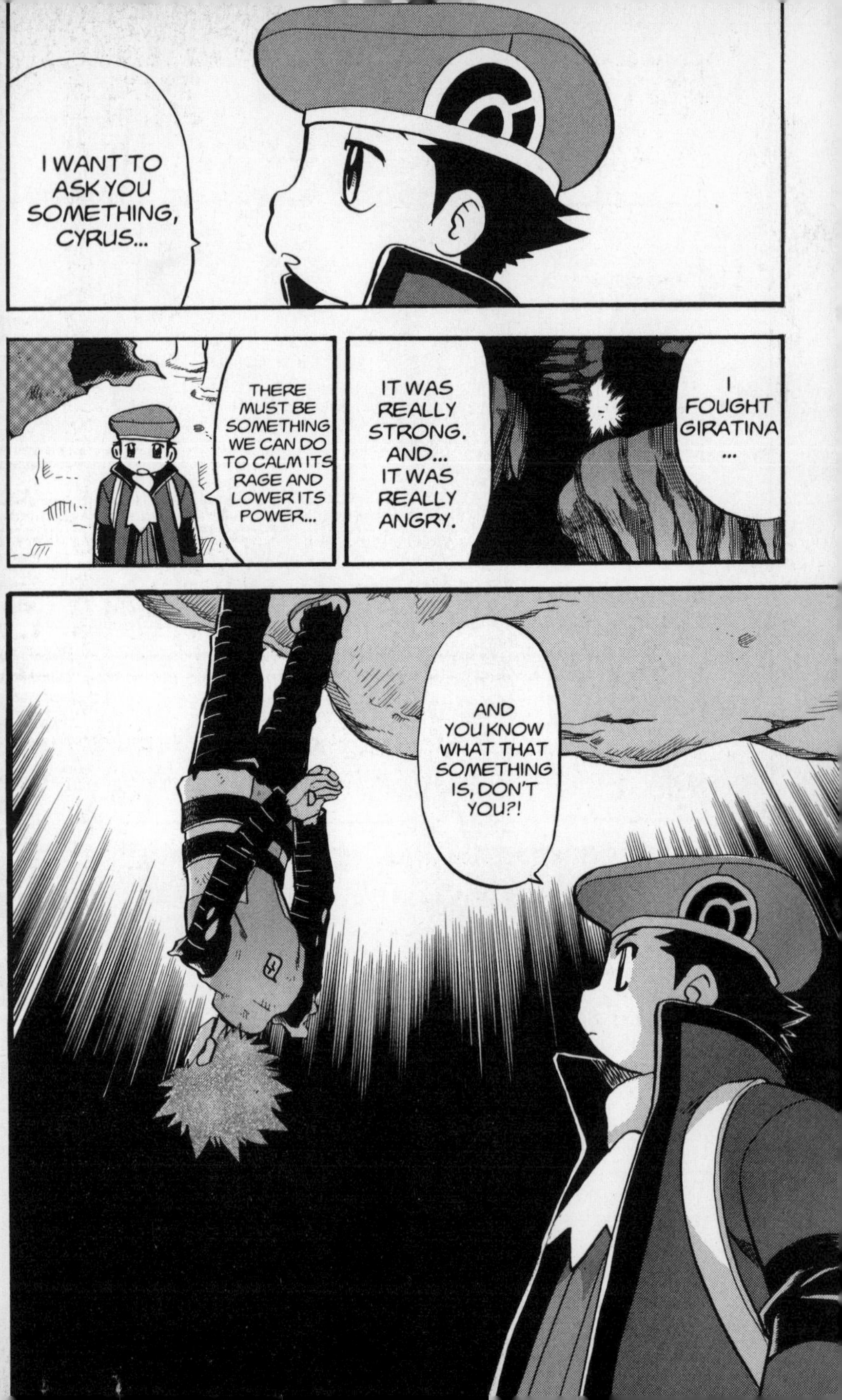
I WANT TO ASK YOU SOMETHING, CYRUS...
I FOUGHT GIRATINA...
IT WAS REALLY STRONG. AND... IT WAS REALLY ANGRY.
THERE MUST BE SOMETHING WE CAN DO TO CALM ITS RAGE AND LOWER ITS POWER...
AND YOU KNOW WHAT THAT SOMETHING IS, DON'T YOU?!

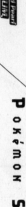

POKÉMON STATS

TEAM PEARL

Chimler/Infernape ♂

Fire
Fighting

LV. 65 (As of Adventure 100)
Ability: Blaze

Naughty. Likes to run.

A speedy Pokémon who is a perfect match for impetuous Pearl. It's Fighting-type moves have become even stronger after it evolved into its final form!

Chatler/Chatot ♂

Normal
Flying

LV. 50 (As of Adventure 100)
Ability: Tangled Feet

Hasty. Somewhat of a clown.

Chatler has been with Pearl the longest of all his Pokémon. It's a lovable Pokémon who can imitate people's words.

Rayler/Luxray ♂

Electric

LV. 60 (As of Adventure 100)
Ability: Intimidate

Brave. Thoroughly cunning.

It was the leader of a pack of Shinx but eventually joined Pearl's team of Pokémon. Its X-ray vision can be a formidable weapon.

POKÉMON ON TEAM PEARL 1

TEAM PEARL 1

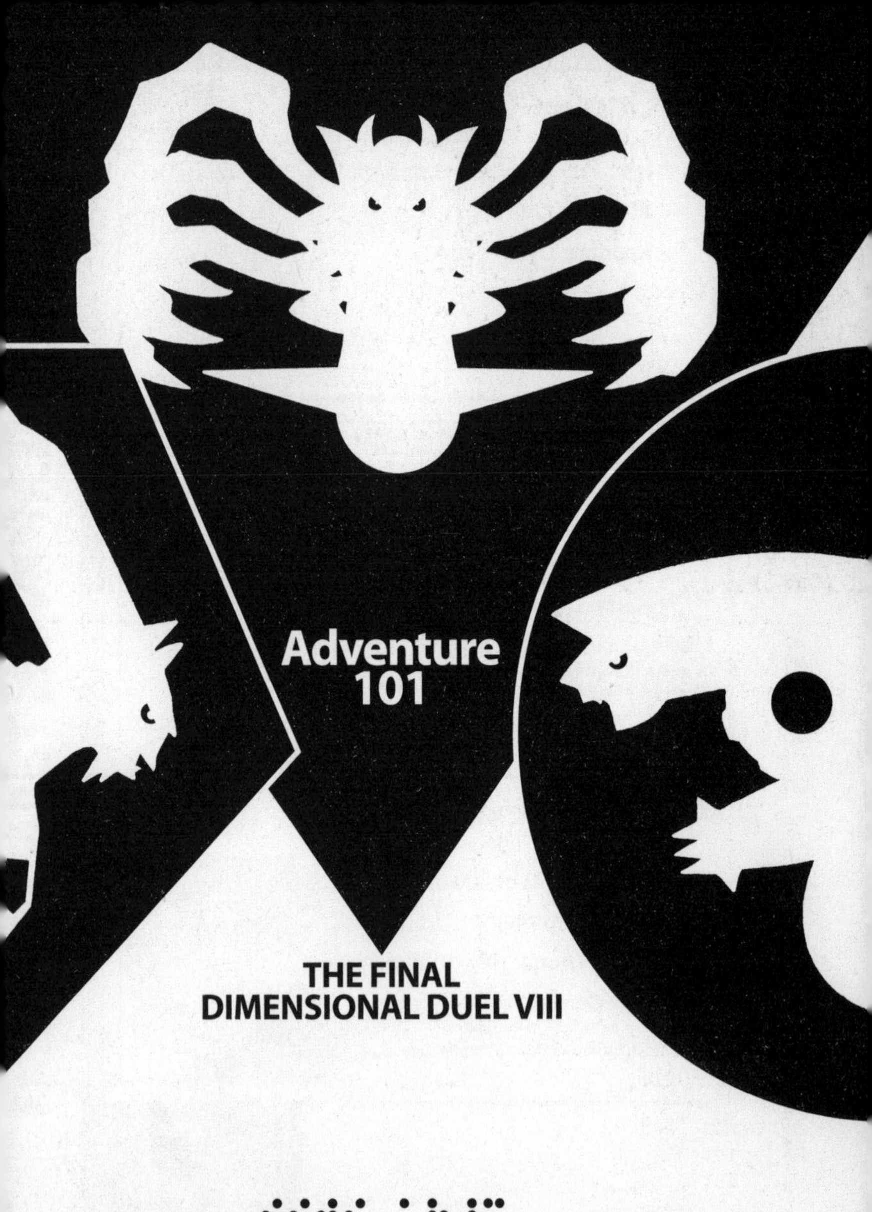

Adventure 101

THE FINAL DIMENSIONAL DUEL VIII

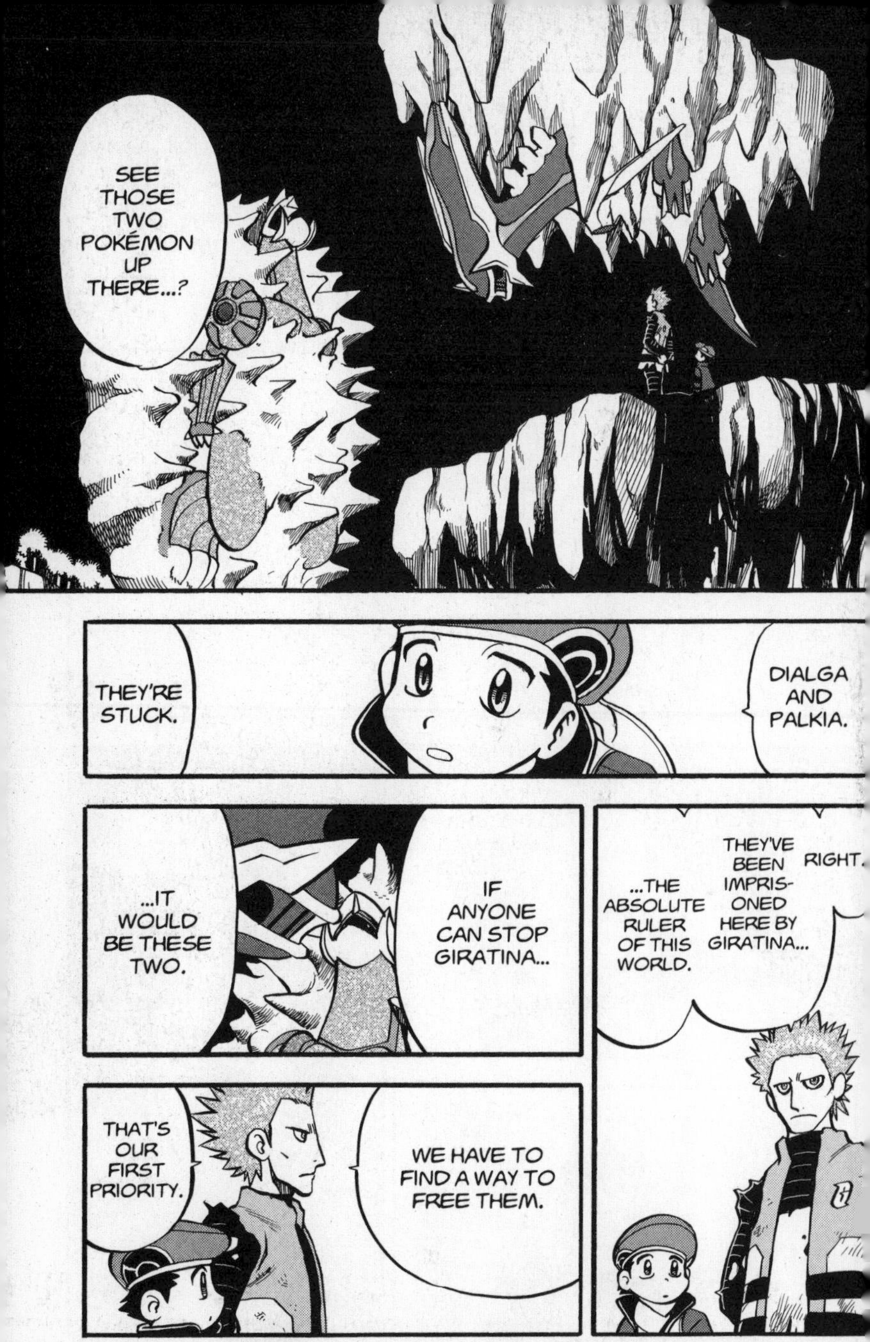
SEE THOSE TWO POKÉMON UP THERE...?
DIALGA AND PALKIA.
THEY'RE STUCK.
RIGHT.
THEY'VE BEEN IMPRIS-ONED HERE BY GIRATINA...
...THE ABSOLUTE RULER OF THIS WORLD.
IF ANYONE CAN STOP GIRATINA...
...IT WOULD BE THESE TWO.
WE HAVE TO FIND A WAY TO FREE THEM.
THAT'S OUR FIRST PRIORITY.

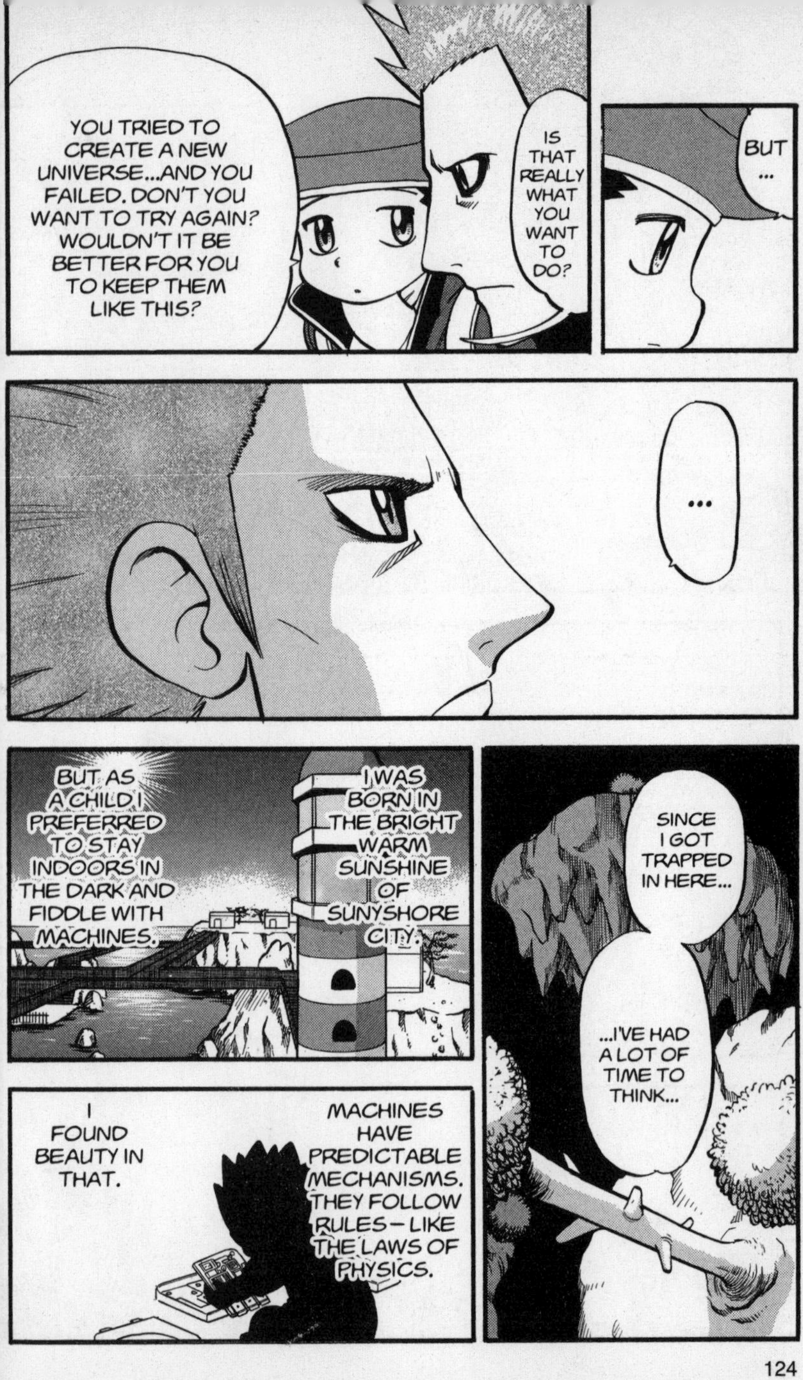
BUT ...
IS THAT REALLY WHAT YOU WANT TO DO?
YOU TRIED TO CREATE A NEW UNIVERSE...AND YOU FAILED. DON'T YOU WANT TO TRY AGAIN? WOULDN'T IT BE BETTER FOR YOU TO KEEP THEM LIKE THIS?
...
SINCE I GOT TRAPPED IN HERE...
...I'VE HAD A LOT OF TIME TO THINK...
I WAS BORN IN THE BRIGHT WARM SUNSHINE OF SUNYSHORE CITY.
BUT AS A CHILD I PREFERRED TO STAY INDOORS IN THE DARK AND FIDDLE WITH MACHINES.
MACHINES HAVE PREDICTABLE MECHANISMS. THEY FOLLOW RULES—LIKE THE LAWS OF PHYSICS.
I FOUND BEAUTY IN THAT.

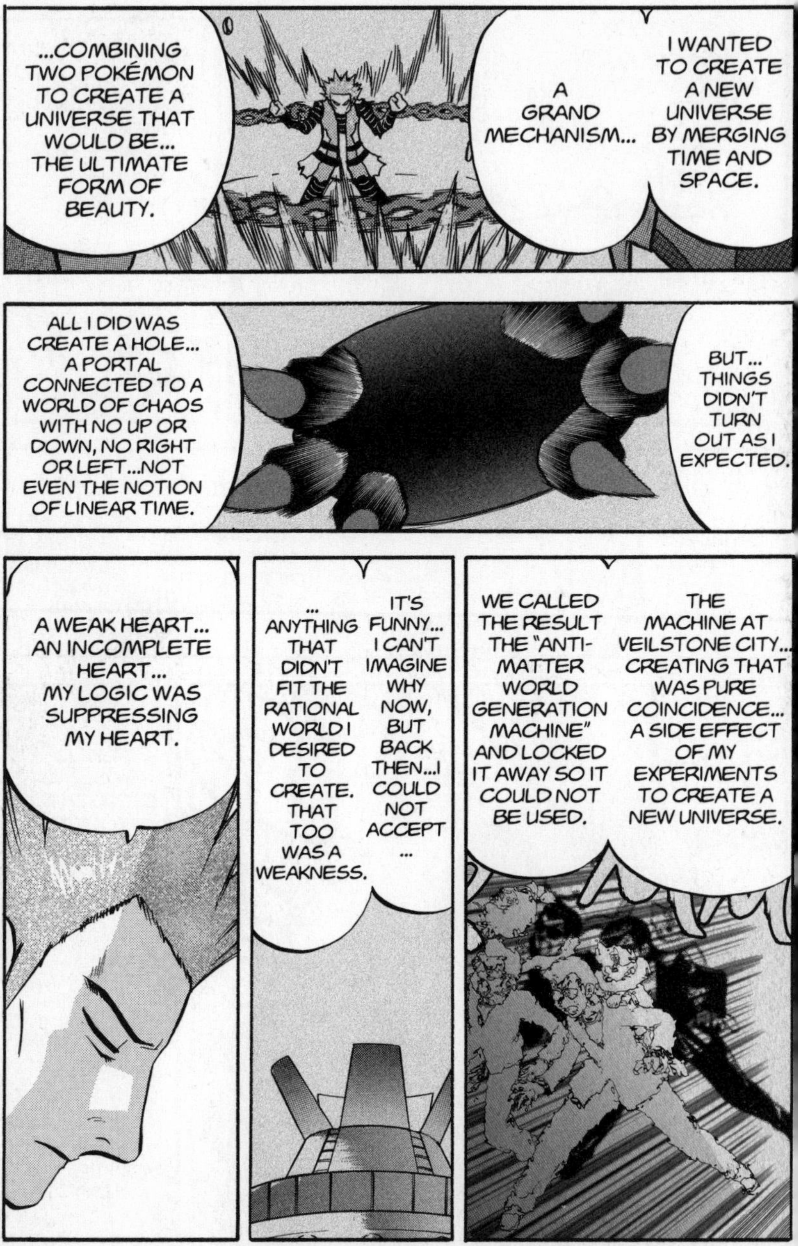
I WANTED TO CREATE A NEW UNIVERSE BY MERGING TIME AND SPACE.
A GRAND MECHANISM...
...COMBINING TWO POKÉMON TO CREATE A UNIVERSE THAT WOULD BE... THE ULTIMATE FORM OF BEAUTY.
BUT... THINGS DIDN'T TURN OUT AS I EXPECTED.
ALL I DID WAS CREATE A HOLE... A PORTAL CONNECTED TO A WORLD OF CHAOS WITH NO UP OR DOWN, NO RIGHT OR LEFT...NOT EVEN THE NOTION OF LINEAR TIME.
THE MACHINE AT VEILSTONE CITY... CREATING THAT WAS PURE COINCIDENCE... A SIDE EFFECT OF MY EXPERIMENTS TO CREATE A NEW UNIVERSE.
WE CALLED THE RESULT THE "ANTI-MATTER WORLD GENERATION MACHINE" AND LOCKED IT AWAY SO IT COULD NOT BE USED.
IT'S FUNNY... I CAN'T IMAGINE WHY NOW, BUT BACK THEN...I COULD NOT ACCEPT...
... ANYTHING THAT DIDN'T FIT THE RATIONAL WORLD I DESIRED TO CREATE. THAT TOO WAS A WEAKNESS.
A WEAK HEART... AN INCOMPLETE HEART... MY LOGIC WAS SUPPRESSING MY HEART.

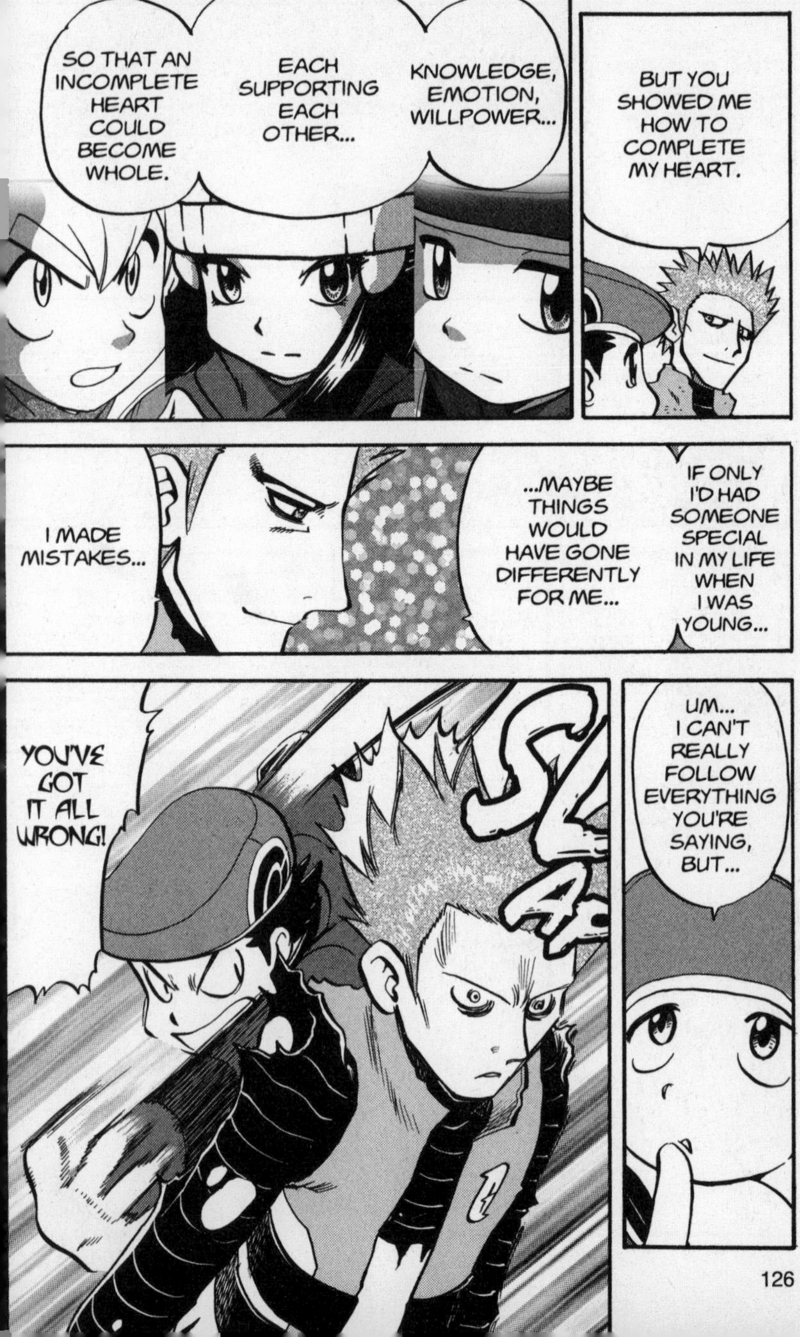
BUT YOU SHOWED ME HOW TO COMPLETE MY HEART.
KNOWLEDGE, EMOTION, WILLPOWER...
EACH SUPPORTING EACH OTHER...
SO THAT AN INCOMPLETE HEART COULD BECOME WHOLE.
IF ONLY I'D HAD SOMEONE SPECIAL IN MY LIFE WHEN I WAS YOUNG...
...MAYBE THINGS WOULD HAVE GONE DIFFERENTLY FOR ME...
I MADE MISTAKES...
UM... I CAN'T REALLY FOLLOW EVERYTHING YOU'RE SAYING, BUT...
YOU'VE GOT IT ALL WRONG!

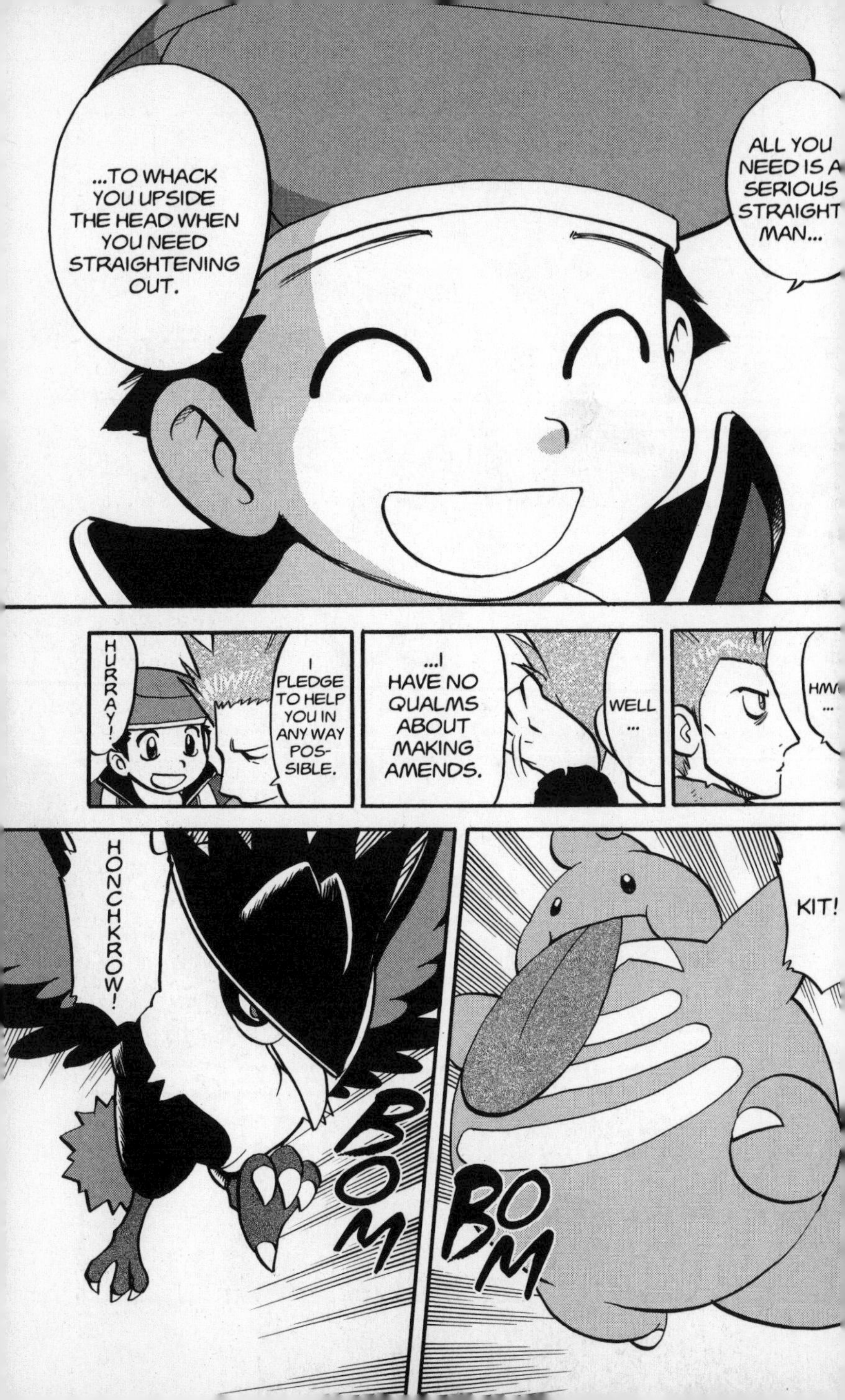
ALL YOU NEED IS A SERIOUS STRAIGHT MAN...
...TO WHACK YOU UPSIDE THE HEAD WHEN YOU NEED STRAIGHTENING OUT.
HM...
WELL ...
...I HAVE NO QUALMS ABOUT MAKING AMENDS.
I PLEDGE TO HELP YOU IN ANY WAY POS-SIBLE.
HURRAY!
KIT!
BOOM
HONCHKROW!
BOOM

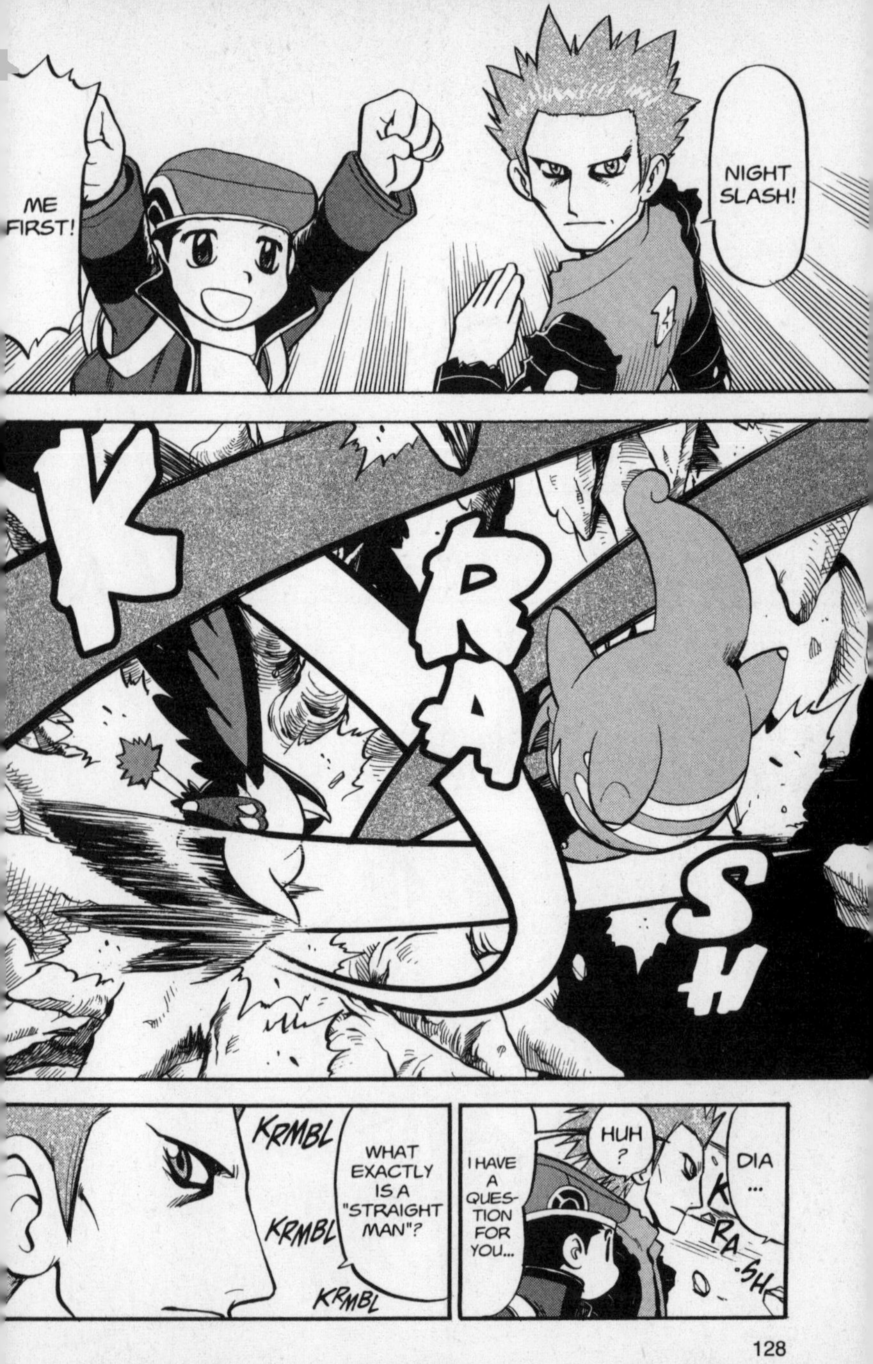
NIGHT SLASH!
ME FIRST!
KRASH
DIA ...
HUH ?
I HAVE A QUESTION FOR YOU...
KRASH
WHAT EXACTLY IS A "STRAIGHT MAN"?
KRMBL
KRMBL
KRMBL

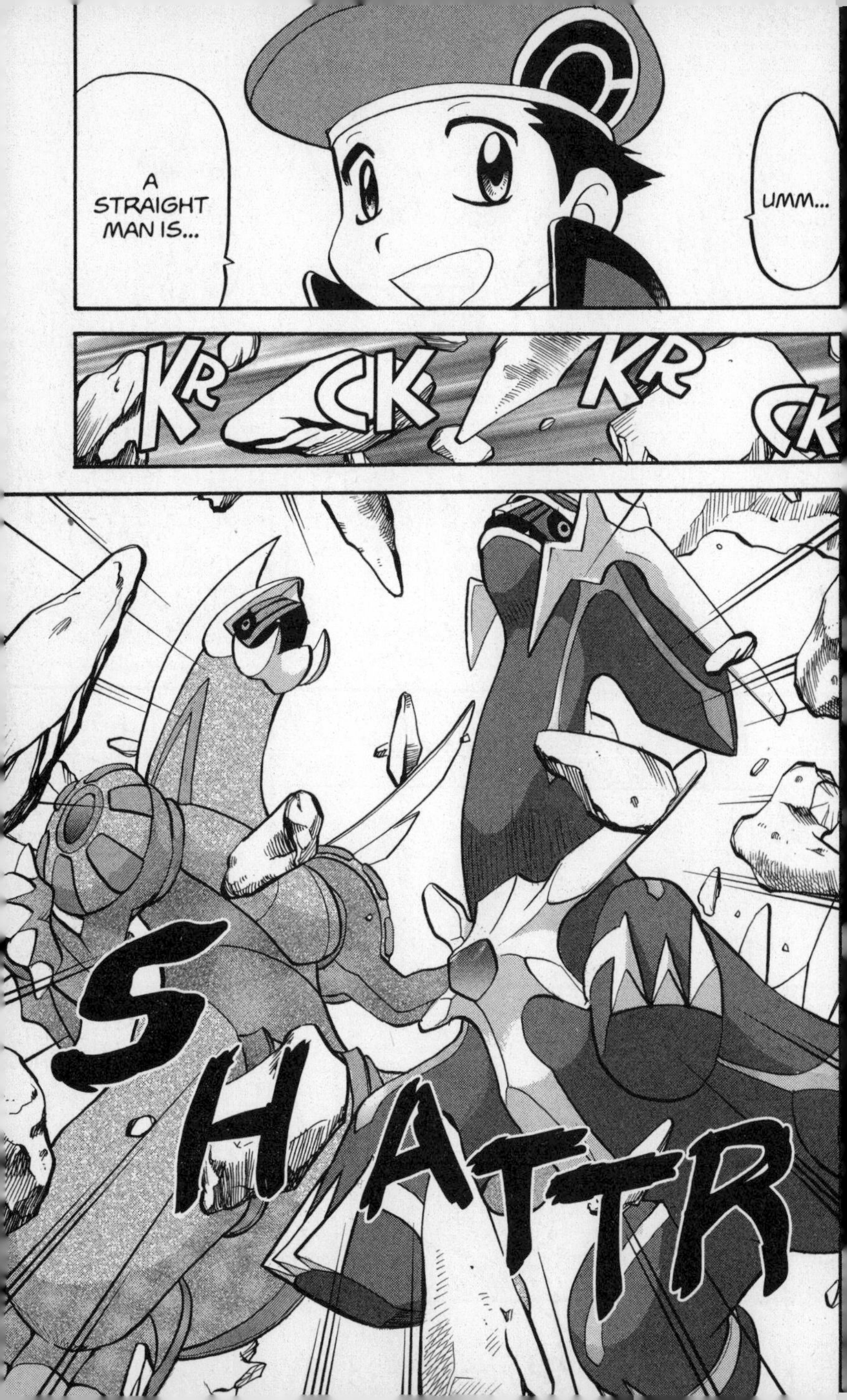
UMM...
A STRAIGHT MAN IS...
KR CK KR CK
SHATTR

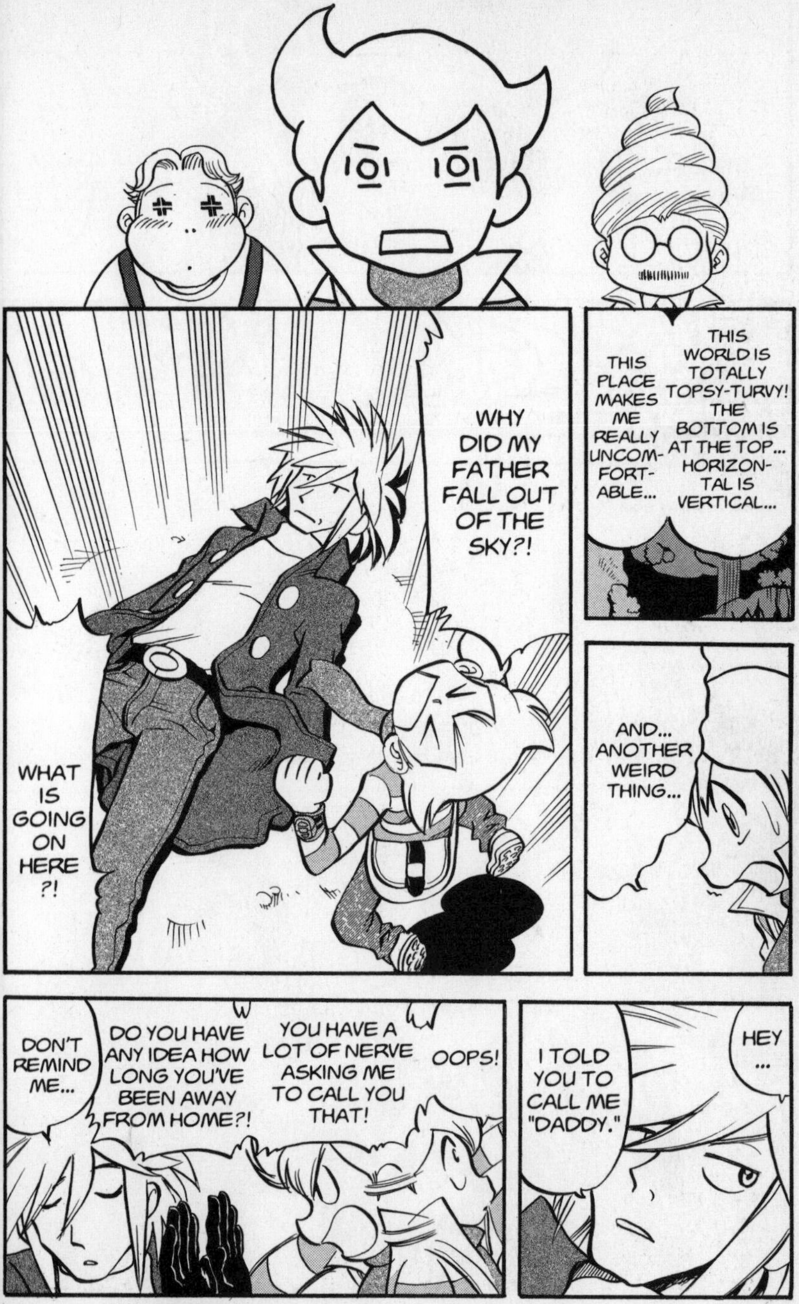
THIS WORLD IS TOTALLY TOPSY-TURVY! THE BOTTOM IS AT THE TOP... HORIZONTAL IS VERTICAL...
THIS PLACE MAKES ME REALLY UNCOMFORTABLE...
AND... ANOTHER WEIRD THING...
WHY DID MY FATHER FALL OUT OF THE SKY?!
WHAT IS GOING ON HERE?!
HEY...
I TOLD YOU TO CALL ME "DADDY."
OOPS!
YOU HAVE A LOT OF NERVE ASKING ME TO CALL YOU THAT!
DO YOU HAVE ANY IDEA HOW LONG YOU'VE BEEN AWAY FROM HOME?!
DON'T REMIND ME...

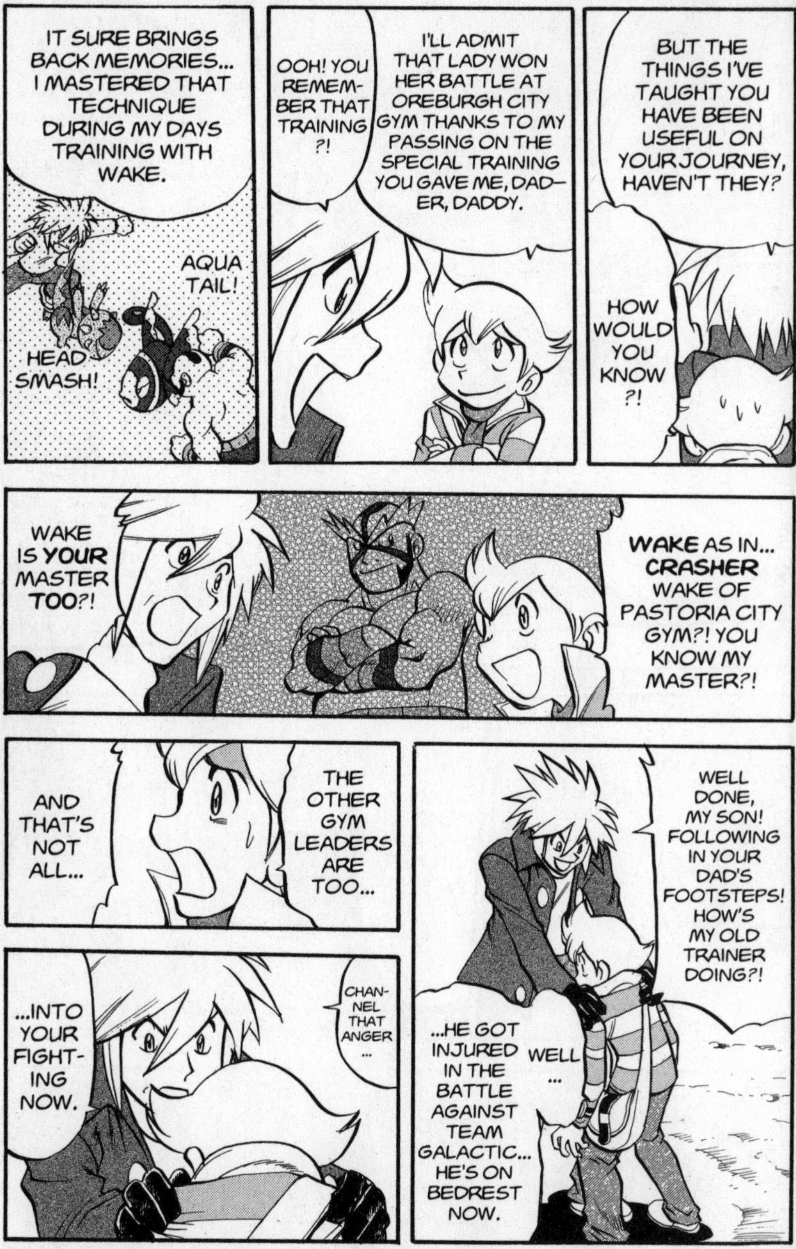

IT SURE BRINGS BACK MEMORIES... I MASTERED THAT TECHNIQUE DURING MY DAYS TRAINING WITH WAKE.
AQUA TAIL!
HEAD SMASH!
OOH! YOU REMEMBER THAT TRAINING?!
I'LL ADMIT THAT LADY WON HER BATTLE AT OREBURGH CITY GYM THANKS TO MY PASSING ON THE SPECIAL TRAINING YOU GAVE ME, DAD-ER, DADDY.
BUT THE THINGS I'VE TAUGHT YOU HAVE BEEN USEFUL ON YOUR JOURNEY, HAVEN'T THEY?
HOW WOULD YOU KNOW?!
WAKE AS IN... **CRASHER** WAKE OF PASTORIA CITY GYM?! YOU KNOW MY MASTER?!
WAKE IS **YOUR** MASTER **TOO**?!
AND THAT'S NOT ALL...
THE OTHER GYM LEADERS ARE TOO...
WELL DONE, MY SON! FOLLOWING IN YOUR DAD'S FOOTSTEPS! HOW'S MY OLD TRAINER DOING?!
WELL...
...HE GOT INJURED IN THE BATTLE AGAINST TEAM GALACTIC... HE'S ON BEDREST NOW.
CHANNEL THAT ANGER...
...INTO YOUR FIGHTING NOW.

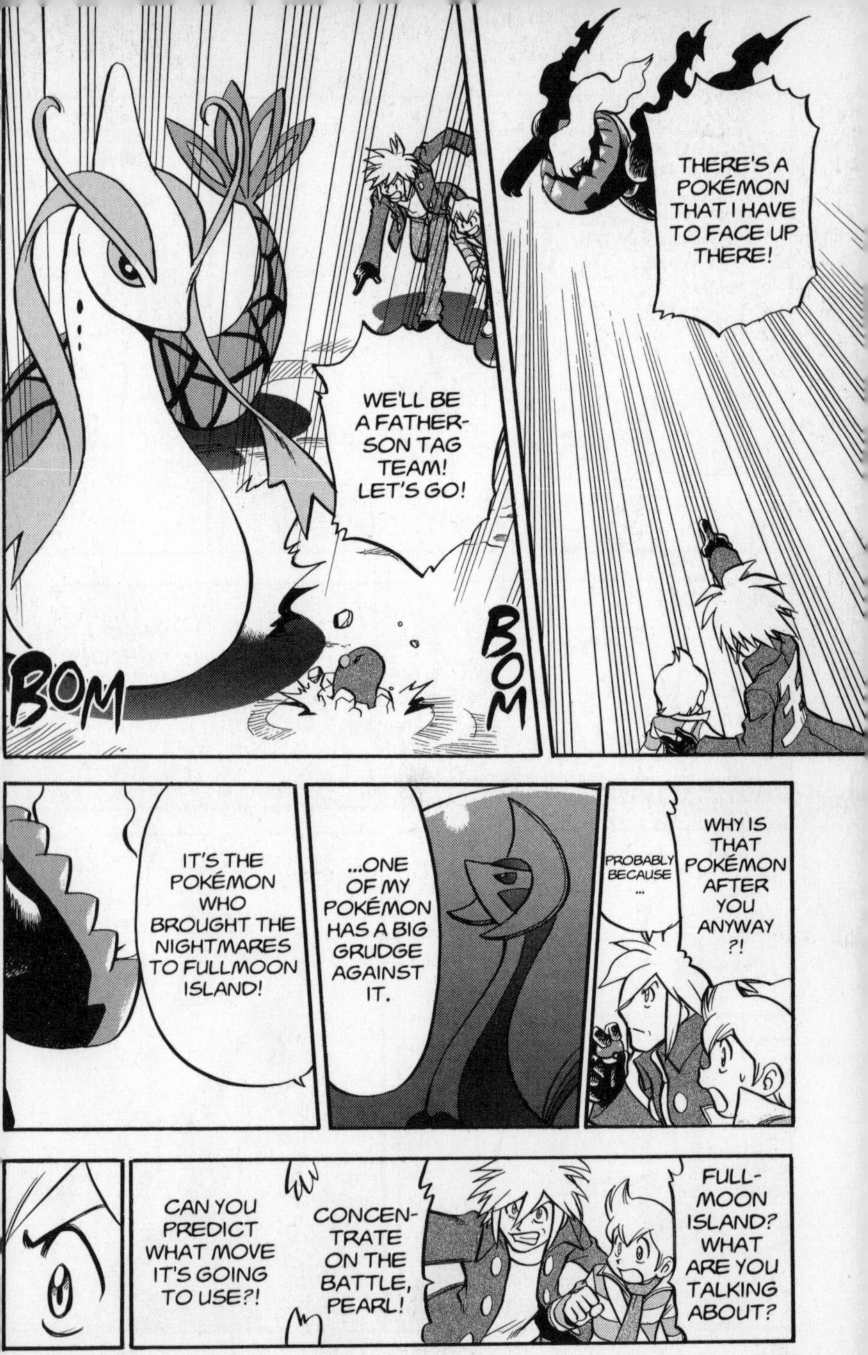
THERE'S A POKÉMON THAT I HAVE TO FACE UP THERE!
WE'LL BE A FATHER-SON TAG TEAM! LET'S GO!
BOM
BOM
WHY IS THAT POKÉMON AFTER YOU ANYWAY?!
PROBABLY BECAUSE ...
...ONE OF MY POKÉMON HAS A BIG GRUDGE AGAINST IT.
IT'S THE POKÉMON WHO BROUGHT THE NIGHTMARES TO FULLMOON ISLAND!
FULL-MOON ISLAND? WHAT ARE YOU TALKING ABOUT?
CONCEN-TRATE ON THE BATTLE, PEARL!
CAN YOU PREDICT WHAT MOVE IT'S GOING TO USE?!

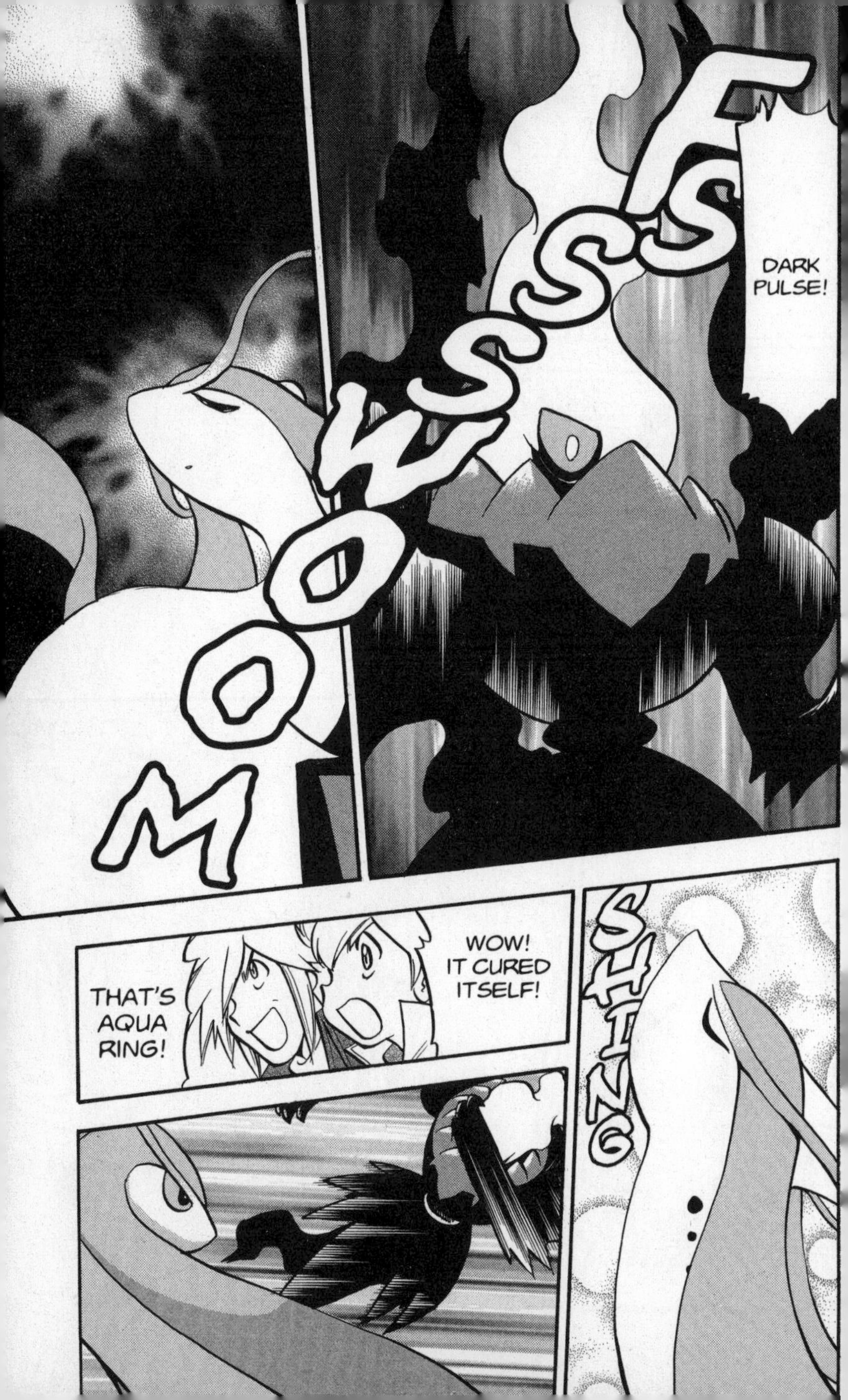
DARK PULSE!
FSSSWOOM
SHING
WOW! IT CURED ITSELF!
THAT'S AQUA RING!

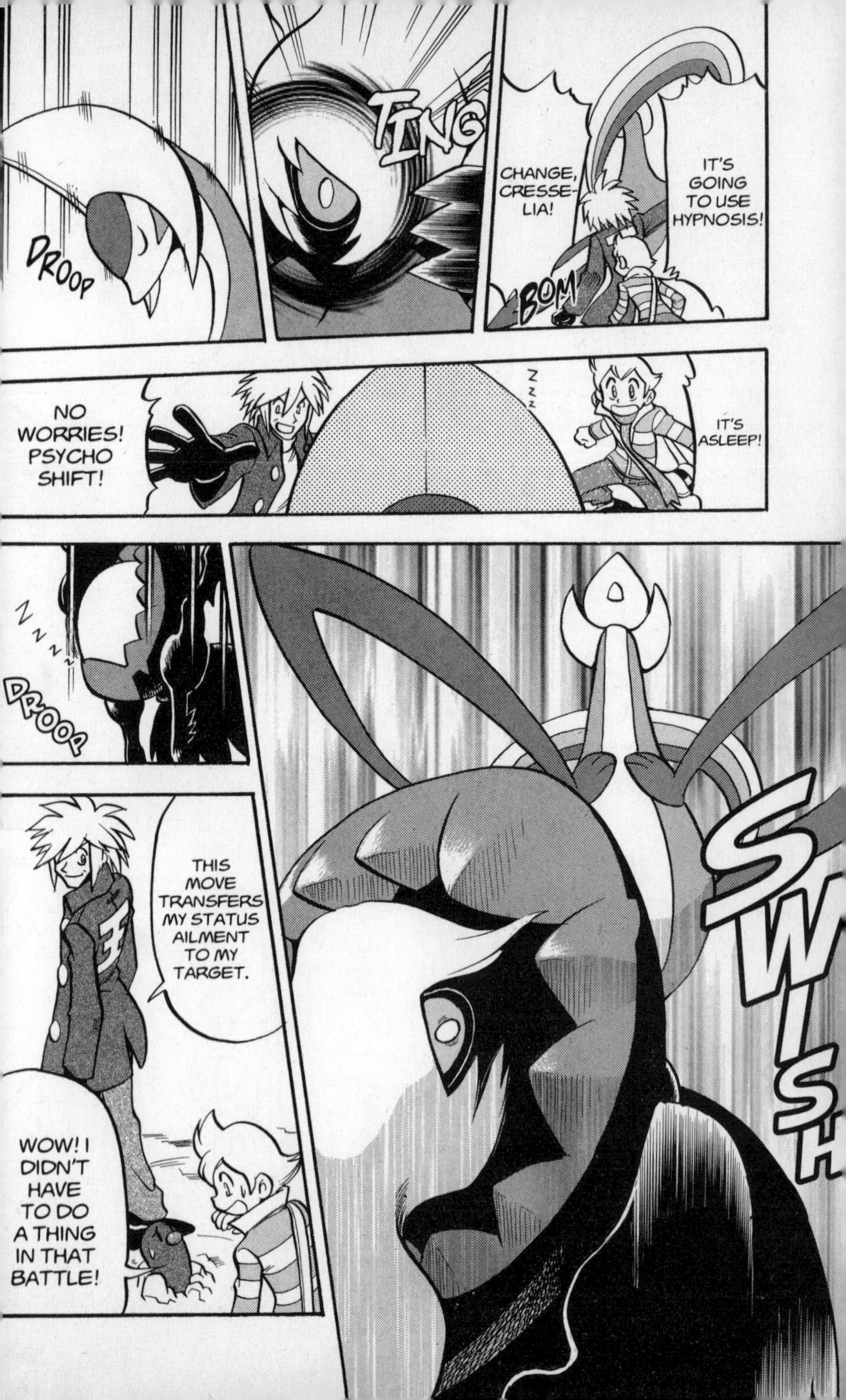
IT'S GOING TO USE HYPNOSIS!
CHANGE, CRESSELIA!
BOM
TING
DROOP
IT'S ASLEEP!
ZZZ
NO WORRIES! PSYCHO SHIFT!
SWISH
ZZZZ
DROOP
THIS MOVE TRANSFERS MY STATUS AILMENT TO MY TARGET.
WOW! I DIDN'T HAVE TO DO A THING IN THAT BATTLE!

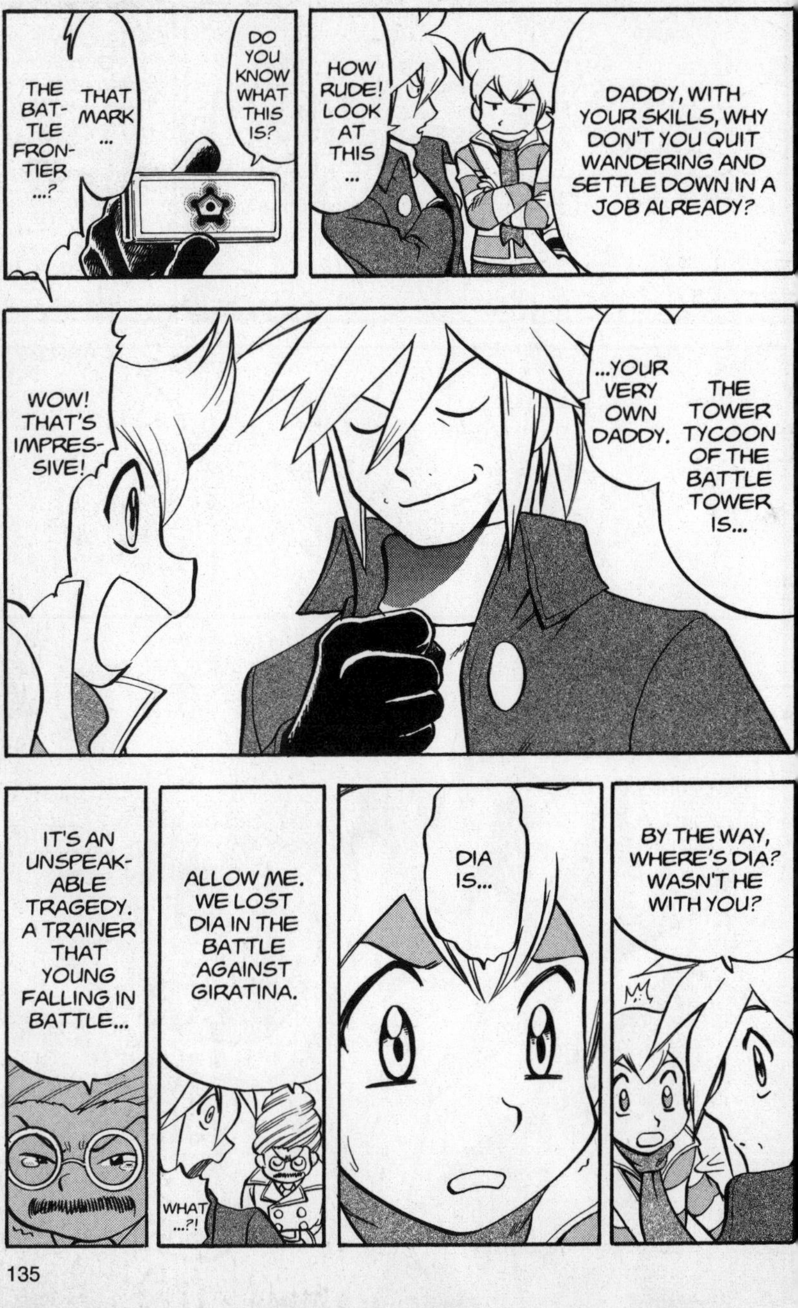
DADDY, WITH YOUR SKILLS, WHY DON'T YOU QUIT WANDERING AND SETTLE DOWN IN A JOB ALREADY?
HOW RUDE! LOOK AT THIS...
DO YOU KNOW WHAT THIS IS?
THAT MARK...
THE BATTLE FRONTIER...?
THE TOWER TYCOON OF THE BATTLE TOWER IS...
...YOUR VERY OWN DADDY.
WOW! THAT'S IMPRESSIVE!
BY THE WAY, WHERE'S DIA? WASN'T HE WITH YOU?
DIA IS...
ALLOW ME. WE LOST DIA IN THE BATTLE AGAINST GIRATINA.
WHAT...?!
IT'S AN UNSPEAKABLE TRAGEDY. A TRAINER THAT YOUNG FALLING IN BATTLE...

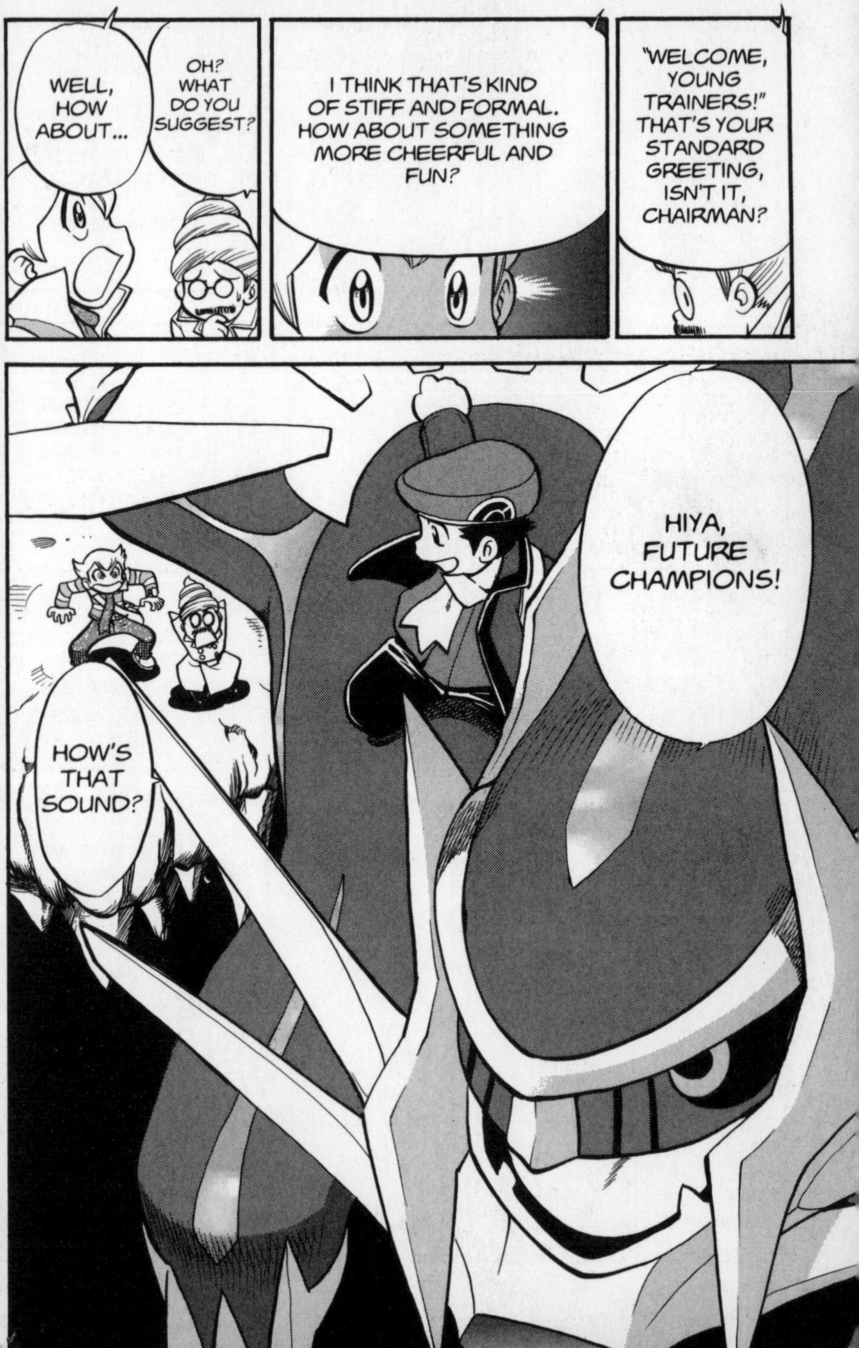
"WELCOME, YOUNG TRAINERS!" THAT'S YOUR STANDARD GREETING, ISN'T IT, CHAIRMAN?
I THINK THAT'S KIND OF STIFF AND FORMAL. HOW ABOUT SOMETHING MORE CHEERFUL AND FUN?
OH? WHAT DO YOU SUGGEST?
WELL, HOW ABOUT...
HIYA, FUTURE CHAMPIONS!
HOW'S THAT SOUND?

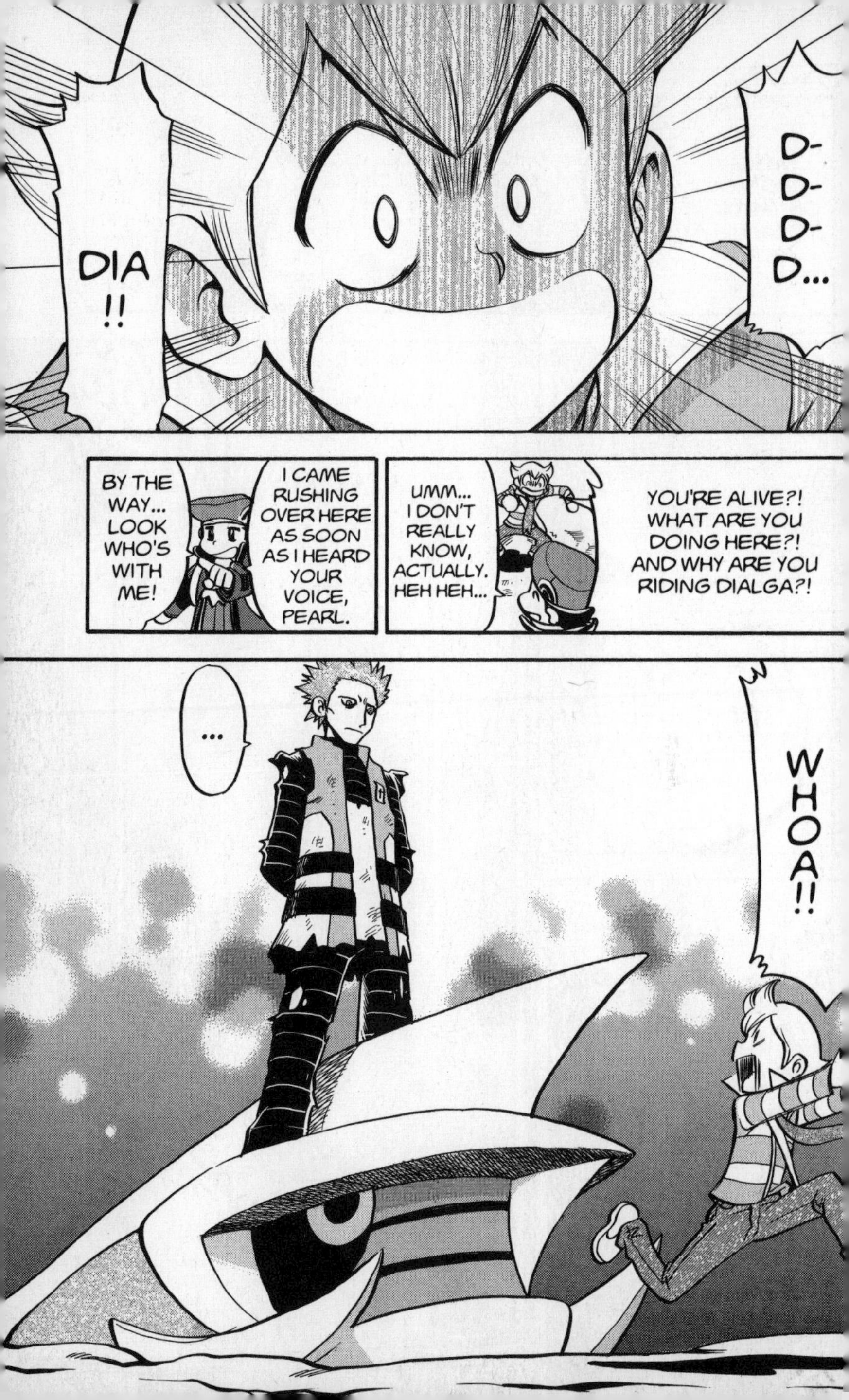
D-D-D-D...
DIA!!
YOU'RE ALIVE?! WHAT ARE YOU DOING HERE?! AND WHY ARE YOU RIDING DIALGA?!
UMM... I DON'T REALLY KNOW, ACTUALLY. HEH HEH...
I CAME RUSHING OVER HERE AS SOON AS I HEARD YOUR VOICE, PEARL.
BY THE WAY... LOOK WHO'S WITH ME!
WHOA!!
...

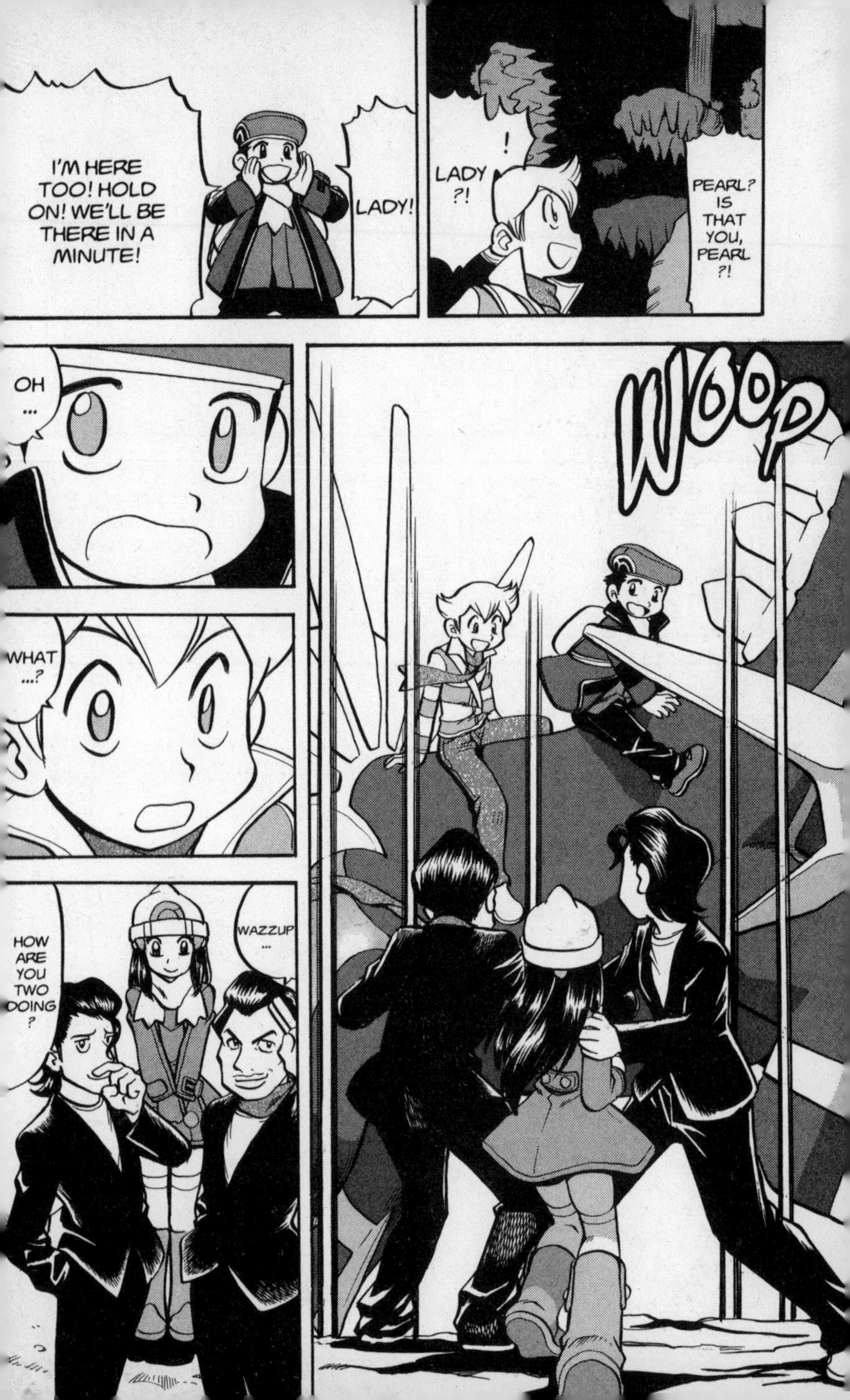
PEARL? IS THAT YOU, PEARL?!
!
LADY?!
LADY!
I'M HERE TOO! HOLD ON! WE'LL BE THERE IN A MINUTE!
WOOP
OH...
WHAT...?
WAZZUP...
HOW ARE YOU TWO DOING?

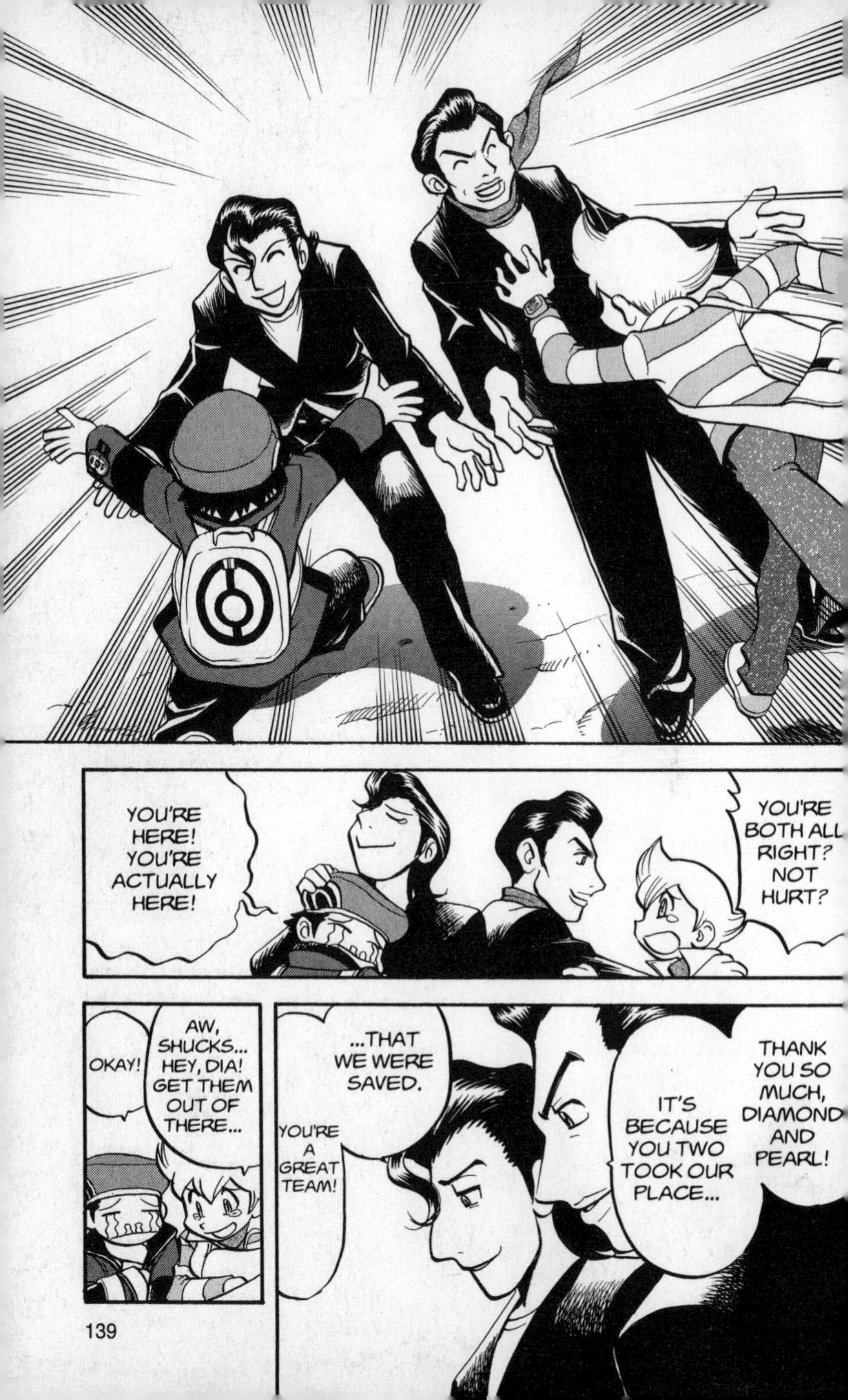
YOU'RE BOTH ALL RIGHT? NOT HURT?
YOU'RE HERE! YOU'RE ACTUALLY HERE!
THANK YOU SO MUCH, DIAMOND AND PEARL!
IT'S BECAUSE YOU TWO TOOK OUR PLACE...
...THAT WE WERE SAVED.
YOU'RE A GREAT TEAM!
AW, SHUCKS... HEY, DIA! GET THEM OUT OF THERE...
OKAY!

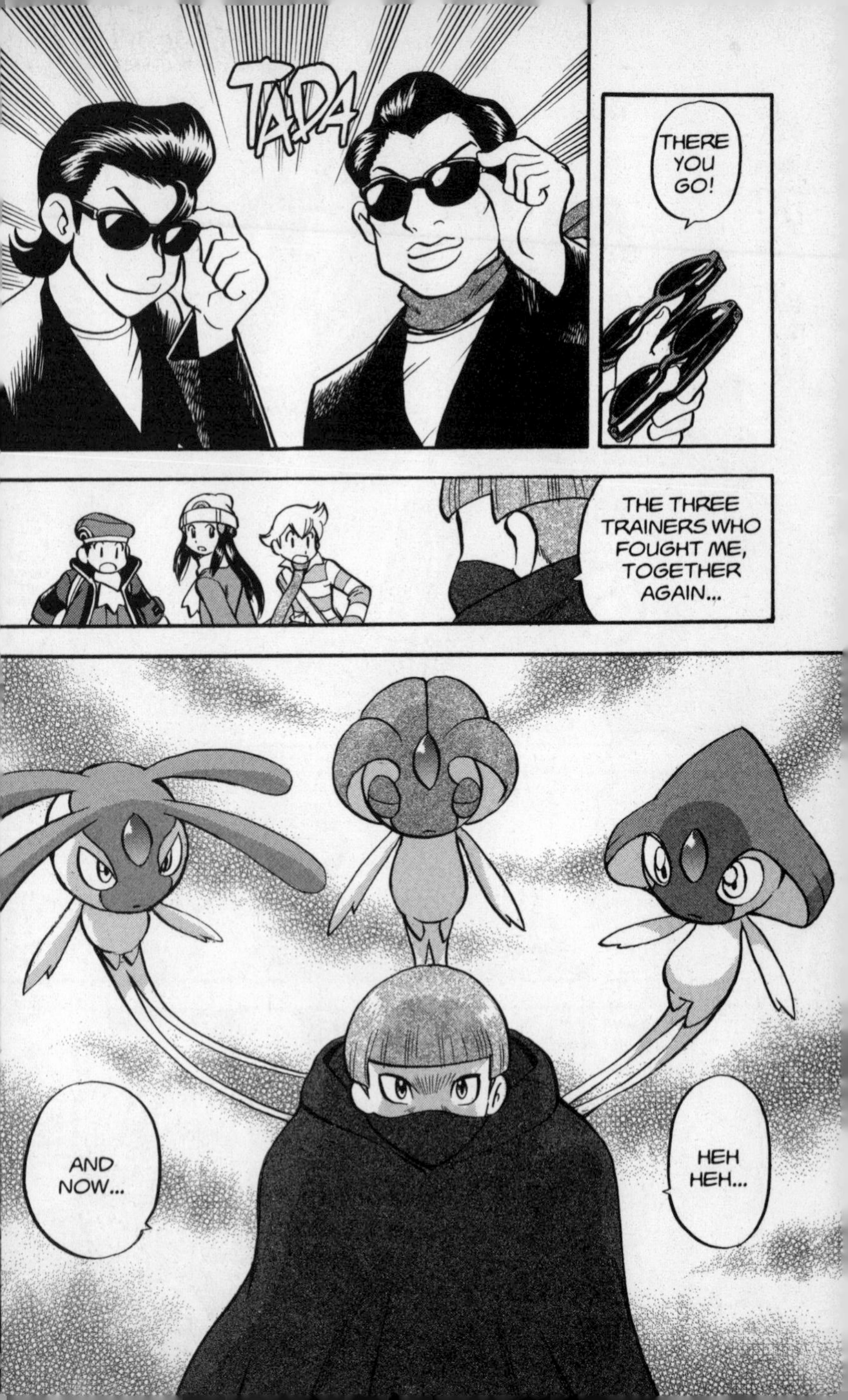
THERE YOU GO!
TADA
THE THREE TRAINERS WHO FOUGHT ME, TOGETHER AGAIN...
HEH HEH...
AND NOW...

Pokémon
ADVENTURES

Diamond and Pearl
PLATINUM

Zeller/Buizel ♂

Water

- **LV. 53** (As of Adventure 101)
- **Ability: Swift Swim**
- **Stubborn. Likes to fight.**

It used to live near Lake Valor, but was forced to flee when the Galactic Bomb was detonated. Thus it is very angry...

Tauler/Tauros ♂

Normal

- **LV. 58** (As of Adventure 101)
- **Ability: Anger Point**
- **Cheerful and robust.**

Pearl captured Tauler during his training with Wake. Its powerful charges are strong enough to break down doors.

Digler/Diglett ♂

Ground

- **LV. 48** (As of Adventure 101)
- **Ability: Sand Veil**
- **Bashful. Quick to run away.**

Although small, this Pokémon can make the ground shake. It works well with the other five Pokémon of Pearl's team and is ready for the final battle.

POKÉMON ON TEAM PEARL | 2

P o k é m o n   S t a t s

TEAM PEARL

TEAM PEARL 2

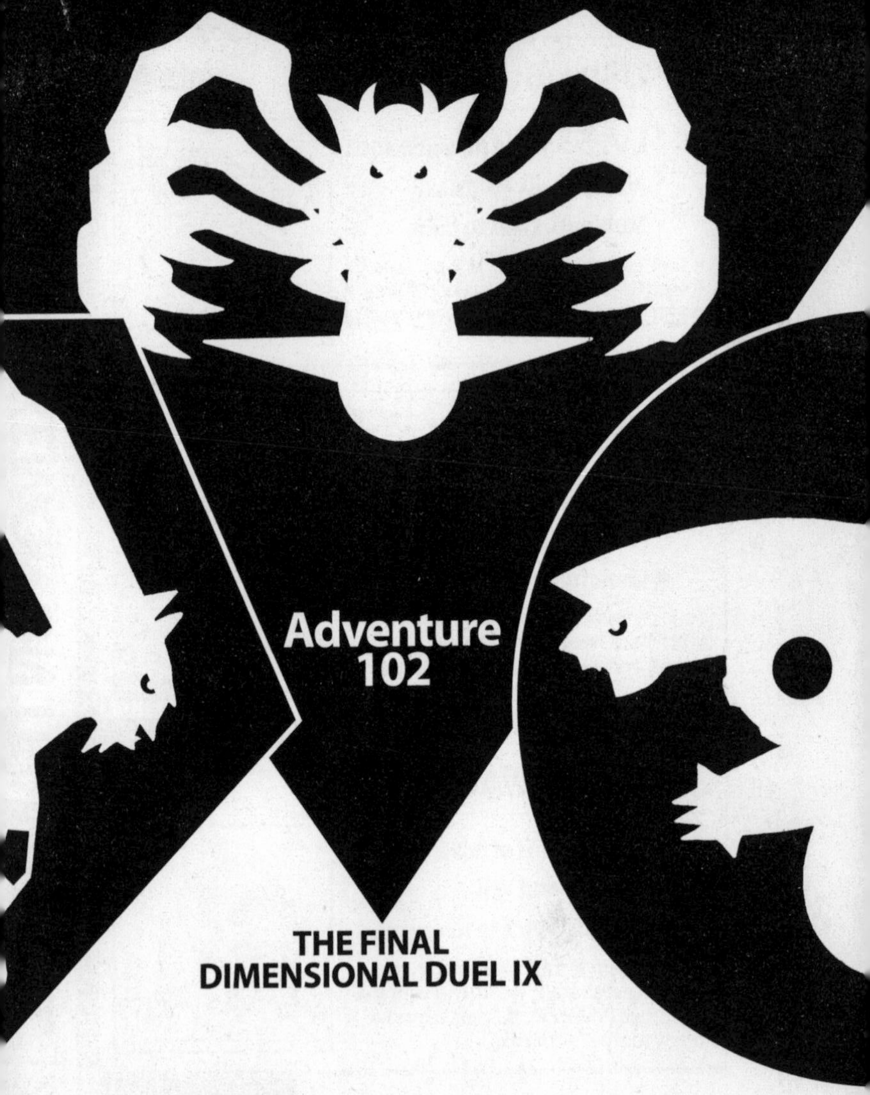

Adventure 102

THE FINAL DIMENSIONAL DUEL IX

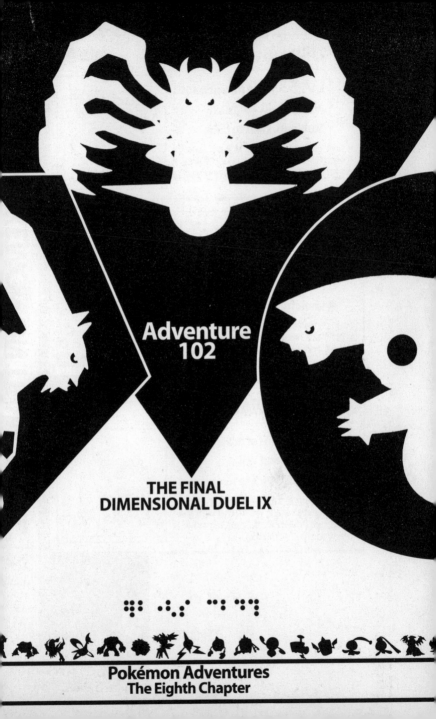

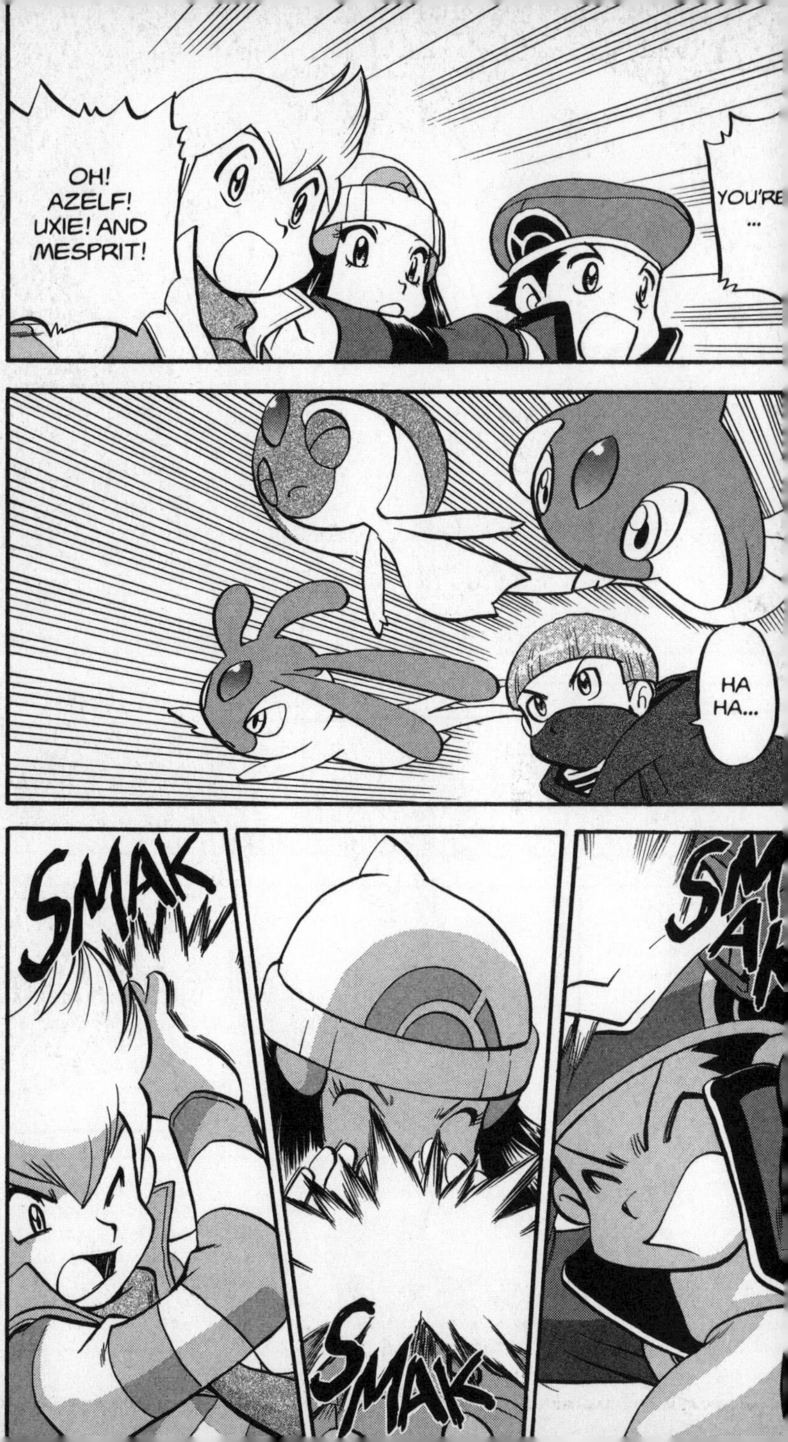
YOU'RE ...
OH! AZELF! UXIE! AND MESPRIT!
HA HA...
SMAK
SMAK
SMAK

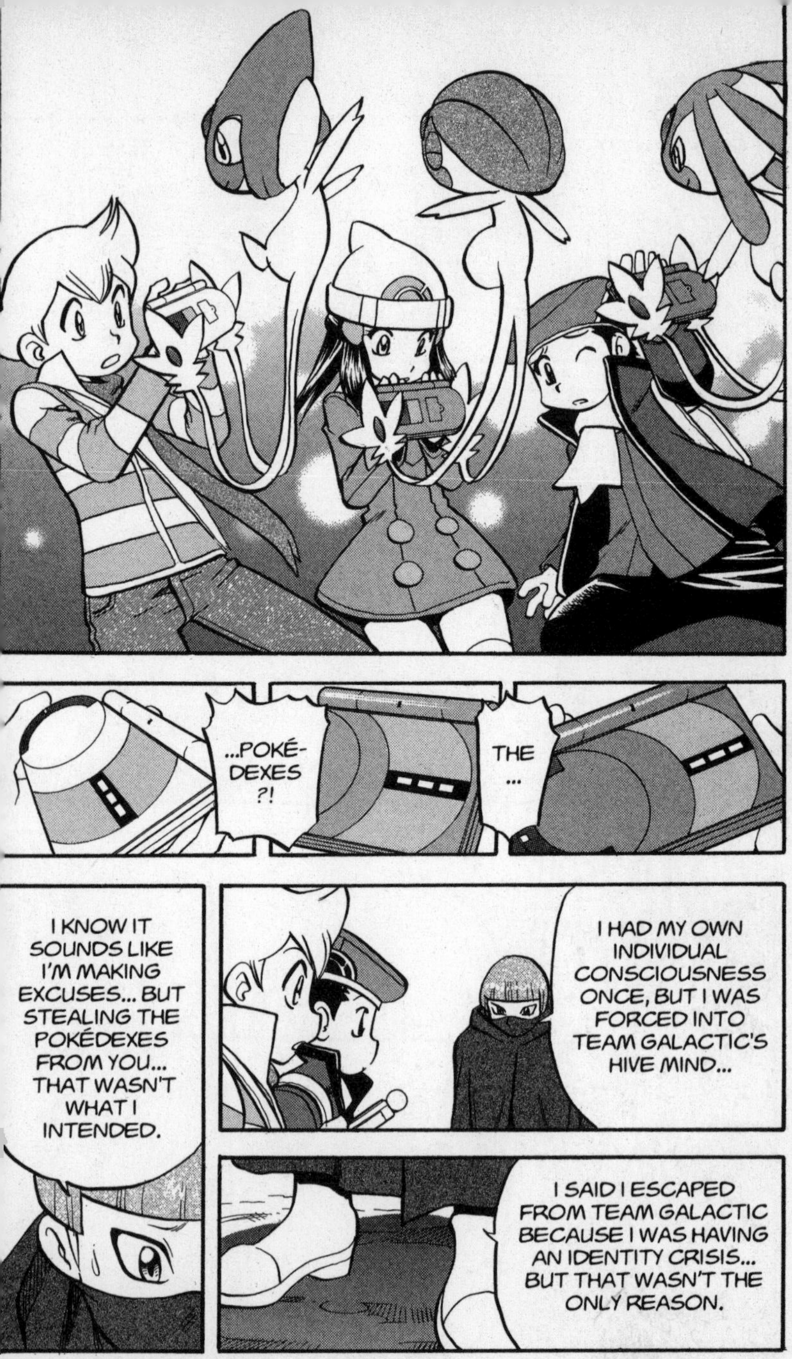
THE ...
...POKÉ-DEXES ?!
I HAD MY OWN INDIVIDUAL CONSCIOUSNESS ONCE, BUT I WAS FORCED INTO TEAM GALACTIC'S HIVE MIND...
I SAID I ESCAPED FROM TEAM GALACTIC BECAUSE I WAS HAVING AN IDENTITY CRISIS... BUT THAT WASN'T THE ONLY REASON.
I KNOW IT SOUNDS LIKE I'M MAKING EXCUSES... BUT STEALING THE POKÉDEXES FROM YOU... THAT WASN'T WHAT I INTENDED.

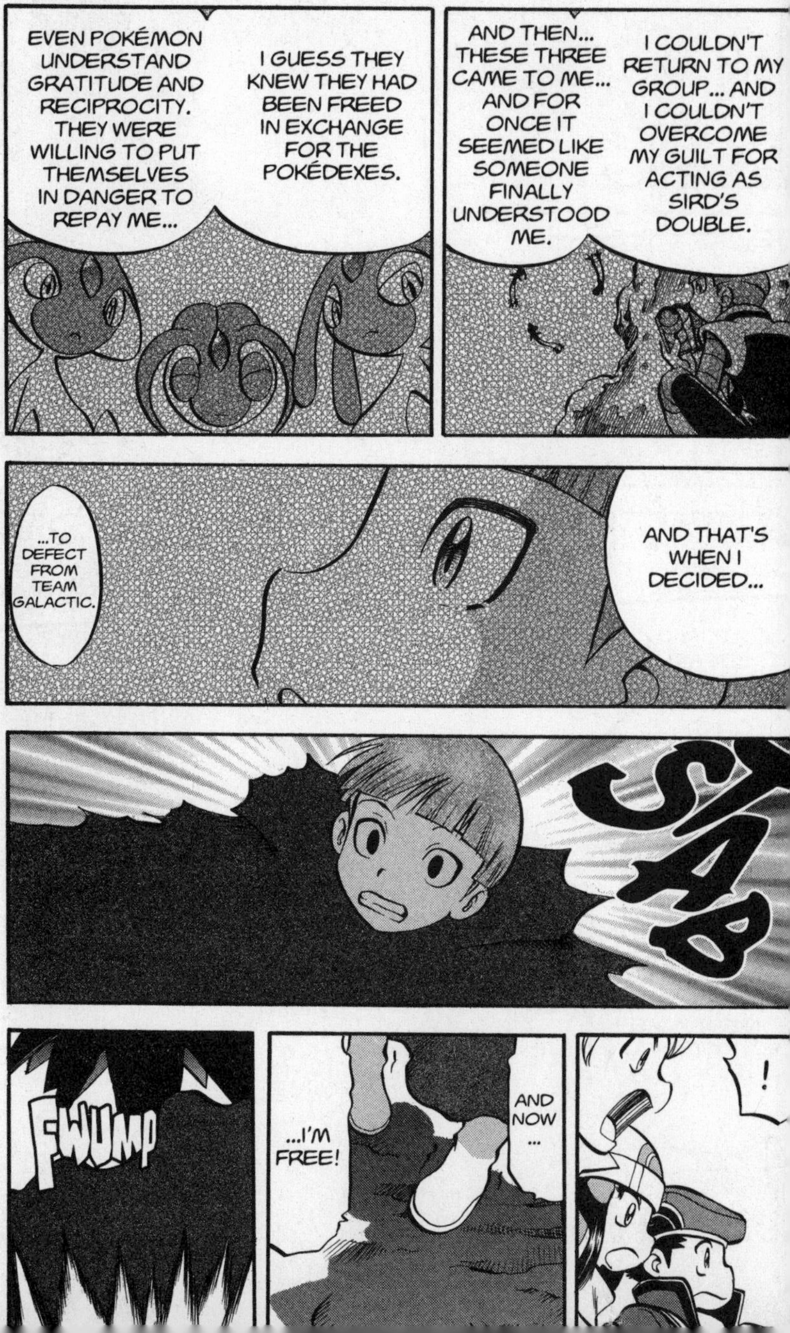
I COULDN'T RETURN TO MY GROUP... AND I COULDN'T OVERCOME MY GUILT FOR ACTING AS SIRD'S DOUBLE.
AND THEN... THESE THREE CAME TO ME... AND FOR ONCE IT SEEMED LIKE SOMEONE FINALLY UNDERSTOOD ME.
I GUESS THEY KNEW THEY HAD BEEN FREED IN EXCHANGE FOR THE POKÉDEXES.
EVEN POKÉMON UNDERSTAND GRATITUDE AND RECIPROCITY. THEY WERE WILLING TO PUT THEMSELVES IN DANGER TO REPAY ME...
AND THAT'S WHEN I DECIDED...
...TO DEFECT FROM TEAM GALACTIC.
STAB
!
AND NOW...
...I'M FREE!
FWUMP

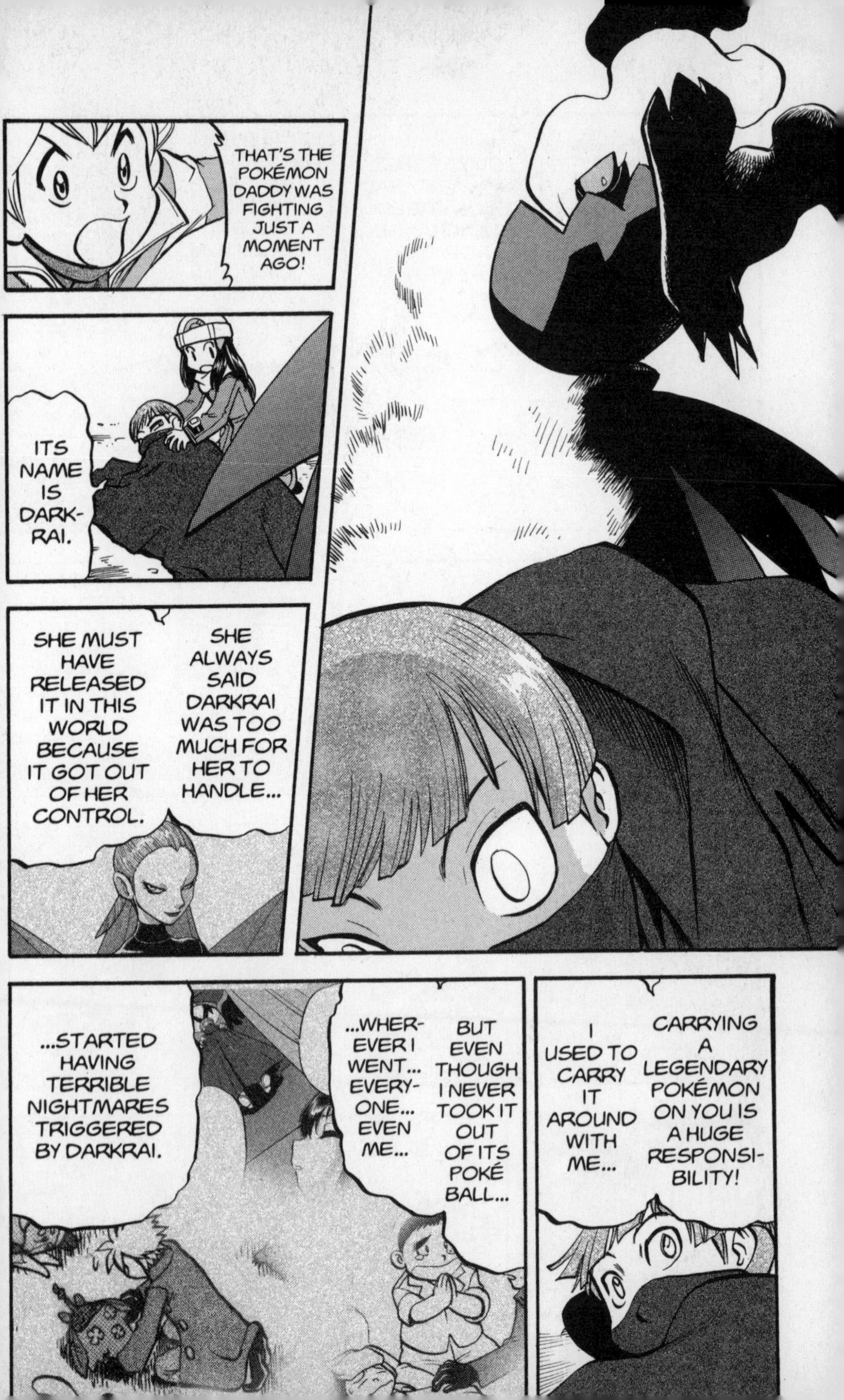
THAT'S THE POKÉMON DADDY WAS FIGHTING JUST A MOMENT AGO!
ITS NAME IS DARK-RAI.
SHE ALWAYS SAID DARKRAI WAS TOO MUCH FOR HER TO HANDLE...
SHE MUST HAVE RELEASED IT IN THIS WORLD BECAUSE IT GOT OUT OF HER CONTROL.
CARRYING A LEGENDARY POKÉMON ON YOU IS A HUGE RESPONSI-BILITY!
I USED TO CARRY IT AROUND WITH ME...
BUT EVEN THOUGH I NEVER TOOK IT OUT OF ITS POKÉ BALL...
...WHER-EVER I WENT... EVERY-ONE... EVEN ME...
...STARTED HAVING TERRIBLE NIGHTMARES TRIGGERED BY DARKRAI.

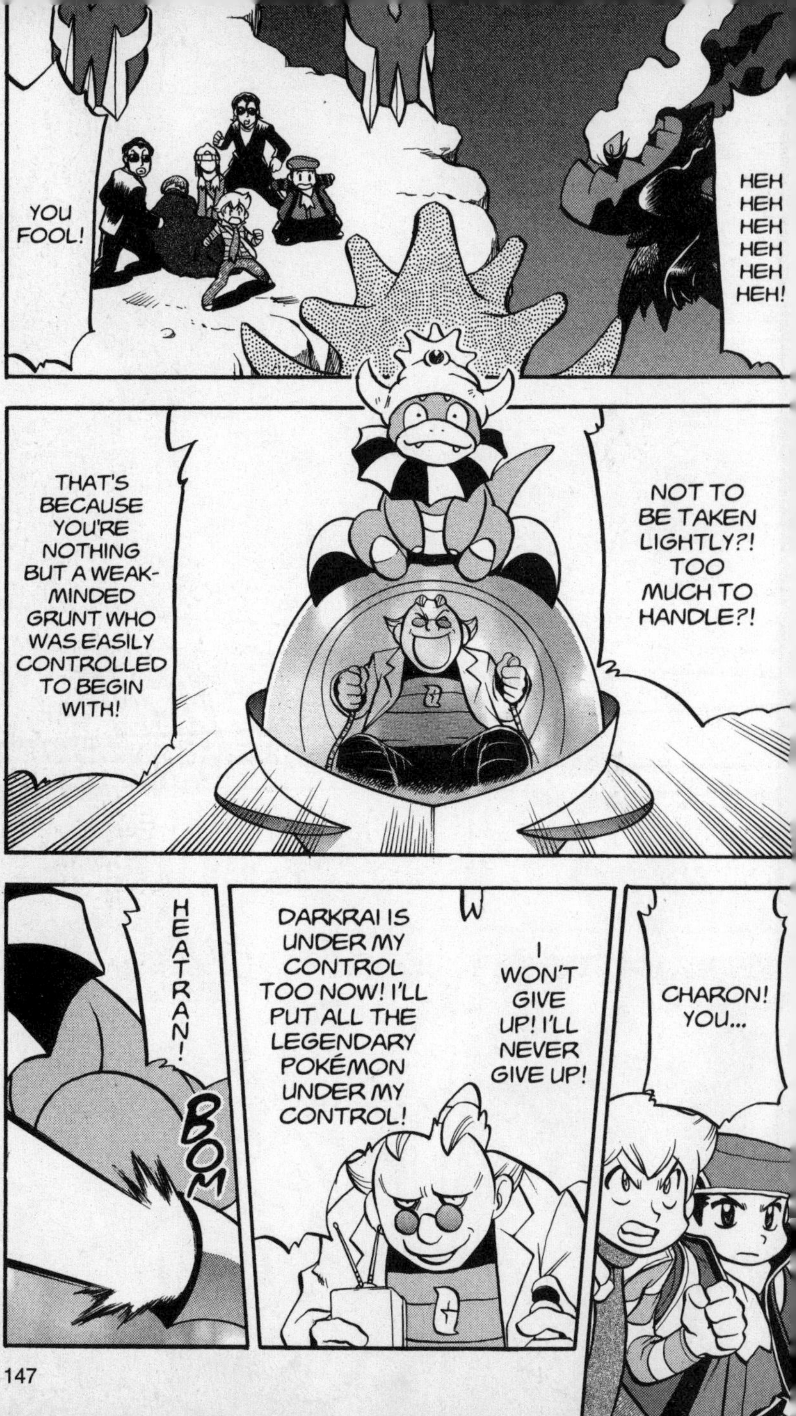
HEH HEH HEH HEH HEH HEH!
YOU FOOL!
NOT TO BE TAKEN LIGHTLY?! TOO MUCH TO HANDLE?!
THAT'S BECAUSE YOU'RE NOTHING BUT A WEAK-MINDED GRUNT WHO WAS EASILY CONTROLLED TO BEGIN WITH!
CHARON! YOU...
I WON'T GIVE UP! I'LL NEVER GIVE UP!
DARKRAI IS UNDER MY CONTROL TOO NOW! I'LL PUT ALL THE LEGENDARY POKÉMON UNDER MY CONTROL!
HEATRAN!
BOM

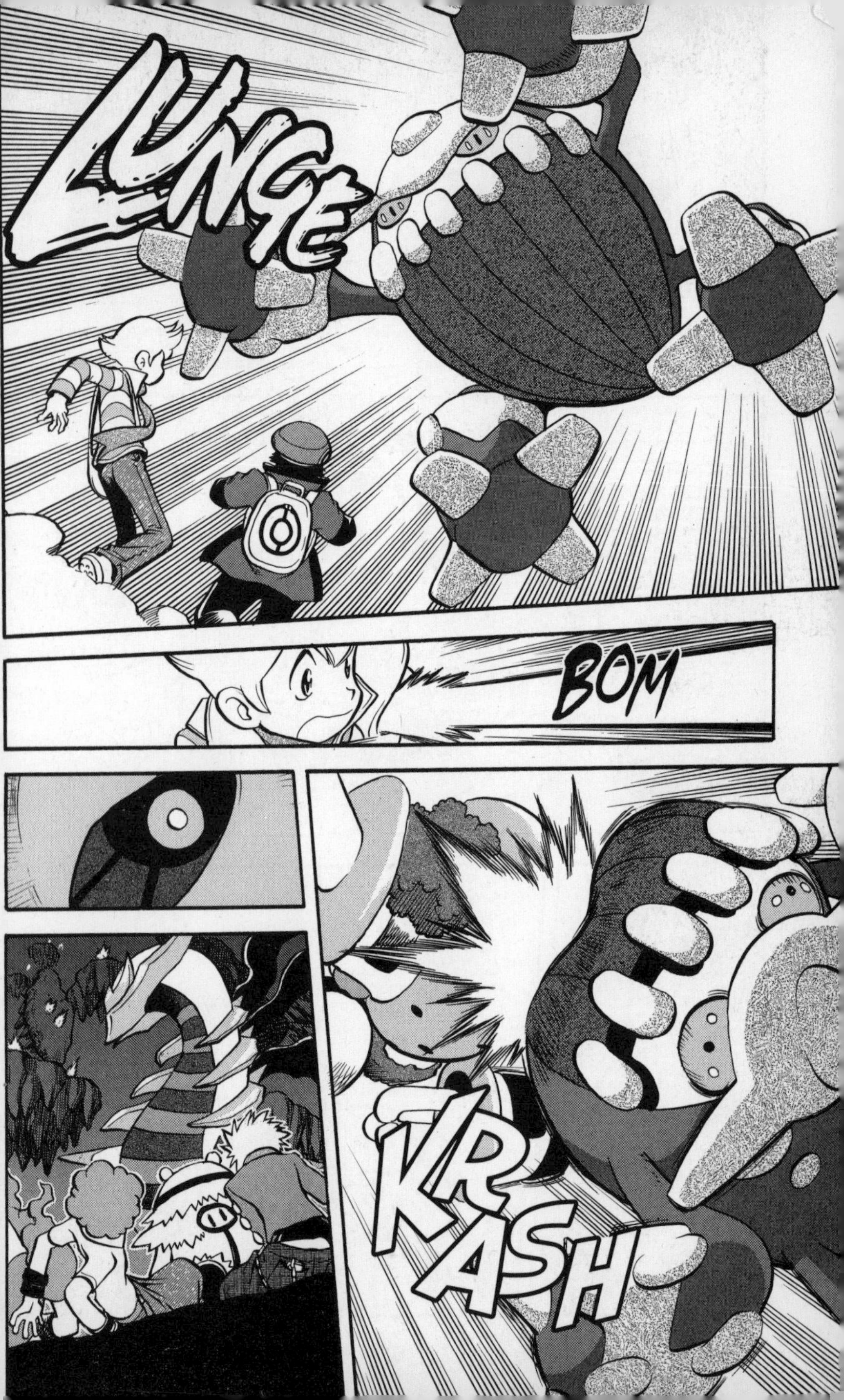
LUNGE
BOM
KRASH

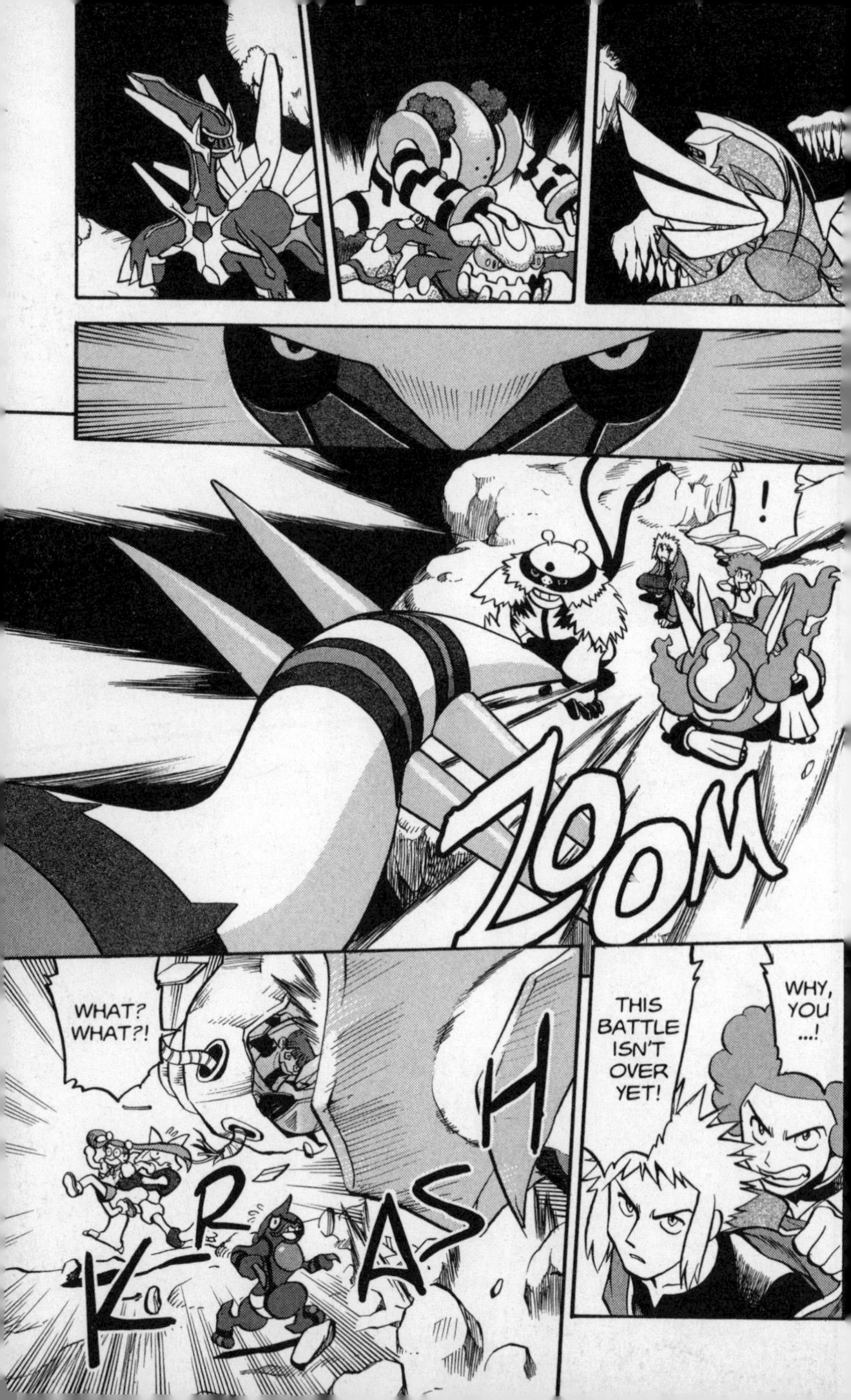
!
ZOOM
WHY, YOU ...!
THIS BATTLE ISN'T OVER YET!
WHAT? WHAT?!
KRASH

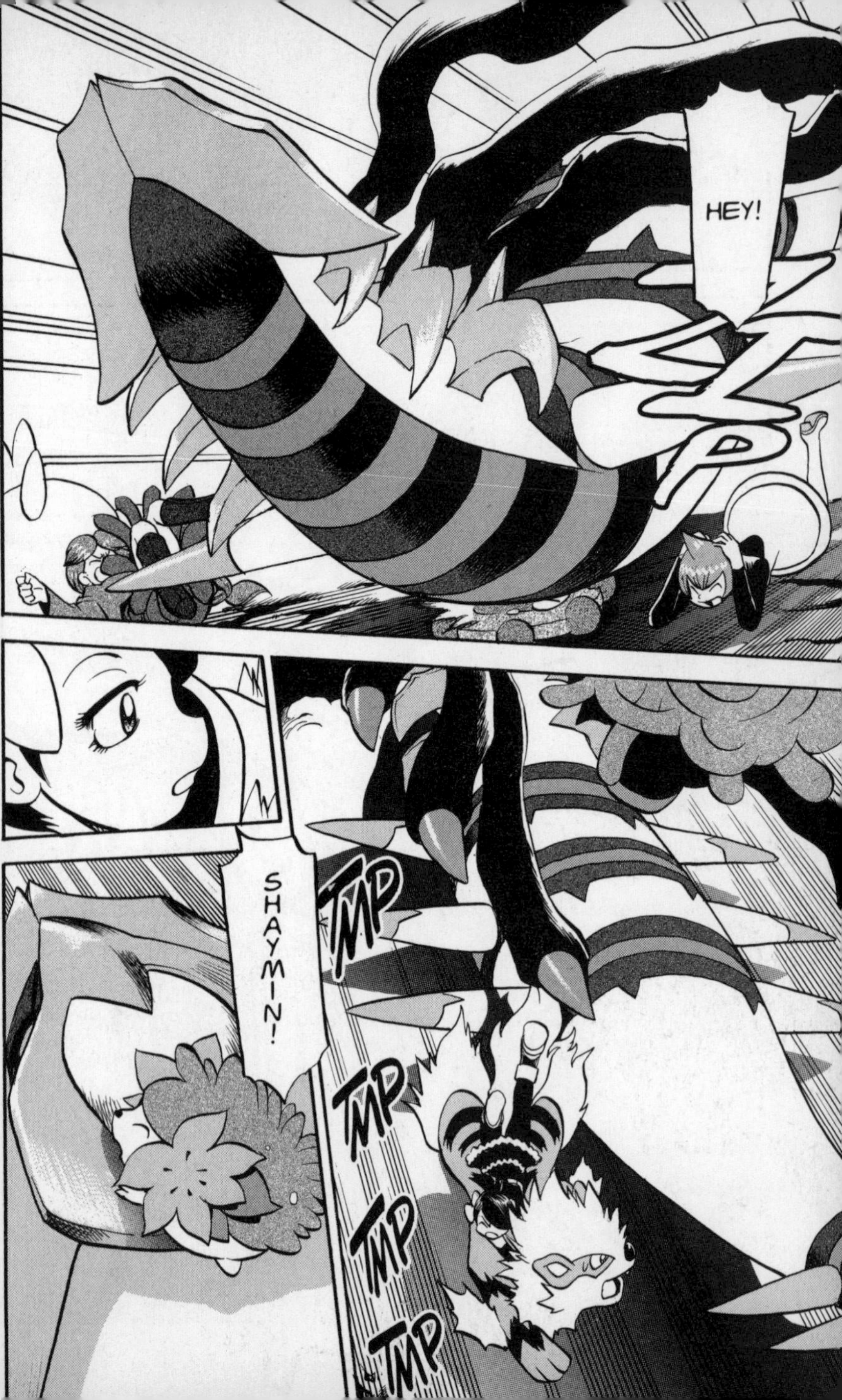
HEY!
SHAYMIN!
TMP
TMP
TMP
TMP

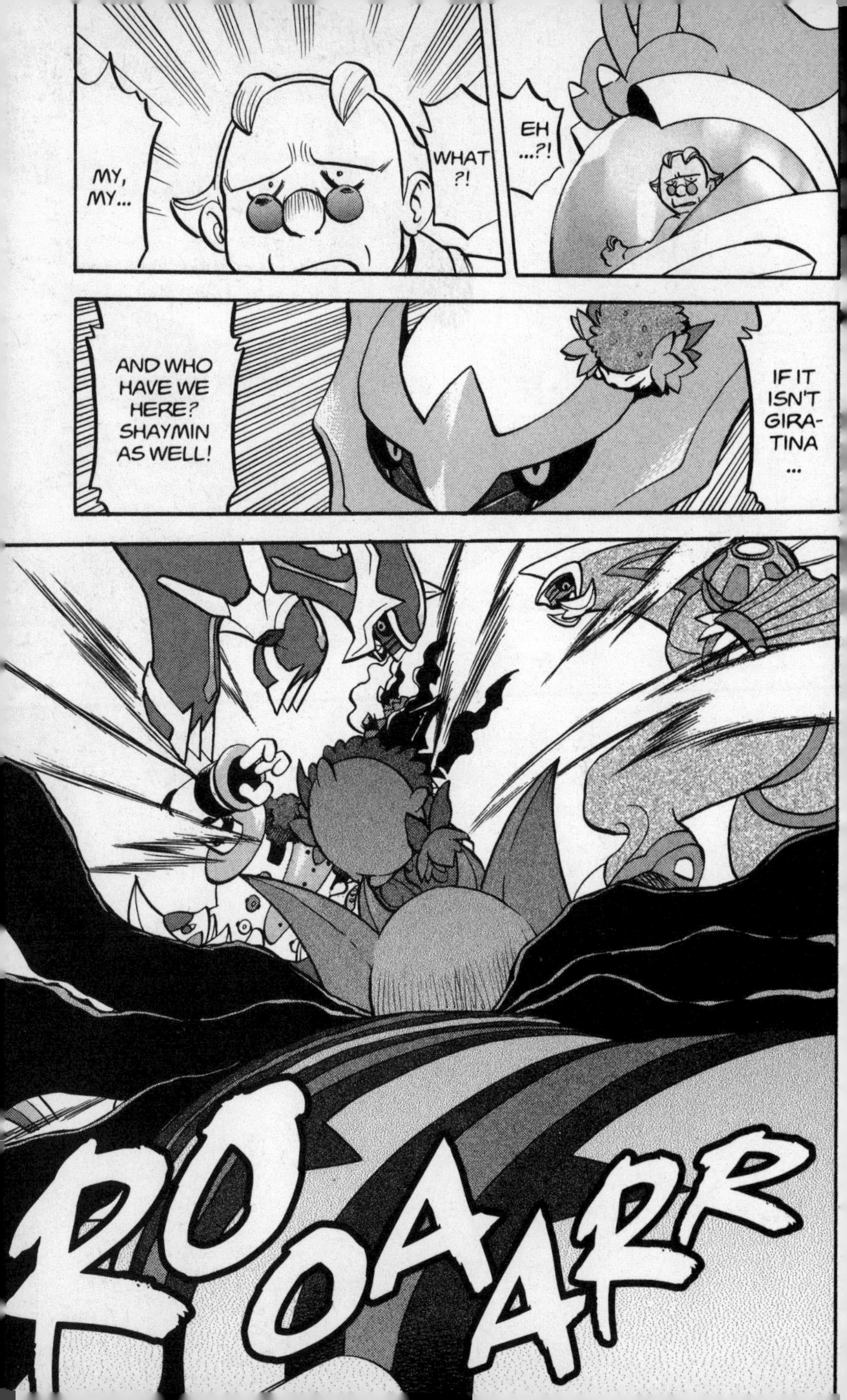
EH ...?!
WHAT ?!
MY, MY...
IF IT ISN'T GIRA-TINA ...
AND WHO HAVE WE HERE? SHAYMIN AS WELL!
ROOAARR

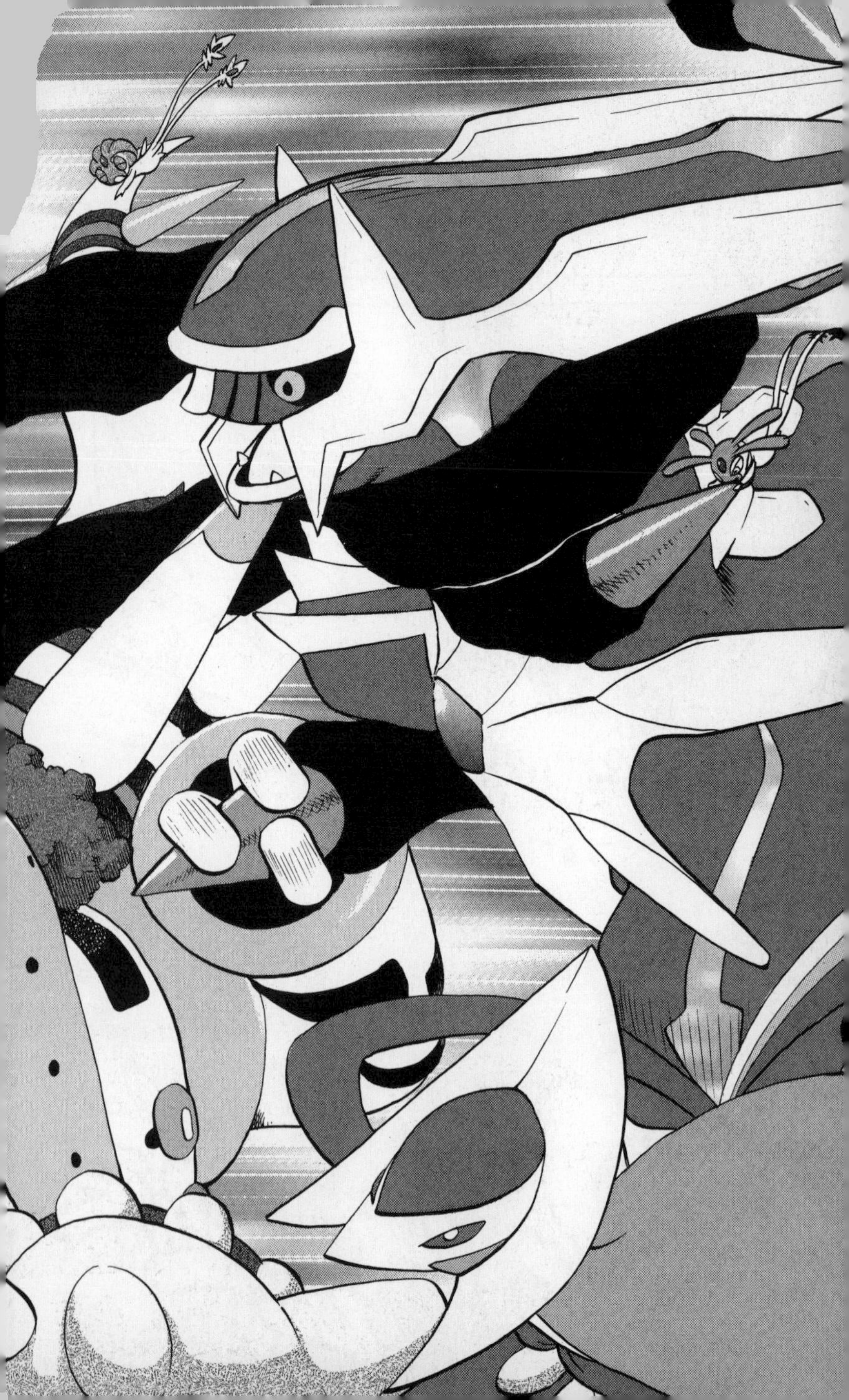

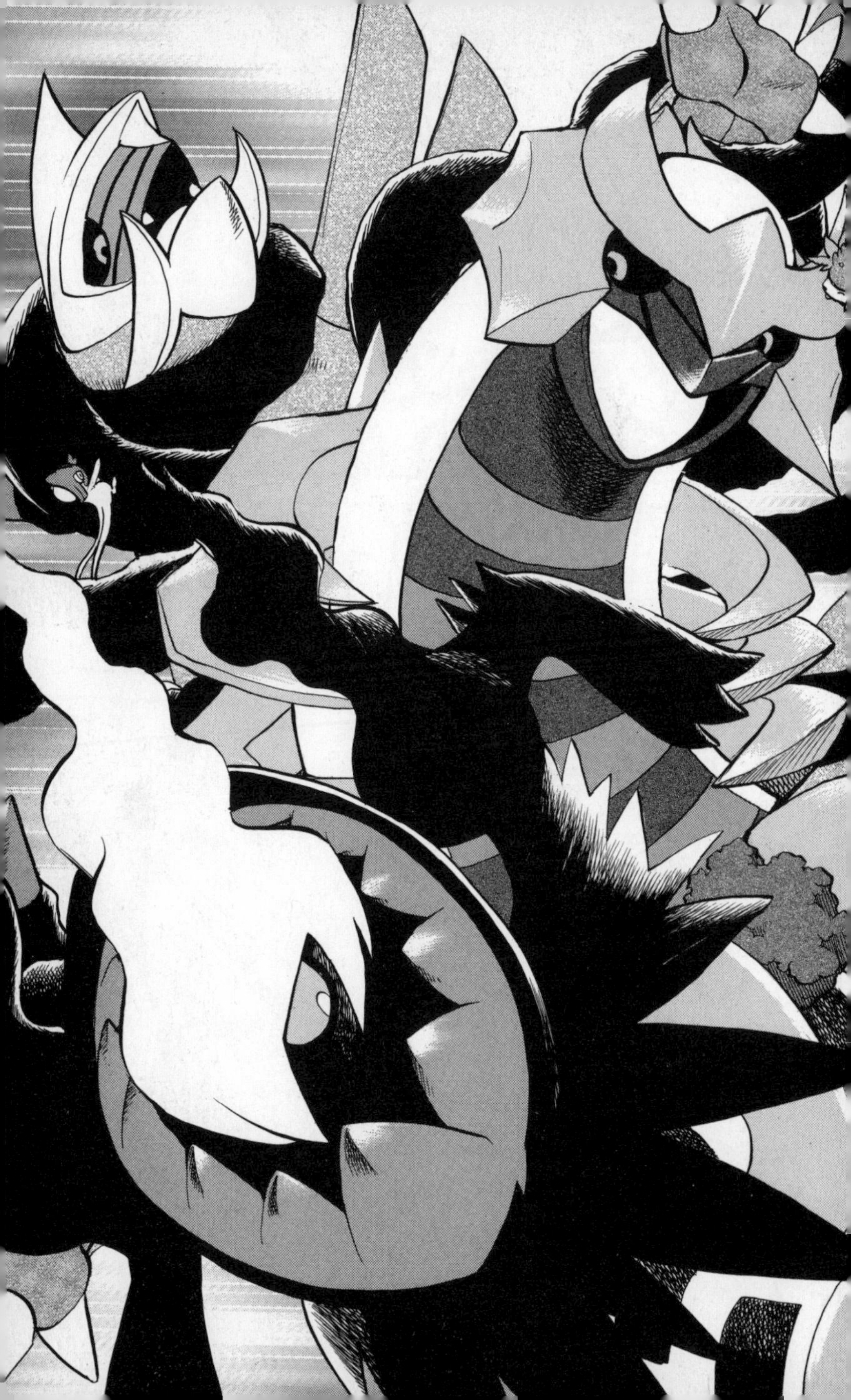

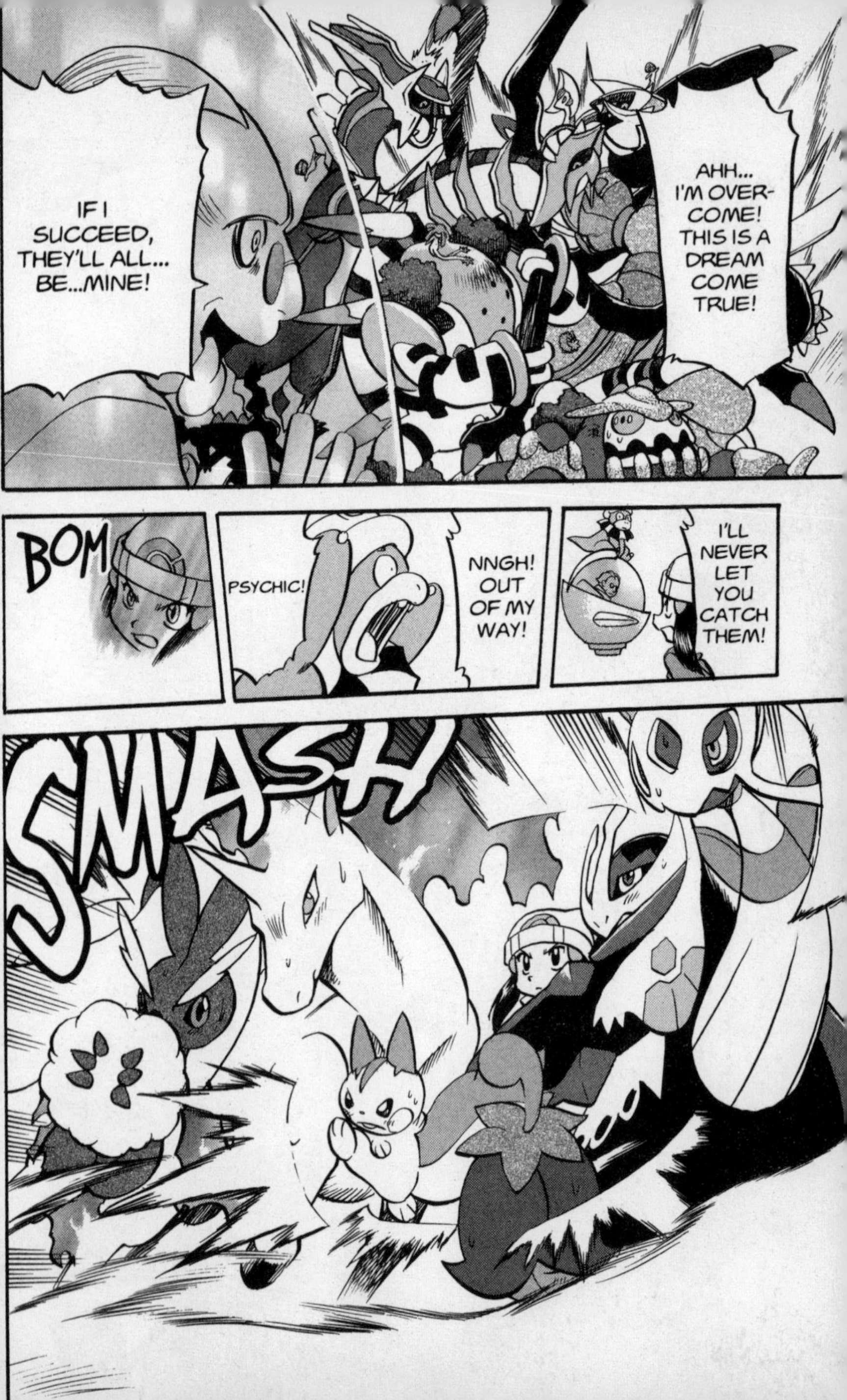
AHH... I'M OVER-COME! THIS IS A DREAM COME TRUE!
IF I SUCCEED, THEY'LL ALL... BE...MINE!
I'LL NEVER LET YOU CATCH THEM!
NNGH! OUT OF MY WAY!
PSYCHIC!
BOM
SMASH

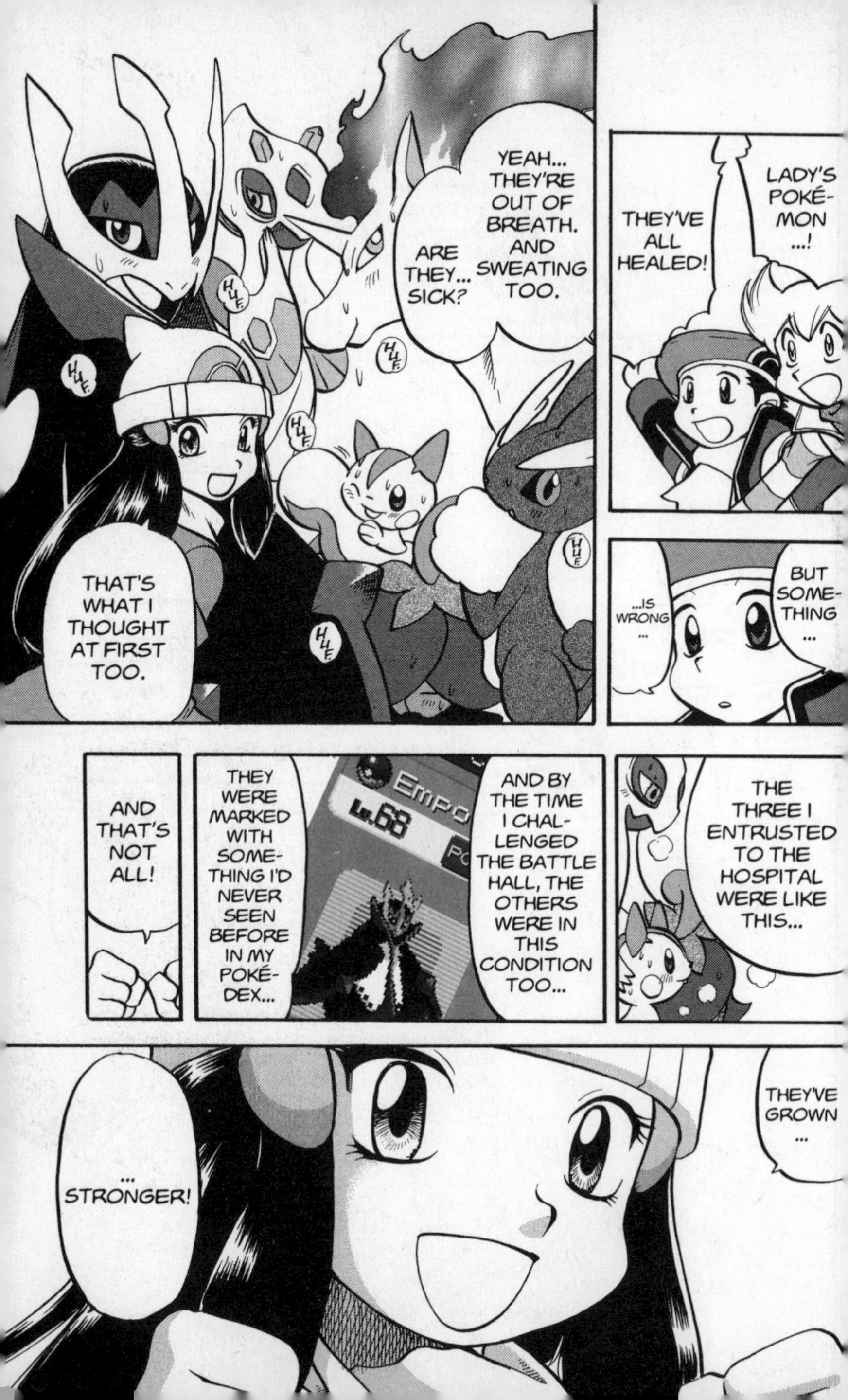
LADY'S POKÉ-MON ...!
THEY'VE ALL HEALED!
BUT SOME-THING ...
...IS WRONG ...
YEAH... THEY'RE OUT OF BREATH. AND SWEATING TOO.
ARE THEY... SICK?
HUF
HUF
HUF
HUF
HUF
HUF
THAT'S WHAT I THOUGHT AT FIRST TOO.
THE THREE I ENTRUSTED TO THE HOSPITAL WERE LIKE THIS...
AND BY THE TIME I CHAL-LENGED THE BATTLE HALL, THE OTHERS WERE IN THIS CONDITION TOO...
THEY WERE MARKED WITH SOME-THING I'D NEVER SEEN BEFORE IN MY POKÉ-DEX...
AND THAT'S NOT ALL!
THEY'VE GROWN ...
... STRONGER!

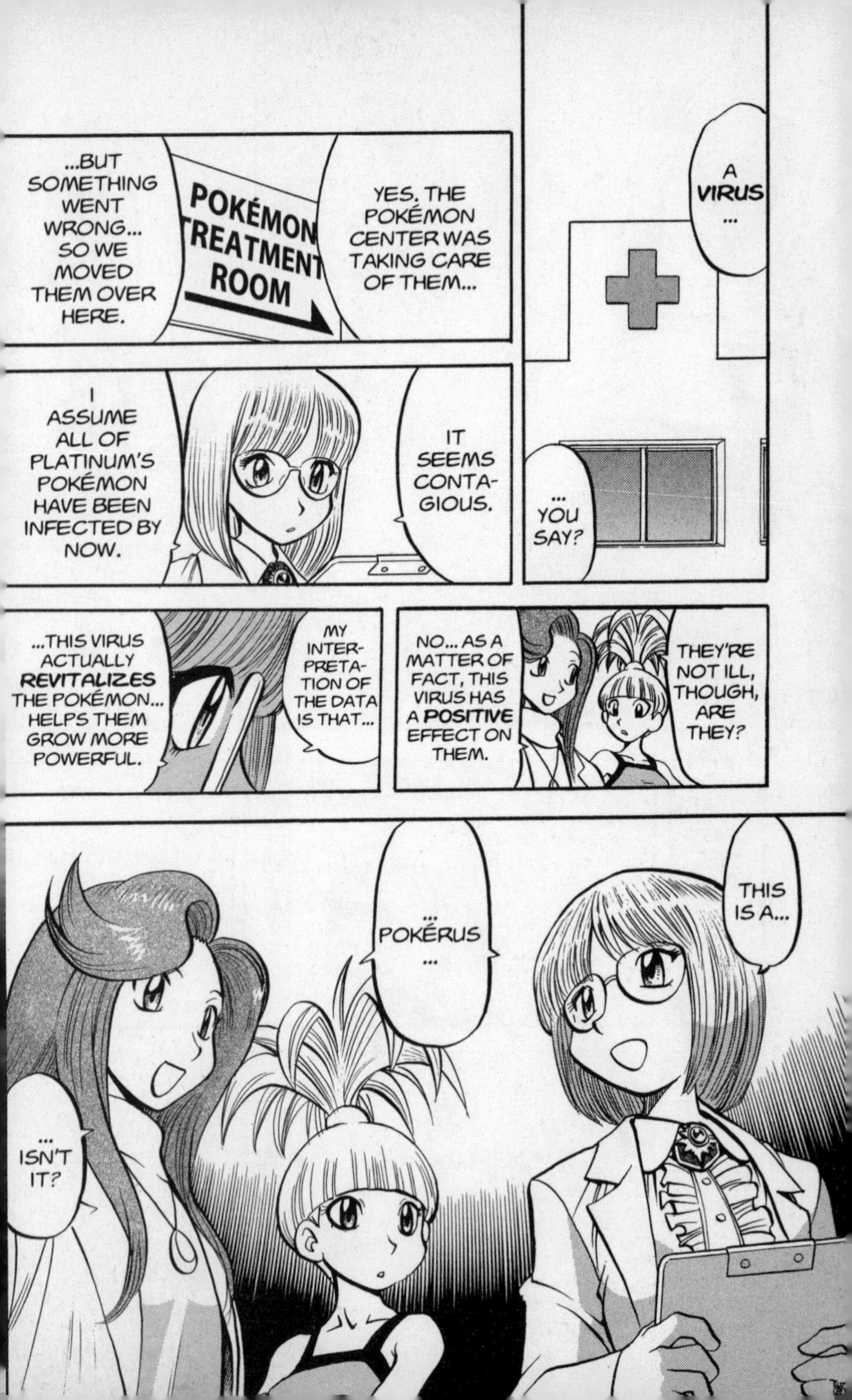
A VIRUS...
...YOU SAY?
YES. THE POKÉMON CENTER WAS TAKING CARE OF THEM...
POKÉMON TREATMENT ROOM
...BUT SOMETHING WENT WRONG... SO WE MOVED THEM OVER HERE.
IT SEEMS CONTAGIOUS.
I ASSUME ALL OF PLATINUM'S POKÉMON HAVE BEEN INFECTED BY NOW.
THEY'RE NOT ILL, THOUGH, ARE THEY?
NO... AS A MATTER OF FACT, THIS VIRUS HAS A POSITIVE EFFECT ON THEM.
MY INTERPRETATION OF THE DATA IS THAT...
...THIS VIRUS ACTUALLY REVITALIZES THE POKÉMON... HELPS THEM GROW MORE POWERFUL.
THIS IS A...
...POKÉRUS...
...ISN'T IT?

Pokémon Adventures Diamond and Pearl Platinum

CHARACTER PROFILE

PLATINUM

LADY

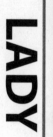

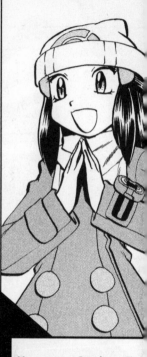

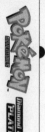

THE DAUGHTER OF THE PRESTIGIOUS BERLITZ FAMILY, WHO HAVE LIVED IN THE SINNOH REGION FOR OVER 200 YEARS. TRADITION DICTATES THAT THE HEIR OF THE FAMILY TRAVEL TO MT. CORONET TO GATHER MATERIALS TO CREATE A SPECIAL EMBLEM SHAPED LIKE THE FAMILY CREST. PLATINUM HEADS OUT ON THIS TRADITIONAL JOURNEY AND GETS CAUGHT UP IN AN EPIC BATTLE. NOW SHE HAS DISCOVERED THE SECRET BEHIND A PLACE KNOWN AS THE DISTORTION WORLD. SHE USED TO BE A SHELTERED GIRL WITH LITTLE KNOWLEDGE OF THE OUTSIDE WORLD, BUT SHE HAS GAINED MUCH PRACTICAL EXPERIENCE ON HER JOURNEY WITH DIA AND PEARL. HER BONDS WITH HER POKÉMON HAVE GROWN STRONGER AND SHE HAS GATHERED ALL EIGHT GYM BADGES AS WELL. AS A MEMBER OF THE SCHOLARLY BERLITZ FAMILY, SHE BROUGHT WITH HER AN ABUNDANT KNOWLEDGE THAT HAS BEEN A GREAT ASSET ON THEIR JOURNEY. HER REAL NAME IS PLATINUM BERLITZ.

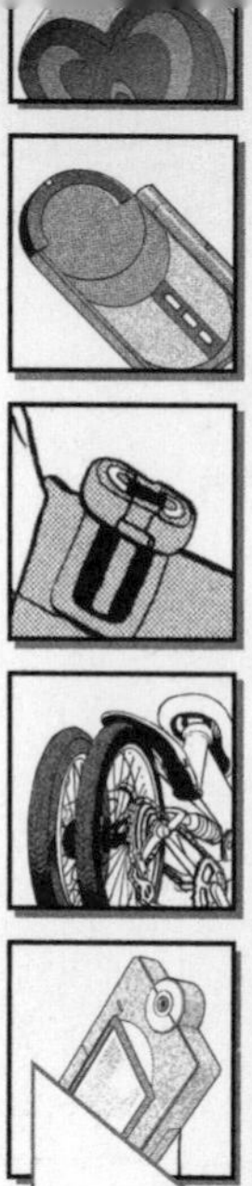

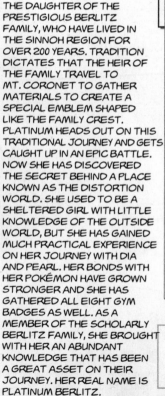

Hometown: Sandgem Tow

Birthday: October 27th

Age: 12 (As of Adventure 10

Blood-type: A

Special Skill: Reading

Family: Mother (Yanase), Father (Mr. Berlitz)

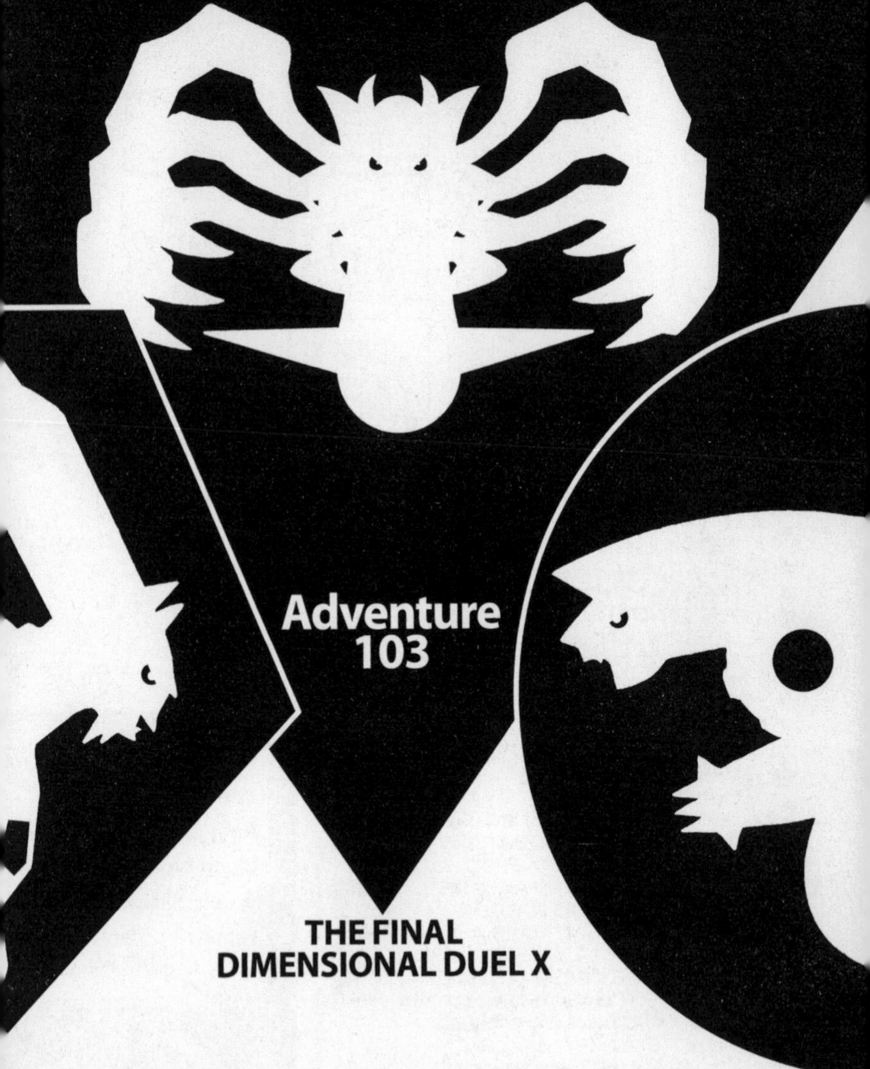

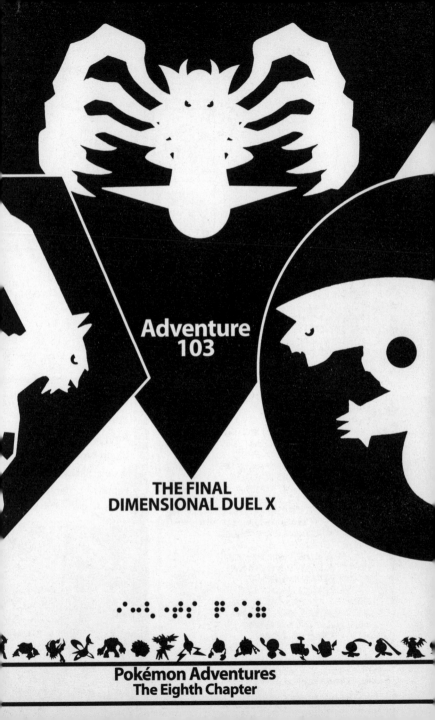

Adventure 103

THE FINAL DIMENSIONAL DUEL X

Pokémon Adventures
The Eighth Chapter

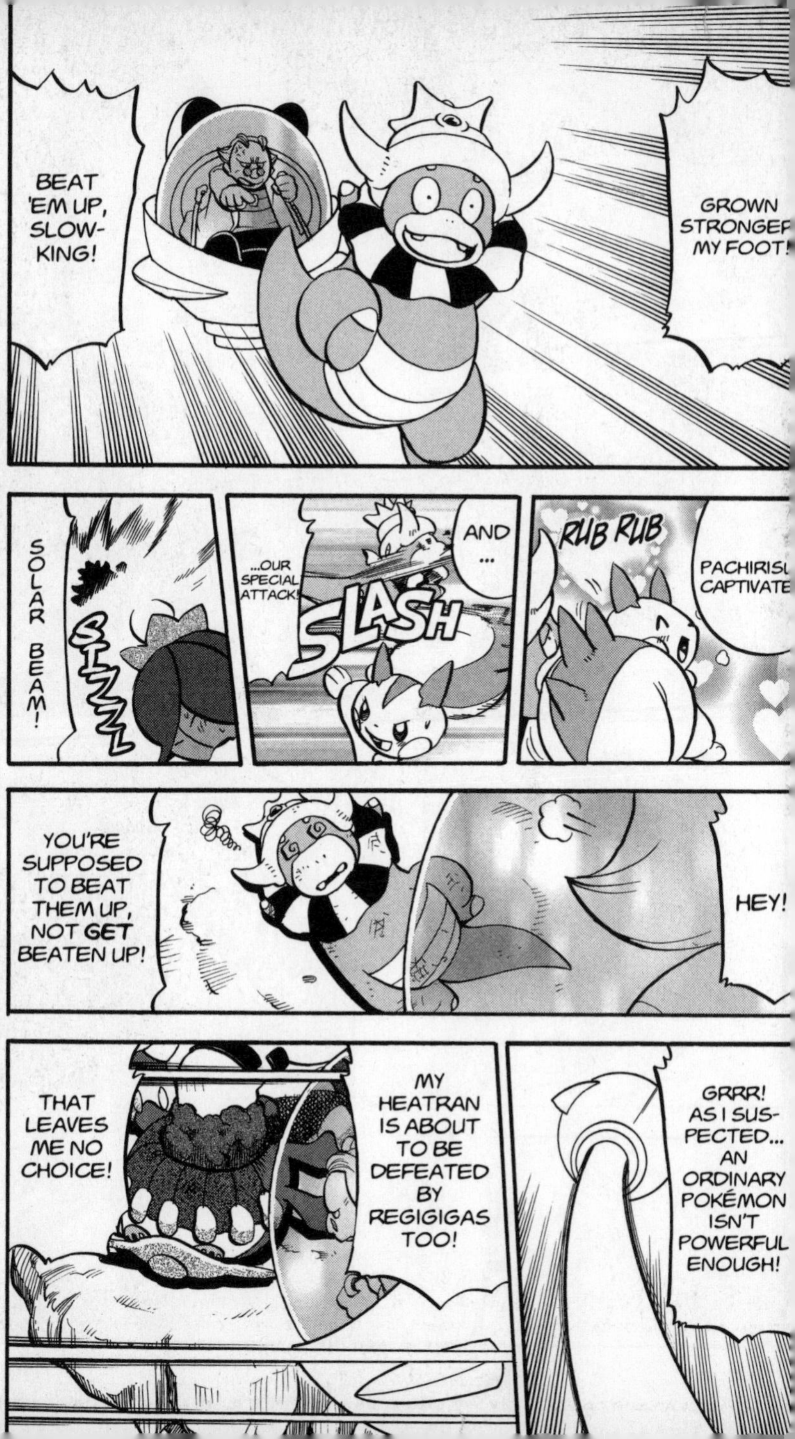
GROWN STRONGER MY FOOT!
BEAT 'EM UP, SLOW-KING!
RUB RUB
PACHIRISU CAPTIVATE
AND ...
...OUR SPECIAL ATTACK!
SLASH
SOLAR BEAM!
SIZZZL
HEY!
YOU'RE SUPPOSED TO BEAT THEM UP, NOT GET BEATEN UP!
GRRR! AS I SUS-PECTED... AN ORDINARY POKÉMON ISN'T POWERFUL ENOUGH!
MY HEATRAN IS ABOUT TO BE DEFEATED BY REGIGIGAS TOO!
THAT LEAVES ME NO CHOICE!

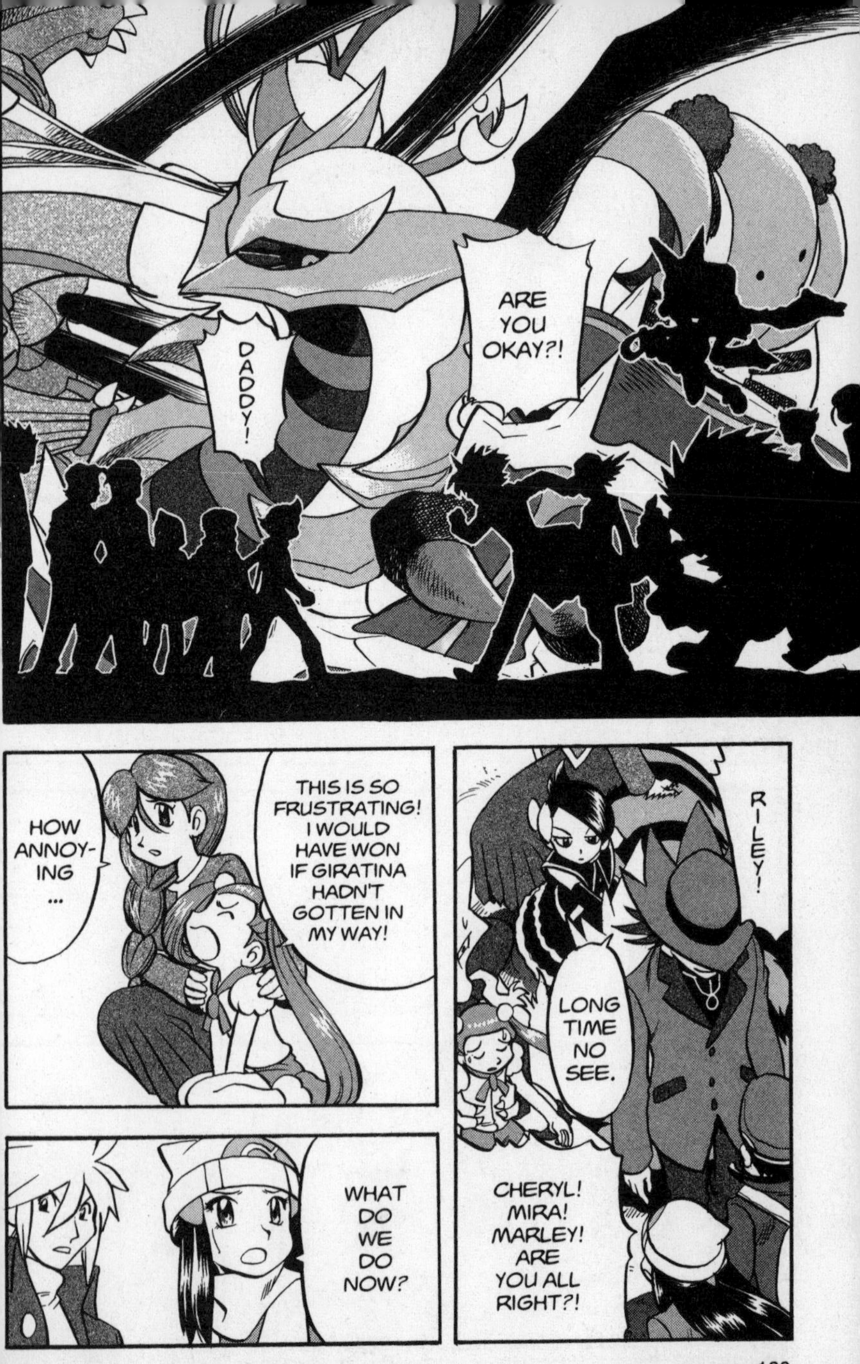
ARE YOU OKAY?!
DADDY!
RILEY!
LONG TIME NO SEE.
CHERYL! MIRA! MARLEY! ARE YOU ALL RIGHT?!
THIS IS SO FRUSTRATING! I WOULD HAVE WON IF GIRATINA HADN'T GOTTEN IN MY WAY!
HOW ANNOY-ING...
WHAT DO WE DO NOW?

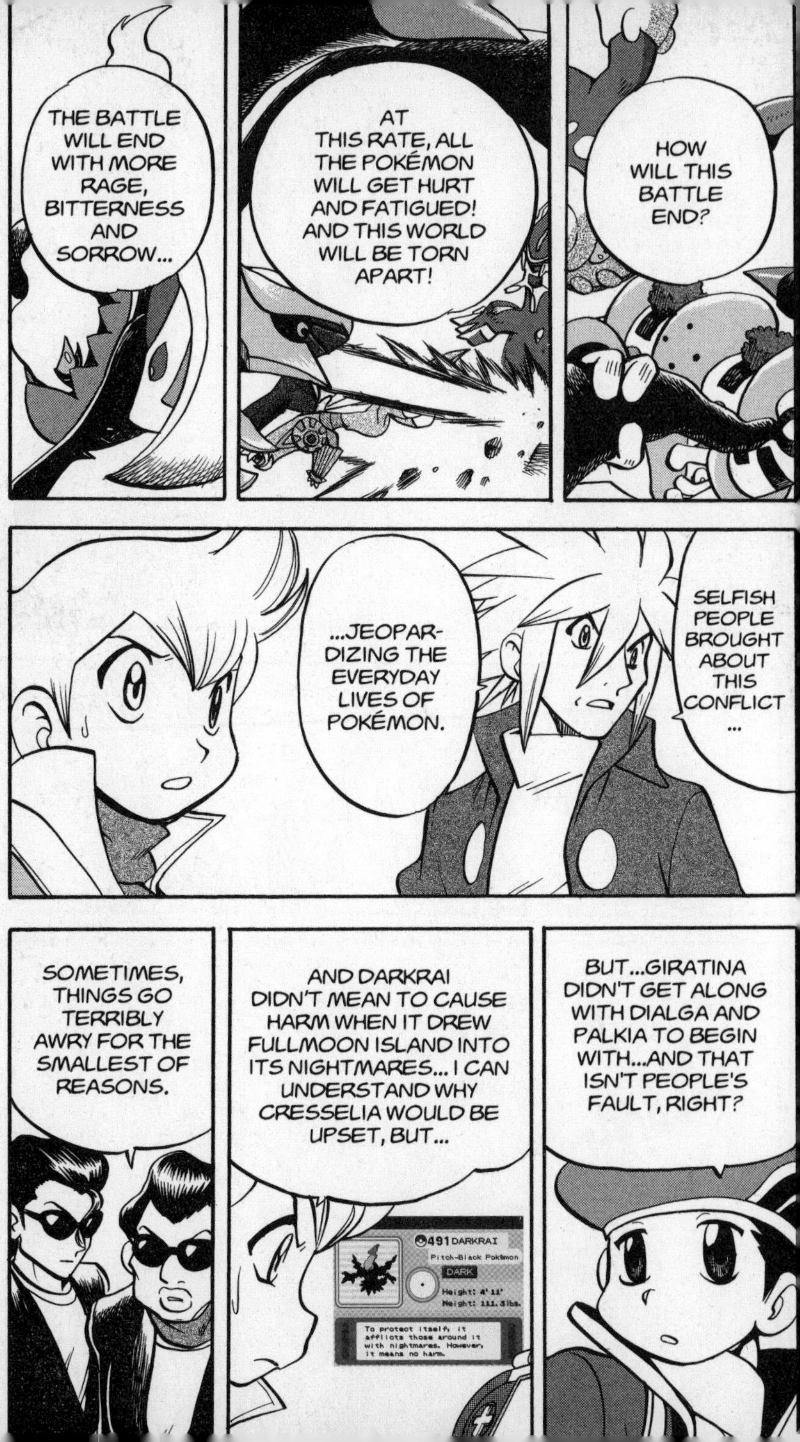
HOW WILL THIS BATTLE END?
AT THIS RATE, ALL THE POKÉMON WILL GET HURT AND FATIGUED! AND THIS WORLD WILL BE TORN APART!
THE BATTLE WILL END WITH MORE RAGE, BITTERNESS AND SORROW...
SELFISH PEOPLE BROUGHT ABOUT THIS CONFLICT ...
...JEOPARDIZING THE EVERYDAY LIVES OF POKÉMON.
BUT...GIRATINA DIDN'T GET ALONG WITH DIALGA AND PALKIA TO BEGIN WITH...AND THAT ISN'T PEOPLE'S FAULT, RIGHT?
AND DARKRAI DIDN'T MEAN TO CAUSE HARM WHEN IT DREW FULLMOON ISLAND INTO ITS NIGHTMARES... I CAN UNDERSTAND WHY CRESSELIA WOULD BE UPSET, BUT...
491 DARKRAI
Pitch-Black Pokémon
DARK
Height: 4'11"
Weight: 111.3 lbs.
To protect itself, it afflicts those around it with nightmares. However, it means no harm.
SOMETIMES, THINGS GO TERRIBLY AWRY FOR THE SMALLEST OF REASONS.

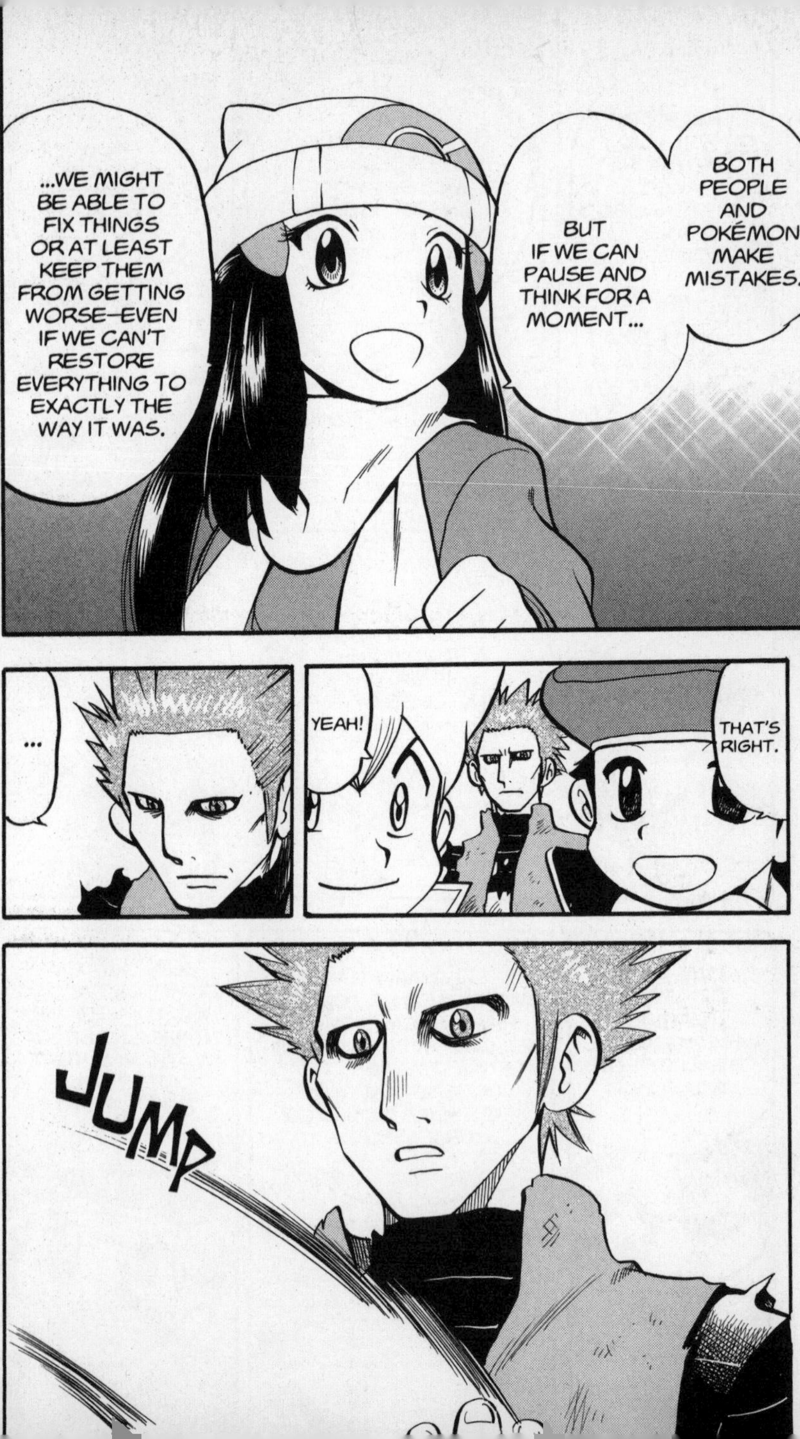
BOTH PEOPLE AND POKÉMON MAKE MISTAKES.
BUT IF WE CAN PAUSE AND THINK FOR A MOMENT...
...WE MIGHT BE ABLE TO FIX THINGS OR AT LEAST KEEP THEM FROM GETTING WORSE—EVEN IF WE CAN'T RESTORE EVERYTHING TO EXACTLY THE WAY IT WAS.
THAT'S RIGHT.
YEAH!
...
JUMP

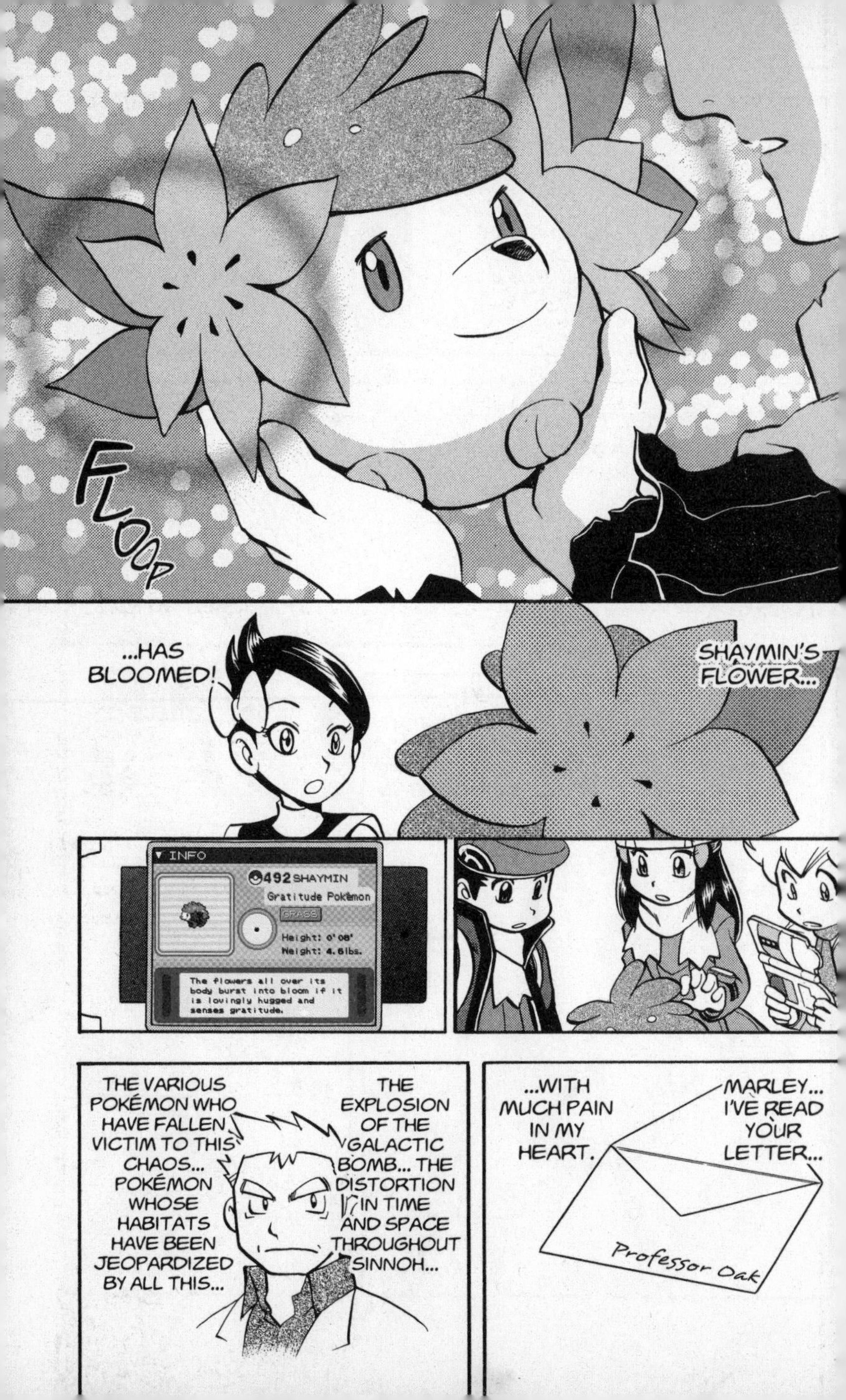
FLOOP
SHAYMIN'S FLOWER...
...HAS BLOOMED!
▼ INFO
492 SHAYMIN
Gratitude Pokémon
GRASS
Height: 0'08"
Weight: 4.6lbs.
The flowers all over its body burst into bloom if it is lovingly hugged and senses gratitude.
MARLEY... I'VE READ YOUR LETTER...
...WITH MUCH PAIN IN MY HEART.
Professor Oak
THE EXPLOSION OF THE GALACTIC BOMB... THE DISTORTION IN TIME AND SPACE THROUGHOUT SINNOH...
THE VARIOUS POKÉMON WHO HAVE FALLEN VICTIM TO THIS CHAOS... POKÉMON WHOSE HABITATS HAVE BEEN JEOPARDIZED BY ALL THIS...

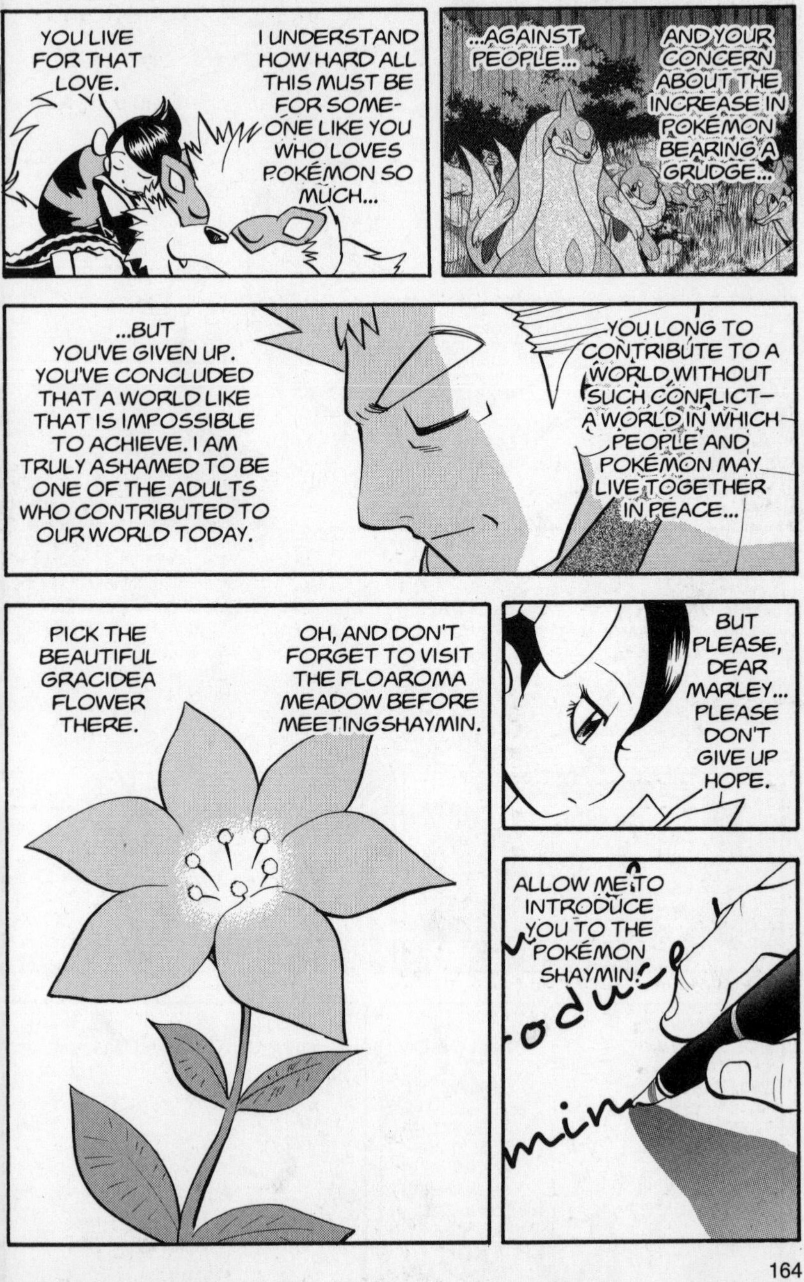
AND YOUR CONCERN ABOUT THE INCREASE IN POKÉMON BEARING A GRUDGE...
...AGAINST PEOPLE...
I UNDERSTAND HOW HARD ALL THIS MUST BE FOR SOMEONE LIKE YOU WHO LOVES POKÉMON SO MUCH...
YOU LIVE FOR THAT LOVE.
YOU LONG TO CONTRIBUTE TO A WORLD WITHOUT SUCH CONFLICT—A WORLD IN WHICH PEOPLE AND POKÉMON MAY LIVE TOGETHER IN PEACE...
...BUT YOU'VE GIVEN UP. YOU'VE CONCLUDED THAT A WORLD LIKE THAT IS IMPOSSIBLE TO ACHIEVE. I AM TRULY ASHAMED TO BE ONE OF THE ADULTS WHO CONTRIBUTED TO OUR WORLD TODAY.
BUT PLEASE, DEAR MARLEY... PLEASE DON'T GIVE UP HOPE.
ALLOW ME TO INTRODUCE YOU TO THE POKÉMON SHAYMIN.
OH, AND DON'T FORGET TO VISIT THE FLOAROMA MEADOW BEFORE MEETING SHAYMIN.
PICK THE BEAUTIFUL GRACIDEA FLOWER THERE.

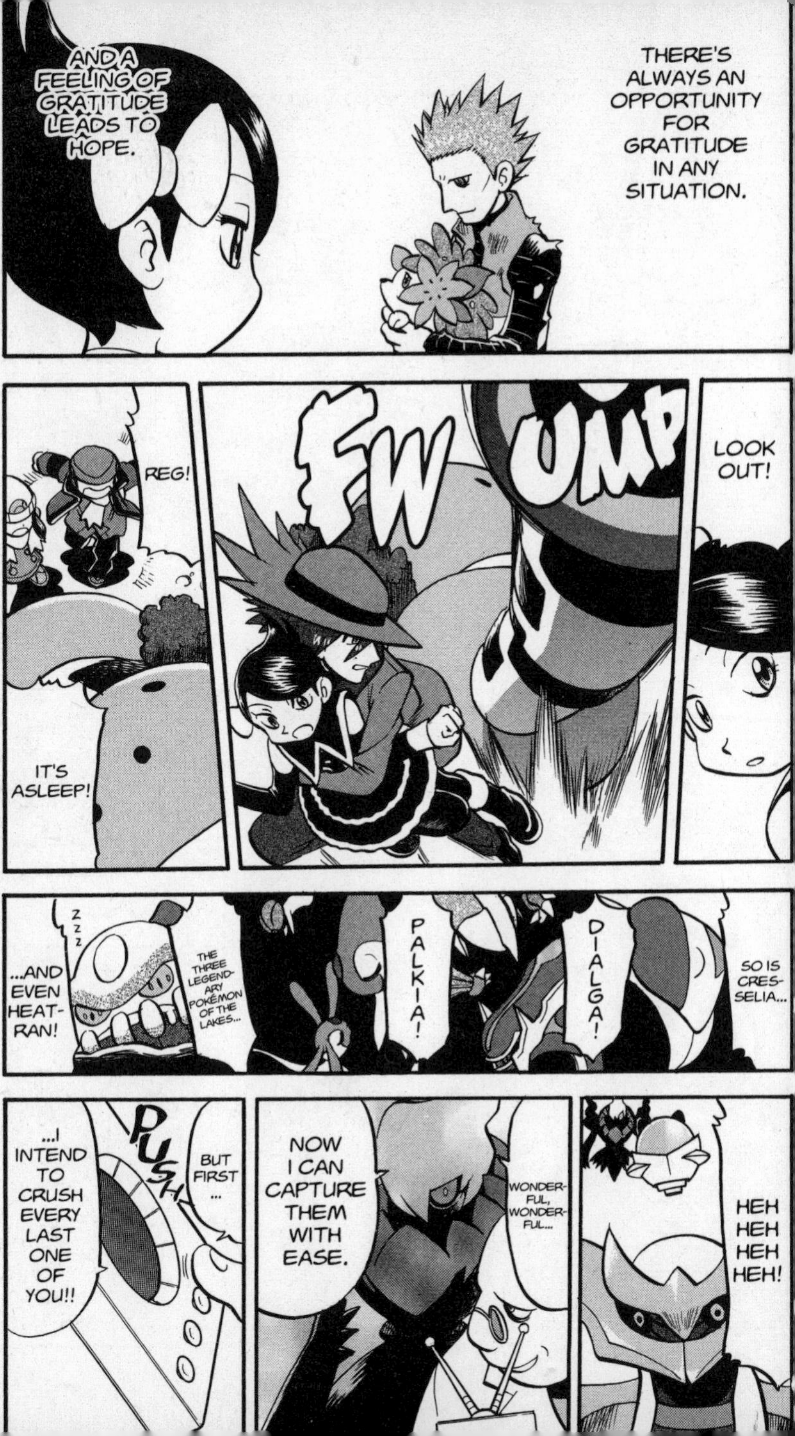
THERE'S ALWAYS AN OPPORTUNITY FOR GRATITUDE IN ANY SITUATION.
AND A FEELING OF GRATITUDE LEADS TO HOPE.
LOOK OUT!
FWUMP
REG!
IT'S ASLEEP!
SO IS CRES-SELIA...
DIALGA!
PALKIA!
THE THREE LEGENDARY POKÉMON OF THE LAKES...
...AND EVEN HEATRAN!
Z Z Z
HEH HEH HEH HEH!
WONDERFUL, WONDERFUL...
NOW I CAN CAPTURE THEM WITH EASE.
BUT FIRST...
PUSH
...I INTEND TO CRUSH EVERY LAST ONE OF YOU!!

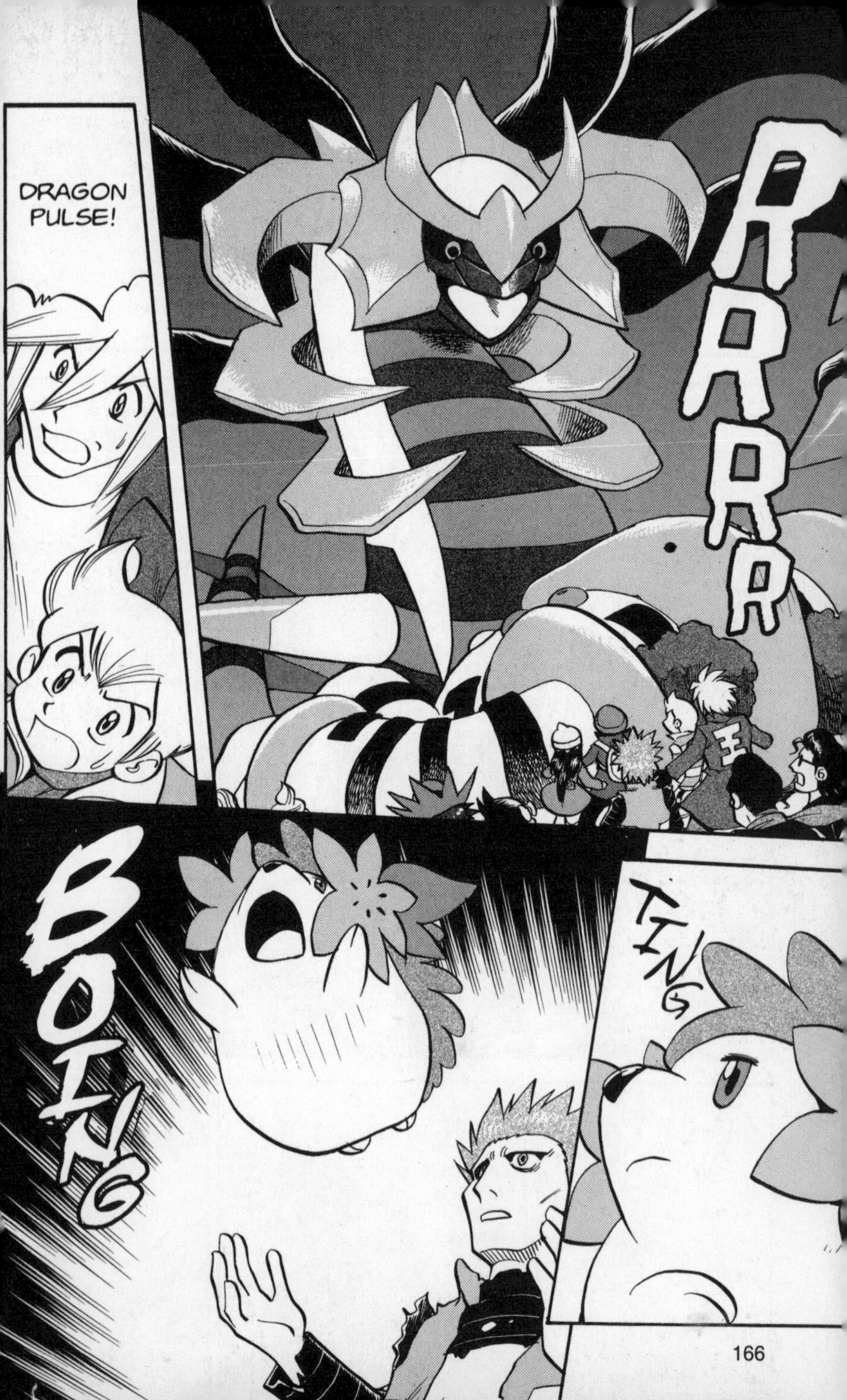
RRRRR
DRAGON PULSE!
TING
BOING

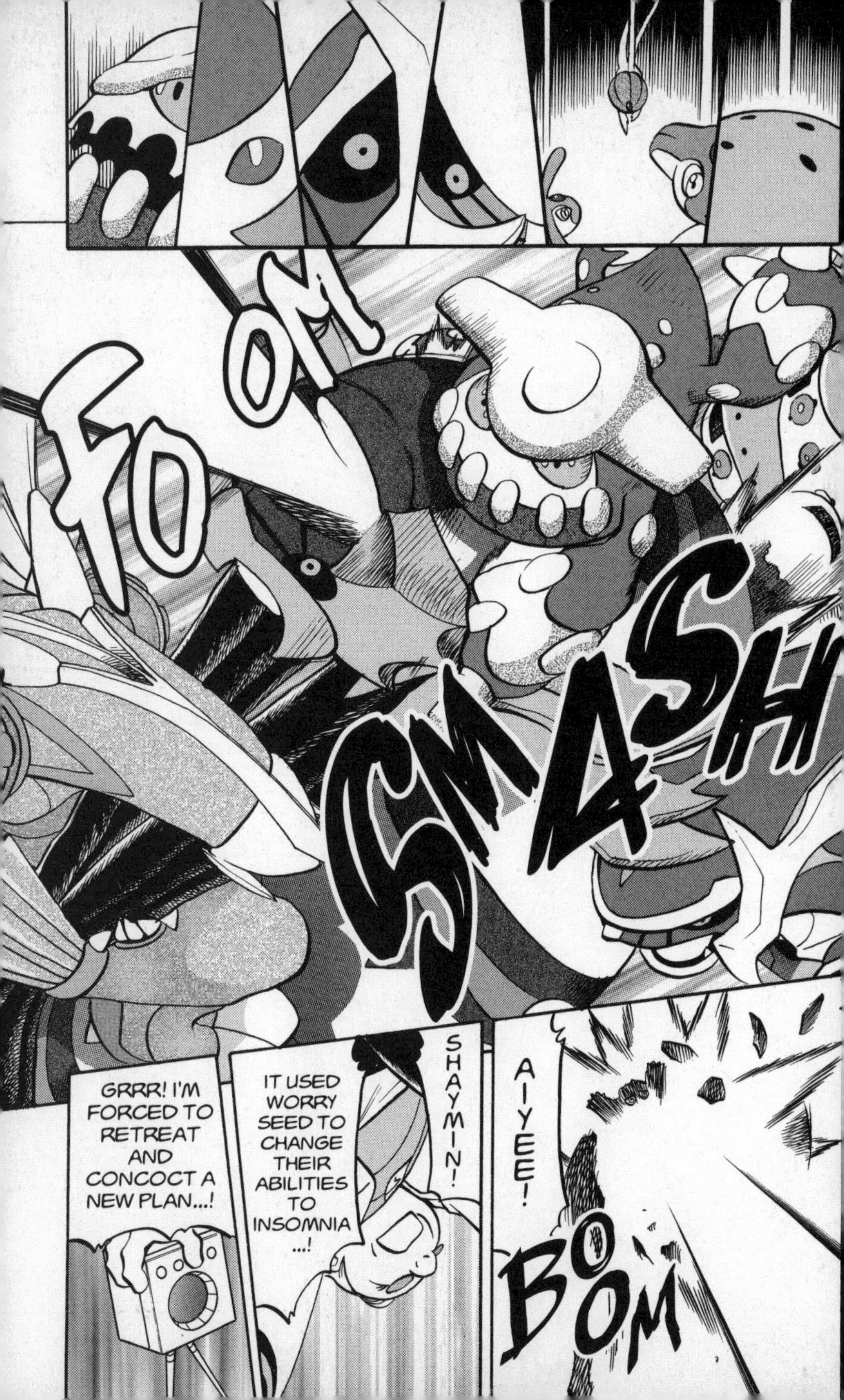
FOOM
SMASH
AIYEE!
BOOM
SHAYMIN!
IT USED WORRY SEED TO CHANGE THEIR ABILITIES TO INSOMNIA...!
GRRR! I'M FORCED TO RETREAT AND CONCOCT A NEW PLAN...!

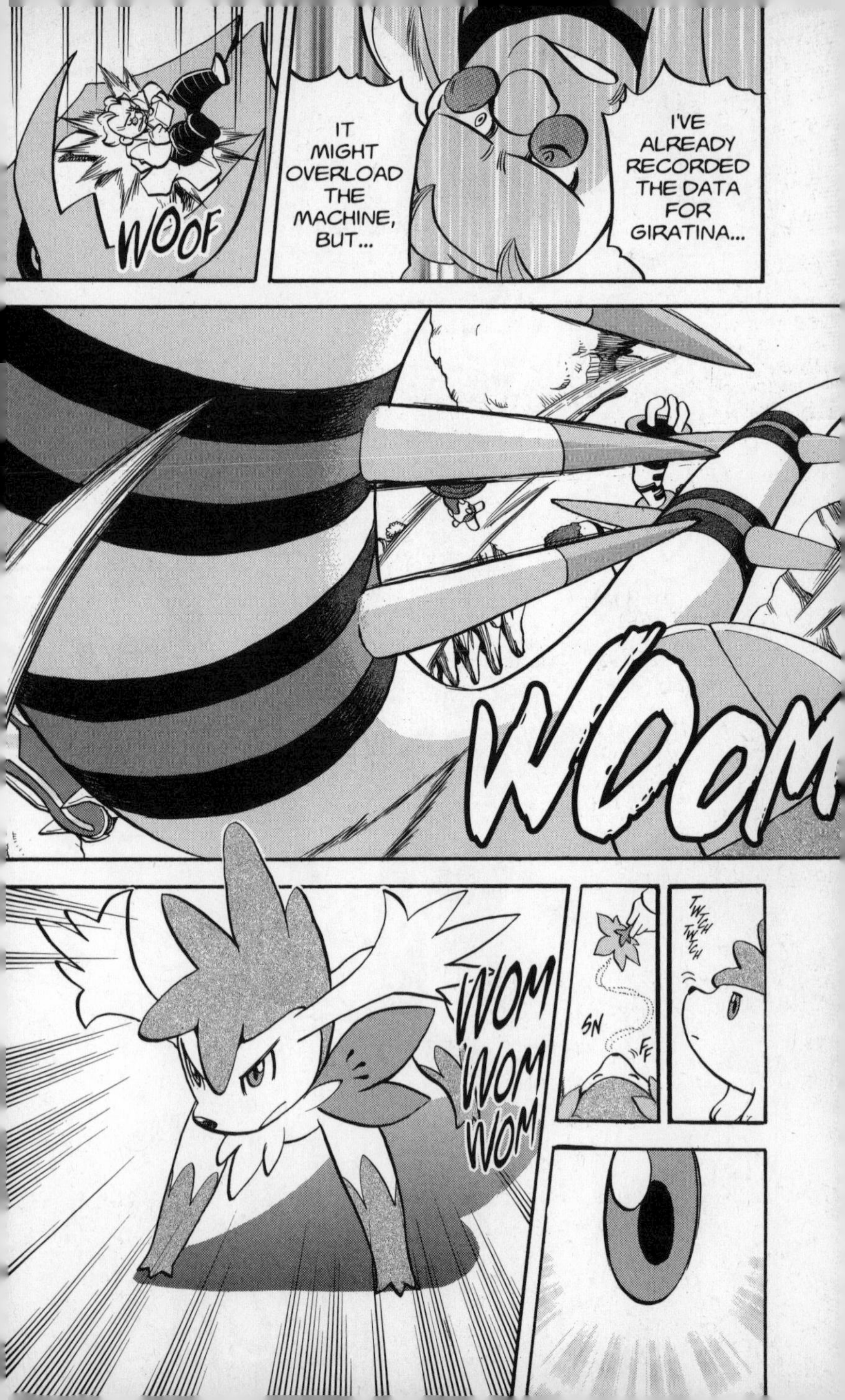
I'VE ALREADY RECORDED THE DATA FOR GIRATINA...
IT MIGHT OVERLOAD THE MACHINE, BUT...
WOOF
WOOM
TWITCH TWITCH
SN FF
WOM WOM WOM

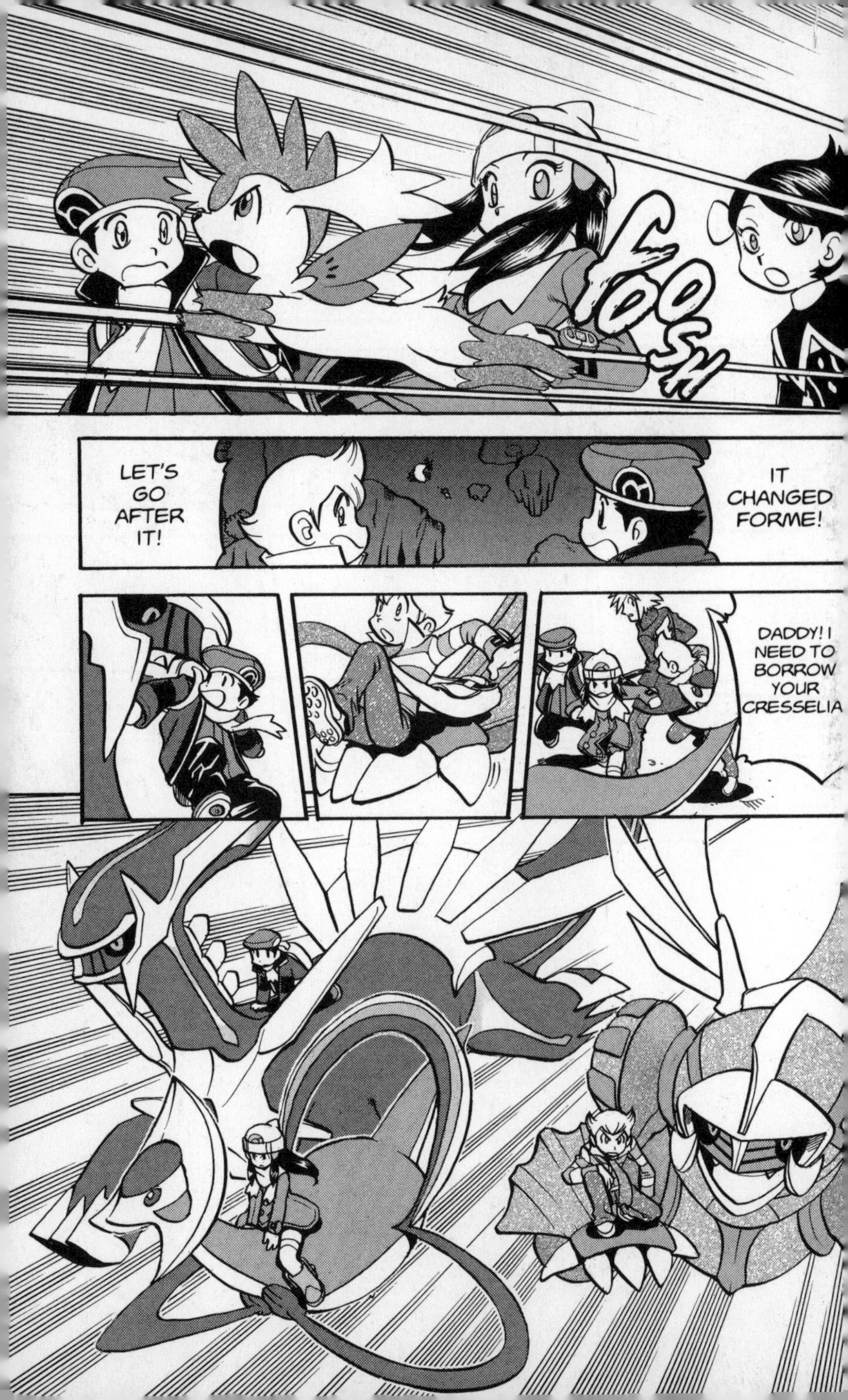
WOOSH
IT CHANGED FORME!
LET'S GO AFTER IT!
DADDY!! I NEED TO BORROW YOUR CRESSELIA

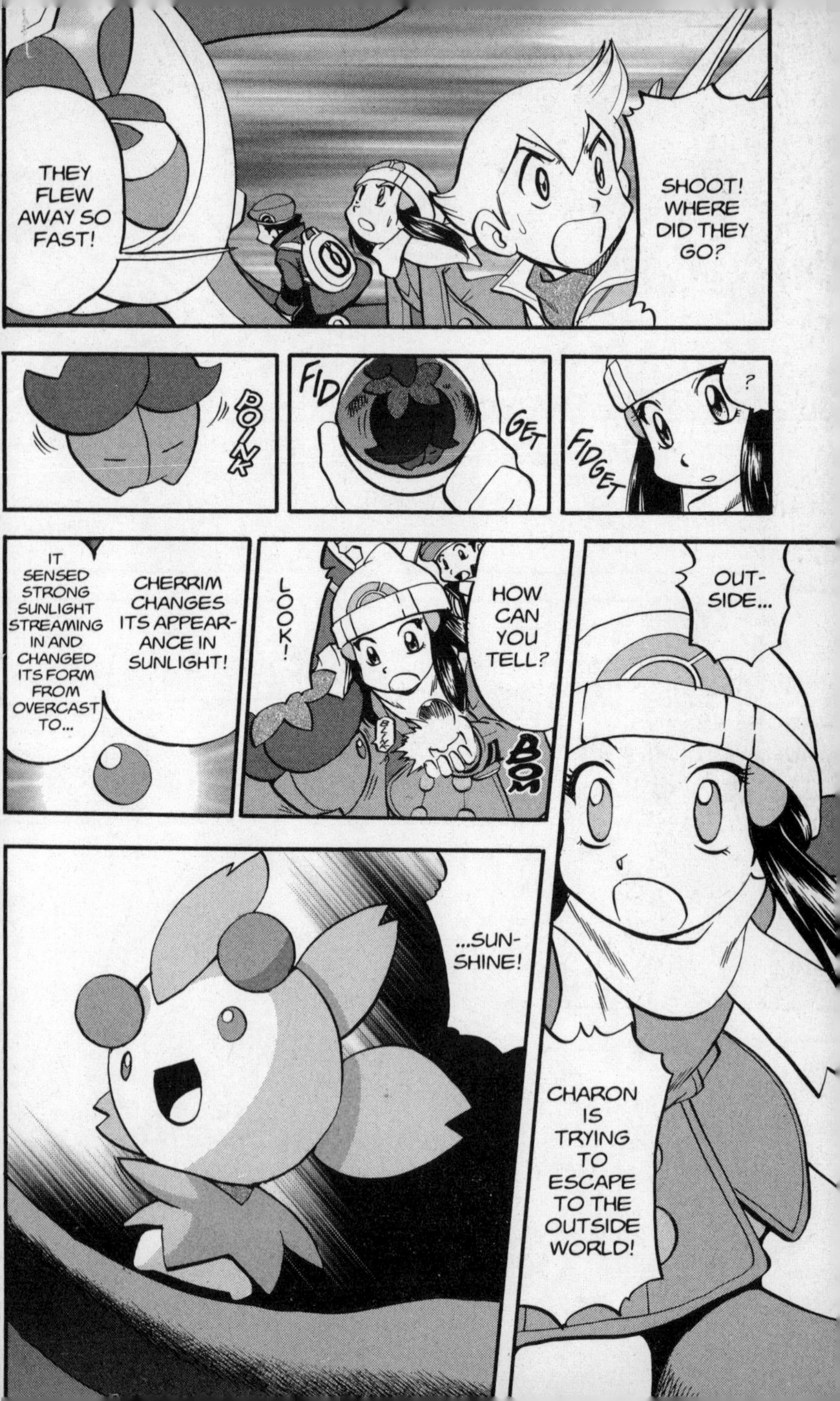
SHOOT! WHERE DID THEY GO?
THEY FLEW AWAY SO FAST!
?
FIDGET
GET
FID
POINK
OUT-SIDE...
CHARON IS TRYING TO ESCAPE TO THE OUTSIDE WORLD!
HOW CAN YOU TELL?
LOOK!
BOM
CHERRIM CHANGES ITS APPEARANCE IN SUNLIGHT!
IT SENSED STRONG SUNLIGHT STREAMING IN AND CHANGED ITS FORM FROM OVERCAST TO...
...SUN-SHINE!

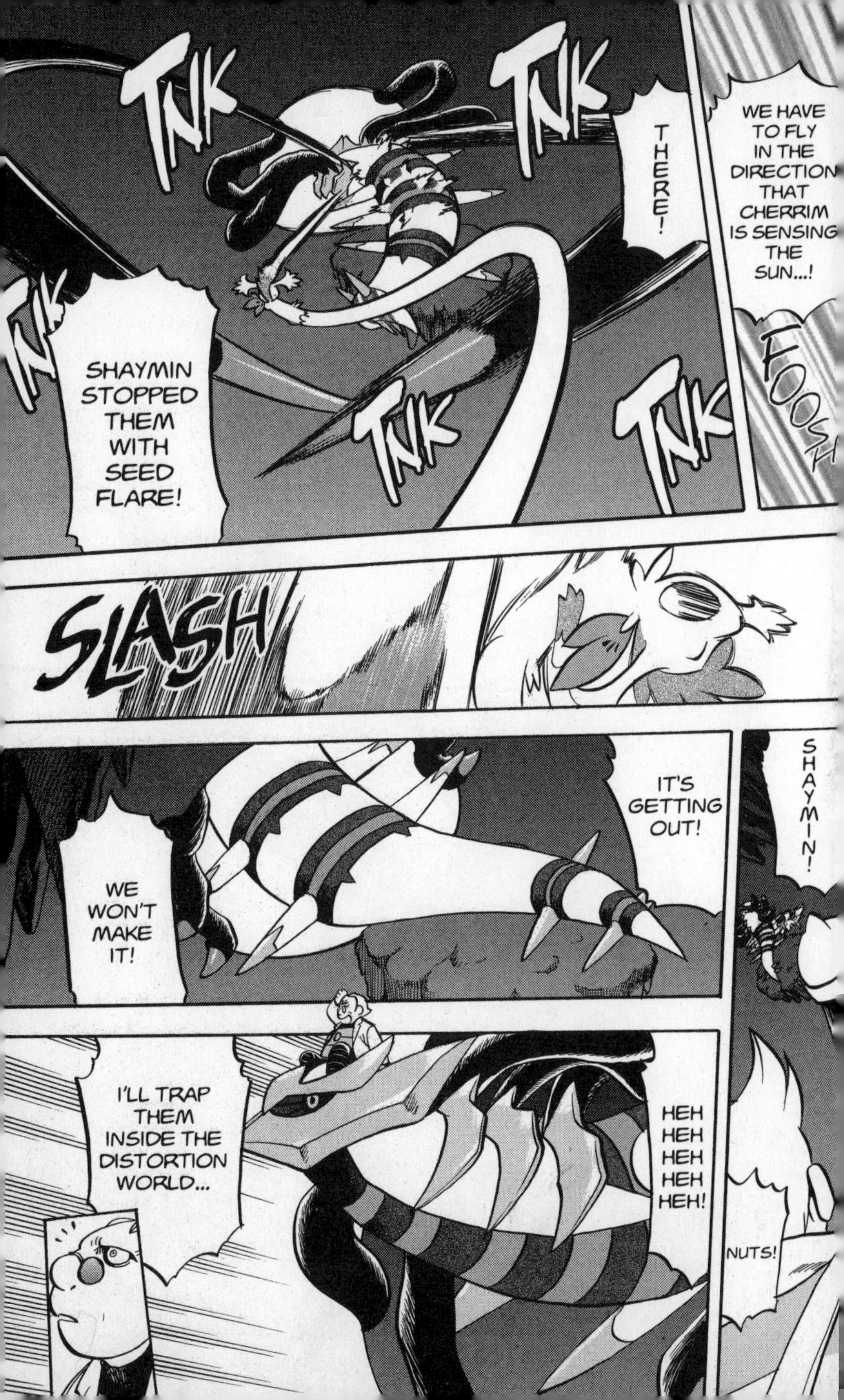
WE HAVE TO FLY IN THE DIRECTION THAT CHERRIM IS SENSING THE SUN...!
FOOOSH
TNK
THERE!
TNK
TNK
SHAYMIN STOPPED THEM WITH SEED FLARE!
TNK
TNK
SLASH
SHAYMIN!
IT'S GETTING OUT!
WE WON'T MAKE IT!
NUTS!
HEH HEH HEH HEH HEH!
I'LL TRAP THEM INSIDE THE DISTORTION WORLD...

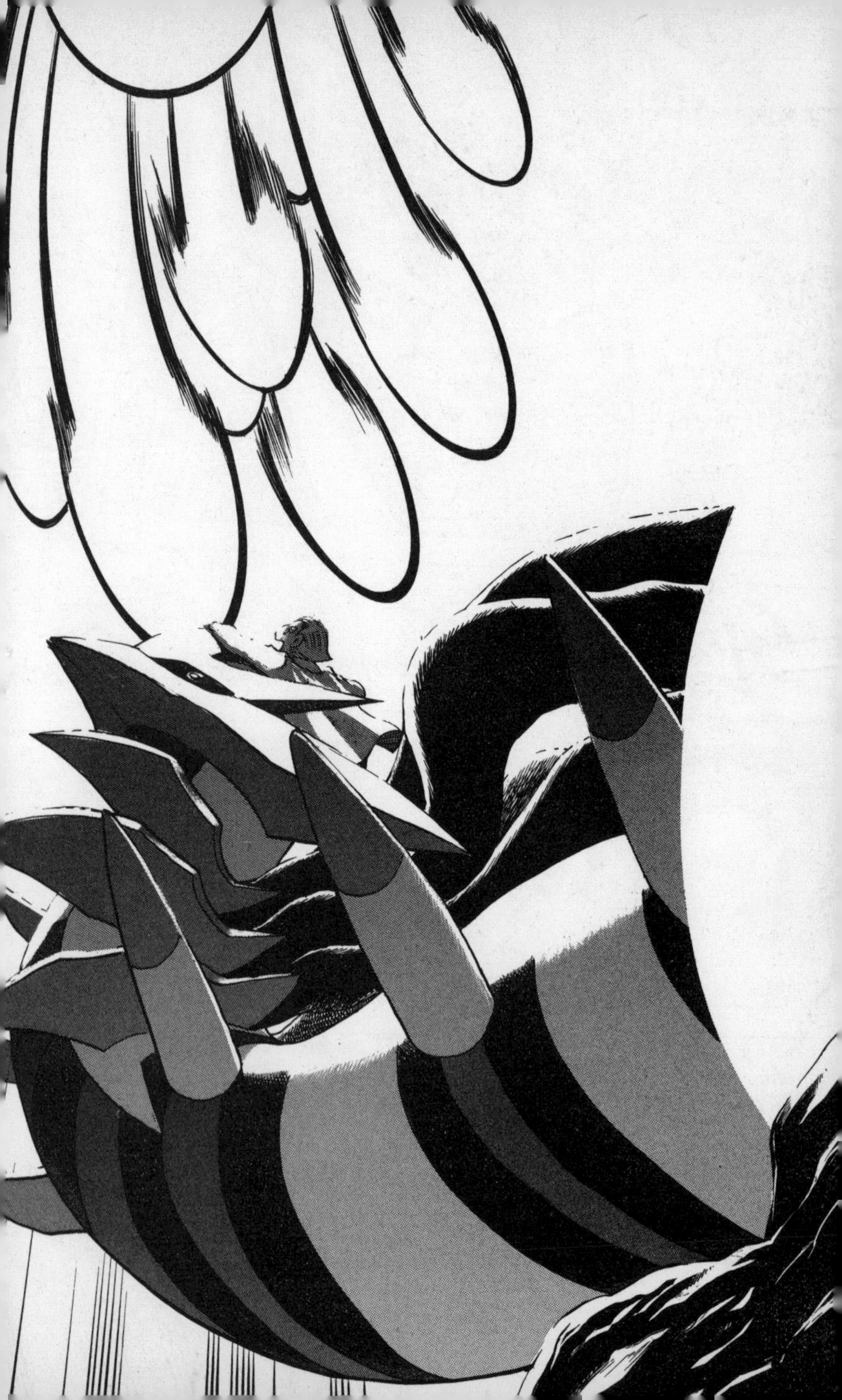

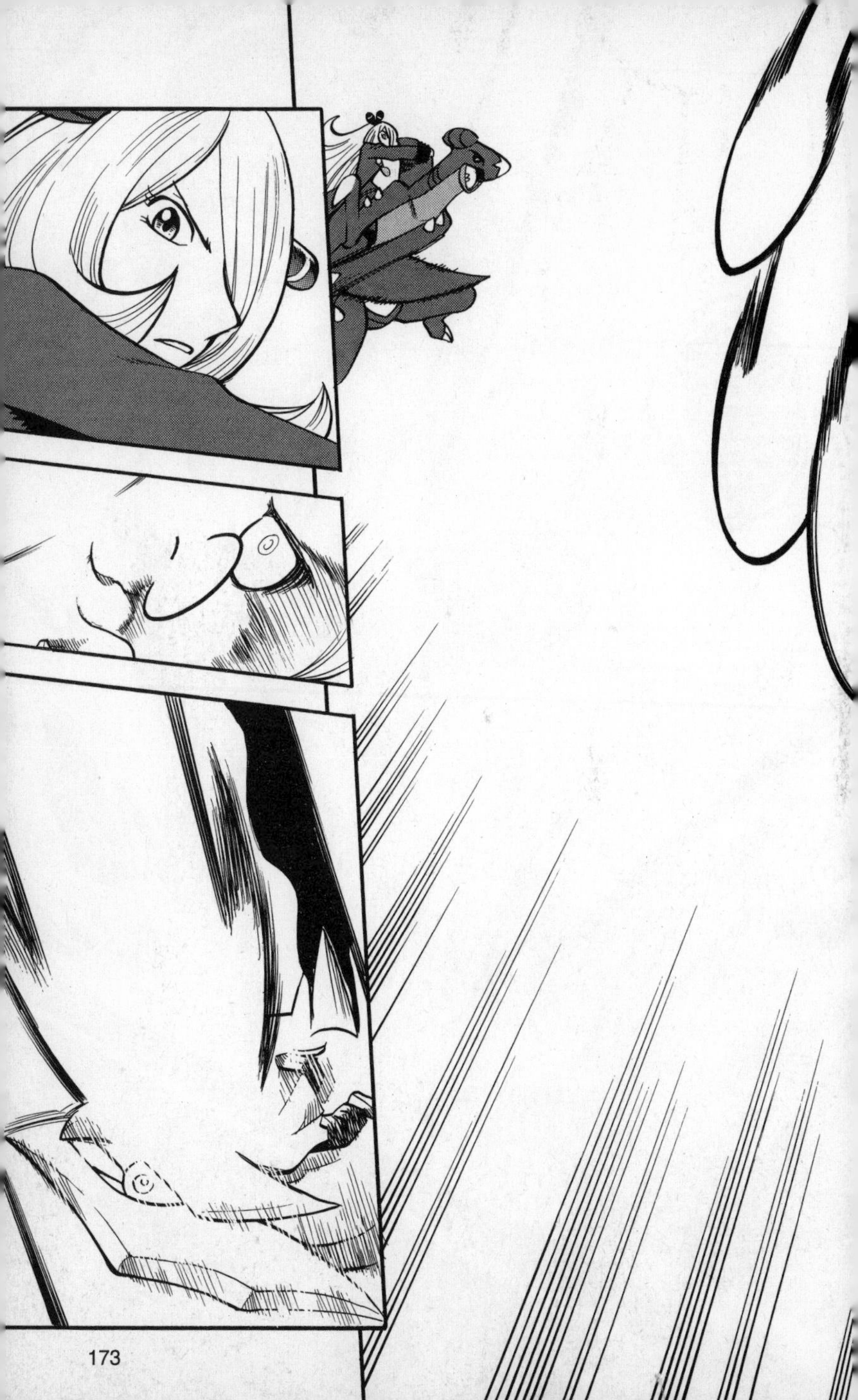

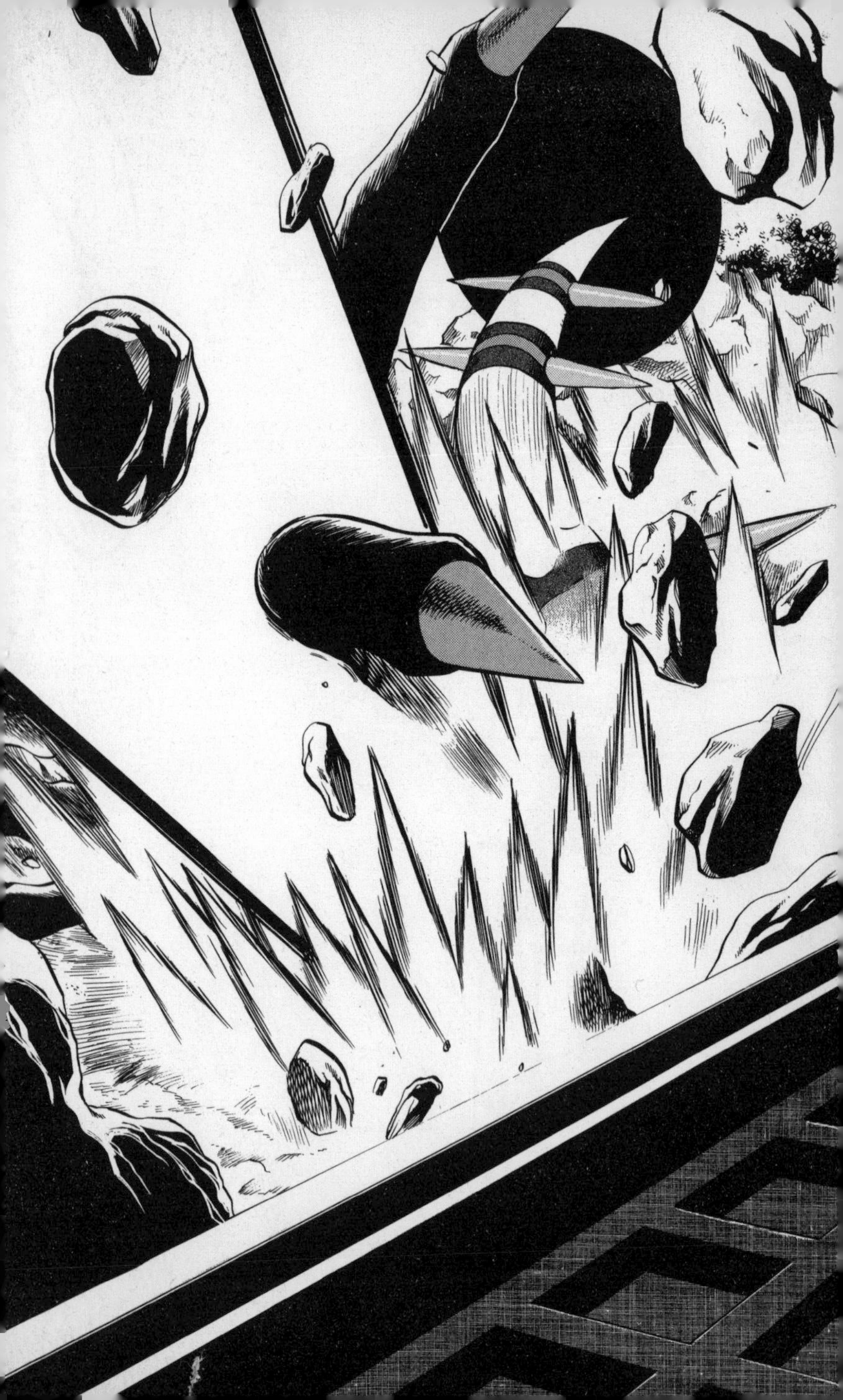

Diamond and Pearl
PLATINUM

POKÉMON STATS

TEAM PLATINUM

Empoleon/Empoleon ♀

Water
Steel

LV. 68 (As of Adventure 103)

Ability: Torrent

Serious. A little quick tempered.

The Piplup that Lady received from Professor Rowan has evolved into Empoleon, a proud and powerful Pokémon well qualified to be her main fighter.

Rapidash/Rapidash ♂

Fire

LV. 59 (As of Adventure 103)

Ability: Flash Fire

Modest. Often lost in thought.

Ponyta carried Lady all over the wide Sinnoh region and, after evolving, has proved to be strong in battle...!

Lopunny/Lopunny ♀

Normal

LV. 51 (As of Adventure 103)

Ability: Cute Charm

Mild. Alert to sounds.

Fast and light on its feet, Lopunny brings victory with its distinctive moves such as Healing Wish and its Ability Cute Charm.

POKEMON OF TEAM PLATINUM

TEAM PLATINUM

Pachirisu/Pachirisu ♀

Electric

- **LV. 53** (As of Adventure 103)
- **Ability: Run Away**
- **Quirky. Highly curious.**

This Pokémon has powerful Electric-type moves. It once belonged to a Gym Leader, so it is an experienced member of the team, even though it only joined midway on her journey.

Froslass/Froslass ♀

Ice
Ghost

- **LV. 60** (As of Adventure 103)
- **Ability: Snow Cloak**
- **Quiet. Very finicky.**

This important member of Lady's team was given to her by Gym Leader Candice. Its Poké Ball was destroyed at the Spear Pillar, but that hasn't stopped it from making a comeback.

Cherrim/Cherrim ♀

Grass

- **LV. 49** (As of Adventure 103)
- **Ability: Flower Gift**
- **Docile. Impetuous and silly.**

Cherrim was entrusted to Lady by Gardenia. Its wounds were healed at the Pokémon hospital, and then it was taken to the Battle Frontier. It supports Lady in battle as her only Grass-type Pokémon.

POKÉMON STATS

TEAM PLATINUM

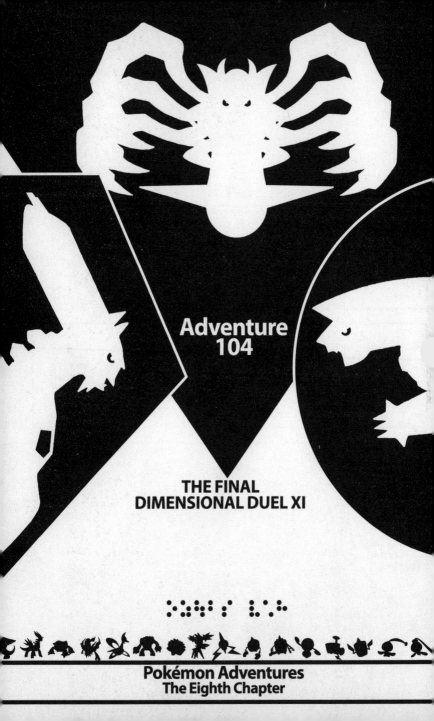

Adventure 104

THE FINAL DIMENSIONAL DUEL XI

Pokémon Adventures
The Eighth Chapter

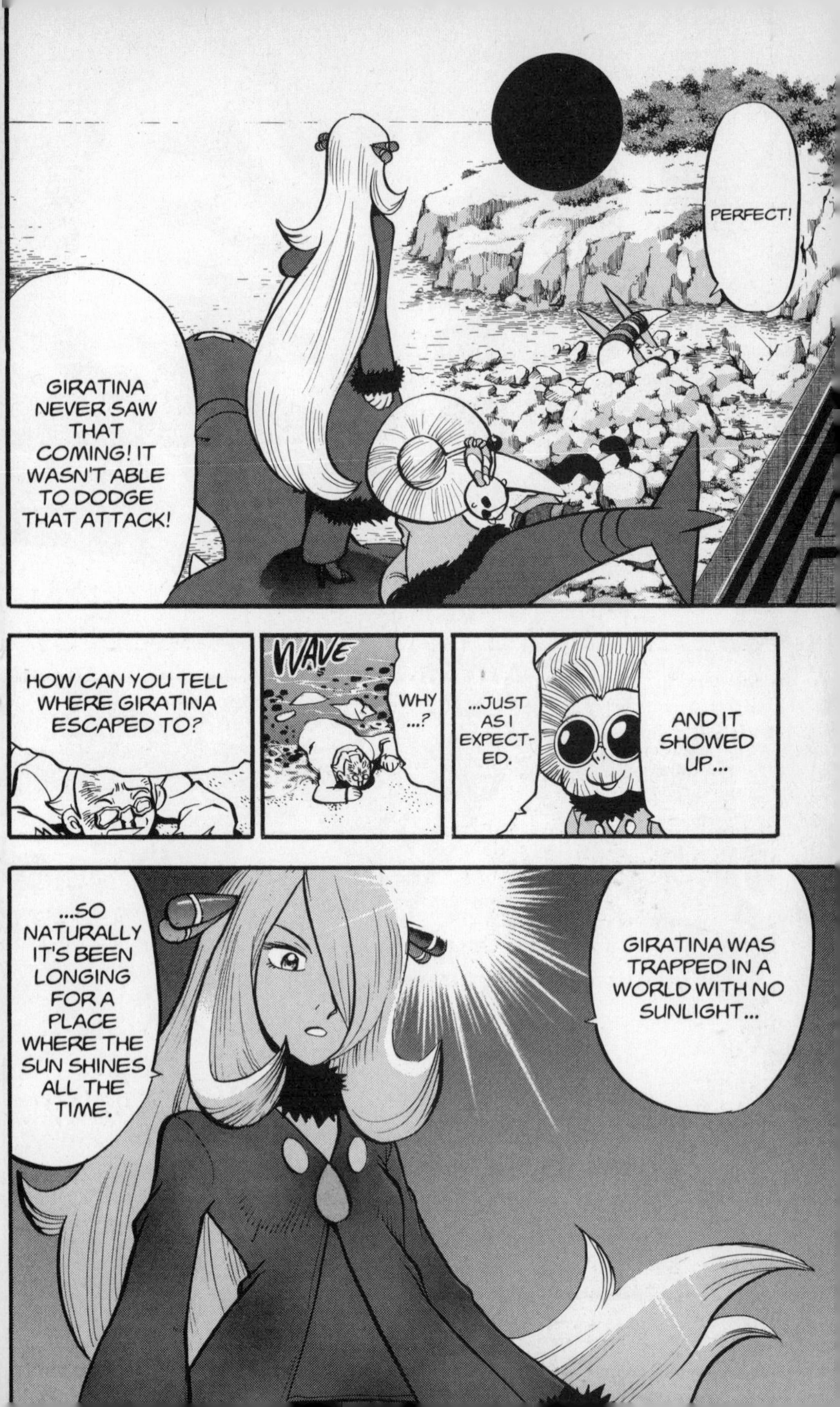
PERFECT!
GIRATINA NEVER SAW THAT COMING! IT WASN'T ABLE TO DODGE THAT ATTACK!
AND IT SHOWED UP...
...JUST AS I EXPECT-ED.
WAVE
WHY ...?
HOW CAN YOU TELL WHERE GIRATINA ESCAPED TO?
GIRATINA WAS TRAPPED IN A WORLD WITH NO SUNLIGHT...
...SO NATURALLY IT'S BEEN LONGING FOR A PLACE WHERE THE SUN SHINES ALL THE TIME.

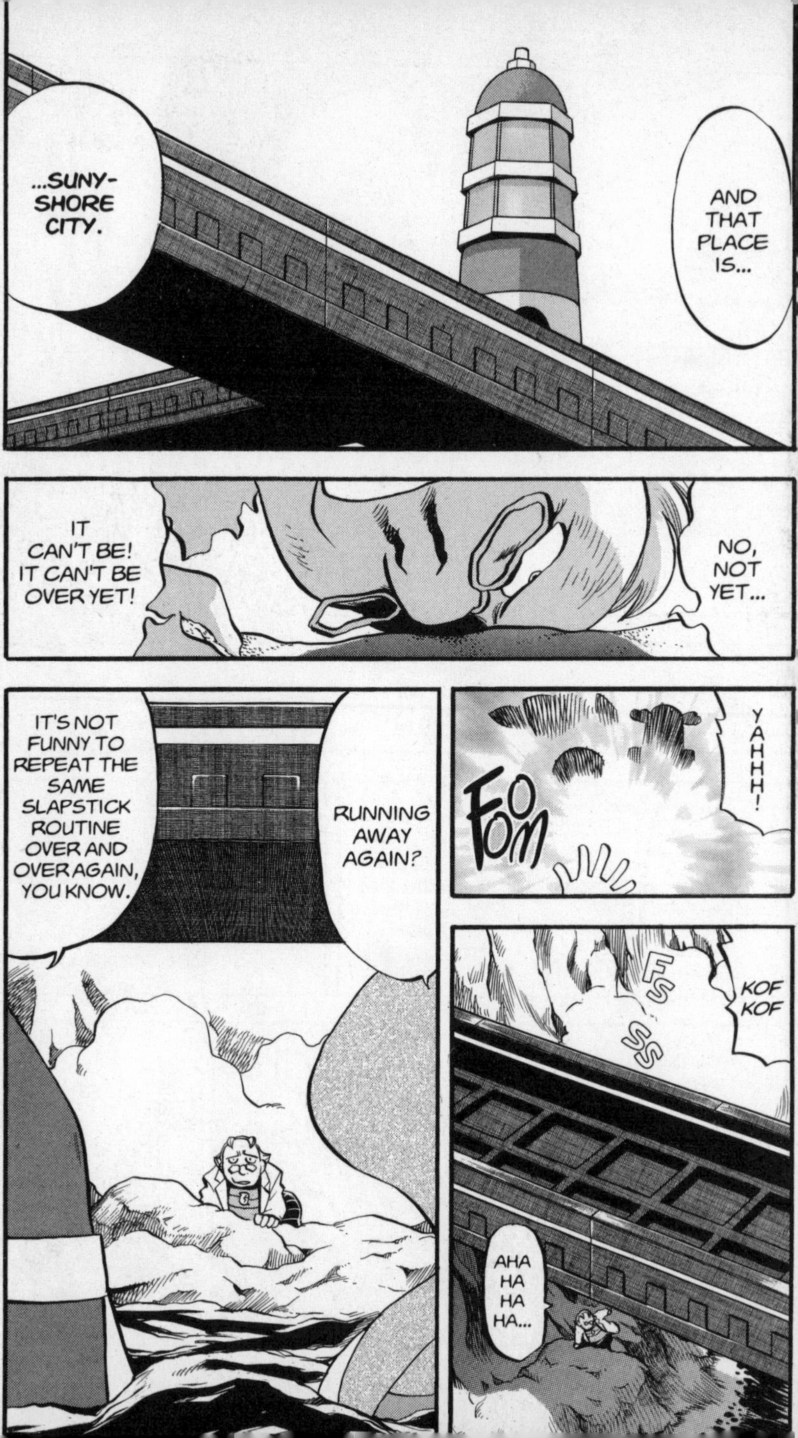
AND THAT PLACE IS...
...SUNY-SHORE CITY.
NO, NOT YET...
IT CAN'T BE! IT CAN'T BE OVER YET!
YAHHH!
FOOM
KOF KOF
FSSSS
AHA HA HA HA...
RUNNING AWAY AGAIN?
IT'S NOT FUNNY TO REPEAT THE SAME SLAPSTICK ROUTINE OVER AND OVER AGAIN, YOU KNOW.

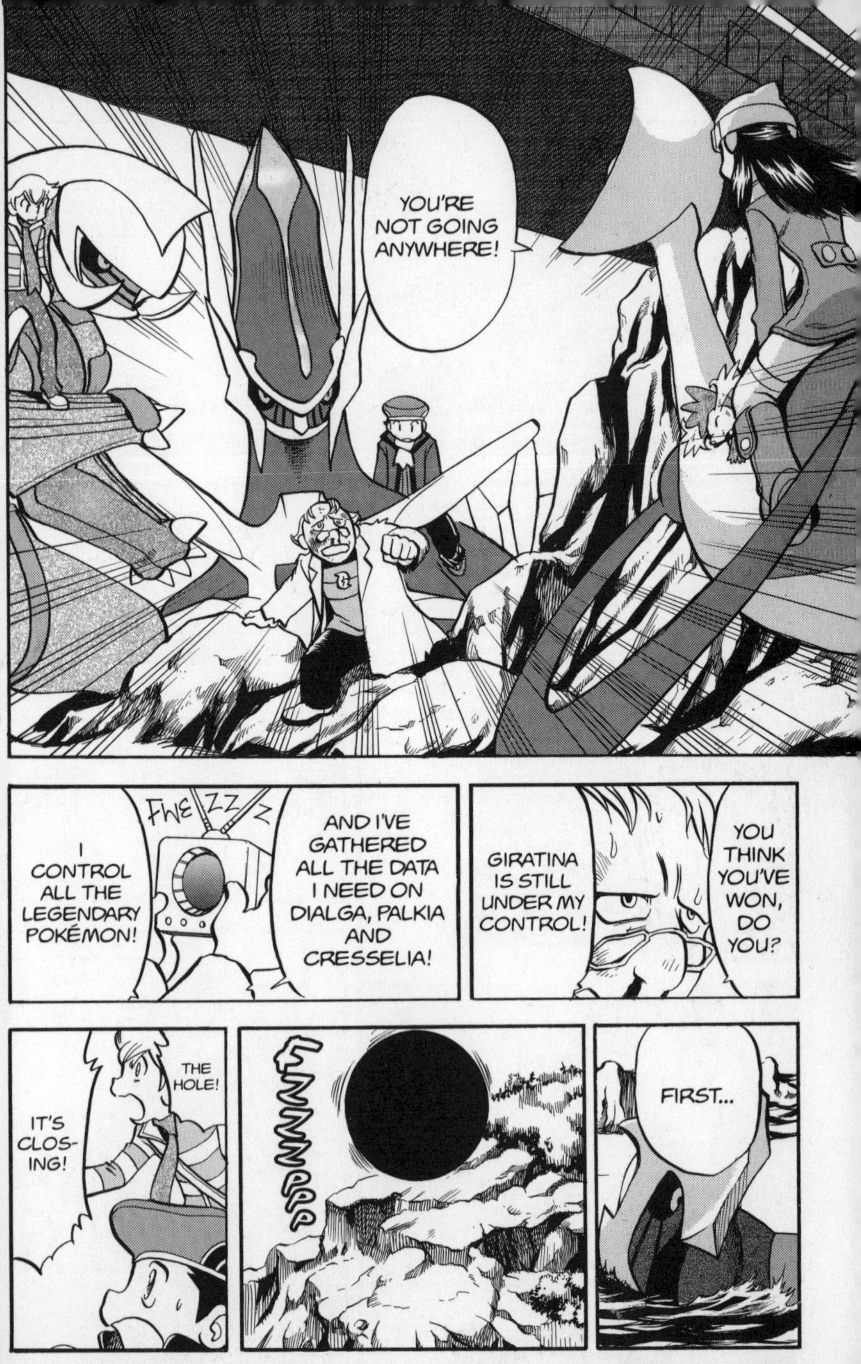
YOU'RE NOT GOING ANYWHERE!
YOU THINK YOU'VE WON, DO YOU?
GIRATINA IS STILL UNDER MY CONTROL!
AND I'VE GATHERED ALL THE DATA I NEED ON DIALGA, PALKIA AND CRESSELIA!
FWEZZZ
I CONTROL ALL THE LEGENDARY POKÉMON!
FIRST...
THE HOLE!
IT'S CLOSING!

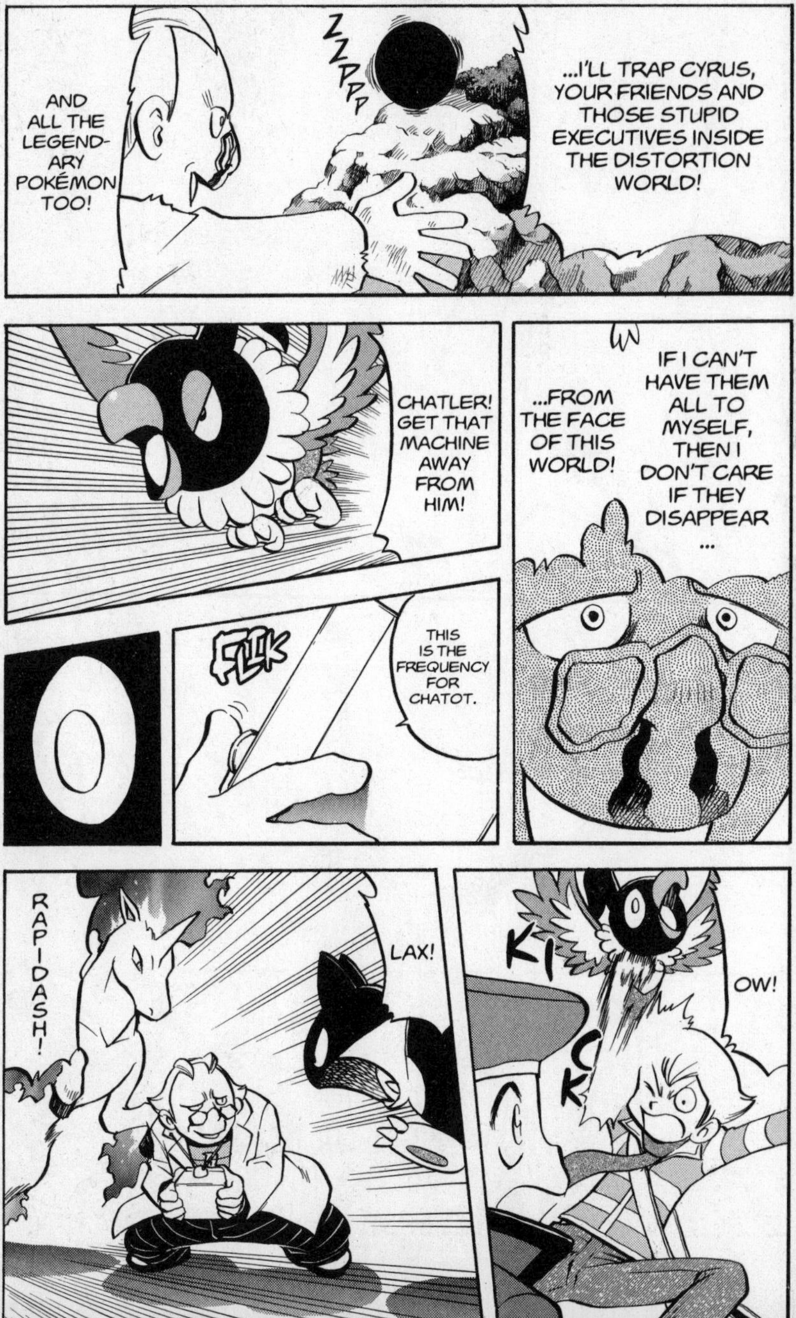
...I'LL TRAP CYRUS, YOUR FRIENDS AND THOSE STUPID EXECUTIVES INSIDE THE DISTORTION WORLD!
ZZZPPP
AND ALL THE LEGEND-ARY POKÉMON TOO!
IF I CAN'T HAVE THEM ALL TO MYSELF, THEN I DON'T CARE IF THEY DISAPPEAR ...
...FROM THE FACE OF THIS WORLD!
CHATLER! GET THAT MACHINE AWAY FROM HIM!
THIS IS THE FREQUENCY FOR CHATOT.
FLIK
OW!
KICK
LAX!
RAPIDASH!

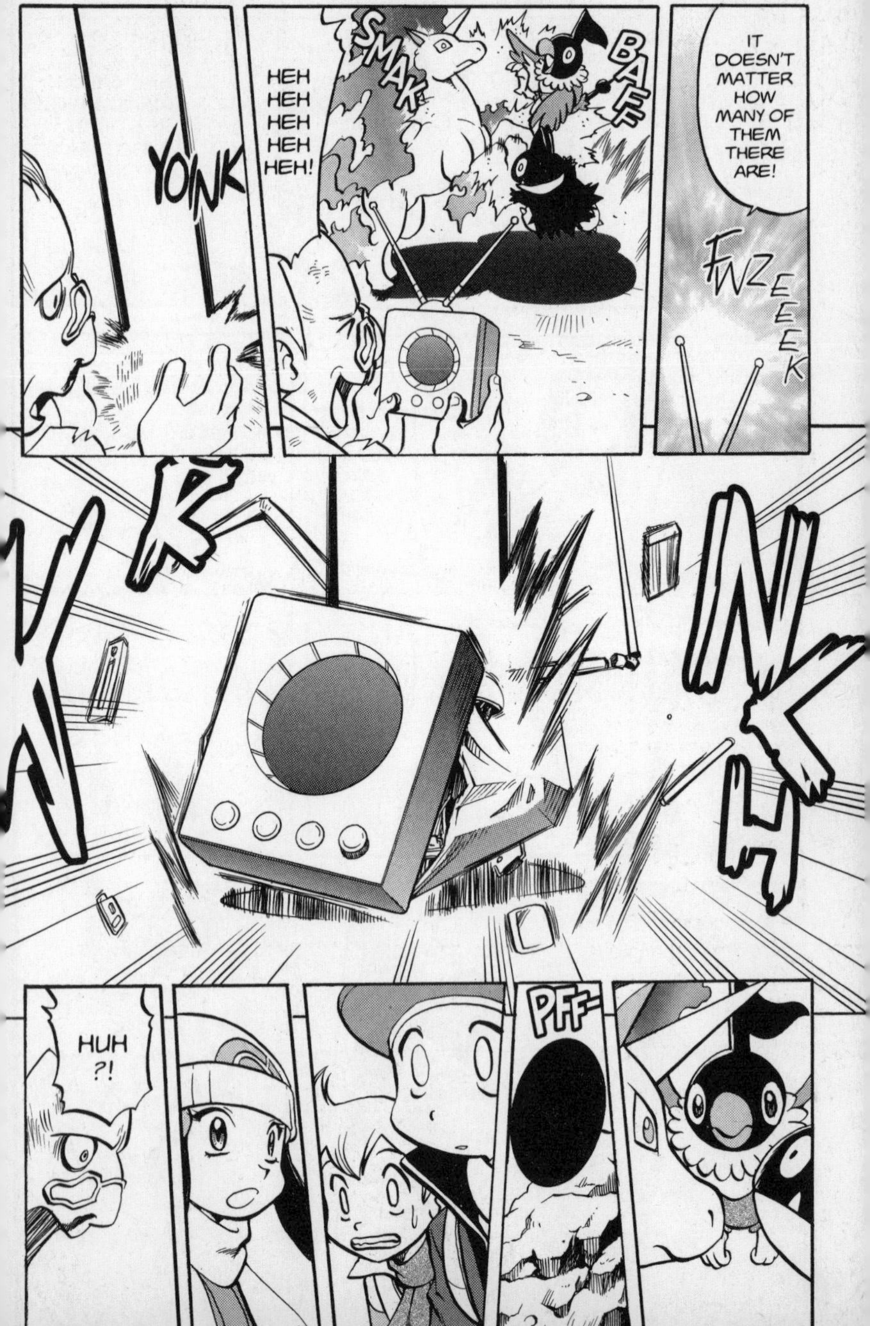
IT DOESN'T MATTER HOW MANY OF THEM THERE ARE!
FWZEEEEK
BAFF
SMAK
HEH HEH HEH HEH HEH!
YOINK
PFF-
HUH ?!

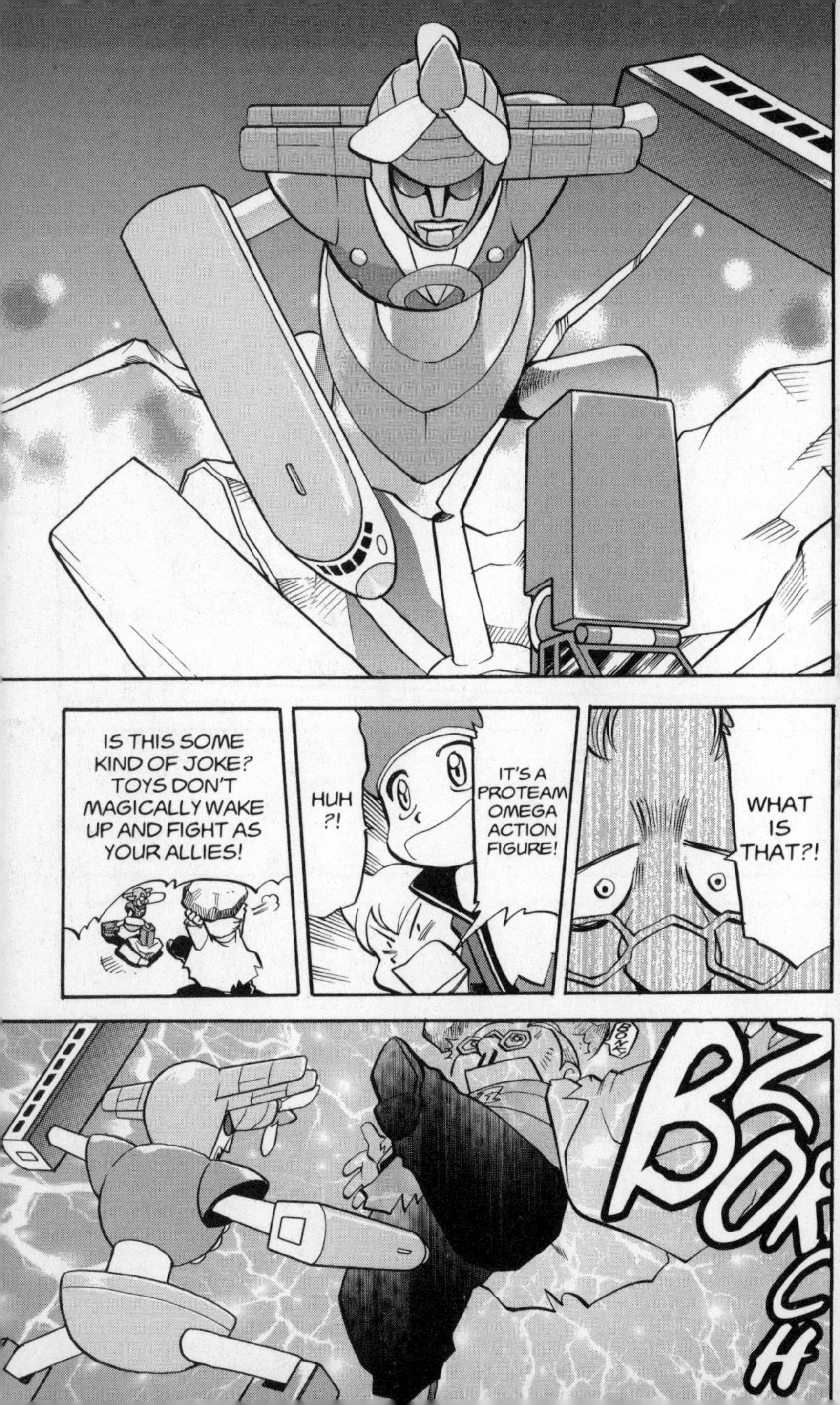
WHAT IS THAT?!
IT'S A PROTEAM OMEGA ACTION FIGURE!
HUH ?!
IS THIS SOME KIND OF JOKE? TOYS DON'T MAGICALLY WAKE UP AND FIGHT AS YOUR ALLIES!
BONK

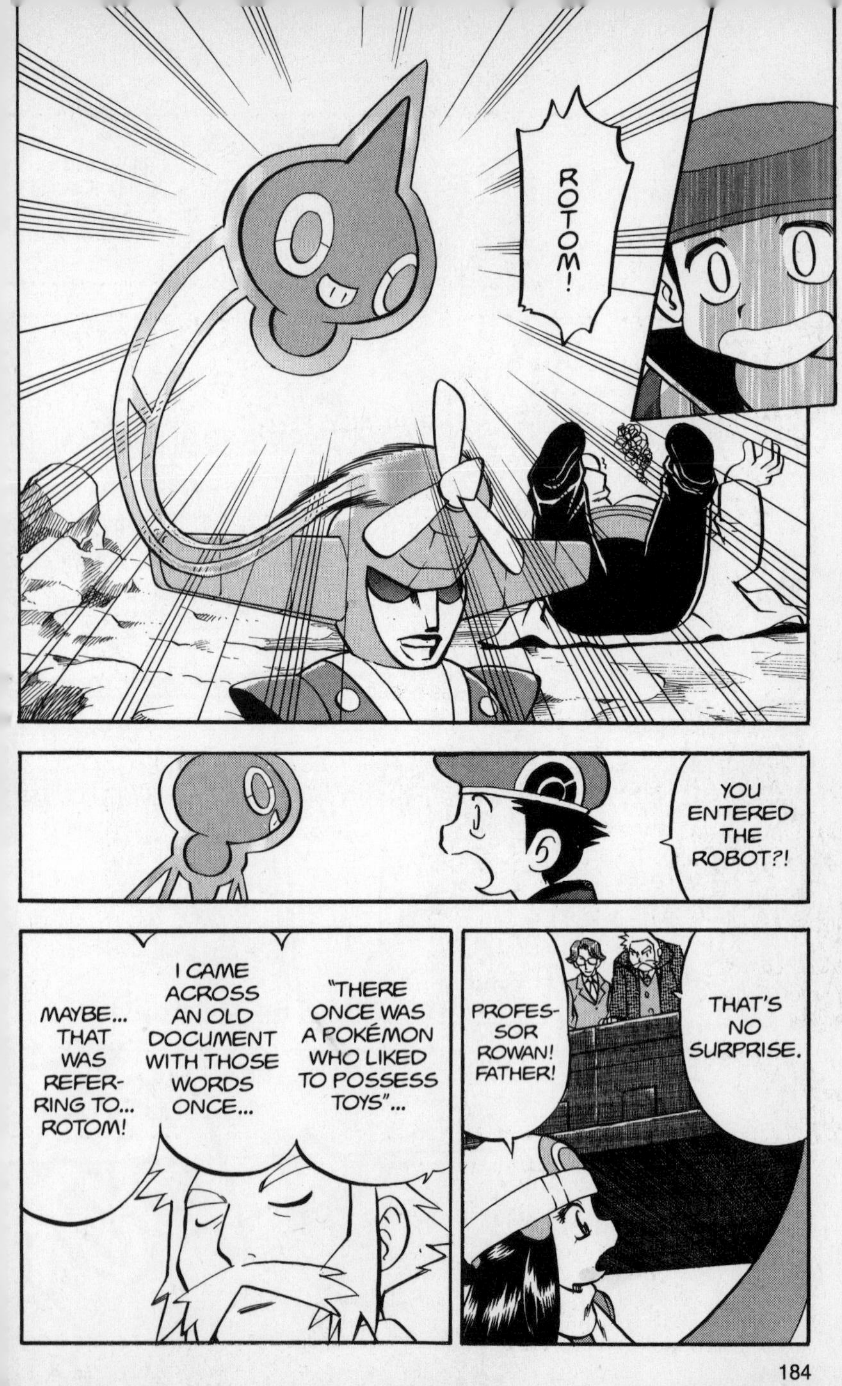
ROTOM!
YOU ENTERED THE ROBOT?!
THAT'S NO SURPRISE.
PROFES-SOR ROWAN! FATHER!
"THERE ONCE WAS A POKÉMON WHO LIKED TO POSSESS TOYS"...
I CAME ACROSS AN OLD DOCUMENT WITH THOSE WORDS ONCE...
MAYBE... THAT WAS REFER-RING TO... ROTOM!

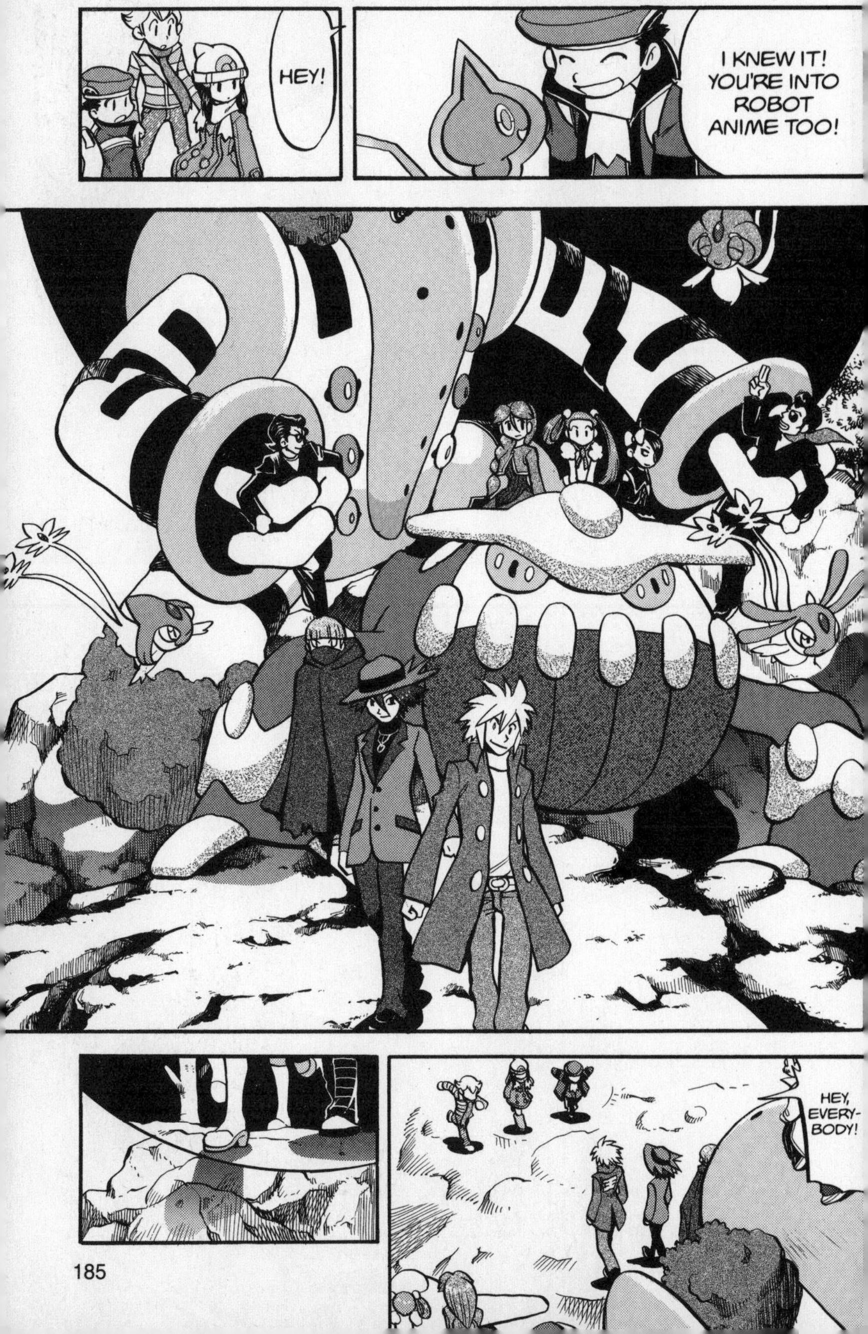
I KNEW IT! YOU'RE INTO ROBOT ANIME TOO!
HEY!
HEY, EVERY-BODY!

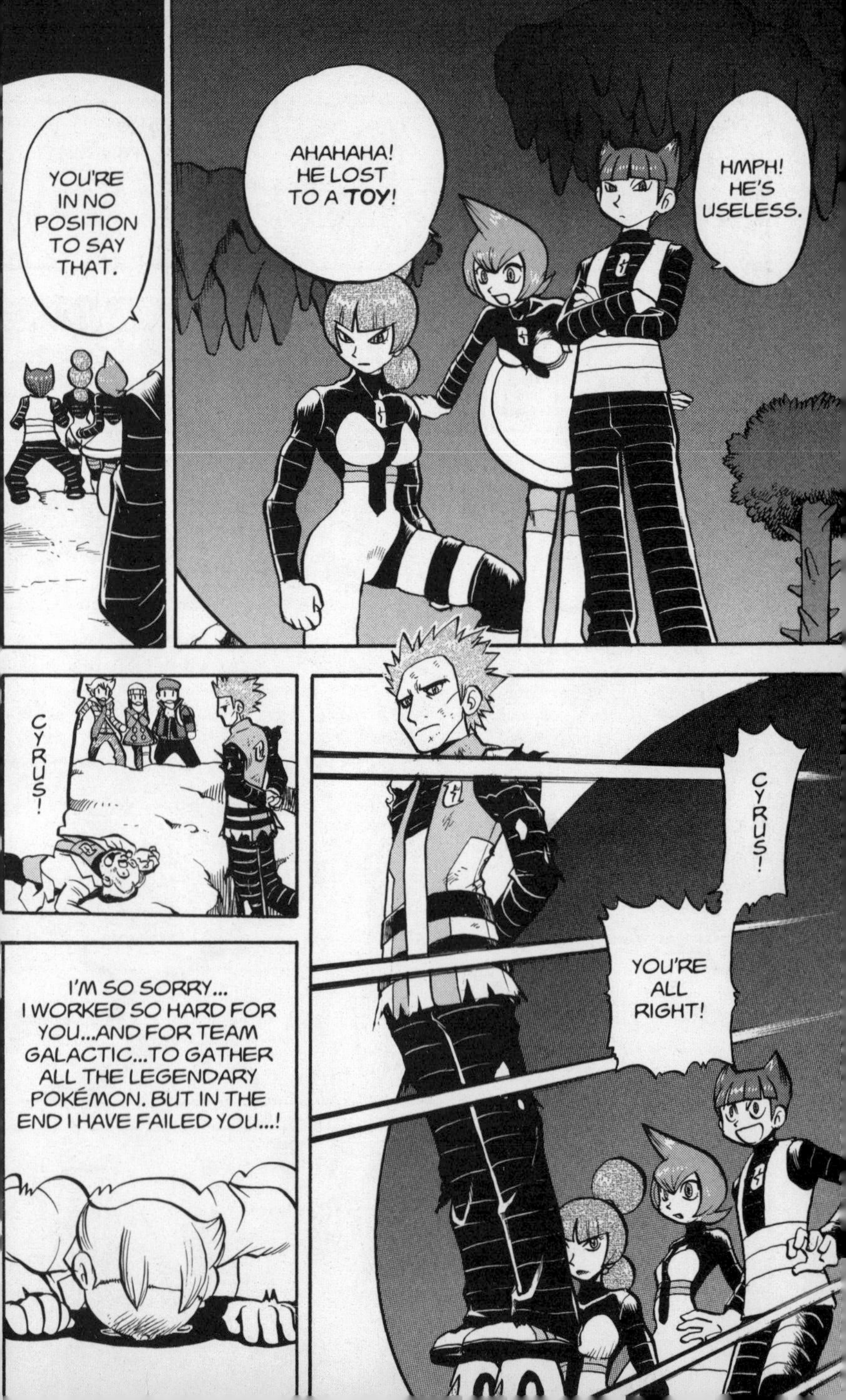
HMPH! HE'S USELESS.
AHAHAHA! HE LOST TO A TOY!
YOU'RE IN NO POSITION TO SAY THAT.
CYRUS!
YOU'RE ALL RIGHT!
CYRUS!
I'M SO SORRY... I WORKED SO HARD FOR YOU...AND FOR TEAM GALACTIC...TO GATHER ALL THE LEGENDARY POKÉMON. BUT IN THE END I HAVE FAILED YOU...!

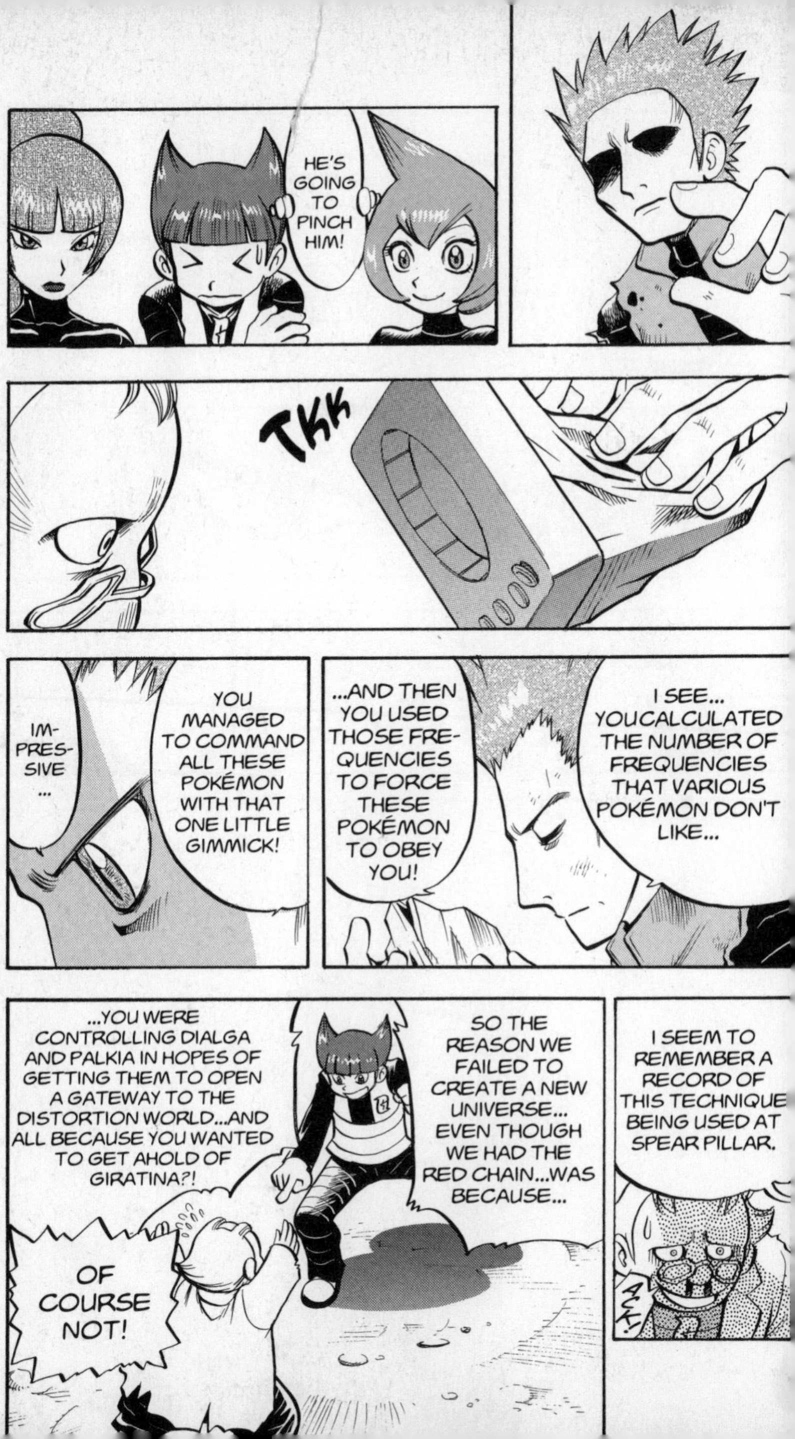
HE'S GOING TO PINCH HIM!
TKK
I SEE... YOU CALCULATED THE NUMBER OF FREQUENCIES THAT VARIOUS POKÉMON DON'T LIKE...
...AND THEN YOU USED THOSE FRE-QUENCIES TO FORCE THESE POKÉMON TO OBEY YOU!
YOU MANAGED TO COMMAND ALL THESE POKÉMON WITH THAT ONE LITTLE GIMMICK!
IM-PRES-SIVE...
I SEEM TO REMEMBER A RECORD OF THIS TECHNIQUE BEING USED AT SPEAR PILLAR.
AUK!
SO THE REASON WE FAILED TO CREATE A NEW UNIVERSE... EVEN THOUGH WE HAD THE RED CHAIN...WAS BECAUSE...
...YOU WERE CONTROLLING DIALGA AND PALKIA IN HOPES OF GETTING THEM TO OPEN A GATEWAY TO THE DISTORTION WORLD...AND ALL BECAUSE YOU WANTED TO GET AHOLD OF GIRATINA?!
OF COURSE NOT!

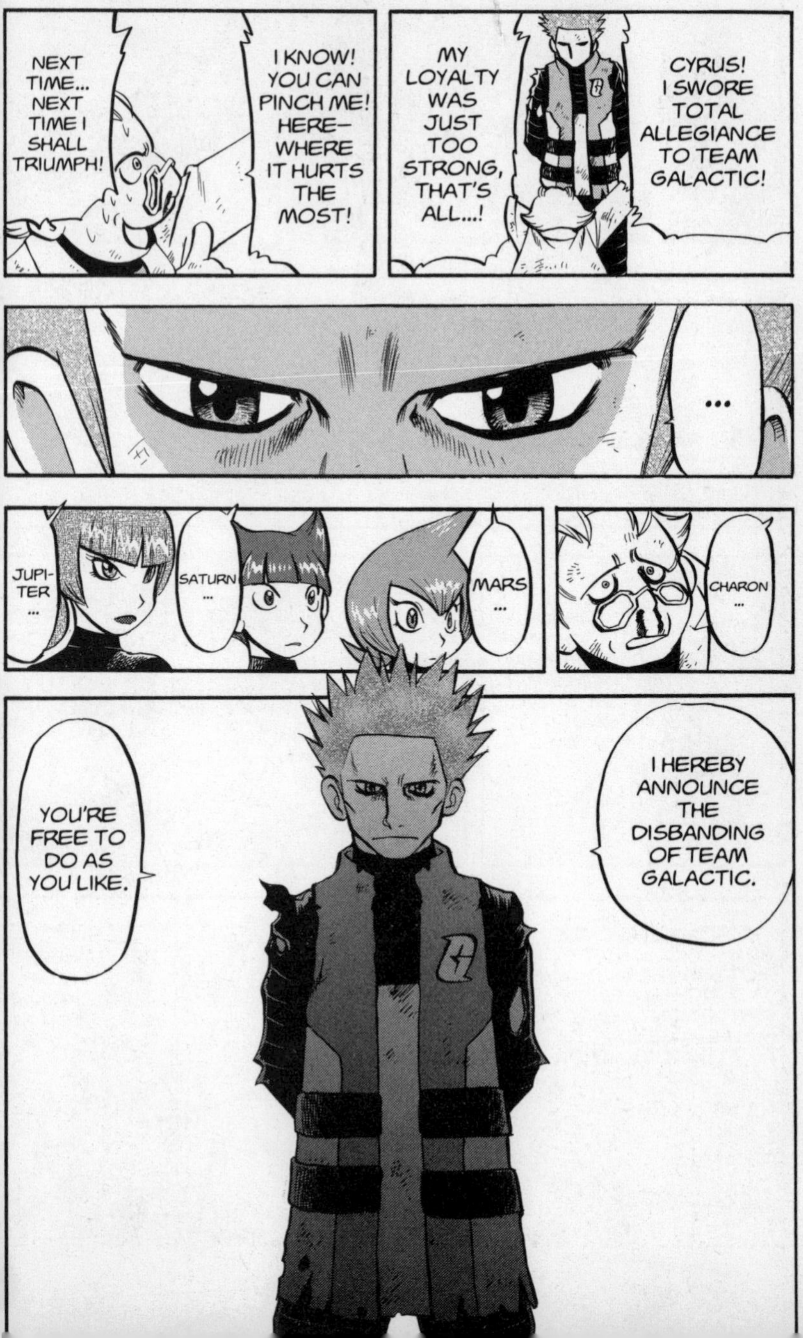
CYRUS! I SWORE TOTAL ALLEGIANCE TO TEAM GALACTIC!
MY LOYALTY WAS JUST TOO STRONG, THAT'S ALL...!
I KNOW! YOU CAN PINCH ME! HERE—WHERE IT HURTS THE MOST!
NEXT TIME... NEXT TIME I SHALL TRIUMPH!
...
CHARON ...
MARS ...
SATURN ...
JUPI-TER ...
I HEREBY ANNOUNCE THE DISBANDING OF TEAM GALACTIC.
YOU'RE FREE TO DO AS YOU LIKE.

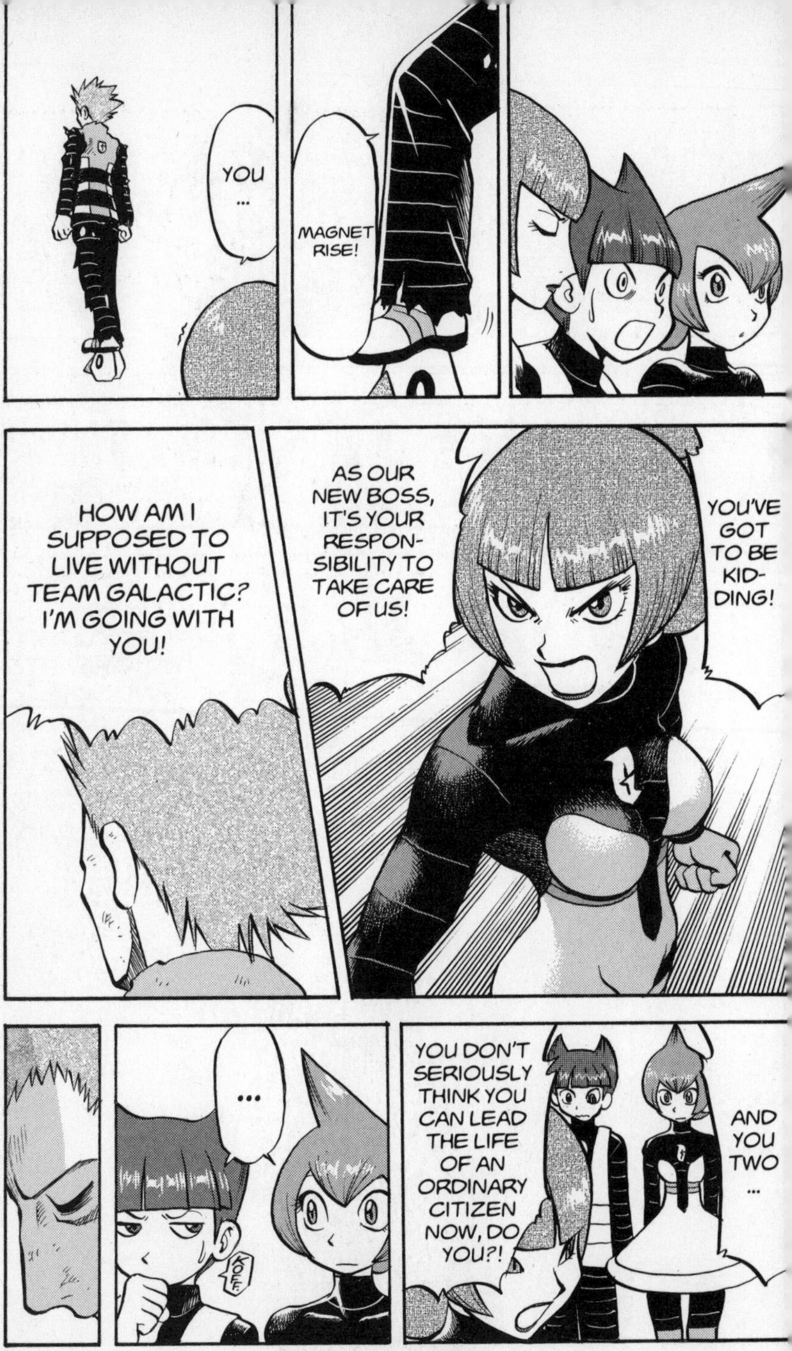
MAGNET RISE!
YOU ...
YOU'VE GOT TO BE KID-DING!
AS OUR NEW BOSS, IT'S YOUR RESPON-SIBILITY TO TAKE CARE OF US!
HOW AM I SUPPOSED TO LIVE WITHOUT TEAM GALACTIC? I'M GOING WITH YOU!
AND YOU TWO ...
YOU DON'T SERIOUSLY THINK YOU CAN LEAD THE LIFE OF AN ORDINARY CITIZEN NOW, DO YOU?!
...
KOFF

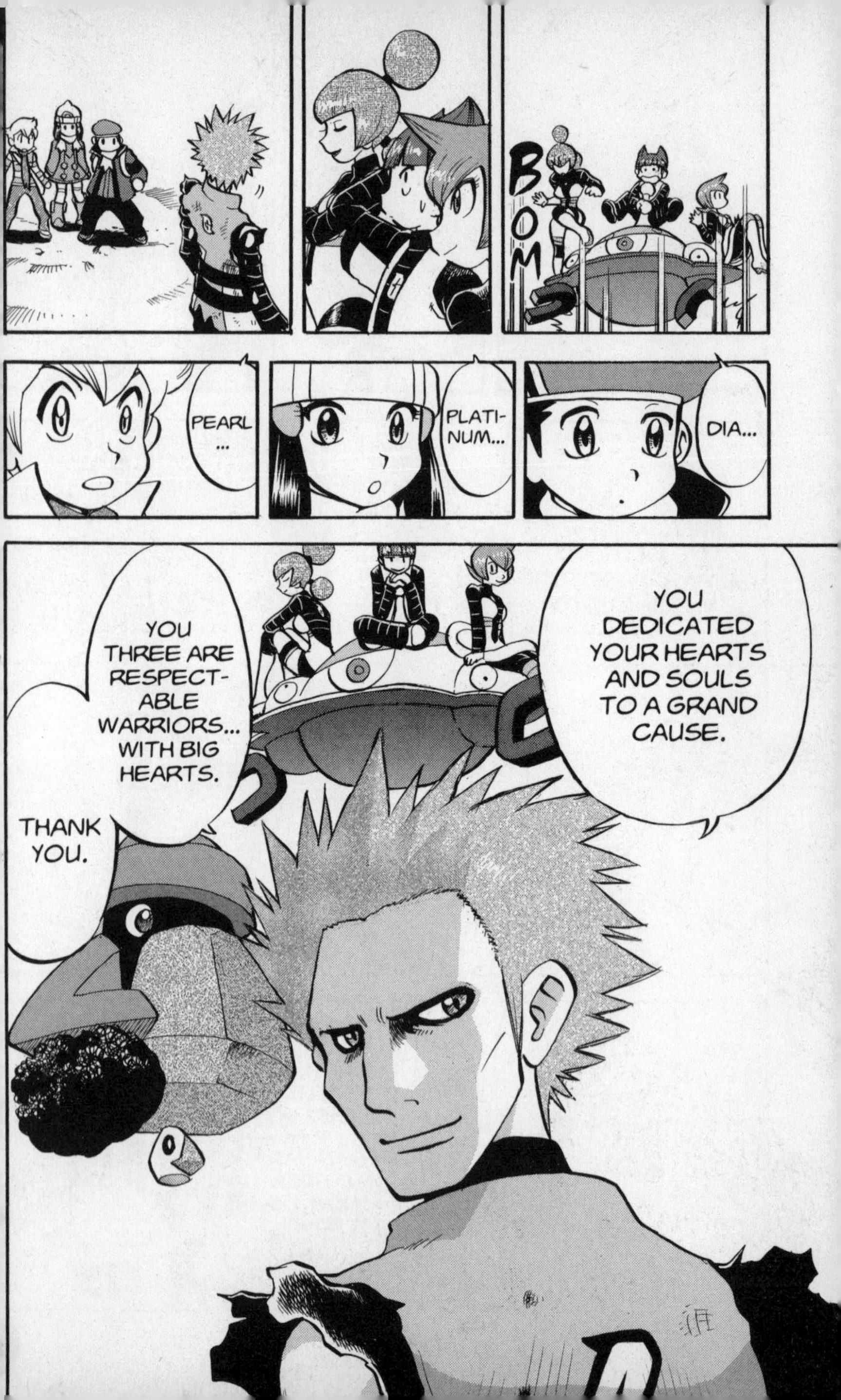
BOM
DIA...
PLATI-NUM...
PEARL...
YOU DEDICATED YOUR HEARTS AND SOULS TO A GRAND CAUSE.
YOU THREE ARE RESPECT-ABLE WARRIORS... WITH BIG HEARTS.
THANK YOU.

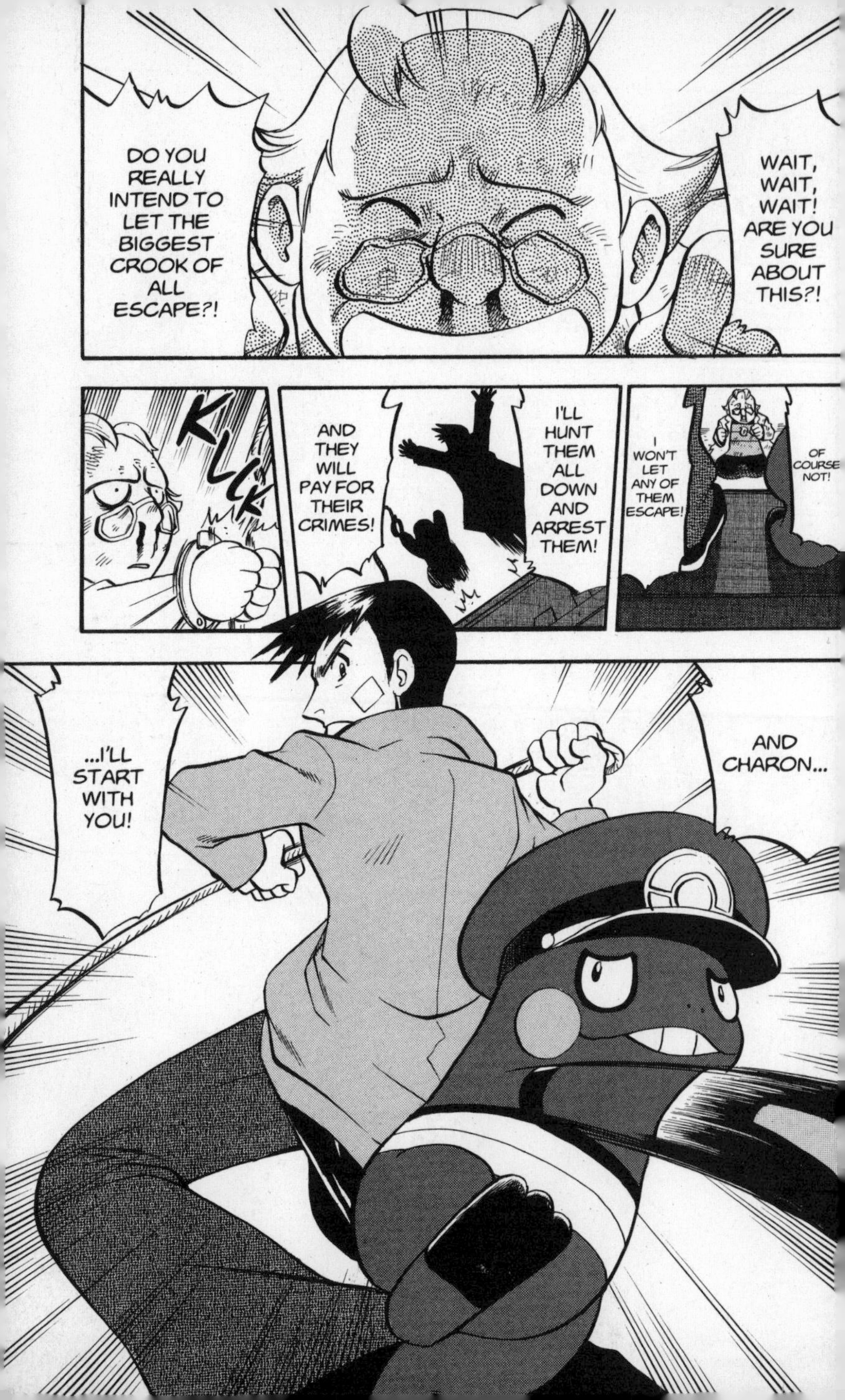
WAIT, WAIT, WAIT! ARE YOU SURE ABOUT THIS?!
DO YOU REALLY INTEND TO LET THE BIGGEST CROOK OF ALL ESCAPE?!
OF COURSE NOT!
I WON'T LET ANY OF THEM ESCAPE!
I'LL HUNT THEM ALL DOWN AND ARREST THEM!
AND THEY WILL PAY FOR THEIR CRIMES!
KLIK
AND CHARON...
...I'LL START WITH YOU!

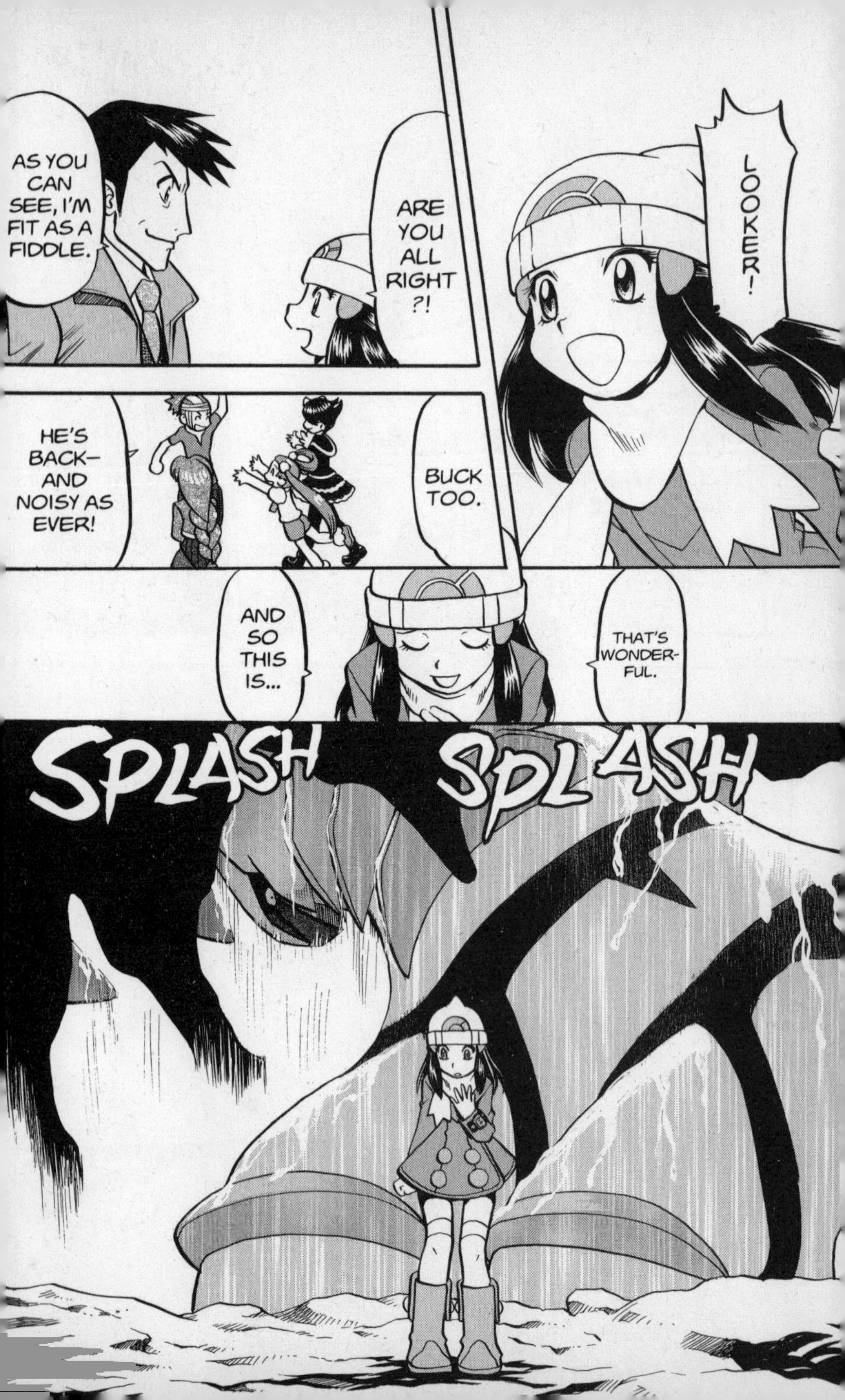
LOOKER!
ARE YOU ALL RIGHT?!
AS YOU CAN SEE, I'M FIT AS A FIDDLE.
BUCK TOO.
HE'S BACK—AND NOISY AS EVER!
THAT'S WONDER-FUL.
AND SO THIS IS...
SPLASH
SPLASH

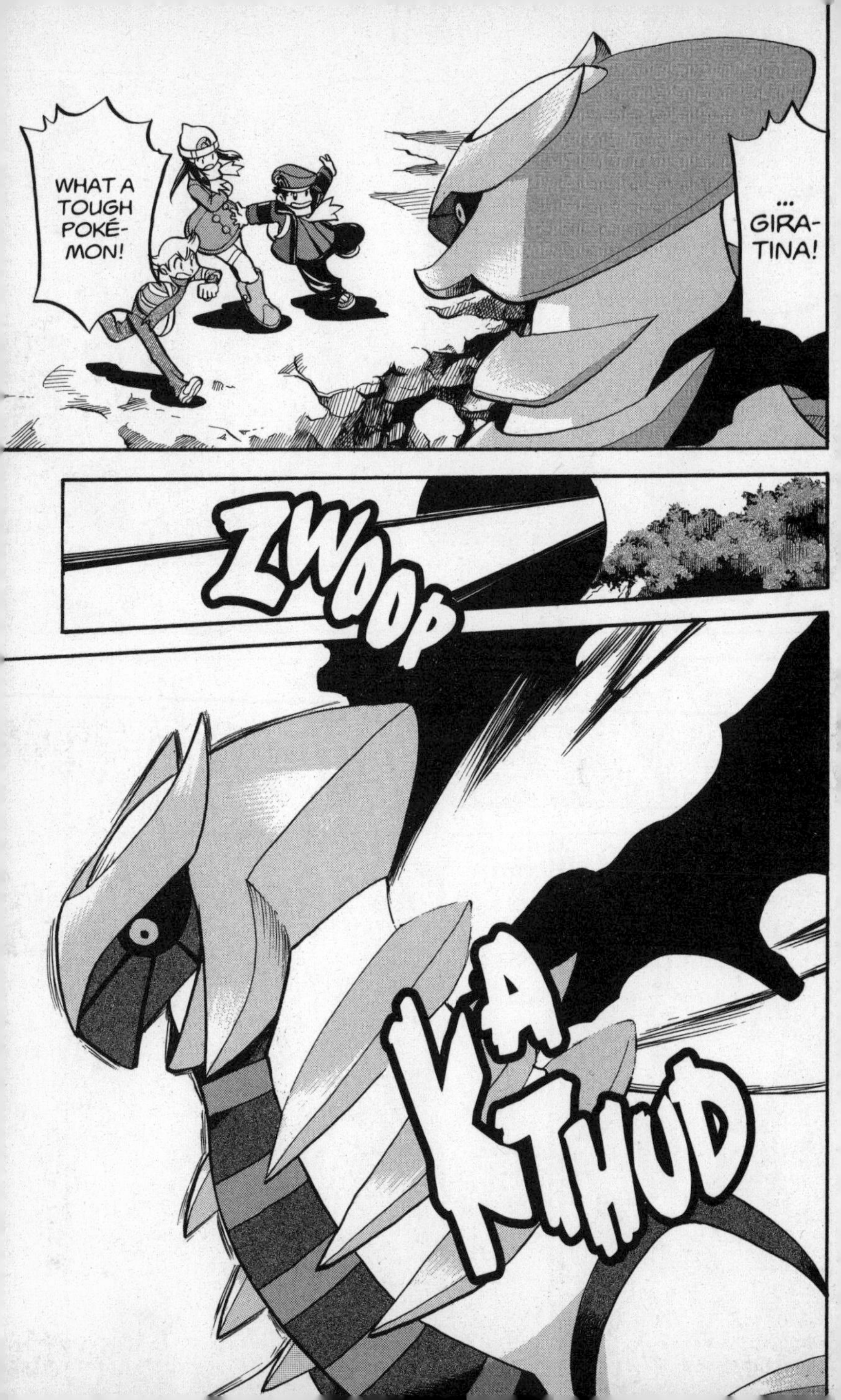
... GIRA-TINA!
WHAT A TOUGH POKÉ-MON!
ZWOOP
KA THUD

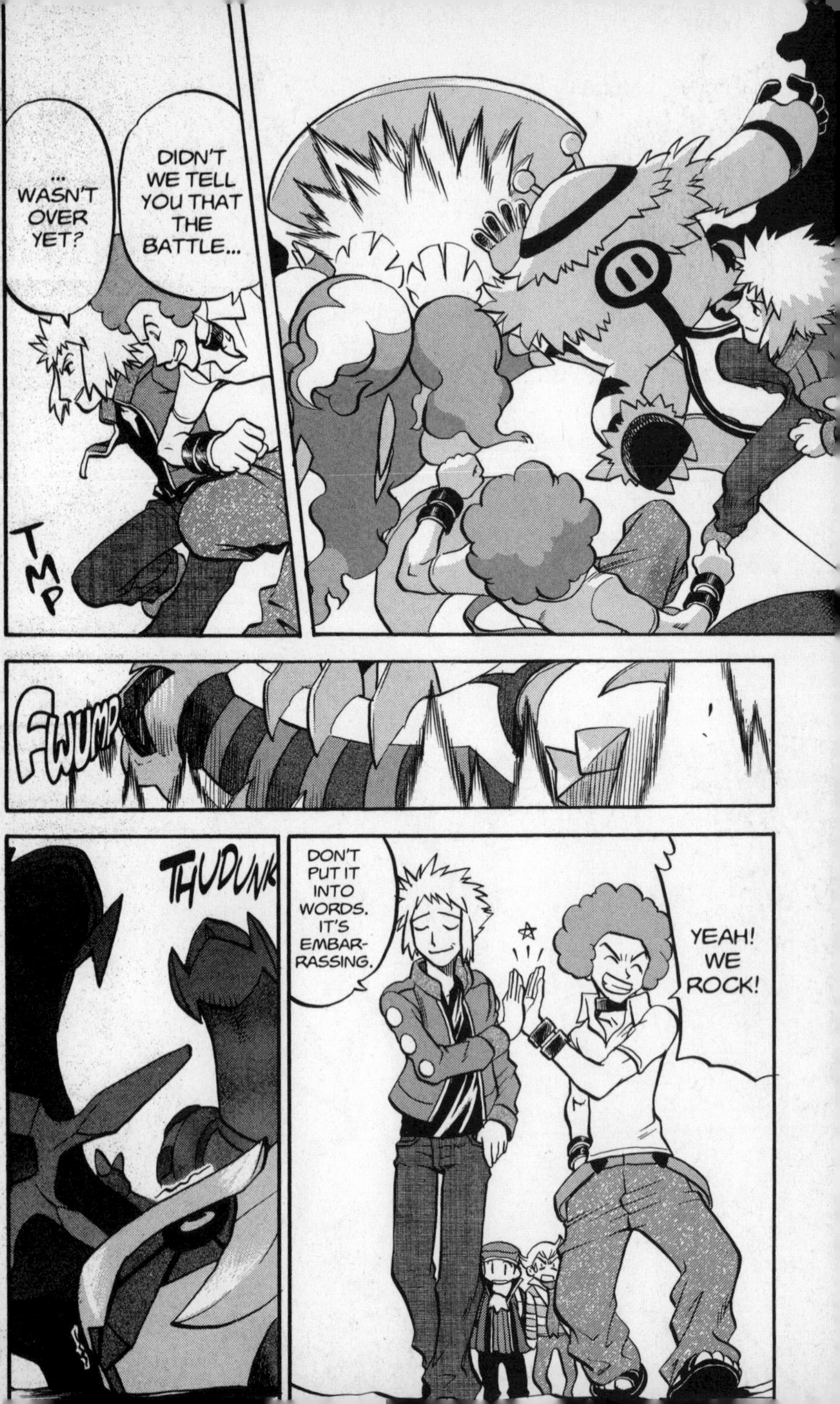
DIDN'T WE TELL YOU THAT THE BATTLE...
...WASN'T OVER YET?
TMP
FWUMP
YEAH! WE ROCK!
DON'T PUT IT INTO WORDS. IT'S EMBAR-RASSING.
THUDUNK

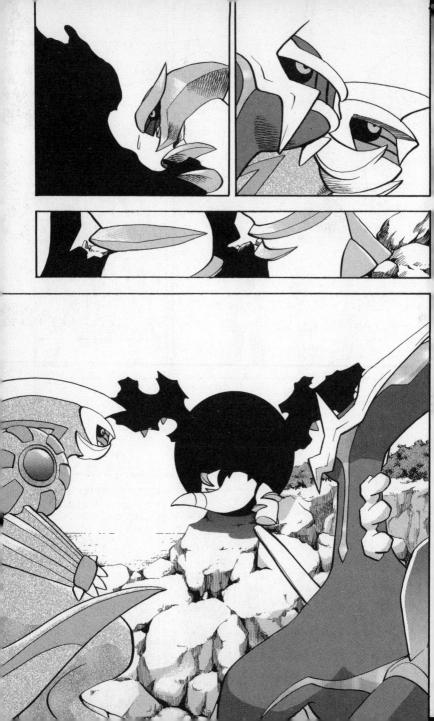

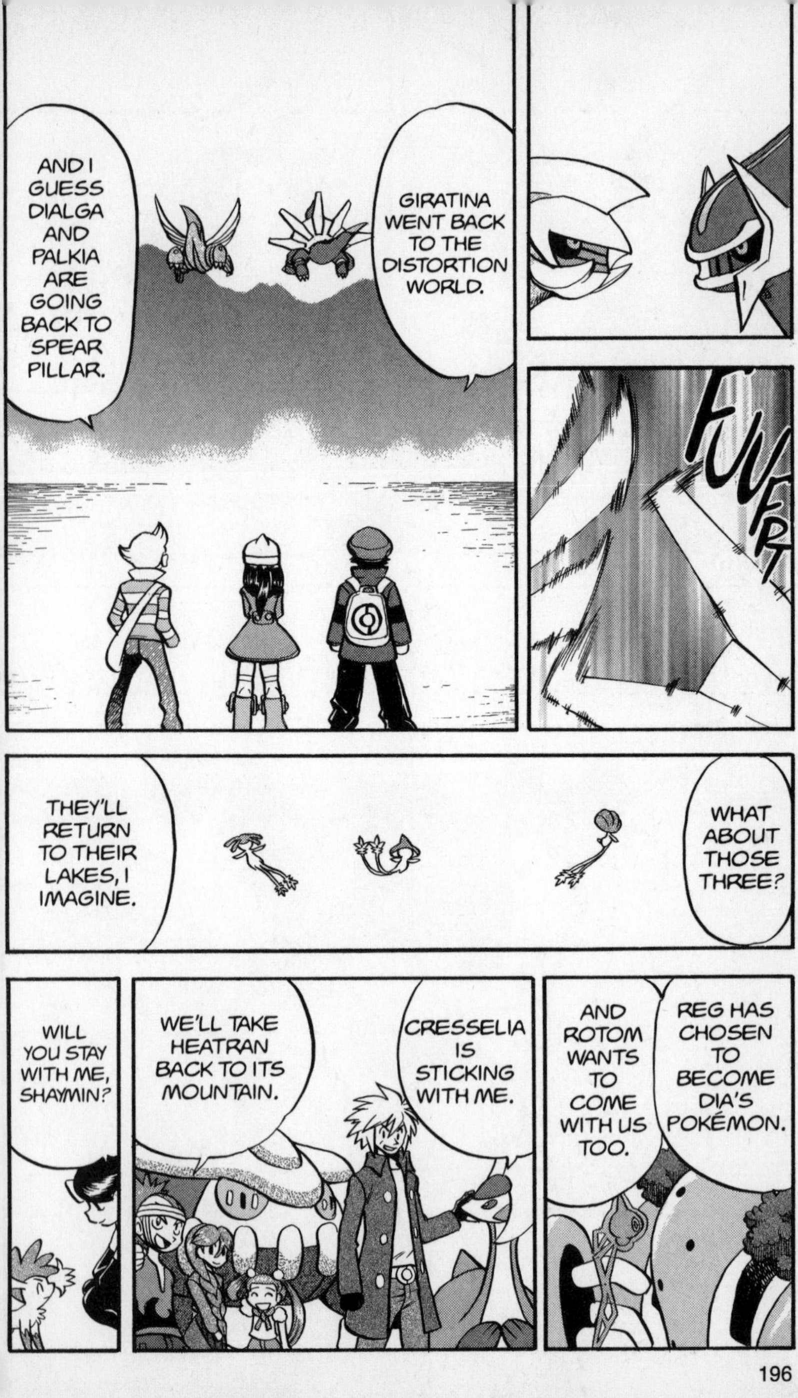
FUUFRT
GIRATINA WENT BACK TO THE DISTORTION WORLD.
AND I GUESS DIALGA AND PALKIA ARE GOING BACK TO SPEAR PILLAR.
WHAT ABOUT THOSE THREE?
THEY'LL RETURN TO THEIR LAKES, I IMAGINE.
REG HAS CHOSEN TO BECOME DIA'S POKÉMON.
AND ROTOM WANTS TO COME WITH US TOO.
CRESSELIA IS STICKING WITH ME.
WE'LL TAKE HEATRAN BACK TO ITS MOUNTAIN.
WILL YOU STAY WITH ME, SHAYMIN?

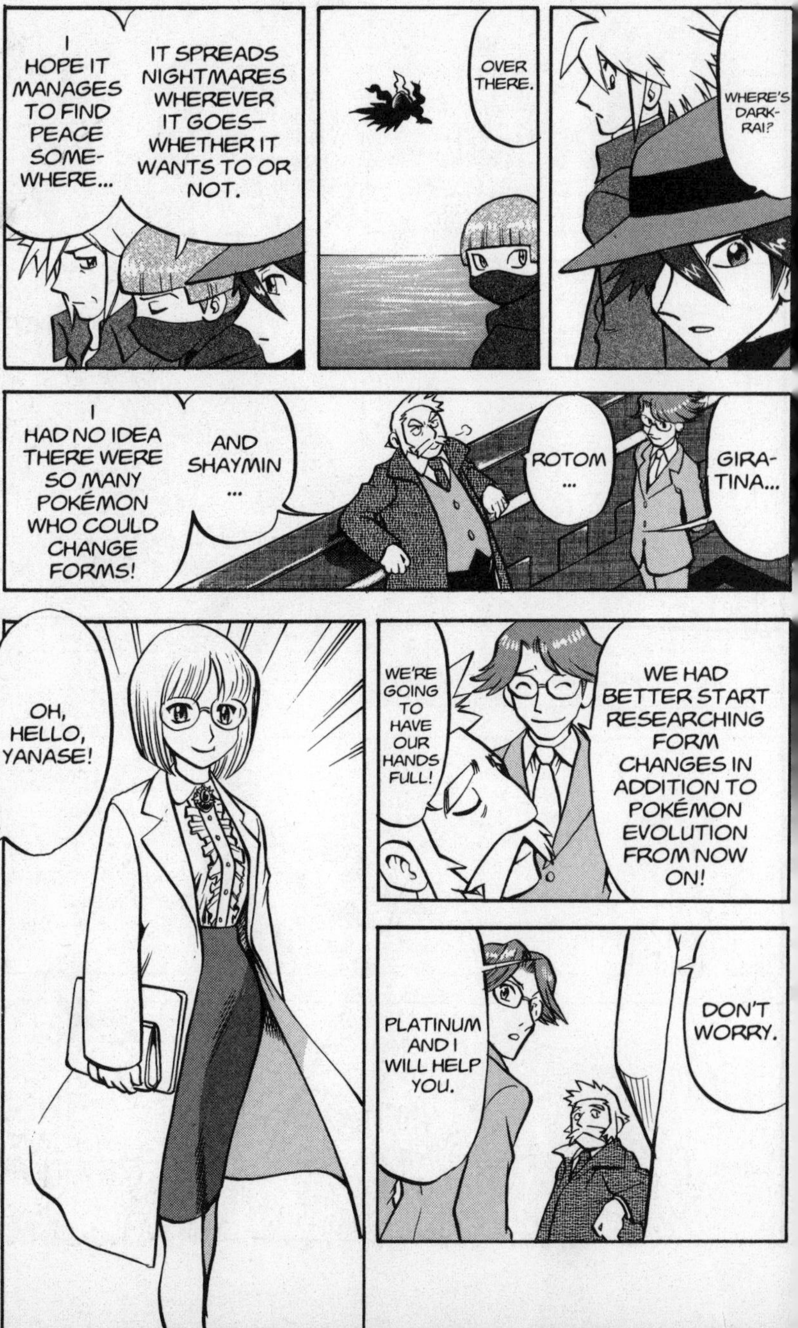
WHERE'S DARK-RAI?
OVER THERE.
IT SPREADS NIGHTMARES WHEREVER IT GOES—WHETHER IT WANTS TO OR NOT.
I HOPE IT MANAGES TO FIND PEACE SOME-WHERE...
GIRA-TINA...
ROTOM ...
AND SHAYMIN ...
I HAD NO IDEA THERE WERE SO MANY POKÉMON WHO COULD CHANGE FORMS!
WE HAD BETTER START RESEARCHING FORM CHANGES IN ADDITION TO POKÉMON EVOLUTION FROM NOW ON!
WE'RE GOING TO HAVE OUR HANDS FULL!
DON'T WORRY.
PLATINUM AND I WILL HELP YOU.
OH, HELLO, YANASE!

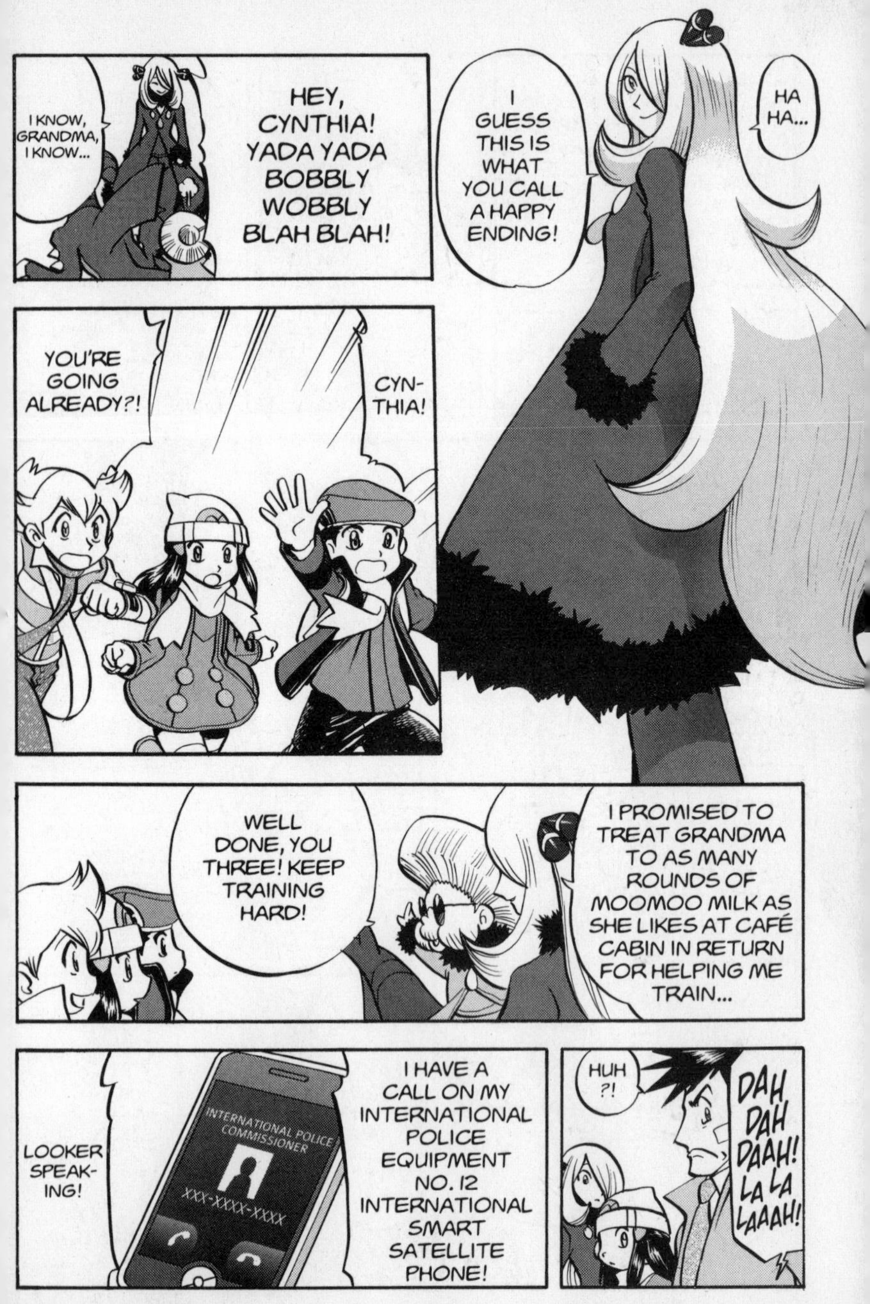
HA HA...
I GUESS THIS IS WHAT YOU CALL A HAPPY ENDING!
HEY, CYNTHIA! YADA YADA BOBBLY WOBBLY BLAH BLAH!
I KNOW, GRANDMA, I KNOW...
CYN-THIA!
YOU'RE GOING ALREADY?!
I PROMISED TO TREAT GRANDMA TO AS MANY ROUNDS OF MOOMOO MILK AS SHE LIKES AT CAFÉ CABIN IN RETURN FOR HELPING ME TRAIN...
WELL DONE, YOU THREE! KEEP TRAINING HARD!
HUH ?!
DAH DAH DAAH! LA LA LAAAH!
I HAVE A CALL ON MY INTERNATIONAL POLICE EQUIPMENT NO. 12 INTERNATIONAL SMART SATELLITE PHONE!
INTERNATIONAL POLICE COMMISSIONER
XXX-XXXX-XXXX
LOOKER SPEAK-ING!

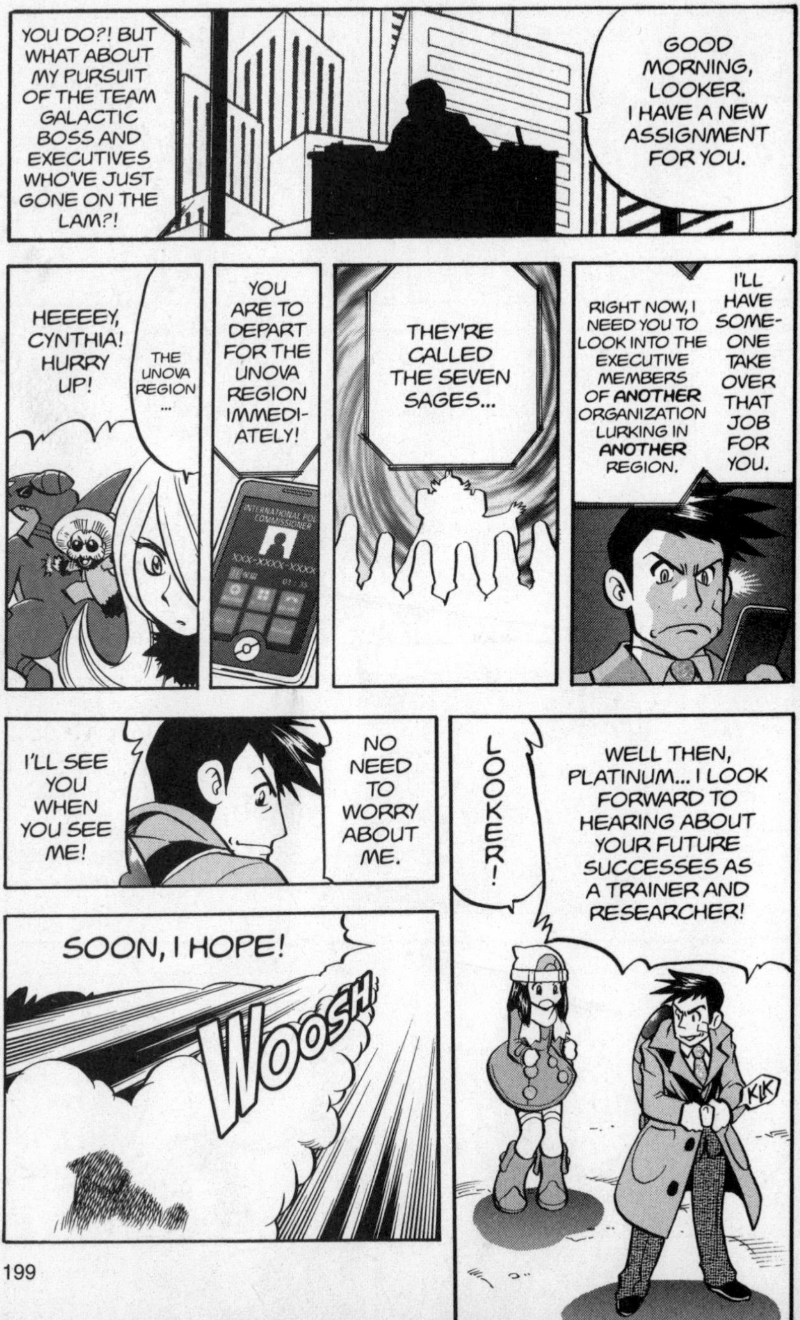
GOOD MORNING, LOOKER. I HAVE A NEW ASSIGNMENT FOR YOU.
YOU DO?! BUT WHAT ABOUT MY PURSUIT OF THE TEAM GALACTIC BOSS AND EXECUTIVES WHO'VE JUST GONE ON THE LAM?!
I'LL HAVE SOME-ONE TAKE OVER THAT JOB FOR YOU.
RIGHT NOW, I NEED YOU TO LOOK INTO THE EXECUTIVE MEMBERS OF **ANOTHER** ORGANIZATION LURKING IN **ANOTHER** REGION.
THEY'RE CALLED THE SEVEN SAGES...
YOU ARE TO DEPART FOR THE UNOVA REGION IMMEDI-ATELY!
COMMISSIONER
THE UNOVA REGION ...
HEEEEY, CYNTHIA! HURRY UP!
WELL THEN, PLATINUM... I LOOK FORWARD TO HEARING ABOUT YOUR FUTURE SUCCESSES AS A TRAINER AND RESEARCHER!
LOOKER!
KLIK
NO NEED TO WORRY ABOUT ME.
I'LL SEE YOU WHEN YOU SEE ME!
SOON, I HOPE!
WOOSH

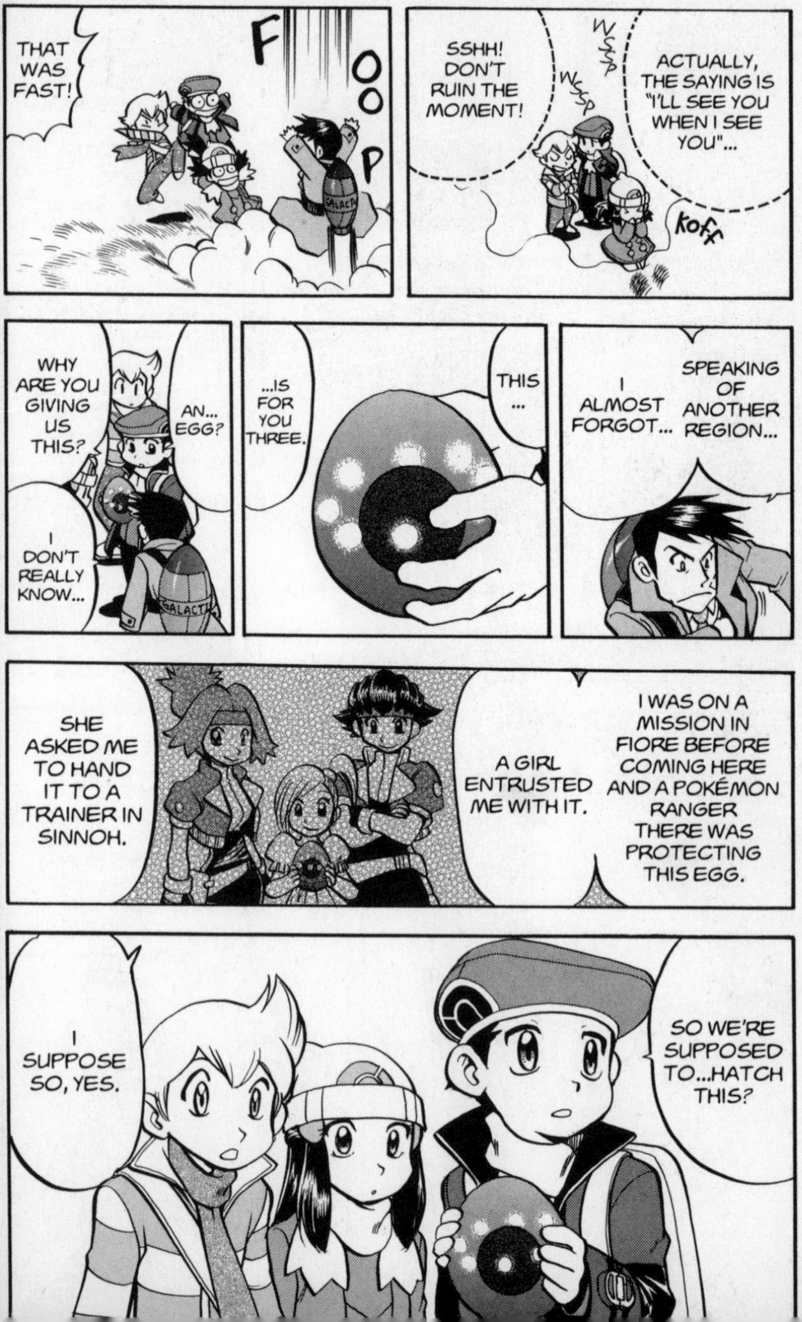
ACTUALLY, THE SAYING IS "I'LL SEE YOU WHEN I SEE YOU"...
WSSP
WSSP
SSHH! DON'T RUIN THE MOMENT!
koff
FOOP
THAT WAS FAST!
SPEAKING OF ANOTHER REGION...
I ALMOST FORGOT...
THIS...
...IS FOR YOU THREE.
AN... EGG?
WHY ARE YOU GIVING US THIS?
I DON'T REALLY KNOW...
I WAS ON A MISSION IN FIORE BEFORE COMING HERE AND A POKÉMON RANGER THERE WAS PROTECTING THIS EGG.
A GIRL ENTRUSTED ME WITH IT.
SHE ASKED ME TO HAND IT TO A TRAINER IN SINNOH.
SO WE'RE SUPPOSED TO...HATCH THIS?
I SUPPOSE SO, YES.

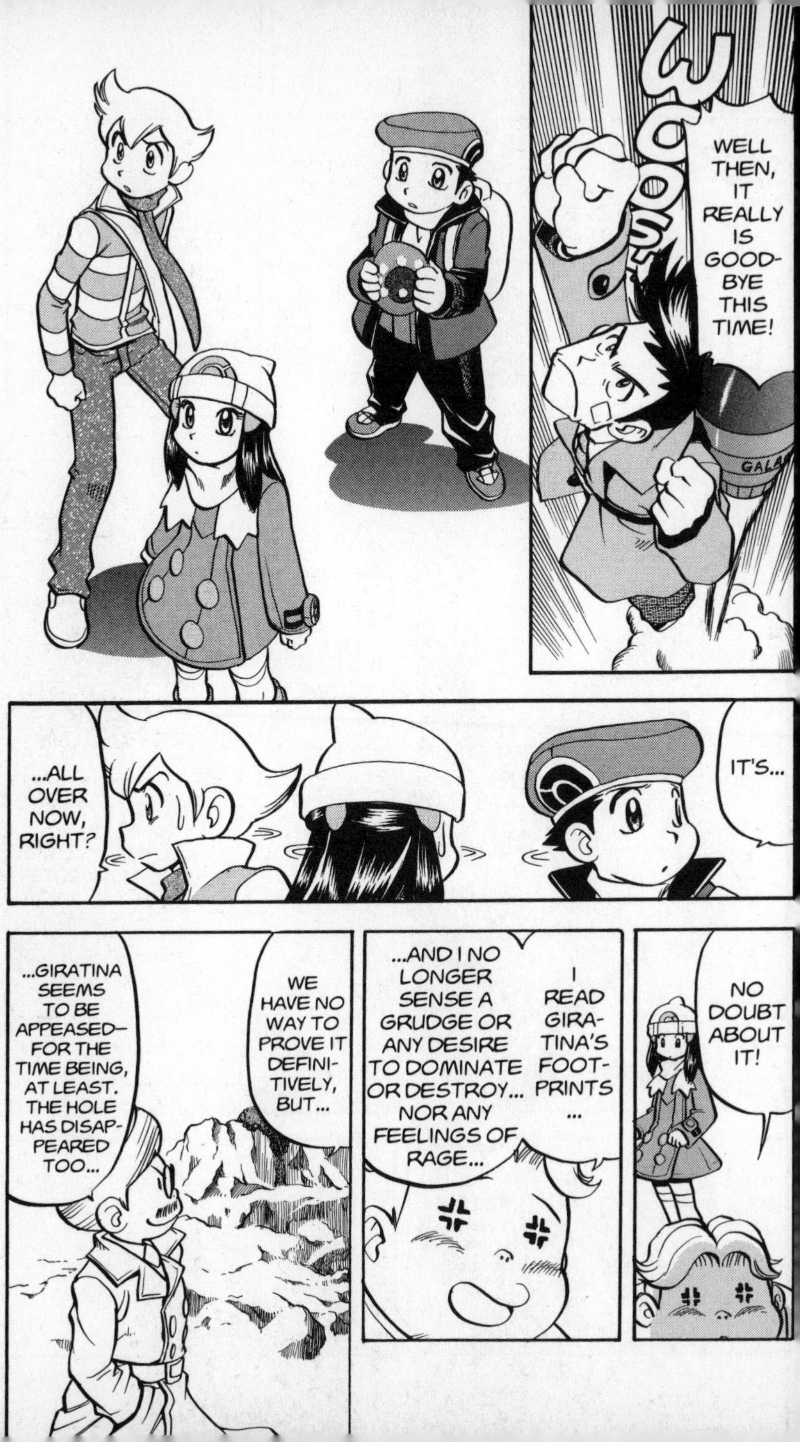
WOOSH!
WELL THEN, IT REALLY IS GOOD-BYE THIS TIME!
IT'S...
...ALL OVER NOW, RIGHT?
NO DOUBT ABOUT IT!
I READ GIRA-TINA'S FOOT-PRINTS...
...AND I NO LONGER SENSE A GRUDGE OR ANY DESIRE TO DOMINATE OR DESTROY... NOR ANY FEELINGS OF RAGE...
WE HAVE NO WAY TO PROVE IT DEFINI-TIVELY, BUT...
...GIRATINA SEEMS TO BE APPEASED—FOR THE TIME BEING, AT LEAST. THE HOLE HAS DISAP-PEARED TOO...

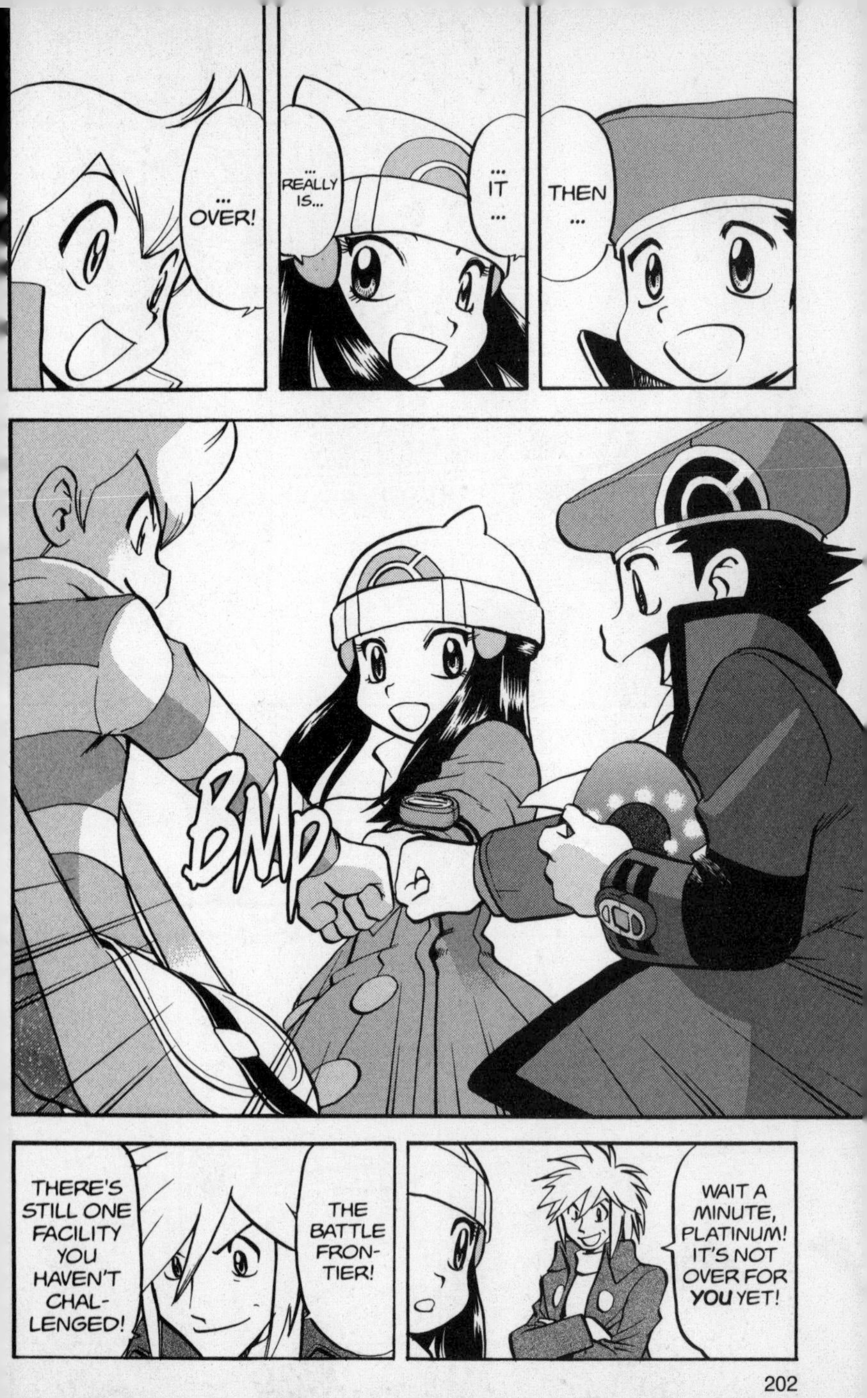
THEN ...
... IT ...
... REALLY IS...
... OVER!
BMP
WAIT A MINUTE, PLATINUM! IT'S NOT OVER FOR **YOU** YET!
THE BATTLE FRON-TIER!
THERE'S STILL ONE FACILITY YOU HAVEN'T CHAL-LENGED!

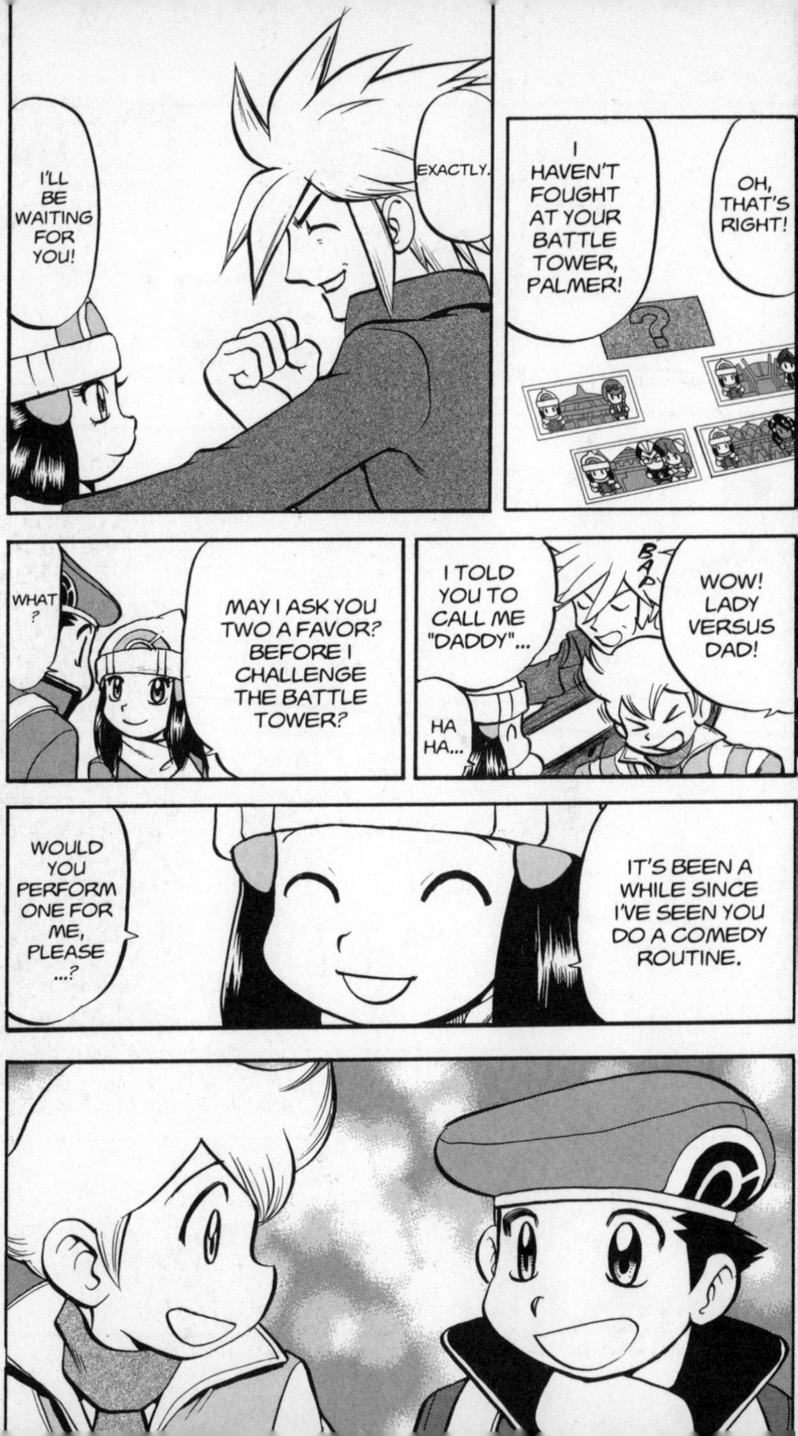
OH, THAT'S RIGHT!
I HAVEN'T FOUGHT AT YOUR BATTLE TOWER, PALMER!
EXACTLY.
I'LL BE WAITING FOR YOU!
WOW! LADY VERSUS DAD!
BAP
I TOLD YOU TO CALL ME "DADDY"...
HA HA...
MAY I ASK YOU TWO A FAVOR? BEFORE I CHALLENGE THE BATTLE TOWER?
WHAT?
IT'S BEEN A WHILE SINCE I'VE SEEN YOU DO A COMEDY ROUTINE.
WOULD YOU PERFORM ONE FOR ME, PLEASE ...?

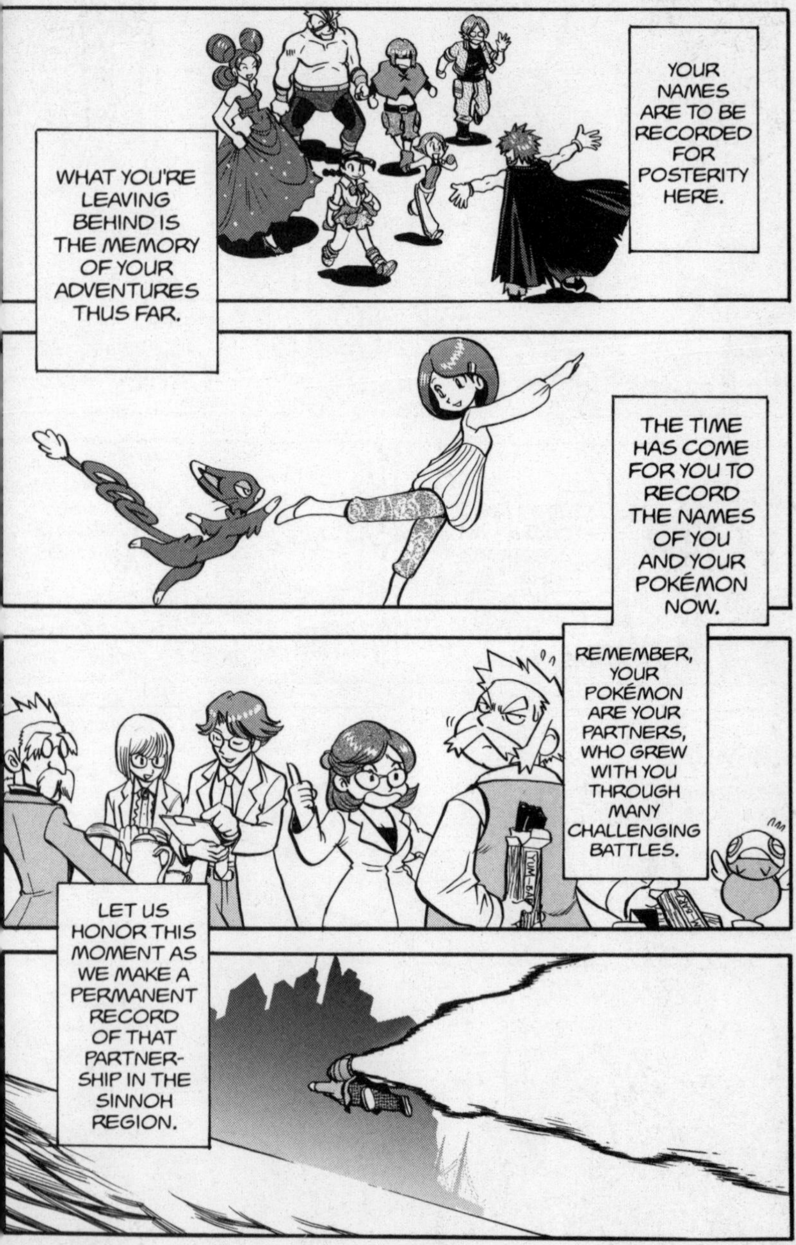
YOUR NAMES ARE TO BE RECORDED FOR POSTERITY HERE.
WHAT YOU'RE LEAVING BEHIND IS THE MEMORY OF YOUR ADVENTURES THUS FAR.
THE TIME HAS COME FOR YOU TO RECORD THE NAMES OF YOU AND YOUR POKÉMON NOW.
REMEMBER, YOUR POKÉMON ARE YOUR PARTNERS, WHO GREW WITH YOU THROUGH MANY CHALLENGING BATTLES.
YUM-BAR
LET US HONOR THIS MOMENT AS WE MAKE A PERMANENT RECORD OF THAT PARTNERSHIP IN THE SINNOH REGION.

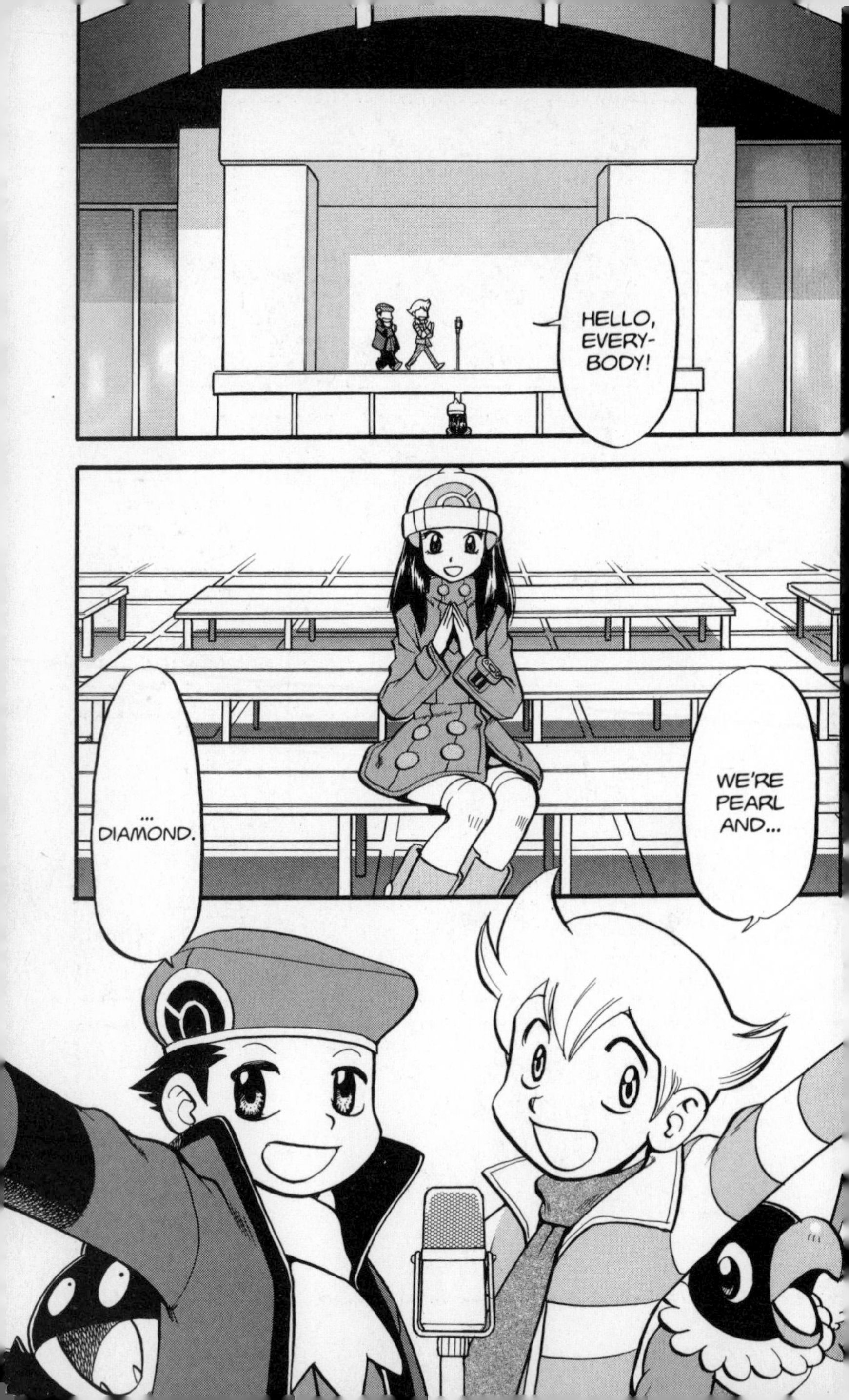
HELLO, EVERY-BODY!
WE'RE PEARL AND...
... DIAMOND.

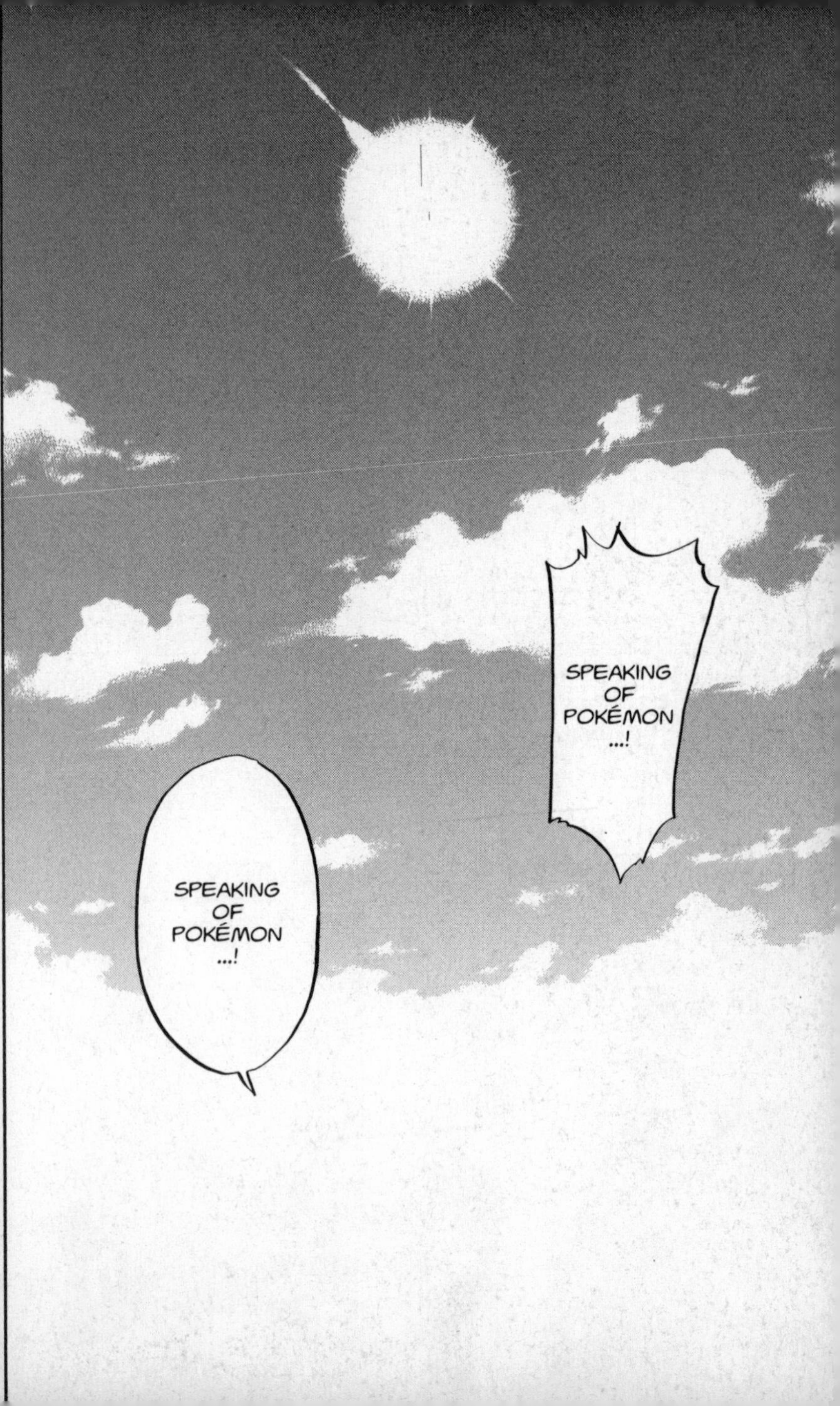
SPEAKING OF POKÉMON ...!
SPEAKING OF POKÉMON ...!

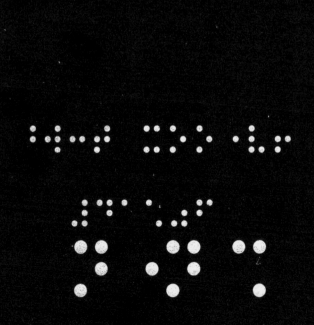

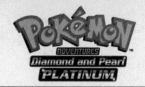

The Seventh Chapter

7 Secret Japanese-Braille Subtitles Decoded!

VOL. 1

Adventure 1: Pearl and Diamond
Adventure 2: Bidoof and Lady
Adventure 3: The Straight Man and Rhythm
Adventure 4: Piplup and Pride
Adventure 5: Roark and Oreburgh Gym
Adventure 6: The Meadow and Sweet Honey
Adventure 7: The Power Plant and the Sandstorm
Adventure 8: The Forest and the Chateau
Adventure 9: Training and First-Time Evolution

Team Galactic Makes Their Move
Continues in Vol. 2...

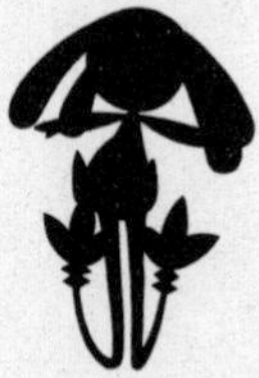

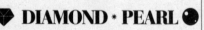

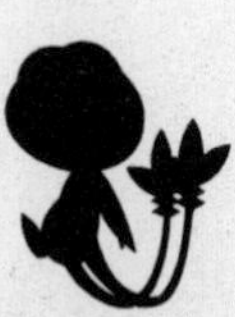

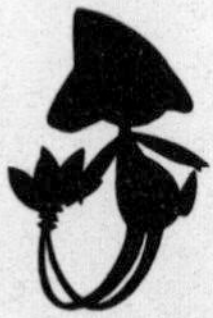

VOL. 2

Adventure 10: Roserade and the Poisonous Thorn
Adventure 11: The Bicycle and Stunky
Adventure 12: Sinnoh and Mt. Coronet
Adventure 13: Lady and the Contest
Adventure 14: The President and the Trio
Adventure 15: Fantina and the Lost Tower
Adventure 16: Paka and Uji
Adventure 17: The Newspaper Company and the Mysterious Writing
Adventure 18: Unown and the Ancient Ruin

A True Bodyguard
Continues in Vol. 3...

VOL. 3

Adventure 19: The Slot Machine and Maylene
Adventure 20: The Gym Battle and Game Corner
Adventure 21: Lady and the Bodyguard
Adventure 22: Foe and Friend
Adventure 23: End and Beginning
Adventure 24: Rain and Footprints
Adventure 25: Light and Memory
Adventure 26: Lake and Shadow
Adventure 27: The Great Marsh and the Safari Zone

Attack on Celestic Town
Continues in Vol. 4...

DIAMOND • PEARL
Subtitles List

VOL. 6

Adventure 48: Arrow and X-Ray Vision
Adventure 49: Snowcapped Mountain and a
            Gym Leader
Adventure 50: Snowpoint and Candice
Adventure 51: Newcomer and Victory
Adventure 52: The Universe and the G-Symbol
Adventure 53: Pokétch and Campaign
Adventure 54: Lickilicky and Treasure
Adventure 55: Big House and the Butler
Adventure 56: The Laboratory and Roseanne
Adventure 57: Flapping Wings and Shock Wave

The Dropping of the Galactic Bomb
Continues in Vol. 7...

6

VOL. 4

Adventure 28: Crasher Wake and Pastoria City
Adventure 29: Victory and Fight Money
Adventure 30: Psyduck and the Secret Potion
Adventure 31: Celestic Town and the Town Elder
Adventure 32: Mural and Assailant
Adventure 33: Willpower and Emotion
Adventure 34: Conference and Kidnapping
Adventure 35: Hearthome Gym and a Math
            Problem
Adventure 36: Illusion and Reality
Adventure 37: Daughter and Father

The Truth Is Revealed
Continues in Vol. 5...

4

VOL. 5

Adventure 38: Truth and Deception
Adventure 39: Resolution and Confession
Adventure 40: Parting and Departure
Adventure 41: The S.S. Sinnoh and Setting Sail
Adventure 42: Riley and Iron Island
Adventure 43: The Cave and an Assignment
Adventure 44: Speed and Razor Leaf
Adventure 45: Malice and Aura
Adventure 46: Ironworks and Contract
Adventure 47: The Furnace and the Moving Floor

The Heartbeat of a Legend
Continues in Vol. 6...

5

◆ DIAMOND ✶ PEARL ●
Subtitles List

VOL. 9

Adventure 76: Roar of Time and Spacial Rend
Adventure 77: Grunt and Individual Will
Adventure 78: Complete and Incomplete
Adventure 79: Dia and Pearl

The Renegade Dragon
Continues on the next page...

VOL. 7

Adventure 58: Lake Acuity and Jupiter
Adventure 59: A Formidable Enemy & Girl Trio
Adventure 60: The Bomb and the Countdown
Adventure 61: The Three Pokémon and Their
Invisible Bond
Adventure 62: Fierce Battle and Defeat
Adventure 63: Downpour and Helping Hand
Adventure 64: Capture and Pupil
Adventure 65: Cyrus and the Perfect World
Adventure 66: Pearl and the New Team
Adventure 67: Enemy Headquarter and Intruder

Divide and Conquer
Continues in Vol. 8...

9

7

VOL. 8

Adventure 68: Strength and Experience
Adventure 69: Spacey and Flakey
Adventure 70: Disguise and Infiltration
Adventure 71: Pokédex and the Morning Sound
Adventure 72: Champion and Boss
Adventure 73: Three Pokémon and Freedom
Adventure 74: Fate and Spear Pillar
Adventure 75: Time and Space

The Other Side of the World
Continues in Vol. 9...

◆ **DIAMOND ✳ PEARL** ●
S u b t i t l e s   L i s t

8

VOL. 11

Adventure 94: Giratina the Renegade
Adventure 95: The Warriors Set Out
Adventure 96: An Attack from the Shadow
Adventure 97: The Form Change of Anger
Adventure 98: The Master of the Spyeye
Adventure 99: The Beginning of a Group Battle
Adventure 100: The World of Antimatter
Adventure 101: Where One's Heart Lies
Adventure 102: The Virus of Justice
Adventure 103: A Letter from Oak
Adventure 104: The Shining Souls

Return to Johto!
Continues in *Pokémon Adventures*
HeartGold/SoulSilver Vol. 1...

11

VOL. 9

Adventure 80: Waiting at the Resort
Adventure 81: Managing Points
Adventure 82: The Brain of the Castle
Adventure 83: Careless Butler
Adventure 84: Battleground Buck
Adventure 85: The Treasure of Stark Mountain

The Renegade Dragon
Continues in Vol. 10...

9

PLATINUM
Subtitles List

VOL. 10

Adventure 86: The Swapping Panel
Adventure 87: The Awakening
Adventure 88: Charon's Ambition
Adventure 89: Rental Facility
Adventure 90: Jamming
Adventure 91: A Request from Palmer
Adventure 92: The Fierce Battle Hall
Adventure 93: Five House Electronics

Legends!
Continues in Vol. 11...

10

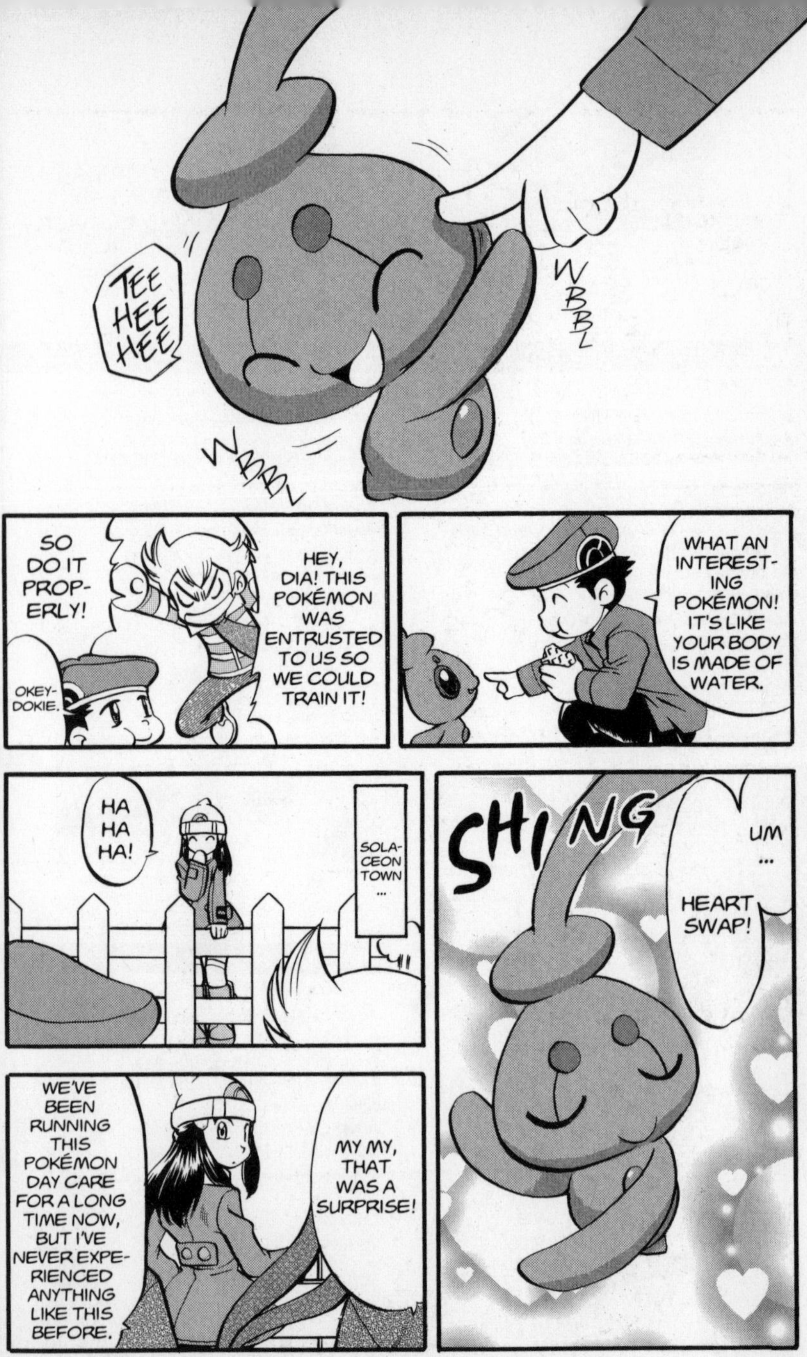
TEE HEE HEE
WBBL
WBBL
WHAT AN INTERESTING POKÉMON! IT'S LIKE YOUR BODY IS MADE OF WATER.
HEY, DIA! THIS POKÉMON WAS ENTRUSTED TO US SO WE COULD TRAIN IT!
SO DO IT PROPERLY!
OKEY-DOKIE.
SHING
UM ... HEART SWAP!
SOLACEON TOWN ...
HA HA HA!
MY MY, THAT WAS A SURPRISE!
WE'VE BEEN RUNNING THIS POKÉMON DAY CARE FOR A LONG TIME NOW, BUT I'VE NEVER EXPERIENCED ANYTHING LIKE THIS BEFORE.

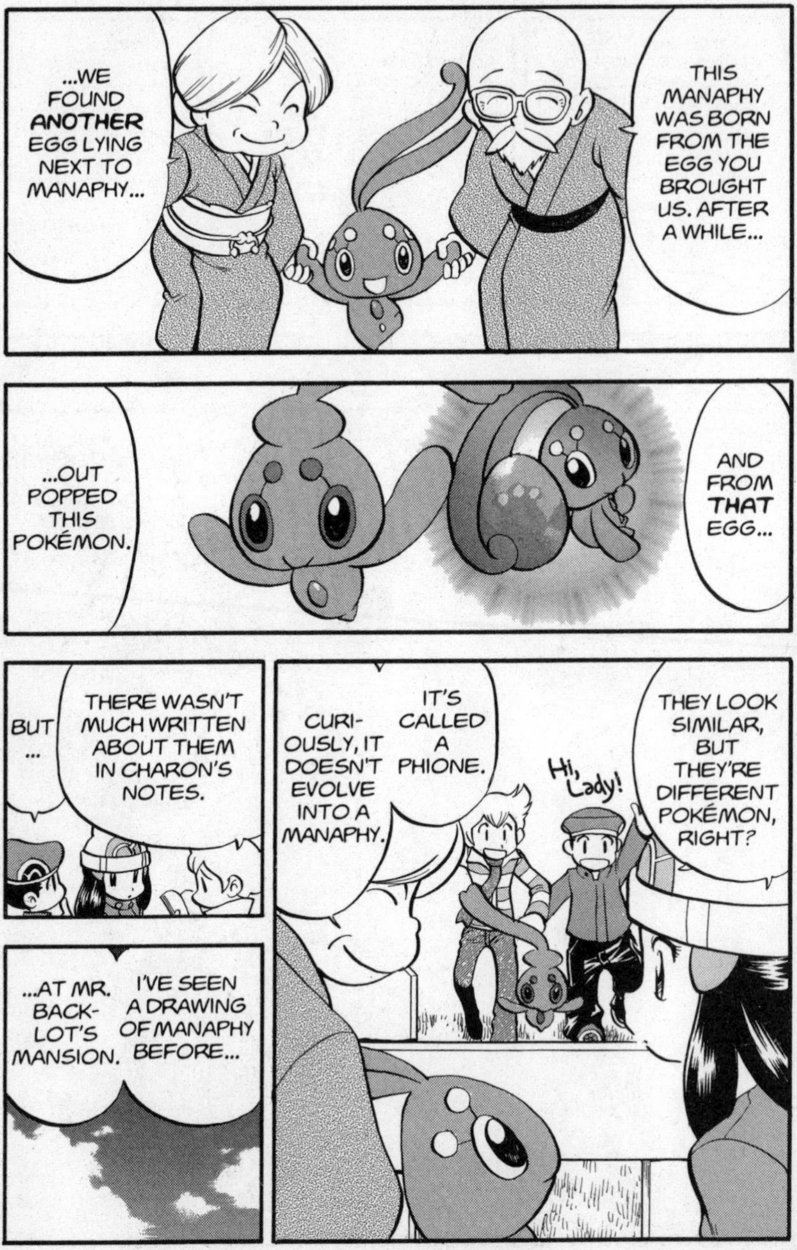
THIS MANAPHY WAS BORN FROM THE EGG YOU BROUGHT US. AFTER A WHILE...
...WE FOUND **ANOTHER** EGG LYING NEXT TO MANAPHY...
AND FROM **THAT** EGG...
...OUT POPPED THIS POKÉMON.
THEY LOOK SIMILAR, BUT THEY'RE DIFFERENT POKÉMON, RIGHT?
Hi, Lady!
IT'S CALLED A PHIONE.
CURI-OUSLY, IT DOESN'T EVOLVE INTO A MANAPHY.
THERE WASN'T MUCH WRITTEN ABOUT THEM IN CHARON'S NOTES.
BUT ...
I'VE SEEN A DRAWING OF MANAPHY BEFORE...
...AT MR. BACK-LOT'S MANSION.

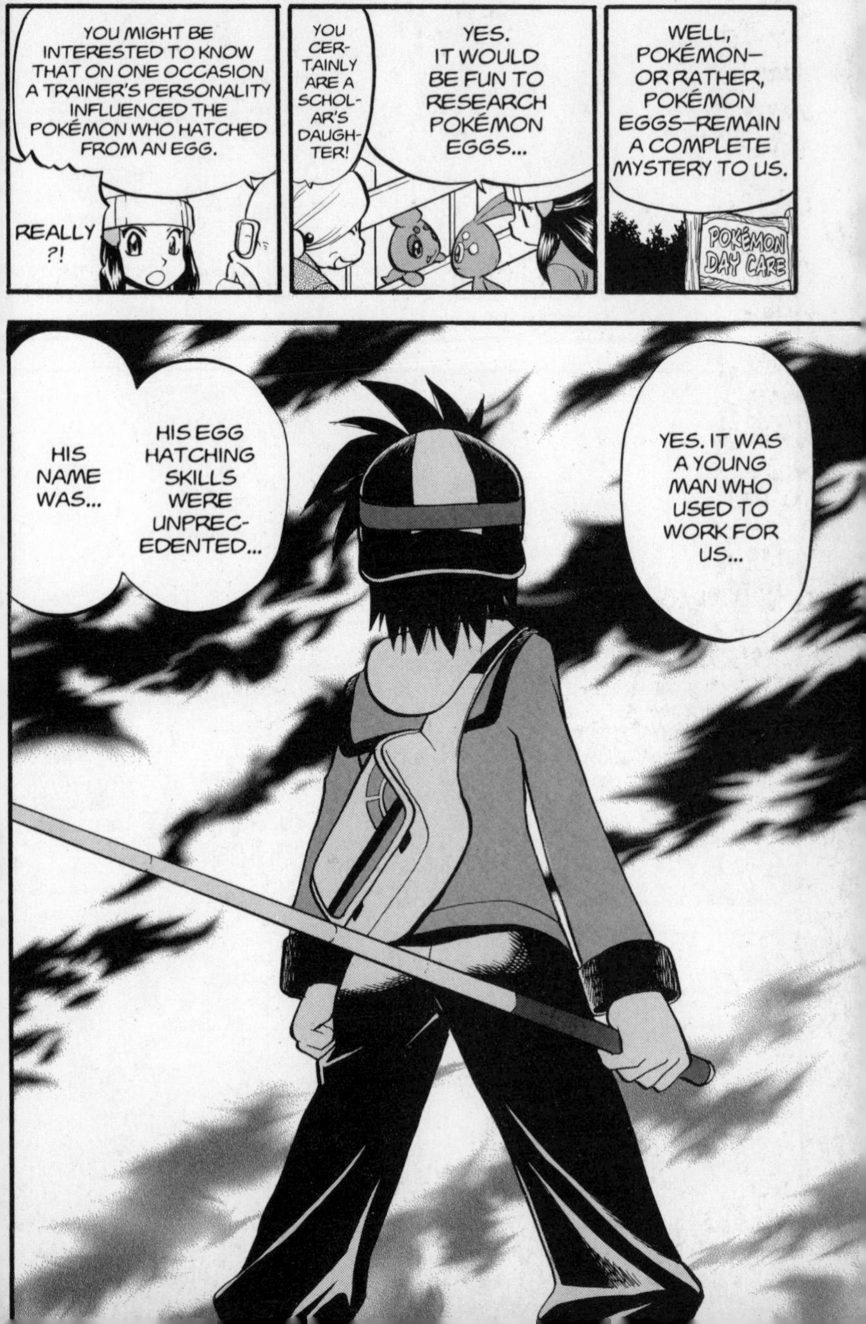
WELL, POKÉMON—OR RATHER, POKÉMON EGGS—REMAIN A COMPLETE MYSTERY TO US.
POKÉMON DAY CARE
YES. IT WOULD BE FUN TO RESEARCH POKÉMON EGGS...
YOU CER-TAINLY ARE A SCHOL-AR'S DAUGH-TER!
YOU MIGHT BE INTERESTED TO KNOW THAT ON ONE OCCASION A TRAINER'S PERSONALITY INFLUENCED THE POKÉMON WHO HATCHED FROM AN EGG.
REALLY ?!
YES. IT WAS A YOUNG MAN WHO USED TO WORK FOR US...
HIS EGG HATCHING SKILLS WERE UNPREC-EDENTED...
HIS NAME WAS...

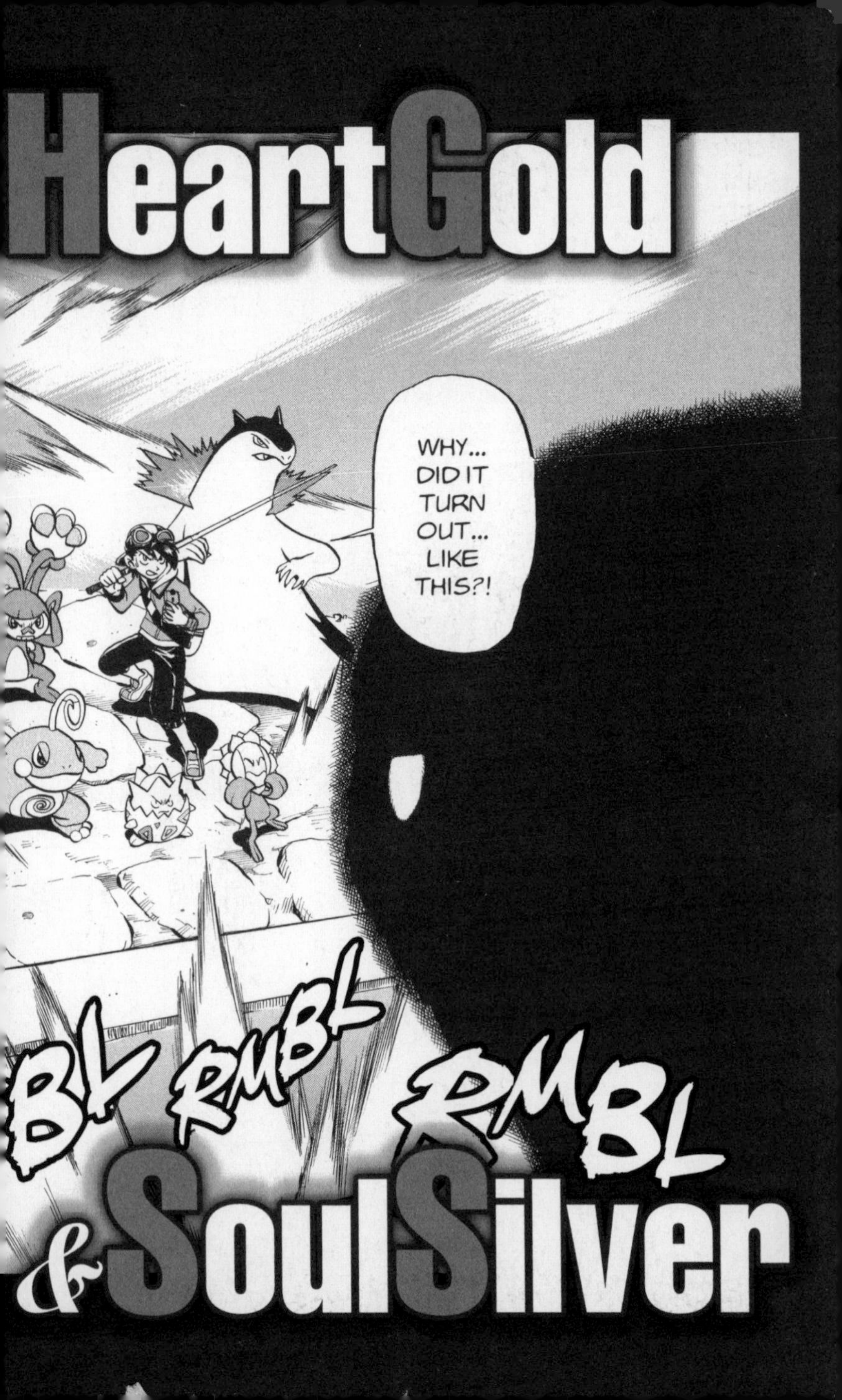
HeartGold
WHY... DID IT TURN OUT... LIKE THIS?!
BL RMBL
RMBL
& SoulSilver

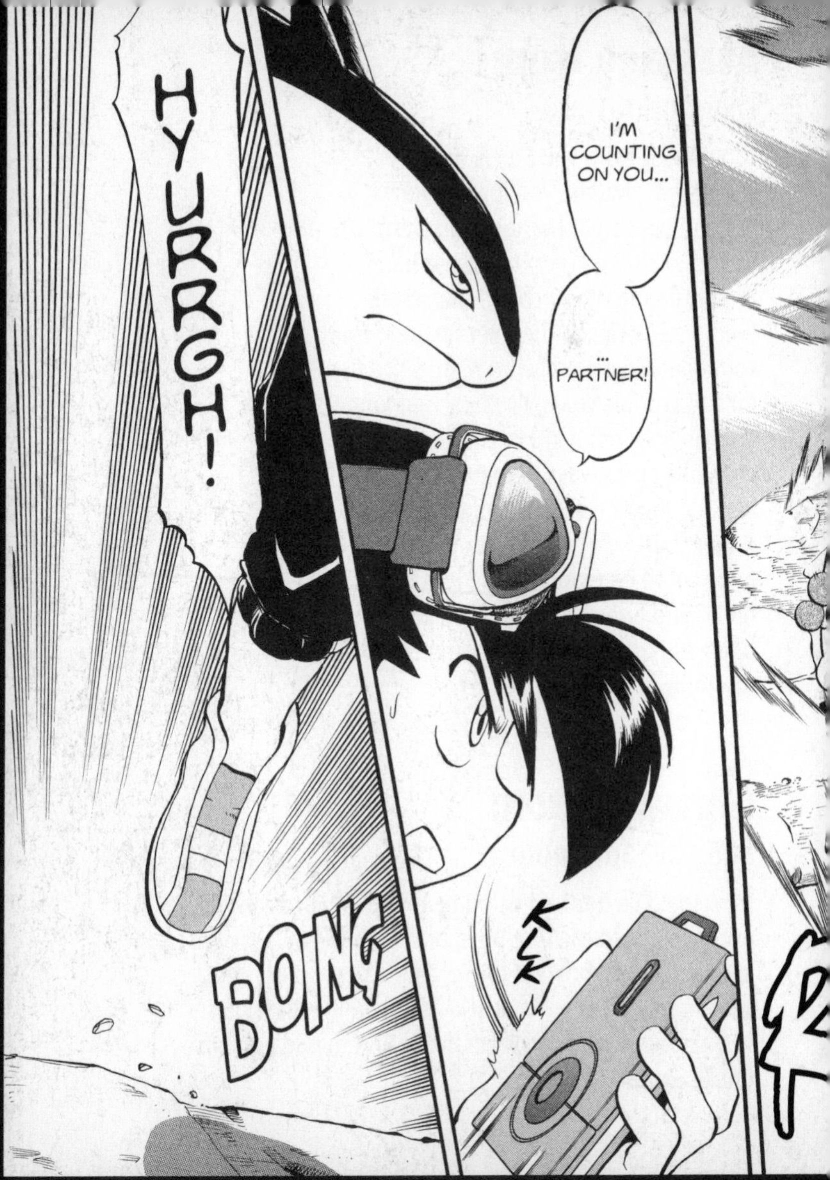
I'M COUNTING ON YOU...
...PARTNER!
HYURRGH!
BOING
KLK

Message from
Hidenori Kusaka

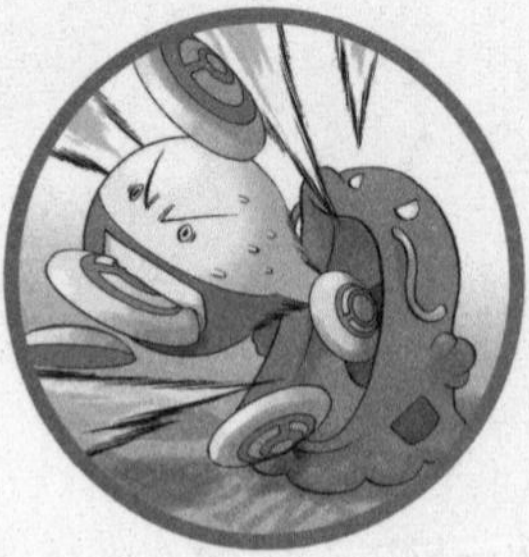

(Continued from vol. 10.) A friend suggested, "Maybe you mix up your left and your right because you were forced to change from being left-handed to right-handed as a child." Interesting theory... I searched the Internet and found some people with this problem. Since then, for the last five years, I've been working on using my left hand to eat (to hold my chopsticks). I always thought I was right-handed, but it feels a lot more natural to use my left hand. At the same time, I've started to be more conscious of the left side of my body, and I don't confuse right and left as often as I used to! The human brain is a mysterious thing.

Message from
Satoshi Yamamoto

Now that I've finished working on the *Platinum* story arc, it seems to me that the theme is the search for a sun that shines only on oneself. It's a story about those who search all over the world and the other side of the world for a light to shine on them. And this search has finally come to an end.

AVAILABLE NOW!

Your favorite Pokémon Trainers Gold and Silver are back! Crystal too! And so is Team Rocket...

In this two-volume thriller, troublemaker Gold and feisty Silver must team up again to find their old enemy Lance and the Legendary Pokémon Arceus.

Meanwhile, Team Rocket is on the rampage digging up, stealing and collecting 16 mysterious plates for some nefarious purpose known only to them...

What is the hidden power of the 16 plates, and what do they symbolize...?

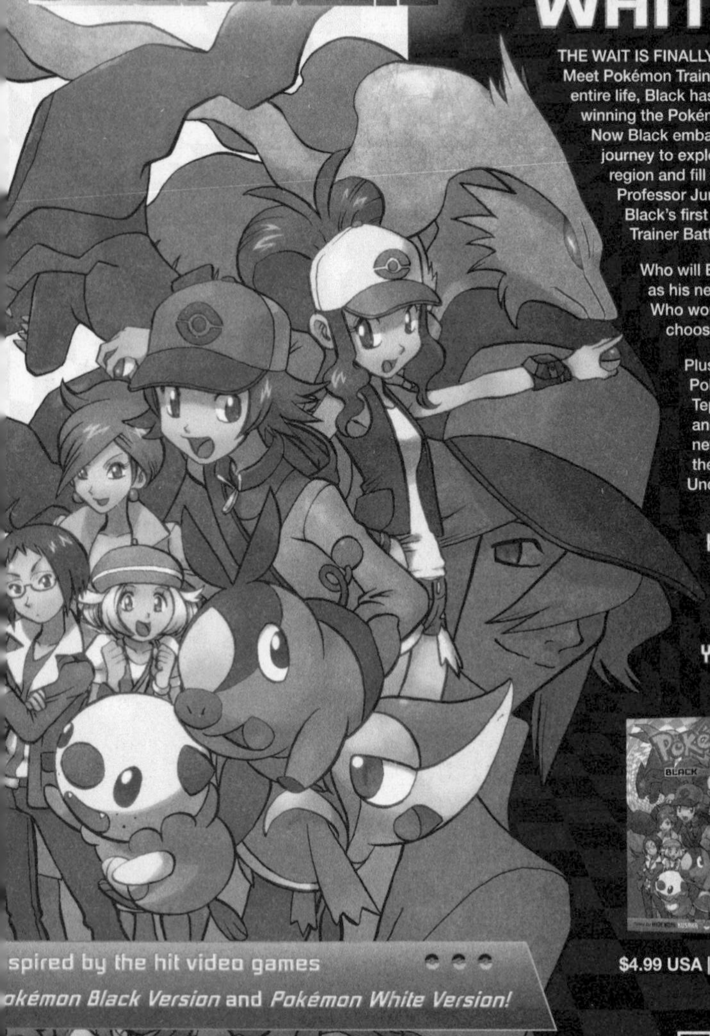

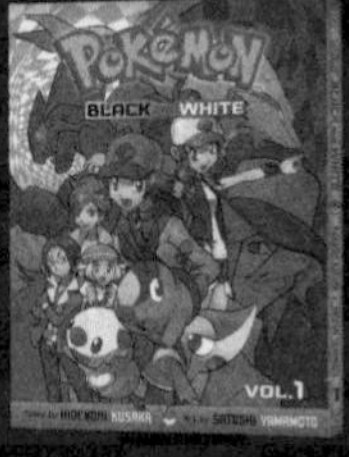

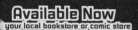

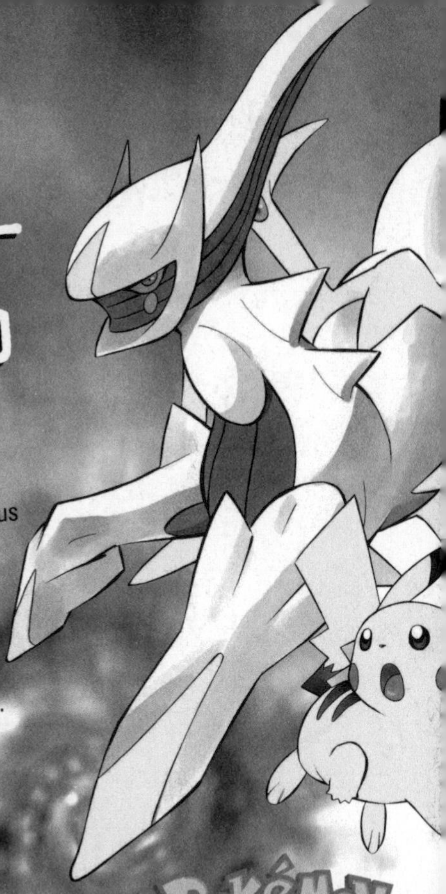

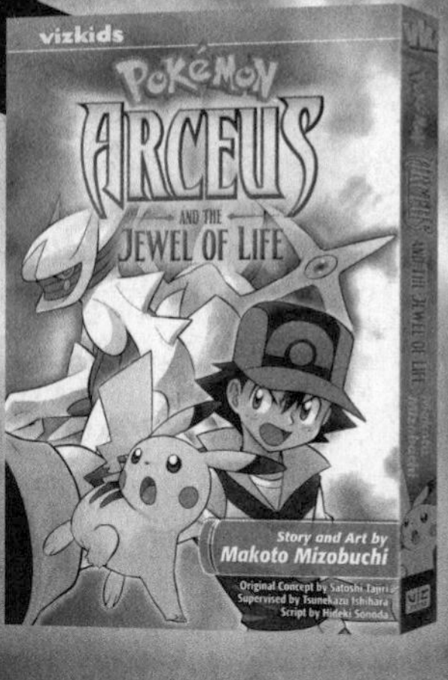

vizkids
Pokémon
ARCEUS
AND THE
JEWEL OF LIFE
Story and Art by
Makoto Mizobuchi
Original Concept by Satoshi Tajiri
Supervised by Tsunekazu Ishihara
Script by Hideki Sonoda

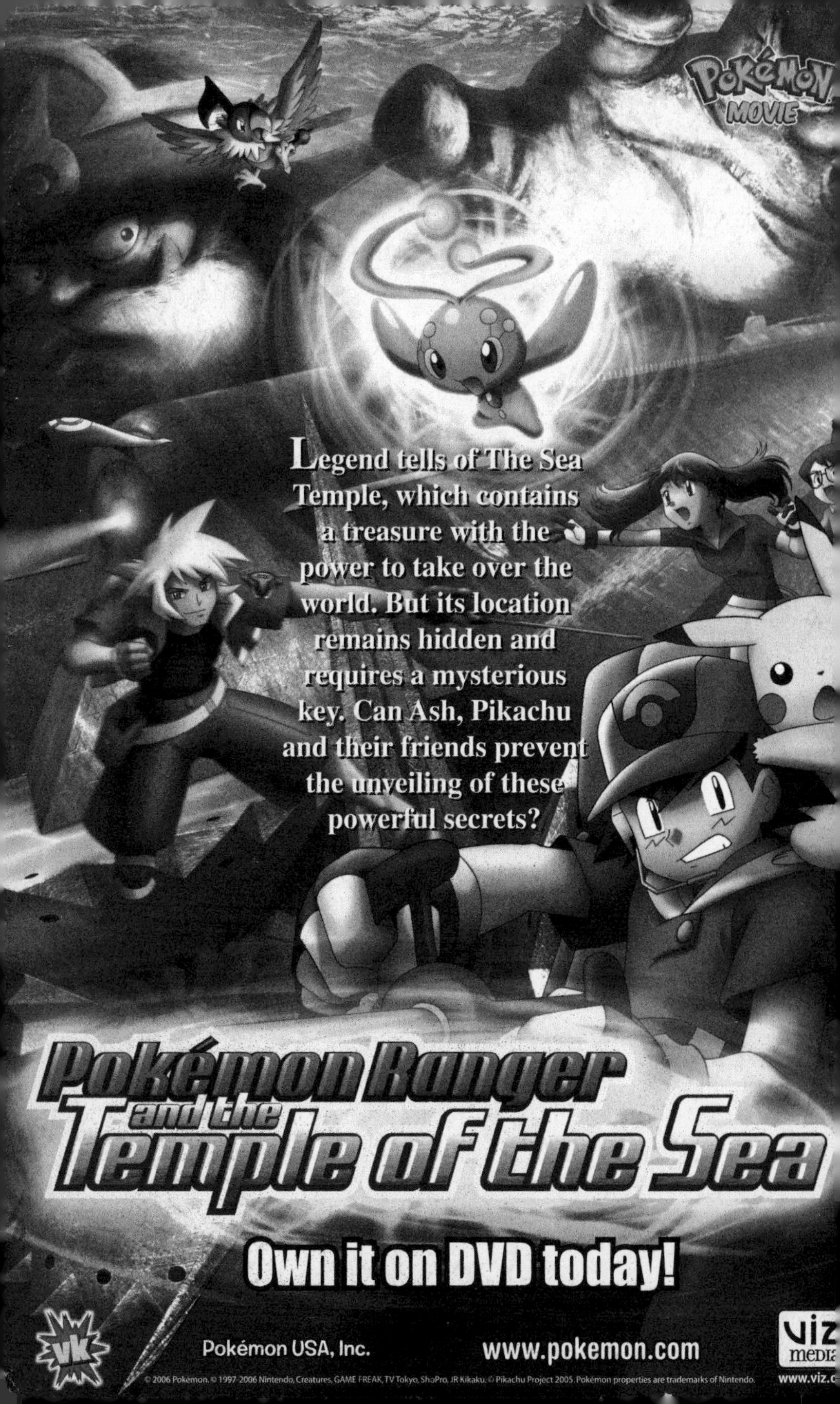
POKÉMON MOVIE
Legend tells of The Sea Temple, which contains a treasure with the power to take over the world. But its location remains hidden and requires a mysterious key. Can Ash, Pikachu and their friends prevent the unveiling of these powerful secrets?
Pokémon Ranger and the Temple of the Sea
Own it on DVD today!
Pokémon USA, Inc.
www.pokemon.com
© 2006 Pokémon. © 1997-2006 Nintendo, Creatures, GAME FREAK, TV Tokyo, ShoPro, JR Kikaku. © Pikachu Project 2005. Pokémon properties are trademarks of Nintendo.

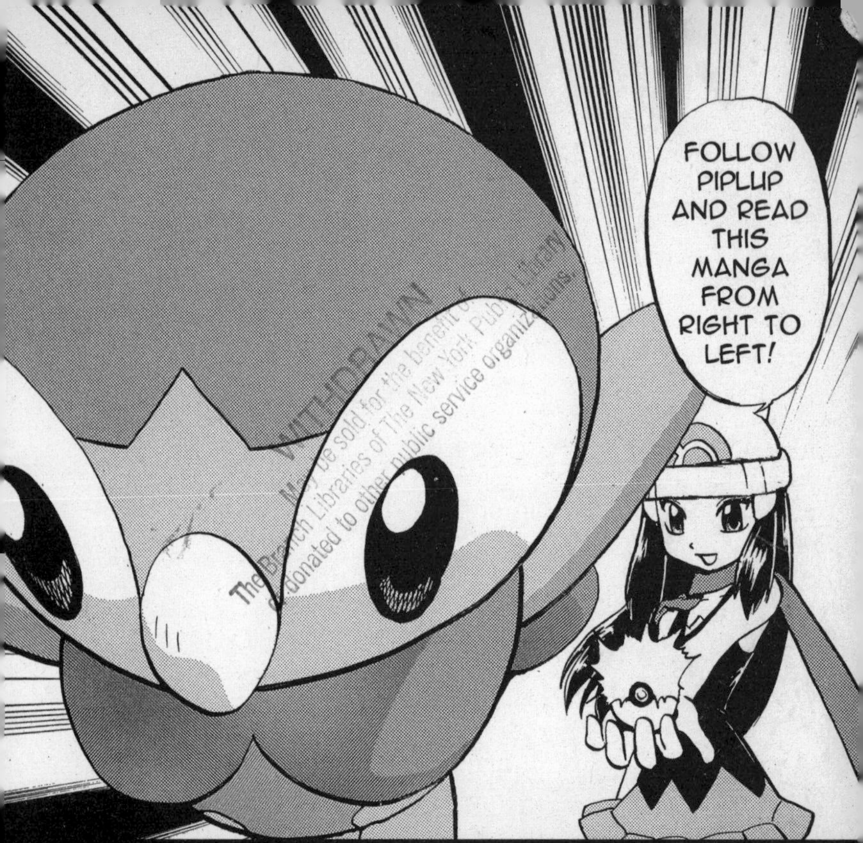
FOLLOW PIPLUP AND READ THIS MANGA FROM RIGHT TO LEFT!

THIS IS THE END OF THIS GRAPHIC NOVEL!

To properly enjoy this VIZ Media graphic novel, please turn it around and begin reading from right to left.

This book has been printed in the original Japanese format in order to preserve the orientation of the original artwork. Have fun with it!

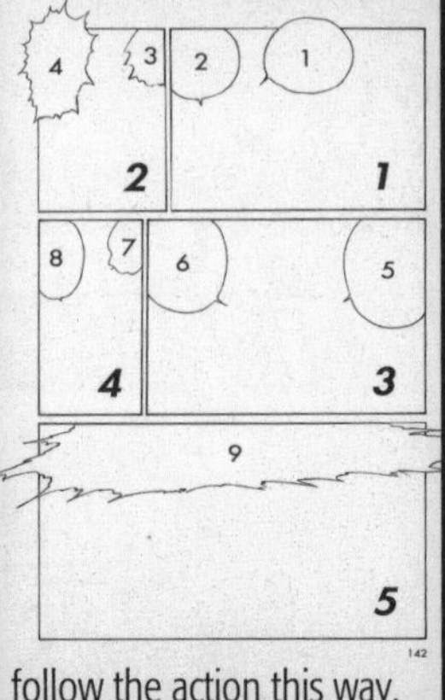

follow the action this way.